MW00658681

The Garland Library of Medieval Literature

General Editors
James J. Wilhelm, Rutgers University
Lowry Nelson, Jr., Yale University

Literary Advisors
Ingeborg Glier, Yale University
William W. Kibler, University of Texas
Norris J. Lacy, Washington University
Giuseppe Mazzotta, Yale University
Fred C. Robinson, Yale University
Aldo Scaglione, University of North Carolina

Art Advisor
Elizabeth Parker McLachlan, Rutgers University

Music Advisor
Hendrik van der Werf, Eastman School of Music

Plate 1. Daniel of the Blossoming Valley defends the Lady of the Dark Mountain against the dwarf Juran. *Illustration by Alfred S. Schwartz.*

Der Stricker

Daniel of the Blossoming Valley (Daniel von dem Blühenden Tal)

translated by
MICHAEL RESLER

Volume 58
Series B
GARLAND LIBRARY OF MEDIEVAL LITERATURE

This volume first appeared in 1990 in the

GARLAND LIBRARY OF
MEDIEVAL LITERATURE

Edited by

PROFESSOR JAMES J. WILHELM

Rutgers University

Copyright © 2005 by Michael Resler
All rights reserved
Printed in the United States of America

Library of Congress Cataloging-in-Publication Data

Stricker, 13th cent.
[Daniel von dem Blühenden Tal. English]
Daniel of the Blossoming Valley (Daniel von dem Blühenden Tal)
Der Stricker; translated by Michael Resler.
p. cm. — (The Garland library of medieval literature; v. 58. Series B)
Translation of: Daniel von dem Blühenden Tal.
Includes bibliographical references.
ISBN 0-9760873-1-6
1. Arthurian romances. I. Resler, Michael. II. Title.
III. Series: Garland library of medieval literature; v. 58.
PT1653.D3E5 1990
831'.2—dc20 *89—28774*
CIP

Cover design by Michael Swanson and Kimberly Dunfey

For

PROFESSOR ALEXANDER KALLOS

dem houbetman der wâren zuht.
des site was vor valsche ein fluht.

Wolfram von Eschenbach
Parzival (vv. 162, 23-24)

Preface of the General Editors

The Garland Library of Medieval Literature was established to make available to the general reader modern translations of texts in editions that conform to the highest academic standards. All of the translations are originals, and were created especially for this series. The translations attempt to render the foreign works in a natural idiom that remains faithful to the originals.

The Library is divided into two sections: Series A, texts and translations; and Series B, translations alone. Those volumes containing texts have been prepared after consultation of the major previous editions and manuscripts. The aim in the edition has been to offer a reliable text with a minimum of editorial intervention. Significant variants accompany the original, and important problems are discussed in the Textual Notes. Volumes without texts contain translations based on the most scholarly texts available, which have been updated in terms of recent scholarship.

Most volumes contain Introductions with the following features: (1) a biography of the author or a discussion of the problem of authorship, with any pertinent historical or legendary information; (2) an objective discussion of the literary style of the original, emphasizing any individual features; (3) a consideration of sources for the work and its influence; and (4) a statement of the editorial policy for each edition and translation. There is also a Select Bibliography, which emphasizes recent criticism on the works. Critical writings are often accompanied by brief descriptions of their importance. Selective glossaries, indices, and footnotes are included where appropriate.

The Library covers a broad range of linguistic areas, including all of the major European languages. All of the important literary forms and genres are considered, sometimes in anthologies or selections.

The General Editors hope that these volumes will bring the general reader a closer awareness of a richly diversified area that has for too long been closed to everyone except those with precise academic training, an area that is well worth study and reflection.

James J. Wilhelm
Rutgers University

Lowry Nelson, Jr.
Yale University

CONTENTS

LIST OF ILLUSTRATIONS

INTRODUCTION

Sometime during the early decades of the thirteenth century—probably between the years 1210 and 1225—a German poet, der Stricker, set about composing an Arthurian romance, *Daniel of the Blossoming Valley* (*Daniel von dem Blühenden Tal*). He wrote his story in Middle High German, a language which had already become the vehicle for a great flowering of German chivalric literature during the high Middle Ages.

While falling short of the lofty literary achievement of his two great Arthurian predecessors in Germany—Hartmann von Aue and Wolfram von Eschenbach—der Stricker nevertheless earned his place in the annals of German medieval literature. For he appears to have formulated his tale in a radically new fashion. Prior to der Stricker's *Daniel*, German poets writing about King Arthur and his knights of the Round Table had for several decades been relying upon French models for the basic outlines of their own works. In fact, the earliest German Arthurian romance—Hartmann's *Erec* (ca. 1185)—was a free adaptation of Chrétien de Troyes' Old French *Erec et Enide*. With *Daniel*, however, der Stricker established an abrupt break with this imitative pattern, since no French source has ever been uncovered for *Daniel*. Indeed, despite der Stricker's claim—in the prologue—that he derived his story from the French poet Alberich de Besançon, scholars are convinced that the story of *Daniel* was largely the product of poetic phantasy. The translation which follows in this volume is the first full English rendition of that story, thought to be the first original, freely invented Arthurian romance in the German tradition.

Introduction

THE POET

We possess very few hard facts about the life of der Stricker. Indeed, this holds true for most of the German poets of the high Middle Ages, even the most prominent among them. For generally they were not accorded any degree of celebrity status during their lifetimes, nor did they have biographers to record the external details of their lives. As for der Stricker, even his name appears to be an assumed one, and there have been numerous attempts to explain its origins. Goedeke (p. 105), for instance, attempted to derive Stricker from the verb *strîchen* ("to rove about," "to wander"). This would, of course, call to mind a *vagus* or travelling poet. But the name attested in the manuscripts is *strickære*, and not *strichære*, which Goedeke's *strîchen* would demand (Pfeiffer, p. 498). Instead, there is a general consensus that this *nom de plume*, if it is that, was intended to suggest not an "itinerant," but rather a "weaver" or a "knitter." Among those who ascribe to this theory, Pfeiffer (p. 498) was the first to propose that such a pseudonym may have referred to the function of the poet as a weaver of stories.

But was the name necessarily a pseudonym, or might it perhaps have been the patronymic of an historically traceable family? In fact, a document uncovered by Pfeiffer (p. 499) makes mention of a certain Heinricus Strichaere, who was attested ca. 1190 in Austria. Meier (p. 220) proffered a further possibility in the person of Godefridus Stricker, whose name was listed in 1216 in a document from the parish of Adenau in the Eifel. The various forms of evidence therefore suggest two possible interpretations of the name: it may have been a family name, or it may simply have been an adopted pseudonym. Most scholars lean towards the latter theory, but in the final analysis both possibilities remain open.

It is nonetheless certain that der Stricker must have spent at least some part of his life in Austria. Several allusions in his later poems to events in that region of the German-speaking world provide the basis for this theory. For example, in the poem "Klage" (ed. Moelleken, *Kleindichtung*, vol. 5, pp. 189-218), the poet states:

min chlage ist ein ursprinc,
dar uz manic chlage fliuzet
und so grozlich begiuzet,
daz min chlage wirt erchant
noch verrer denne in osterlant. (vv. 40-44)

My lament is a fountain
from which many a lament flows
and [which] pours forth so much water
that my lament is recognized
much farther than in Osterlant.

"Osterlant," as Pfeiffer (p. 499) points out, refers generally to eastern lands, but more specifically to the area beginning around Melk and continuing along the Danube—in other words, to parts of present-day Austria. However, it is conceivable that this passage could be interpreted in two different ways: (1) as Pfeiffer maintains: "I shall raise my lament that it be heard far beyond here in Austria," indicating that the poet was speaking in Austria; or (2) "I shall raise my lament that it be heard even farther away from here than in Austria," here implying that der Stricker himself was far from Austria, and that he would be pleased if persons in Austria and beyond could hear his lament.

The second interpretation of the cited passage notwithstanding, other references do make it appear highly probable that der Stricker actually did live in Austria. In the poem "Die Gauhühner" (ed. Moelleken, *Kleindichtung*, vol. 2, pp. 264-71), for example, he refers to the castle Kirchling, which he says in this warning to the nobility, had been stormed by angry peasants (Pfeiffer, p. 499). Kirchling(en), the present-day Kierling, is situated near Vienna, in the vicinity of Klosterneuburg (Pfeiffer, p. 499). Moreover, the story of the blind Herzog Heinrich (ed. Hahn, *Kleinere Gedichte*, pp. 51f.), which der Stricker tells as an admonition against superstitious beliefs, points to

Austria—particularly if one accepts Lachmann's view that this Heinrich was the younger of the Medlinger Heinrichs († ca. 1227-29). Finally, the poem "Die Herren zu Österreich" (ed. Moelleken, *Kleindichtung*, vol. 1, pp. 149-56) makes unambiguous reference to Austria and provides further testimony to corroborate the theory that der Stricker spent perhaps a considerable part of his lifetime there.

But was der Stricker also native to Austria? Or might he have been born elsewhere and have travelled to Austria at some later point? Any attempt to address these questions must first consider additional evidence. For one thing, it is generally accepted—despite the unlikelihood of the etymology: "Stricker" < *strîchære* ("itinerant")—that der Stricker was a professional travelling poet. Convincing proof of this can be found in a number of his writings (see Rosenhagen, *Untersuchungen*, p. 110; and Bartsch, ed. *Karl*, p. xxxi). Perhaps the most frequently cited passage in this regard is the following, from the poem "Frauenehre" (ed. Moelleken, *Kleindichtung*, vol. 1, pp. 15-91):

> Ditz ist ein scho(e)n mere,
> daz ouch nu der strickêre
> die vrowen wil bekennen.
> [...]
> sin leben und vrowen pris,
> die sint ein ander unbekant.
> ein pfert und alt gewant,
> die stunden baz in sinem lobe. (vv. 137-45)
>
> This is a nice piece of news:
> that even der Stricker
> now wishes to acknowledge the ladies.
> [...]
> His [der Stricker's] habits and the praise of ladies
> are strangers to one another.
> A horse and an old piece of clothing
> would be a more fitting topic for his praise.

These words are spoken in the poem by an adversary of der Stricker, who indirectly characterizes our poet as a wandering minstrel; for two objects are mentioned here which are typical of the sort of rewards thought to have been offered such professional artists: "a horse and an old piece of clothing." Further evidence to support the notion that der Stricker was an itinerant poet is found in a passage (p. 157) near the end of *Daniel*, in which der Stricker states, through the voice of his narrator:

> There is one thing which shall ever amaze me: that King Arthur was so generous and the lords nowadays are so miserly. King Arthur did well to relinquish a land as wealthy as Cluse.

This lament, which is reminiscent of similar utterances by Walther von der Vogelweide, seems to bespeak a wandering poet dependent upon the generosity of the various lords at whose courts he performed. Thus, it is entirely conceivable that, as a wandering poet, der Stricker may have travelled to Austria, where he then remained for a time. This, in turn, leaves open the possibility that he may not, as was long assumed, necessarily have been Austrian by birth.

Gustav Rosenhagen, through his inquiries into the dialect of *Daniel*, first brought to light compelling linguistic evidence that located der Stricker's roots outside of Austria. In fact, Rosenhagen's greatest service with regard to der Stricker's language lies in his rebuttal of the long-standing belief that (1) the dialect of *Daniel* was Austrian, and (2) der Stricker was a native Austrian. Rosenhagen (*Untersuchungen*, p. 35) pointed out that numerous early scholars (e.g., Bartsch, ed. *Karl*, p. i; Pfeiffer, pp. 498f.; Jensen, p. 30; and Khull, p. 313) had simply mouthed the traditional opinion that der Stricker's language bore strong Austrian characteristics—often without any sound factual basis for such claims. Of course, der Stricker's references to events and places in Austria are unmistakable, but it does not necessarily follow from this that he also composed in an Austrian dialect. As a result of his examination of the *Daniel* manuscripts, Rosenhagen (*Untersuchungen*, pp. 42f.) uncovered certain Middle German traits in the language. (In this context, "middle" is not a chronological designation [as in "Middle High German"], but rather a geographical term indicating a more centrally located region lying to the north of Austria.) On the basis of Rosenhagen's evidence, there is every reason to believe that *Daniel* was originally written in one of the Middle German dialects.

At one point in his treatment of this question, Rosenhagen is prudent enough to emphasize the "impossibility of making any more precise determination within the Middle German region" (*Untersuchungen*, p. 43). Yet several pages later he departs from this cautious stance and attempts to link der Stricker with the Franciscan Lamprecht von Regensburg, who lived and wrote in eastern Franconia (an area which falls within the rather comprehensive parameters of "Middle Germany"). In any event, any conclusion that der Stricker was born in eastern Franconia and that the local dialect of that area influenced *Daniel* is—while not altogether implausible—at this point still unsubstantiated.

Nonetheless, even localizing the language of *Daniel* somewhere within the very broad Middle German dialect region may offer some important clues as to where der Stricker was born. The reasoning for this is quite simple. As we shall see, *Daniel* was one of his early works, if not his very first. As such, it was more likely than the later poems to retain the seminal dialect features of the poet's birthplace. (The later stories, especially if written elsewhere, would have been more subject to the natural linguistic "contamination" which arises from travelling—and especially living—in other areas.) Thus, since *Daniel* is an early work and if it is written in a Middle German dialect, then it follows from this that der Stricker may very well have been born somewhere in the Middle German region.

The entire question of dialect—in *Daniel* as well as in the poet's other works—is enormously complicated by the fact that virtually no extant Stricker manuscript is written in the dialect of the original work. Scholars are therefore almost solely dependent upon rhyme analysis in unravelling the enigmas surrounding der Stricker's dialect. For now, the most that can be said with relative certainty concerning this question of locale and dialect is: (1) that *Daniel* very likely was originally composed not in Austrian dialect, but in one of the dialects of the Middle German region; (2) that der Stricker may possibly have been born in this same region; and finally (3) that our poet then lived or travelled in Austria, perhaps even acquiring certain dialect habits there which surface in his later works. A great deal of the conjecturality attending these various hypotheses could be alleviated by a comprehensive and definitive study of der Stricker's dialect—in itself a formidable task which has yet to be undertaken.

Despite the uncertainty surrounding the dialect of der Stricker, the fact remains that—wherever his birthplace and whatever his native idiom—he crafted his version of Middle High German into numerous poems and tales. For *Daniel* is by no means the only story for which der Stricker is noted. On the contrary, he composed a large number of other works—a total of nearly 170, according to one tally (Wailes, "Stricker and *Prudentia*," p. 136). Moreover, the wide variety of different genres in which he wrote is quite striking. His only other long work was the 12,000-line epic *Karl der Große*, an adaptation of Pfaffe Konrad's *Rolandslied* (ca. 1170), which in turn was a German version of the French *Chanson de Roland*. Most of der Stricker's other writings—with the exception of *Pfaffe Amîs* (the comic story of a priest named Amis) and several medium-length stories—are significantly shorter. Among these are prayers, beast fables, numerous didactic poems and sixteen *Mären* ("stories" or "tales").

Der Stricker's present-day reputation as a poet rests more upon his shorter tales than upon his two lengthy works *Daniel* and *Karl* (though the latter is transmitted in more than forty manuscripts—a fairly reliable barometer of its popularity during the Middle Ages). Modern readers are most likely to be acquainted with the *Mären*—a particular form of literature for which der Stricker is widely regarded as having laid the groundwork in Germany. Der Stricker's *Mären* tend to focus on the comical side of everyday life; they often deal with such topics as ludicrous misunderstandings or the conflict between husband and wife. And most of the *Mären* contain an underlying—or sometimes more overtly expressed—moral or philosophical message. In fact, der Stricker's *Mären* and other short poems, in particular, leave the firm impression that this poet must have been a man of some education, for he betrays here a knowledge of theological issues and of legal niceties, as well as a grounding in the principles of rhetoric.

It would therefore not be surprising that a poet who evinced such learning would be welcome at the courts of prominent patrons. In fact, many of the major German poets of the high Middle Ages wrote under the aegis of wealthy lords, who commonly accorded them various sorts of material assistance. However, unlike many of his contemporaries der Stricker left no firm clues as to just who his patrons might have been. Certainly it is difficult to imagine that his longer works, in particular, could have been undertaken without some such support. But precisely who those sponsors were, we simply cannot say. In a very general sense, der Stricker's many religiously oriented poems have given rise to speculation that he might have composed under the sponsorship of an ecclesiastical patron (indeed, his name has been linked—albeit somewhat tenuously—to both the Franciscan and the Dominican orders [Wailes, "Stricker and *Prudentia*," p. 137]). On the other hand, his secular works seem to speak more in favor of a noble (perhaps even princely) backer. In the final analysis, there is no compelling reason to exclude *either* possibility: for given the widely varying themes which der Stricker treats in his many works, it appears altogether plausible that he may have written for diverse audiences under the auspices of various patrons. Yet no single identifiable name has yet emerged incontrovertibly as a patron of our poet.

Der Stricker's period of florescence, on the other hand, is subject to somewhat more precise conclusions: those poems which can be dated fall roughly into the first half of the thirteenth century—in other words, into the latter portion of the great golden age of Middle High German literature, which lasted from about 1170 to 1240. This means that der Stricker was probably born towards the end of the twelfth century. And virtually all scholars concur that the two longer works, *Daniel* and *Karl*, probably constitute the poet's early literary production, and that the shorter fables and verse narratives make up his later work. However, uncertainty arises when one attempts to establish a sequence within either of these two larger groupings, or indeed when one endeavors to assign specific dates of composition to the shorter works (with the exception of those few poems which can be dated on the basis of explicit reference to topical events or persons).

Early critics, in their attempts to fix a relative chronology among the shorter stories, often based their findings upon simplistic and ultimately specious principles: for instance, that the comical tales—by virtue of their levity—must have stemmed from der Stricker's youth, and conversely that the religiously oriented writings were necessarily the fruit of an older, more contemplative poet. Such conjectures can be dismissed on numerous grounds. For one thing, they involve sweeping generalizations—and rather shaky assumptions—concerning human nature. And in any event we possess a paucity of firm biographical information about der Stricker. In a broader sense, however, because medieval literature is largely non-confessional in nature, it is risky at best to attempt to allocate thematically different writings to different "periods" in the life of a poet of the Middle Ages. Instead, as Wailes ("Der Stricker," p. 493) correctly points out, we have to imagine that der Stricker—in his role as a professional travelling poet—was dependent "to some degree on the tastes of others [i.e., of his patrons]" for his choice of subject matter. Thus, he may well have composed "prayers for a religious community" and "comic tales for a bourgeois audience"—all within more or less the same span of time.

If it is virtually impossible to establish even a relative sequence—much less absolute datings—for most of der Stricker's later writings, the problem is not quite so intractable for the earlier *Daniel* and *Karl*. First of all, on the basis of parallel passages, Rosenhagen (*Untersuchungen*, p. 103) established the fact that der Stricker must have been acquainted with Wirnt von Grafenberg's romance *Wigalois*. Since *Wigalois* was completed by 1210, *Daniel* must therefore have been written sometime after the year 1210. Furthermore, another of der Stricker's contemporaries, Rudolf von Ems, makes express reference to *Daniel* in his *Willehalm*. Because Rudolf's *Willehalm* was finished by 1243 at the latest, *Daniel* must likewise have been written prior to that year (Bartsch, ed. *Karl*, pp. iii-viii; and "Margarete," pp. 3f.).

Similarly, modern scholars have been able to date der Stricker's *Karl* to within the years 1217 and 1225. The first of these two dates rests upon Schnell's thesis (pp. 78-80) that Wolfram's *Willehalm* exerted an influence on *Karl*. Since *Willehalm* is thought to have been completed by ca. 1217, *Karl* must therefore have originated sometime after that. Schnell arrives at the latter date, 1225, by linking certain events in *Karl* to the historically documented marriage of Emperor Friedrich II in November of the same year. Further inquiries—by J. Singer (pp. 97-99) and von der Burg (p. 355)—have likewise placed *Karl* within this general time span of 1217-1225.

Since der Stricker's two longer works—*Karl* and *Daniel*—stand in close chronological proximity to one another, scholars have long been divided as to which was written first. However, there are at least some promising clues for arriving at a firm answer. For example, a recent analysis of certain stylistic characteristics of both *Daniel* and *Karl* (specifically, the various ways in which the direct discourse of the characters is incorporated into the narrative) has shown that, in all likelihood, *Daniel* was the earlier of the two (Resler, "Datierung"). With this in mind, it is possible to correlate the dating for *Karl* (1217-1225) with that for *Daniel* (1210-1243) and thereby to narrow appreciably the time span for *Daniel's* composition: quite simply, since *Daniel* is older than *Karl*, *Daniel* must have been written sometime before 1225, the latest possible year for *Karl*. Thus, it can be deduced that *Daniel* was composed between the year 1210 (after Wirnt's *Wigalois*) and the year 1225 (again, prior to the latest possible date for *Karl*).

Thus, one must imagine der Stricker working on his *Daniel* as a relatively young man (or at least early in his career), probably at some point during the second or third decades of the thirteenth century. Though he was never again to return specifically to the Arthurian mythology for his inspiration, der Stricker's later writings still resonate incontestably with one important feature prominent in the *Daniel* story: the same moralizing and didactic voice of the *Daniel* narrator finds its way into many of the later works and serves as a link between the initial, somewhat tentative stirrings of der Stricker's literary muse and the subsequent ripening of his art.

One final piece may be added to what is still a rather fuzzy and tenuous biographical mosaic: unlike Hartmann and Wolfram—indeed, unlike many of the German courtly poets of the high Middle Ages—der Stricker appears not to have been a knight. Evidence for this can best be unearthed by appealing directly to the text of *Daniel*. For in contrast to the romances of both Hartmann and Wolfram, which fairly teem with the daily minutiae of the chivalric way of life, *Daniel* contains precious little "insider's knowledge" of the nuts and bolts of chivalry. Such knowledge—which, if present in *Daniel*, might lead to the conclusion that der Stricker was a member of the knightly order—is simply not evident. Instead, as we have already established, it is probably best to picture der Stricker in the role of an itinerant professional poet.

All in all, relatively few concrete facts are known about this poet: His real name may or may not have been Stricker—more likely not. Born in the late twelfth century—probably in Middle Germany and, within that broad region, perhaps in Franconia—he appears to have later lived and plied his trade for some considerable time in Austria. Since the last of the relatively few poems which can be reliably dated seem to cluster around the mid-point of the thirteenth century, we are probably justified in assuming that he died about 1250. A reasonably well educated man, his learning shines through in many of his writings. Der Stricker was clearly not a knight (in fact, it is commonly accepted that he was not even a member of the nobility, but that he belonged instead to the middle class). Nor was he a wealthy man, as he seems to have depended for his livelihood upon the generosity of certain unnamed patrons—some of whom may have been secular lords, others perhaps attached in some way to the church. And finally, while der Stricker never attained the soaring heights of a Wolfram or the stylistic polish of a Gottfried von Strassburg, he displayed an uncommon originality and a broad versatility in his prodigious literary efforts.

Sources and Influence

At first glance it would appear that one need not look very far in order to find the direct source for der Stricker's *Daniel*. For in his prologue, the poet states (p. 3), quite plainly and straightforwardly:

> Master Alberich of Besançon has brought to me a story from the French which I have translated that it might be heard in German whenever entertainment suits the occasion. Let no one criticize me: for only if Alberich has lied to me, do I pass falsehood on to you.

Yet as indicated previously, modern scholars have been virtually unanimous in their rejection of this claim. In fact, the notion that a

French work by Alberich of Besançon served as der Stricker's prototype is now believed to be fully as improbable as is Wolfram's celebrated appeal to a certain Kyot as the precursor for his *Parzival.*

The question now arises: why is it that we do not simply take der Stricker at his word when he names Alberich as the source for his story? For one thing, there is no evidence whatsoever that Alberich, who is known chiefly for his romance *Alexander*, ever even composed a *Daniel*. Moreover, der Stricker appears to have lifted the passage in which he refers to Alberich almost verbatim from the German *Alexanderlied* of Pfaffe Lamprecht. Writing around the middle of the twelfth century, Lamprecht states in his prologue:

> Alberich of Besançon has brought this song to us. He wrote it in Welsh [i.e. French], and now I shall report it to you in German. Let no one criticize me, for only if he [Alberich] has lied, do I also lie.

The extent of der Stricker's borrowing from the German *Alexanderlied* is evident when one compares these lines with the passage cited from *Daniel*. Yet why is there this apparent equivocation on the part of der Stricker? One possible explanation lies in the fact that, by this point in the development of the courtly romance in Germany, the appeal to a source had become virtually canonical among poets. Hence der Stricker's claim in this passage can probably best be viewed primarily as a formulaic necessity. (Seen from a much broader perspective, of course, the careful appeal to *auctoritas*, or established authority, is very much characteristic of medieval composition.) At any rate, what matters most in the final analysis is that scholars have never been able to unearth any Romance version of the Daniel story. Thus, in a sense, part of the significance of der Stricker's *Daniel* lies in the simple fact that it was—the reference to Alberich of Besançon notwithstanding—freely invented and not based upon a French model.

This is not to say that der Stricker was unaware of either contemporary or earlier literary traditions, both inside and outside of Germany. Much to the the contrary. For, while apparently fabricating the general story-line of *Daniel*, der Stricker drew liberally and broadly from the motifs, episodes and at times even specific wordings both of Middle High German works of his own age and of various legends and stories from classical antiquity. Rosenhagen, in his *Untersuchungen* and in the ancillary notes to his edition, documents in some detail the individual passages which most specifically point to der Stricker's close acquaintance with (and extensive borrowings from) Middle High German literature. Chief among the poets and stories which contributed in this fashion to *Daniel* are: Pfaffe Konrad, whose *Rolandslied* supplied much of the imagery and vocabulary for the mass battle scenes in *Daniel* (and which was later to provide the direct impetus for der Stricker's *Karl der Große*); Hartmann von Aue, who with his two pioneering Arthurian romances *Erec* and *Iwein*, had set the stage for both der Stricker and the other subsequent Arthurian poets in Germany; Wirnt von Grafenberg, whose Arthurian romance *Wigalois* is echoed in a number of different passages in *Daniel*; Heinrich von Veldeke, who with his early courtly epic *Eneide* (an adaptation of Virgil's *Aeneid*) had explored the demonic, destructive side of love—a motif which plays a significant role in *Daniel*; and Ulrich von Zazikhoven, whose *Lanzelet* seems to have had a direct bearing upon—among many other things in *Daniel*—the wondrous fountain standing at the entrance to Cluse and King Arthur's custom of refusing all food until hearing of some marvelous adventure.

Of all of these more or less contemporary works, Hartmann's *Iwein* has been shown (see Rosenhagen, *Untersuchungen*; and Kern) to have exerted by far the single most pervasive influence upon *Daniel*. In addition to numerous similarities in the prologues of the two works and in their respective depictions of the Arthurian court and its cast of characters, certain other prominent features point incontrovertibly to der Stricker's deep indebtedness to Hartmann's *Iwein*. In both romances, for example, the action is initially launched into motion by a report of adventure: in *Iwein* this comes from the story told by the knight Kalogrenant, and in *Daniel* from the lengthy account by the messenger giant. Moreover, both heroes set out alone and unnoticed from the Arthurian court in order to take up the trail of adventure. Also, the statue of the wailing beast standing beneath a lime tree near the entrance to Cluse fulfills a strikingly similar function to that of the magic fountain (likewise situated beneath a lime tree!) in *Iwein*. Indeed, even the effects are the same once the two fountains have been activated: in each case, there quickly ensues an ominous storm with a paralyzing display of lightning and thunder, whereupon the lord of the land angrily rides up, ready to do battle with all intruders. Moreover, in both stories, the hero, just on the verge of embarking upon a perilous adventure, is delayed by another petitioner and is faced with a wrenching choice between conflicting obligations. There also exist notable points of overlap between Daniel's adventure with the dwarf Juran and Iwein's struggle against the giant Harpin (see Kern, pp. 34-36). And finally, both heroes—Daniel and Iwein—ultimately rule over the kingdoms of their defeated opponents and marry (after remarkably hasty reconciliations) the widows of those same knights.

The broad and pervasive range of influence on *Daniel* from the classical literature of antiquity was first detailed by Bartsch (ed., *Karl*, pp. xxxivf.). For one thing, the blinding of Matur's giant by the knights of the Round Table is a clear echo of the saga of Polyphemus, the Cyclops from the *Odyssey* who is robbed of his eyesight by Odysseus and his men. Furthermore, the lethal head (the mere sight of which is enough to inflict death on any beholder) is an apparent allusion to the head of Medusa. And the diseased creature who terrorizes the Land of the Green Meadow, and whose voice robs victims of their senses, is reminiscent of the Sirens; likewise, the sorceress Circe appears to have been a model for the capacity of this same monster to transform human beings into various sorts of animals. Finally, the notion that bathing in human blood can have a certain curative quality is a motif central to various legends of ancient times (and indeed one which was still quite popular during the high Middle Ages). Given the demonstrably pervasive influence on *Daniel* by classical literature, the question arises as to just how der Stricker might have established his contact with these various stories. The answer to this question is quite simple: at the time of *Daniel's* composition, the literature of ancient Greece and Rome was familiar in many learned and aristocratic circles in Germany. Thus, der Stricker could readily have become acquainted with all of these legends, in one form or another, at the courts where he in all likelihood plied his trade.

From all of this there emerges the inevitable assessment that, while *Daniel* marks an important break with compositional tradition in Germany, it is clearly not a work which arose in a literary vacuum. By the same token, der Stricker did not fail to grasp—and exploit for purposes of his story—the enchantment with things French which had captivated German courtiers of the high Middle Ages. For he seems consciously to have set about investing his tale with certain trappings of the exemplary French romances. Nowhere is this more evident than in his choice of proper names in *Daniel*. In fact, some of the more non-Germanic sounding names appear to have come down to der Stricker from French romances of the day. In the notes to his *Daniel* edition, Rosenhagen proffers possible sources for some of these manifestly Francophone names. In addition, much new information can also be adduced to supplement Rosenhagen's findings. For instance, Linval (v. 248) may have derived from Marie de France's *Lanval* (Rosenhagen, *Daniel*, p. 181); however, the name also occurs in yet another work, *Les Merveilles de Rigomer* (vv. 4494 and 7087), thought to date from sometime during the first half of the thirteenth century. Rosenhagen also offers possible models for the Dark Mountain (*Daniel*, p. 179); to these must be added the *mont dolereus* contained in Chrétien's *Erec* (v. 1694) and in Guillaume le Clerc's *Fergus* (though the latter may possibly have postdated *Daniel*). The dwarf Juran, for whose name Rosenhagen is unable to offer an explanation, may well have come to der Stricker by way of the late twelfth-century *Folie Tristan d'Oxford*, in which a giant named Urgan appears. Furthermore, Danise—the widow of King Matur and Daniel's eventual queen—is in all likelihood a name designedly chosen by der Stricker to correspond phonetically to Daniel (Rosenhagen, *Daniel*, p. 181); and yet even here an altogether plausible French model offers itself in Dyonise, one of the damsels at the court (vv. 6331 and 6525) in *Durmart le Galois*, which dates from the first third of the thirteenth century. Even more compelling—and likewise overlooked by Rosenhagen—is the origin of the name Beladigant, which is attested in *Le Bel Inconnu* from the early thirteenth century; in this instance the name survives virtually unaltered from the French work, in which, significantly, the eponymous character is one of King Arthur's knights.

The name of the title hero Daniel is likewise clearly non-Germanic in origin. Although der Stricker is generally thought to have derived the name Daniel from the Bible rather than from contemporary courtly literature (Rosenhagen, *Daniel*, p. 179), the name can also be accounted for by searching among literary documents. In the second continuation of *Perceval*, for example, a knight named Daniaus is listed among the members of King Arthur's court. While some doubt persists as to whether this work was composed before or after *Daniel*, the two at any rate are chronologically close to one another. Hence the name might well have been in general circulation. As such, der Stricker could have encountered it in one form or another. One could even pursue this line of conjecture further and imagine that, with the Biblical name in the back of his mind, der Stricker might then have modified Daniaus to Daniel.

All of this demonstrates that, not unlike the older classical literature, the French courtly romances constitute an entire body of poetry which der Stricker might have come to know, most probably through contact with fellow poets at the German courts. Certainly such stories were at this time very much in fashion in Germany. However, it remains wholly within the realm of conjecture as to whether der Stricker was himself able to read Old French, or whether he had perhaps heard the Old French romances performed in Germany. It is of course also conceivable—though this appears even less compelling, for lack of any tangible supporting evidence—that he may have actually been in France himself. Nonetheless, whatever the mode of contact and whatever the level of his proficiency, it seems a reasonably safe conclusion that der Stricker was to some degree conversant with the French literature of his day. Indeed, in his incorporation of French elements—most especially certain proper names—into his *Daniel*, he betrays the same pattern of broad eclecticism which comes to light in his extensive borrowings from contemporary German literature and from the works of classical antiquity.

At first blush the Romance names in *Daniel* might seem to offer encouragement to those wishing to resurrect the theory, despite all evidence to the contrary, that a French source existed for *Daniel*. Certainly this is what der Stricker would have had his audience believe. However, any argument for a French *Daniel du Val Florissant*—as Paris (p. 136) envisioned the title for this apparently non-existent romance—is patently fallacious if based solely upon the presence of French names in the German version. For one thing, Arthurian romance was originally a French genre and as such was invested—virtually of necessity—with a full array of Romance trappings (including just such features as proper names). Moreover, since der Stricker had expressly claimed a French source for his story, it seems that his assigning Romance names to many of his characters was a conscious attempt to align his self-conceived work more convincingly with the

French tradition. Indeed, a further purpose of the Francophone names in *Daniel* might have been to induce audiences to accept more readily the assertion of a French source.

It is apparent from all of this that the outside sources feeding into the story of Daniel were both many and diverse. This fact alone is evidence of the poetic and organizational difficulties with which der Stricker must have had to grapple while working on *Daniel*. In the final analysis, der Stricker perhaps most convincingly earned his poet's laurel for the double role which he played in composing *Daniel*: as integrator and as innovator. For not only did he face the task of weaving all of the diverse motifs and episodes together into a cohesive story, he also achieved something—despite his open disavowal of that achievement—which few other poets in Germany at this time were inclined to undertake: he engaged in a sort of inventive fictionalizing which was very nearly taboo among courtly storytellers of the high Middle Ages.

Such were the various impulses which informed and helped to generate *Daniel*. But what about the reception of this romance by medieval poets and audiences? In order to arrive at any firm conclusions concerning this issue, we must first consider certain factors external to the story itself. For instance, the manuscript transmission is often an authoritative yardstick for the popularity of a work during its own age. And in the case of *Daniel*, it is both sparse and late. Only five *Daniel* manuscripts survived into the twentieth century; and all of these date from the mid- to late fifteenth century, a good 200 or 250 years after the composition of the story. Despite this relative paucity of manuscripts, however, der Stricker's sole Arthurian romance was not entirely without resonance during the Middle Ages. For one thing, a contemporary poet, Rudolf von Ems, refers twice—in his two romances *Alexander* and *Willehalm von Orlens*—to der Stricker and to

Daniel with a distinct measure of admiration. In *Willehalm von Orlens* (ed. Junk, p. 37) Rudolf states:

> Ŏch heti úch der Strikære
> Bas danne ich berihtet,
> Wold er úch han getihtet
> Als Daniel vom blůnden tal. (vv. 2230-33)
>
> In addition, der Stricker would have
> reported to you better than I [would have],
> had he wished to compose poetry for you
> as [did? as he did with?] Daniel of the Blossoming Valley.

While the final line of this passage is somewhat enigmatic (and even suggests that Rudolf may have mistaken "Daniel" for a fellow poet, instead of a story!), nonetheless it is clear that Rudolf intended to offer his praise to der Stricker. However, these lines and the more or less similar passage from *Alexander* together constitute the only truly contemporary external references to *Daniel.*

Nevertheless, during the later Middle Ages the story appears by no means to have fallen into oblivion. For sometime during the latter half of the thirteenth century (perhaps around 1260-1280), another German-speaking poet, der Pleier, appropriated the same tale and reworked it into *Garel vom blühenden Tal.* Der Pleier, who has been linked with the region around Schärding in Austria, composed three quite lengthy Arthurian romances, the other two being *Tandareis und Flordibel* and *Meleranz.* Apparently the earliest of the three, *Garel* betrays affinities to *Daniel* which extend well beyond the nearly homologous names of the two heroes. In fact, there can be no doubt that der Pleier knew *Daniel* first-hand and consciously undertook to imitate—and significantly revise—the story. Indeed, the evidence is striking. As in *Daniel,* the action is first set in motion by the arrival of a messenger giant. Also, in one of his adventures Garel must defend himself against a creature armed with a lethal head ostensibly modelled on the Gorgon-like head carried about in *Daniel* by the intruder in the Land of the Bright Fountain. And at one point in *Garel* the warfare is waged on a massive scale, just as we find in der Stricker's story. Even a casual reading of *Garel* makes it abundantly clear that der Pleier borrowed from his predecessor both the overall story and a number of individual episodes and motifs.

However, along with the striking similarities, there are also some major and noteworthy points of divergence between *Daniel* and *Garel*. In contrast to *Daniel*, in which King Arthur plays an unusually prominent role, in *Garel* it is the title hero himself who occupies center stage for most of the story. King Arthur and the knights of the Round Table recede into the background and assume a more supporting role. Moreover, the hero Garel is—unlike Daniel—very much subject to the power of love; and his chivalric feats are accomplished not so much by the power of *list* (or cunning), to which Daniel resorts time and again, but rather by the more traditional virtues of physical force and knightly prowess. (It is not known for certain whether der Pleier was himself, unlike der Stricker, a knight; the fact that he consciously undertook to restore to the tale of Daniel some of the prime chivalric features which are so notably lacking in der Stricker's version might tend to indicate that he did belong to the knightly order.) Finally, the very name of the protagonist—Garel—has less of a Biblical, otherworldly ring than does Daniel; quite simply, it "sounds" more like the sort of name which an Arthurian knight ought to bear.

These and the myriad other alterations which der Pleier undertook vis à vis der Stricker's *Daniel* appear to share common ground: namely a purposeful design to bring the Daniel/Garel story more into line with the established conventions of the earlier, classical Arthurian romances (see below, ARTISTIC ACHIEVEMENT). For up until the time of der Stricker's *Daniel*, a German audience listening to an Arthurian romance had already come to expect certain fixed ingredients within that story: among other things, that King Arthur should be chiefly a passive background figure, that the hero be at the center of the action, and that his feats should be motivated by love for his spouse. In these (as well as in numerous other) details, der Stricker had missed the mark. Thus, a great many of the changes which der Pleier introduced in his retelling of the tale can be said to constitute a correction of "the violations of norm which der Stricker commited [sic] in his construct" (D. Müller, p. 178). In the simplest terms, der Pleier endeavored to bring the story back into line with the by then familiar conventions of the genre. And it seems that der Pleier's recasting of *Daniel* into *Garel* must have found some measure of resonance among later generations. The best evidence for this are the Garel frescoes in Runkelstein Castle near Bolzano in South Tyrol. Dating from around the year 1400, these drawings illustrate scenes not from der Stricker's *Daniel*, but from the later, more typically "Arthurian" version by der Pleier.

While der Pleier's *Garel* certainly substantiates most strikingly the survival of the Daniel story during the Middle Ages, it is not the only such evidence. At some point after the reworking by der Pleier (perhaps during the second half of the fourteenth century, although the dating entails some considerable conjecture), a Swabian poet by the name of Konrad von Stoffeln wrote a brief Arthurian romance entitled *Gauriel von Muntabel*. Not only is one of the men of the Round Table identified in *Gauriel* as "Daniel von Plüental" (v. 3867), but, as Rosenhagen (*Untersuchungen*, p. 119) points out, another of the knights bears the name Limual, a possible reminiscence of the knight Linval from *Daniel* (v. 248). And perhaps most significantly, the name of the hero Gauriel appears to be—as Rosenhagen (*Untersuchungen*, p. 119) suggests—an amalgamation of Daniel and Garel.

One final and barely audible echo of *Daniel* emanates from the mid-fifteenth century, in the poem *Der Spiegel*. Once mistakenly attributed by earlier scholars to Meister Altswert, this work is now believed to have been written by the Swabian knight/poet Hermann von Sachsenheim. At one point in his tale (ed. Holland and Keller, *Meister Altswert*, p. 164) Hermann says:

Reht als dem konig Matter
Was mir myn hertz versnytten,
Do in hett überstritten
Von Blumendal herr Danyel. (vv. 28-31)

Just as [was the case] with King Matur,
my heart was torn apart
after he [Matur] had been defeated by
Sir Daniel of the Blossoming Valley.

This very brief passage demonstrates that *Daniel*—despite its apparent failure to achieve outright acclaim during the golden age in which it was composed—was nonetheless resilient and memorable enough to have lived on in the collective literary domain of subsequent generations. Moreover, not only did *Daniel* thus endure beyond its own day for a good two centuries and more; it also appears (based upon the allusion in *Der Spiegel* to the conflict between Daniel and King Matur) that even some of the particular details of the story were still in circulation during the fifteenth century (Rosenhagen, *Untersuchungen*, p. 119).

Other than these limited and rather faint reverberations, however, the story of Daniel lay dormant and forgotten for some time, before it was finally brought back to life by philologists of the nineteenth century. What emerges from all of this is the realization that der Stricker's *Daniel* failed to play a major role in the development or dissemination of the Arthurian legend within Germany. Inasmuch as *Daniel* was the work of a poet whose real genius lay in a genre other than Arthurian romance, one can, in a sense, hardly be surprised at this. Furthermore, the relative lack of sweeping appeal which *Daniel* seems to have held for audiences of the Middle Ages is, to some extent, part of a larger circumstance: namely that, by the time der Stricker set about composing *Daniel*, the towering and truly enduring Arthurian romances of the Middle High German language had already been written. All who followed in the footsteps of Wolfram and Hartmann were to fall short, to a greater or lesser measure, of their eminent predecessors. To be sure, the decline in the intrinsic literary merit of the later stories was neither as profound nor as universal as early critics liked to maintain. And yet despite what appears nonetheless to have been a certain degree of erosion, the genre continued to flourish in Germany and more and more Arthurian romances were composed. Indeed, even after most poets had long since turned their attention to other subjects, the tales already recorded about King Arthur and his knights of the Round Table still held the attention of audiences for much of the remainder of the Middle Ages. Wolfram's *Parzival*, for instance, still enjoyed enough residual popularity to find its way from manuscript form onto the printed page as late as the year 1477 (J. Schultz, p. 3). But in the larger perspective Arthurian romance (along with most other things characteristically medieval) was destined to fall wholly out of fashion with the advent of the post-medieval era, in which reason and scientific inquiry began gradually to supplant the older, more rigid ways of thinking ingenerate in the chivalric literature of the Middle Ages.

ARTISTIC ACHIEVEMENT

While the tale of Daniel did not find major resonance during its own age, what reaction it did evoke was, as we have seen, generally favorable. The same cannot be said of *Daniel's* reception by scholars of the nineteenth century, who almost unanimously disparaged it as a poor imitation of the romances of Hartmann. The key to an understanding of this initial derogation of *Daniel* is the word "post-classical"—a term which carries a strong hint of the pronouncedly judgmental attitude of the early scholarship. In effect, critics placed high upon a pedestal the three great German Arthurian romances—Hartmann's *Erec* and *Iwein*, and Wolfram's *Parzival*. Along with the five Old French romances of Chrétien de Troyes, these three German works were viewed as the "classical" examples of the genre.

The problem inherent in this canonical approach is that it made so few representatives of the genre into a universal yardstick by which all other Arthurian stories were to be evaluated. Of course, if no further romances had been written in Germany, then such narrow standards might perhaps have been sufficient to define the whole genre (J. Schultz, p. 5). However, a total of twelve to fifteen German Arthurian romances have come down to us from the high Middle Ages. Nevertheless, it was perhaps inevitable that early critics, by focusing their attention on the ways in which *Daniel* and the other subsequent stories deviated from the "classical" norm, would downgrade these later poets who had also ventured onto the turf of Arthurian romance.

By contrast, more modern scholarship has to a large extent cast off the shackles imposed by these initial devaluations of *Daniel*. Indeed, the often heard charge that *Daniel* lacks any cohesive structure or consistent message has been directly addressed and to a certain degree refuted. For instance, Henderson (*Werkstruktur*) has demonstrated that *Daniel* possesses very highly defined structural characteristics—a finding which belies early notions that it was a primitive, disjointed story. Furthermore, Brall, who examines *Daniel* within its social and historical parameters, uncovers evidence that der Stricker may have composed his romance in direct response to incipient conflicts among different strata of the Austrian nobility. With such reevaluations in mind, it is perhaps most meaningful to return at this point to the original indictment levelled against *Daniel* by earlier scholars: that it is a story which utterly failed to capture the essence of Arthurian romance.

To begin with, it is a patent fact that *Daniel* is markedly different from the stories of Chrétien, Hartmann and Wolfram. To this limited extent the critics were right. However, it is quite another thing to assert (as did early scholarship) that der Stricker therefore must necessarily have misunderstood the spirit of Arthurian literature. As was previously established (see above, SOURCES AND INFLUENCE), der Stricker unquestionably knew intimately and borrowed liberally from the works of Hartmann von Aue. Yet by the same token, the mere fact that der Stricker took the liberty of introducing his own changes does not necessarily mean that he had utterly misread the ethos of Arthurian romance. Instead, it appears altogether conceivable that der Stricker simply went about adapting and reshaping the genre to fit his changed purposes and circumstances.

By examining—non-judgmentally—the various ways in which *Daniel* differs from the accepted norm, one can best uncover some of the unique and admittedly unconventional features of this highly entertaining tale. Such an inquiry will reveal that a strictly conventional Arthurian romance may never have been der Stricker's goal in *Daniel*. Instead, the poet seems to have been intent upon incorporating into *Daniel* a thoroughly different set of ideas—some of them rooted in certain non-Arthurian literary traditions, others more germane to der Stricker's own later writings.

Yet despite the overall unorthodoxy of *Daniel*, it ought to be noted that nothing egregiously "un-Arthurian" occurs during the first eight hundred or so verses. On the contrary, the introduction is quite traditional: a newcomer, Daniel, gains acceptance into King Arthur's fellowship of knights—among whom, characteristically, is the brash and taunting Keii, who meets with humiliating defeat at the hands of the initiate. Even the giant's challenge, which serves to motivate the ensuing plot, corresponds largely to the sort of initial impulse which typically sets Arthurian romances into motion. But then der Stricker's deviation from tradition sets in: during Arthur's council with his men, Gawein proposes that they invite the giant to remain at court for seven days; after this they would then follow him back to his homeland, Cluse, and answer the challenge of his master King Matur. This, at least, is what they are to tell the giant. Gawein's real plan, however, is to muster an army of knights during those seven days, so as to boost their chances in the anticipated battle against Matur's men.

With the introduction of this delusive stratagem, der Stricker severs his initial dependence upon the familiar conventions of the genre. For in place of the more traditional knightly virtues of courage and valor, an element of cunning or trickery now steps to the forefront: the stalling technique is misrepresented to the giant as an opportunity for King Matur to secure a double victory—a victory not only over Arthur himself, but over all of the men of the Round Table as well. As King Arthur himself says to the messenger giant: "They [my followers] ought all to witness the moment when I surrender my land into your lord's hand, such that they—as well as I—may become his vassals" (p. 20). No mention is made of the plot whereby these "vassals" are to form an attack force. Moreover, a second point of departure from convention is embedded in this same scheme: the very fact that King Arthur assembles an army in preparation for the march on Cluse constitutes in itself a sharp break from traditional Arthurian romance. For while King Arthur typically travels about in the company of a large retinue of combat-ready knights, it is nearly always within the parameters of individual, one-on-one encounter that battle is done, whether for sport or in earnest. And in a third area—not yet evident at this early juncture in the story—der Stricker further rejects Arthurian convention, i.e. in the wholesale lack of courtly love (*minne*) as a motivating impulse for his protagonist Daniel.

In summation, der Stricker's chief points of deviation from the established genre can be seen as threefold: (1) cunning (*list*) in place of valor, (2) mass warfare instead of dueling, and (3) absence of *minne*. In effect, these aberrations (as they were initially seen) provided the basis for early denigration of der Stricker's *Daniel*. However, a closer examination will yield some insight into the fact that it may well have been conscious poetic design—and not mere ignorance of convention—

which prompted der Stricker to rethink and to recast certain features of the genre.

First of all, the prominence of *list* in *Daniel* (a topic dealt with in some detail by modern scholars, in particular by de Boor ["Daniel und Garel"], Ragotzky ["Handlungsmodell"] and Moelleken/Henderson) is such that fully seven discrete instances of cunning can be delineated during the course of the story: (1) Gawein's plan to gather an army of knights (pp. 18f.); (2) Daniel's duel with the dwarf Juran (pp. 30-34); (3) Daniel's encounter with the bellyless monster (pp. 38-40); (4) the skirmish between King Arthur's knights and the second giant (pp. 64f.); (5) Daniel's killing of the diseased creature (pp. 85-90); (6) Daniel's activation of the beast's deafening cry so as to dispatch the remaining four armies (pp. 106-108); and (7) Daniel's use of the invisible net to capture the giants' father (pp. 134-140). It is clear from all of this that *list* occupies a remarkably significant position in der Stricker's tale. And at the very least, these repeated applications of cunning stand out as quite "surprising in a chivalric romance" (Wailes, "Stricker and *Prudentia*," p. 152).

At the same time, however, it ought to be emphasized that the more standard Arthurian reliance on knightly strength and valor is not entirely lacking either. For example, in the passage (p. 49) in which Daniel struggles mightily to survive the torrent of water (unleashed when the Count of the Bright Fountain disappears inside the mountain tunnel) we glimpse a typically Arthurian knight in his single-handed bout with adversity. A variation on this can be found in the adventure (pp. 75-77) in which Daniel, with the aid of his invincible sword, duels with a knight protected by the impenetrable skin of a mermaid. In this latter episode, since each combatant possesses a supernatural weapon, the advantages, so to speak, cancel each other out, so that Daniel's eventual victory over this knight can be seen as proof of his superior chivalric prowess. And in a later adventure it is Daniel alone among all of the men of the Round Table who is able to endure the din of the wailing beast long enough to gag it; this act of raw courage—undiluted by any resort to guile—stills the unbearable sound, thereby saving King Arthur and his knights (pp. 55f.). All of these examples demonstrate that, despite the prominence of cunning and trickery, at certain points in the story Daniel does indeed display those chivalric virtues which the genre more typically demands.

In this regard it is interesting to note that *Daniel*, like most other chivalric romances, features a full compliment of supernatural objects: the impenetrable mermaid's skin, Daniel's sword, the invisible net and the magic salve. And although the realm of magic is closely allied with the concept of *list* (Moelleken and Henderson [p. 188], for instance, view magic as an integral component of the Middle High German noun *list*), it does not necessarily follow that the use of such supernatural articles in and of itself constitutes *list*. Indeed, of the seven instances of cunning cited above, those specifically involving one of the supernatural objects (numbers 2, 5, and 7) fall under the rubric of *list* not by virtue of the weapons alone. Instead, these three episodes entail something which transcends mere magic: namely, an artfully conceived plan to employ those weapons in a deceptive manner. It is this—and not the magic properties of the weapons—which embodies *list*. For example, in the episode in which Daniel slays the diseased creature with his magic sword, it is only by cunningly mimicking the derangement of the other captives that he is able to draw near enough to put that sword to use; indeed, it could be argued that from such close range *any* sword would probably suffice. The actual weapon per se, then, does not necessarily comprise this un-Arthurian virtue of *list*. Indeed, viewed from the larger perspective of the genre, supernatural objects are an altogether standard accoutrement of Arthurian romances. Hence it is not in the mere presence of such weapons in *Daniel*, but rather in the clever schemes involved in their application that der Stricker introduced a curious (or at least un-Arthurian) twist to his story.

Der Stricker's break with Arthurian convention is tellingly illustrated in the episode in which Parzival challenges the angry father of the two giants: foolishly placing his faith in the traditional Arthurian virtues of courage and valor, Parzival—that most illustrious of all German Arthurian knights—is helplessly (almost comically!) snapped up by his opponent and disgracefully cast down onto the ledge alongside King Arthur. Daniel, however, possessing the added virtue of *list*, is able to rescue both of his eminent comrades by means of a shrewdly executed ruse: by enticing the giants' father down the mountainside and straight into the invisible net, he almost effortlessly forces the intruder to capitulate.

Though quite rare in Arthurian romance, such artful scheming on the part of the protagonist is by no means unheard of in certain other genres of medieval literature. In fact, Daniel's frequent appeal to *list* brings to mind an earlier form of literature in Germany, the *Spielmannsepik*, which flourished during the latter half of the twelfth century. Variously translated into English as "minstrel's epic" or "minstrelsy," the *Spielmannsepen* are heavily populated by heroes who rely, as does Daniel, just as heavily on cunning as on pure valor or physical strength. Seen in this light, the passage in which Daniel himself lauds the virtues of the intellect over those of the body is strikingly reminiscent of the *Spielmannsepen*: "A man can often accomplish with wisdom full many a thing which he could not achieve by relying upon strength alone" (p. 30). The final culmination of der Stricker's praise of cunning comes in the long didactic excursus in which he states (p. 140), among other things:

> Whatever man has exquisite cunning at his command is deserving of all the more praise from everyone, both men and women alike. For one man alone can accomplish with cunning that which a thousand men, however strong they might be, could never do together.

In one sense, der Stricker's posture here appears to hark back in time to the *Spielmannsepen*. Yet at the same time it also anticipates the rise of the new and shorter genres such as beast fables and *Mären*, in which *list* plays so central a role. Indeed, as has already been established (see above, THE POET), der Stricker himself was to lay the foundations in Germany for these particular forms of literature. Thus, if Daniel's repeated reliance on *list* casts him in a somewhat odd light in the setting of Arthurian romance, this may not be due to der Stricker's nescient misreading of the role of the traditional Arthurian knight. Instead, it may simply betoken the fact that the poet was himself, as Wailes ("Stricker and *Prudentia*," p. 153) puts it, "indifferent to physical hardihood and unimpressed by power." Indeed, to the extent that *Daniel* can be seen as a forerunner of the later didactic poems, der Stricker's consistent design—in *Daniel* as well as in the subsequent shorter works—appears to have been "to extol reason and understanding in contrast to muscle and estate" (Wailes, "Stricker and *Prudentia*," p. 153). Seen in this light, der Stricker's emphasis on *list* in *Daniel* evinces not any misconstruction of Arthurian literature on his part, but rather an articulation of his own very different *Weltanschauung*. Indeed, it seems that in this regard der Stricker was intent on placing his own personal stamp upon the courtly romance.

The mass battle scenes which der Stricker weaves throughout the middle sections of *Daniel* constitute a second very striking point of departure from established Arthurian convention. Early on, critics (Rosenhagen [*Untersuchungen*, pp. 94-96] and de Boor [*Geschichte*, II, 195]) noticed that der Stricker's depiction of large-scale warfare in *Daniel* is modelled, right down to his individual word choice, on the pre-courtly *Rolandslied*—a work which, as previously mentioned, would later provide the direct inspiration for der Stricker's epic *Karl*. Thus, although *Daniel* likely predates *Karl* (see above, THE POET), it would nonetheless appear that, while occupied with his fledgling work

Daniel, der Stricker must already have established a rather close acquaintance with the *Rolandslied.*

At any rate, the scenes of mass combat in *Daniel* are directly related to the unaccustomed role played in the story by King Arthur. To be sure, in Geoffrey of Monmouth's *Historia Regum Brittaniae* (a seminal work in the development of the Arthurian legend) King Arthur is portrayed as a vigorous general personally leading mighty armies of Breton warriors. But already in Chrétien—the real molder of Arthurian legend into Arthurian romance—this aspect had all but disappeared. In fact, with the exception of the Winchester siege in *Cligés*, Chrétien's Arthur is a passive, non-combatant monarch whose knights conduct their fighting individually, and not in concert with one another. Thus, German audiences of the early thirteenth century must surely have been somewhat startled not only by the frequent mentions of King Arthur's "army" (*Daniel* 492, 974, 1109, 2701 and 2960), but also by the extraordinary role which Arthur assumes in *Daniel.* For no longer is he the traditionally non-belligerent monarch. Instead, he emerges here as a robust commander piloting his troops into battle.

Once again, however, this is not to imply that the more commonplace Arthurian ingredients are entirely missing in *Daniel.* For instance, in addition to participating in the larger battles, the hero Daniel also engages in a series of chivalric duels. And even some of the terminology which der Stricker employs to refer to the mass battles is Arthurian in its roots; the first campaign against King Matur's men, for example, is characterized as a *juste*, or "joust" (v. 2964). Furthermore, the duel between Arthur and Matur, which results in Matur's death and which sets off the ensuing large-scale battles, contains elements both familiar and new. For although it is highly unusual for Arthur himself to engage in battle, the form of combat in *Daniel* is that of the traditional duel. What is more, even the wording of this passage (vv. 3007-71) betrays a demonstrable acquaintance on the part of the poet with conventional Arthurian terminology. Moreover, the duel between

Matur and Arthur is fought to the end without the aid of *list* or of supernatural weapons; sheer valor and strength are the sole determining factors. In light of all of this, it can hardly be argued that der Stricker was ignorant of the conventions of comportment for an Arthurian knight in battle. Quite to the contrary, the poet knew and in certain passages even exploited those conventions—yet at the same time seems to have felt utterly unfettered by such constraints.

Nonetheless, it is the large-scale warfare in *Daniel* which stands out—by virtue of its very abnormity in Arthurian romance—as the more memorable mode of battle. Though rather extraordinary in an Arthurian story such as *Daniel*, such broad-based combat would later find more appropriate expression in der Stricker's long epic *Karl*, in which great armies of Christians engage the heathen infidels in battle. This observation brings to light a significant compositional proclivity on the part of the poet: namely that der Stricker, when departing from Arthurian tradition in *Daniel*, tended to utilize poetic stratagems which he would develop further in his later works. Simply put, many important features of the later stories are already prefigured in *Daniel*. In fact, we have already uncovered this pattern with regard to *list*; for just as cunning occupies a central position in *Daniel*, so too does it stand out as a prominent virtue in der Stricker's later poems. And as has just been mentioned, the pre-courtly forms of battle which characterize much of the fighting in *Daniel* would once again reappear in der Stricker's *Karl*.

It is interesting to trace some of the ways in which der Stricker treats these pre-courtly, even heroic battle scenes in his courtly romance *Daniel*. In his depiction of the first battle between the armies of King Arthur and of King Matur (Chapter VIII, pp. 56-68), he offers a lengthy (780 lines) and highly detailed account which is especially rich in metaphor (on this latter point, see I. Hahn [pp. 188-93]). By the time of the second battle (pp. 94-98), however, der Stricker seems to have lost some interest in the minute details of the actual skirmish, inasmuch as only 245 lines (roughly one third the number of the first battle) are devoted to its description. For the third clash (pp. 100f.), the narration is even more dramatically condensed, to a mere 37 lines. However, by the following day word of Matur's death has spread throughout the land, and all four of the remaining armies strike at once, rather than separately over the course of the next four days. As a result, King Arthur's men are sorely outnumbered, and the hardship of conducting battle under such adverse circumstances is reflected in the increased number of lines (238) allotted to this final encounter (pp. 98-102 and 103, or vv. 5468-689 and 5761-78). Of these 238 verses, the overwhelming bulk (221) depicts the first day of battle.

But before this final campaign has a chance to resume after an overnight cease-fire, *list* once again intrudes upon the story. For that same evening Daniel presents his plan to the council of knights: he proposes to loose the deafening wail of the beast-statue, thereby overwhelming the opposition forces (King Arthur's men would already have blocked their ears in protection). The ease with which Arthur's men then proceed to extract surrender from the deafened armies of Cluse is mirrored in the paltry seventeen lines necessary to record the event. Quite significantly, it is cunning—not the sword—which ultimately (indeed, almost effortlessly) wins the war for King Arthur's forces. And der Stricker, by expending such a scant time of narration on the actual reporting of the victory, underscores the ready facility with which this conquest is achieved, thereby implicitly reasserting his praise of *list*. Thus, in this fourth battle in particular we find a curious juxtaposition of heroic/pre-courtly elements (blood, for example, flows most profusely in the final contest: see pp. 99-102, or vv. 5518, 5585, 5628-30, 5669, 5680f.) and Daniel's special brand of cunning, which saves the day and which is again reminiscent of the *Spielmannsepen*.

Interspersed among the four battle scenes are episodes of widely varying origin. At the one extreme stand Daniel's individual adventures; although in many regards un-Arthurian in their essence, these are to a great extent clothed in a vocabulary highly typical of such romances. At the other extreme are the night scenes in King Arthur's encampment, which with its army-like atmosphere and with its absence of courtly ladies is curiously foreign to Arthurian tradition. Thus, in the course of the 2700 lines (32% of the work as a whole) between the beginning of the first battle (v. 3078) and the conclusion of the final one (v. 5778), we can discern an eclectic patchwork of diverse literary strains—including Arthurian, heroic, pre-courtly and *spielmännisch.*

Again, it has been argued that der Stricker—fledgling poet that he was at this point—simply misconstrued the fundamental nature of Arthurian literature. As partial evidence for this, critics have long cited his depiction, in *Daniel*, of the above-mentioned army of knights under the command of King Arthur. This charge—despite recent, more positive interpretations (Brall, W. Schmidt, Ragotzky [*Gattungserneuerung*] and Müller-Ukena)—has never been refuted in any fully definitive way. And yet it seems every bit as possible that the poet was cognizant that *Daniel*, his first work, was quite different from the romances of Hartmann and Wolfram. Indeed, this notion can be corroborated by appealing directly to the story itself. For in the scene where King Arthur attempts to bring about a reconciliation with Matur's widow, he explains to her councilors that he had acted only in self-defense, having been provoked into battle by the messenger giant. He then goes on to add: "I speak truthfully when I say that I would have gladly remained at my court, and that I was driven here contrary to my will" (p. 109). One possible interpretation of this passage is that it represents an apology (or at the very least, an acknowledgement) by der Stricker—an apology both for the highly un-Arthurian warfare waged in *Daniel* and for the unaccustomed conduct of King Arthur. To be sure, it is not utterly unprecedented for Arthur to deviate from his traditional role (for instance, he does battle with the White Knight Gasozein in Heinrich von dem Türlin's *Diu Crône*). However, he is more characteristically portrayed as a passive, seemingly "retired" monarch whose court the most illustrious knights use as a sort of headquarters from which to pursue their own individual adventures. In this passage from *Daniel*, Arthur seems to express his regret at having been forced to abandon that more usual posture. Similarly, the poet—through the voice of Arthur—appears to be declaring his own implicit cognizance that in a more conventional Arthurian romance the king would indeed have remained at home. But *Daniel* is not conventional, and der Stricker seems to have been aware of that fact.

In a third and final area—love—der Stricker likewise embarks upon a rather unorthodox path with his *Daniel*. Among the early scholars, both Bartsch (ed. *Karl*, p. xxxv) and Khull (p. 314) suggested that the absence of courtly love might have been the paramount reason for *Daniel's* failure to attain any enduring popularity during the Middle Ages. Indeed, this appears altogether plausible, given that so many poets of the high Middle Ages (and along with them, presumably, their audiences) seem to have been all but obsessed with love. By contrast, der Stricker shows precious little interest in such matters of the heart. Even in the relatively conventional beginning of his *Daniel*, the very first mention of female beauty (a virtual precondition for love in courtly romances) is made not by a member of King Arthur's court nor even by the narrator, but rather by the messenger giant (pp. 12f.), with reference to the women of Cluse.

As for Daniel himself, while it is true that he encounters and comes to the aid of numerous ladies (and even marries the widow of King Matur), at no point in the story is he ever struck down or even momentarily stunned by the power of *minne*. For instance, after he has heard the plight of the Lady of the Dark Mountain, Daniel's foremost concern is with his own reputation: he fears that, should he continue on to Cluse without stopping to assist her, his good name might perhaps be blackened. The lady and the crisis which she faces are of decidedly secondary import to Daniel. Even when she throws herself at his feet and offers him both her hand in marriage and Juran's magic sword if only he will deliver her from the dwarf, Daniel is still left unaffected by the prospect of possessing her—though he yearns to win the sword.

Moreover, the narrator himself is every bit as insensitive to *minne* as is his protagonist. For throughout this same episode even he, the narrator, withholds all comment on this noblewoman's beauty—comments which are virtually *de rigeur* in such circumstances. And as soon as Daniel has dispatched Juran, his thoughts center not on the lady, but on his newly-won weapon: "That he had acquired the sword from the dwarf pleased Daniel greatly, and he intended to determine conclusively whether it was capable of penetrating the giant's skin" (p. 34). It is precisely at this point in the adventure—when Juran is slain and the immediate peril of the moment has passed—that one might expect Daniel's thoughts to turn finally to the lady. Yet even here (p. 34) the narrator continues to profess ignorance of any possible amorous bonds between Daniel and the lady:

> If the lady had possessed all the world, she would have deemed Daniel worthy of receiving it. And had he desired her hand, as the story relates it, those courtiers would not have refused him.

In this passage, der Stricker employs the contrary-to-fact subjunctive ("had he desired her hand...") as an evasive rhetorical device. For he admits here—albeit only indirectly—that Daniel in fact did not desire the lady's hand. And this is as close as he ever comes to reporting Daniel's own feelings in this prickly situation. What is more, in these same lines the narrator distances himself even further from the whole predicament by disclaiming any omniscience as to the true state of affairs. For instead of basing this part of the narrative on his own knowledge of the story, he takes refuge in his supposed source, with the words "as the story relates it." Indeed, the *Daniel* narrator, here as elsewhere, seems averse to conceding any first-hand knowledge of such matters as marriage—or of its logical antecedent, love. Then, at the end of this adventure when Daniel finally takes his leave of the Lady of the Dark Mountain, the narrator appears almost indifferent towards her: he notes rather matter-of-factly that Daniel's departure "brought great sorrow to the lady and all her retinue" (p. 35).

If *minne* leaves Daniel wholly untouched, quite the opposite can be said of his opponent Juran, whose lust for the Lady of the Dark Mountain ultimately brings about his demise. For, faced with the prospect of finally winning her hand, the dwarf is so utterly blinded by desire that he rashly accepts Daniel's terms for combat, which preclude the use of his invincible sword. Of particular interest is the excursus (p. 31) on *minne* which is inserted at this very crucial juncture in the story; for here der Stricker considers solely the inimical side of love. *Minne* means for der Stricker not the sublime and ennobling (if largely inaccessible) courtly love, but rather a demonic and utterly destructive force. Even Solomon, he states, who was "the wisest man of whom I have ever heard tell" had "both his wisdom and his senses" destroyed by Lady Love (p. 31). In this regard it ought not to be overlooked that der Stricker's articulation here of an altogether cheerless view of *minne* is reminiscent of the Dido scenes in Heinrich von Veldeke's *Eneide*. Indeed, inasmuch as Veldeke depicts in his romance just this very sort of pernicious, ravaging love, scholars have long suspected that the *Eneide* may have exerted an influence—whether direct or indirect—on *Daniel*.

At any rate, Daniel continues, throughout the course of his adventures, to maintain an immunity to any amorous stirrings. For soon after leaving behind the Lady of the Dark Mountain, he encounters the Countess of the Bright Fountain, whose husband is being held captive by the bellyless intruder. As before, there is no indication of any sort of attraction between Daniel and the lady. In fact, this episode is, as Moelleken ("Minne und Ehe," p. 49) points out, the precise antithesis of the scene from Hartmann in which Iwein slays Askalon and marries his widow. In sharp contrast to Hartmann's protagonist, Daniel expends every effort to rescue the husband and return him safely to his spouse! A similar pattern can be discerned in Daniel's third encounter with a lady, this time the Maiden of the Green Meadow. Once again the narrator fails to make note of her beauty. And again Daniel, his thoughts occupied by other pressing matters, stops to ponder whether a refusal to help her might imperil his own honor. The prospect of wooing her never enters his mind. Only when she threatens, in abject despair, to cut off her hair and to sacrifice herself to the diseased creature, does Daniel betray the slightest glimmer of awareness of her femininity: "Your tresses are radiant and blond [...] you must not cut them off" (pp. 87f.), he says, finally consenting to assist her. Then, after Daniel has cut down the diseased creature, the lady's father offers him in effect whatever reward he desires (p. 92). Yet even now—quite characteristically—it never once occurs to him to ask for her hand: *minne* has still failed to touch Daniel.

And finally, Daniel's relationship to Danise—the queen of Cluse and his eventual consort—is equally devoid of amorous attachment. As a preliminary observation, it should be noted that, in the account of this lady's deep lamentation at the death of her husband (pp. 110-112 and 115), der Stricker again dwells upon the dark side of love, here of love lost to death. Then, once she has overcome her grief, she consents to accept Daniel as her second husband. This entire passage is very much at odds with the traditional portrayal of the courtly bliss of the betrothed. For as Moelleken ("Minne und Ehe") has demonstrated, the ensuing marriage between Daniel and Danise is little more than a politically arranged alliance without the faintest trace of *minne*. Of prime significance here is the extent to which King Arthur, and not

Daniel, negotiates the reconciliation with the widowed queen. Once both sides have made peace, Arthur says to her in almost legalistic fashion: "I wish to bestow [Daniel] upon you in atonement" (p. 117), i.e. for the hardship caused by the hostilities and by her subsequent bereavement. Daniel's role in the marriage, then, is little more than that of a reparation in the wake of war! Not insignificantly, the two of them—Daniel and Danise—are then wedded without having ever exchanged a single direct word with one another. And in the process of marrying her, Daniel receives from the officiating priest not only the lady, but also—and perhaps more importantly—"the kingdom and the crown [of Cluse] as well" (p. 118).

The actual depiction of the wedding is, in one respect, aligned with Arthurian tradition: the festival takes place at Whitsuntide and is replete with jousts, "flowers and clover" (p. 121), sumptuous garments, inexhaustible food and drink, and universal merriment. And yet love, a feature normally essential to such courtly festivals, is prominent here only for its absence. Even though der Stricker provides us in these lines with his most extended narratorial reflections on female beauty (p. 121), these observations are clothed in the most general of terms and make no reference to any specific female character in the story. Most tellingly, this same beauty also fails to exert the customary ennobling effect on the knights in attendance. And finally, it is surely significant that neither here nor elsewhere in the story does der Stricker's narrator report of any stirrings of love within Daniel—despite the fact that he does at numerous junctures in the work enter the mind of his protagonist so as to disclose Daniel's inner ponderings. Thus, one must conclude that Daniel is simply immune to the spell of love—a condition quite extraordinary in the chivalric romances of this age.

In seeking to account for the two other points of unorthodoxy (the large-scale warfare and the centrality of cunning) in *Daniel* vis à vis more conventional Arthurian romances, we have been able to uncover a certain pattern. That is to say, over the full course of der Stricker's career as a poet, the "aberrations" within *Daniel* have repeatedly reemerged as germane features of the later works: the mass warfare of *Daniel* is mirrored in *Karl*, and the practice of *list* reappears in the later beast fables and *Mären*. However, as regards *minne*—or more properly, the absence of *minne*—the situation is somewhat more complex. For one thing, it is certainly true that courtly love is hardly a hallmark of der Stricker's later works. Yet it would be sophistic to cite this fact as an "echo" of the lack of *minne* in *Daniel*. The reasoning for this is quite simple: while *minne* is normally endemic to chivalric romances, it is utterly foreign to the genres in which der Stricker later practiced his skills. Hence, it appears that an appeal to der Stricker's later writings will do little to account for his disinterest in the workings of love. Instead, it may in this instance be more efficacious to refer one final time to the rather fragmentary biography which we have pieced together for der Stricker. For if it is true that he was associated, in whatever fashion, with a religious order (and der Stricker has been very tenuously connected with both the Dominicans and the Franciscans; see above, THE POET), then the vow of celibacy incumbent upon any such community might possibly help to account for der Stricker's failure to articulate a personal interest in courtly love. Ultimately, of course, any such hypothesis as this rests heavily on conjecture. Nonetheless, it may offer some clue as to the remarkable absence in *Daniel* of that one central human affect which otherwise so conspicuously captivated the minds of poets and courtiers during the high Middle Ages.

In the final reckoning, der Stricker's *Daniel* leaves the overall impression of a kaleidoscopic hybrid—of a heterogeneous and variegated story seasoned with ingredients from diverse literary strains. While Arthurian in its basic construct, *Daniel* also bears the mark of a great many extra-Arthurian traditions: the pre-courtly *Rolandslied*, the heroic Germanic epic, the *Spielmannsepen*, the early courtly romance *Eneide* by Heinrich von Veldeke, even the beast fables and *Mären* which were to become der Stricker's own forte. At the same time, the strong dose of der Stricker's own poetic phantasy which feeds into the tale of Daniel must likewise be reckoned among the chief ingredients.

Frequently der Stricker has been labelled a poor epigone, even a reactionary for his melding of older, outmoded literary strains with the new and fashionable Arthurian romance. Yet once one discards the artificial standards of the century past, a realization emerges that *Daniel*—the first original, self-conceived German romance centering on the Arthurian legend—is fully able to stand alone and be judged on its own merits. Certainly there is much about *Daniel* that is decidedly un-Arthurian, yet there is reason to believe that at least some of this was consciously and purposefully undertaken. In the final analysis, der Stricker, true to his apparent pseudonym as a "knitter" of tales, has skillfully woven together from widely divergent literary strands a patchwork of a story which, Arthurian or not, has lost none of its appeal despite the passage of nearly eight hundred years. In this vein, it is perhaps most fitting to allow the final word to der Stricker's contemporary Rudolf von Ems, who declares in his *Alexander* (ed. Junk, p. 119):

> swenn er wil der Strickære
> sô macht er guotiu mære. (vv. 3257f.)
>
> Whenever he wishes to,
> der Stricker puts together a good story.

Unencumbered by the preconceptions of earlier generations, we are today in a better position to recognize that der Stricker has created with his *Daniel* precisely that: a good story.

Introduction

PRINCIPLES OF THE TRANSLATION

The following English version of *Daniel* is an essentially conservative translation, though by no means a word-for-word rendering. Unfortunately, a major and significant feature of the original Middle High German text—its verse format with rhymed couplets—is wholly and inevitably sacrificed in the prose translation. In an attempt to offset, in some measure, that loss of rhyme and meter, I have not shied away from drawing upon a richer and more variegated modern English vocabulary than is present—or even possible—in the Middle High German. In a limited way, this probably constitutes some deviation from my stated principle of translational conservatism. It is hoped that such prudently undertaken stylistic enhancement in the English version may help to restore some measure of the sonorous ring of the original text. Nonetheless, the modern reader is urged to bear in mind that der Stricker composed his *Daniel* in a verse form which must have sounded vastly different to the listener of medieval times than does the English prose of this translation.

I have based the translation upon my own critical edition of the *Daniel* text. Just prior to the appearance of that edition in 1983, an important *Daniel* manuscript (Ms. germ. 1340) which had been lost during World War II resurfaced in Cracow. Because the readings of the Cracow manuscript have proved to be crucial for a close understanding of *Daniel*, I have made reference, in the accompanying NOTES, to those passages of my critical text which have been in any way impacted by the rediscovery of this document. Furthermore, I have incorporated the specific emendations proposed by Werner Schröder ("Text von Strickers 'Daniel'"), most particularly where such alterations to the Middle High German text would impinge directly upon the English translation.

Inevitably, certain words, verses and even short passages in *Daniel* have proved utterly resistant to any sort of confident interpretation or precise translation. To a greater or lesser degree, this is unavoidable whenever the better part of eight hundred years separate poet from translator. In all such cases of uncertainty—at times, of genuine bewilderment—I have translated the passage to the best of my judgment, and have sought to examine, in the NOTES, the sources of the uncertainty and/or any possible alternate readings.

Finally, I have taken the liberty of intervening in several different ways on behalf of the modern reader unable to refer to the Middle High German original. First, I have divided the entire work up into fifteen chapters. While the manuscripts generally do not observe any such breaks in the story, it is clear from the very length of *Daniel* (8482 lines in the Middle High German text) that the entire work most certainly could not have been read at one sitting. The chapter divisions which I have imposed upon the story follow what I have judged to be the most naturally occurring breaks in the action. In that regard they may perhaps not deviate so very much from whatever divisions were actually employed by the minstrels in medieval times. Secondly, the paragraph breaks in my translation follow neither the initials in the manuscripts nor the indentations in the critical text. Instead, they are intended solely to anticipate the needs of the modern reader. Thirdly, I have, on several occasions, significantly altered the sequence of verses in the translation. Such realignment is limited to the relatively few passages which would otherwise appear badly disjointed in the English; in all such cases I have made express reference, in the form of a note, to my intervention. And lastly, throughout the work I have replaced, without individual reference in the NOTES, innumerable personal pronouns with proper names. Such substitutions are necessitated by the simple fact that der Stricker, like so many other poets of his age, tended to employ long strings of personal pronouns (often involving two or more persons of the same gender) without reintroducing their antecedents.

Introduction

A work such as this—albeit ultimately a rather solitary undertaking—seldom represents the sole labor of one individual. I would like therefore to express my deep and enduring gratitude to the many organizations and colleagues who contributed in various ways to the completion of this volume: to Professors Eckehard Simon of Harvard University and Theodore M. Andersson of Stanford University, both of whom directed my initial inquiries into der Stricker's *Daniel*; to the Max Niemeyer Verlag in Tübingen for permission to use my critical edition of *Daniel* as the basis for this translation; to the Biblioteka Jagiellońska in Cracow, Poland, for permission to reproduce the miniatures from Ms. germ. 1340; to Mr. Alfred S. Schwartz, who designed and executed the illustration for the frontispiece; to Professor Ingeborg Henderson of the University of California at Davis for her generous and timely loan of a microfilm of the Cracow manuscript; to Ms. Phyllis Korper of Garland Publishing for her valued advice on countless pre-publication details; to the general editor of the Garland Library of Medieval Literature, Professor James J. Wilhelm of Rutgers University, for his cheerful encouragement and for his unfailingly prompt responses to the many inquiries and problems which I sent his way over the course of several years; and, most especially, to Professor Charles P. Lutcavage of Harvard University for the long hours which he spent patiently and critically reading the manuscript in its various stages of completion, as well as for the invaluable and innumerable suggestions which he offered on virtually every aspect of this volume.

Boston, August 1989 *Michael Resler*

SELECT BIBLIOGRAPHY

I. Critical Editions and Translations

Daniel of the Blossoming Valley

Resler, *Daniel*: Resler, Michael, ed. *Der Stricker: Daniel von dem Blühenden Tal.* Altdeutsche Textbibliothek 92. Tübingen: Niemeyer, 1983.

----------, trans. "Middle High German. Der Stricker: *Daniel of the Blossoming Valley.*" *The Romance of Arthur III.* Ed. James J. Wilhelm. New York and London: Garland, 1988. 185-258. [Excerpts.]

Rosenhagen, *Daniel*: Rosenhagen, Gustav, ed. *Daniel von dem blühenden Tal: ein Artusroman von dem Stricker.* Germanistische Abhandlungen 9. Breslau: W. Koebner, 1894. Hildesheim and New York: Georg Olms, 1976.

Related Texts

Altswert, Meister. *Meister Altswert.* Ed. Wilhelm Holland and Adalbert Keller. Bibliothek des Literarischen Vereins in Stuttgart 21. Stuttgart: Literarischer Verein, 1850.

Konrad, Pfaffe. *Das Rolandslied.* Ed. Carl Wesle. Altdeutsche Textbibliothek 69. Tübingen: Niemeyer, 1967.

der Pleier. *Garel von dem blüenden Tal. Ein höfischer Roman aus dem Artussagenkreis von dem Pleier, mit den Fresken des Garelsaales auf Runkelstein.* Ed. M[ichael] Walz. Freiburg im Breisgau: Fr. Wagner'sche Universitäts-Buchhandlung, 1892.

Püterich von Reichertshausen. *Der Ehrenbrief.* Ed. Fritz Behrend and Rudolf Wolkau. Weimar: Gesellschaft der Bibliophilen, 1920.

Rudolf von Ems. *Alexander: ein höfischer Versroman des 13. Jahrhunderts.* Ed. Victor Junk. Leipzig: Hiersemann, 1928-29. Darmstadt: Wissenschaftliche Buchgesellschaft, 1970.

----------. *Willehalm von Orlens.* Ed. Victor Junk. Deutsche Texte des Mittelalters. Berlin: Weidmann, 1905.

der Stricker. *Die bisher unveröffentlichten geistlichen Bîspelreden des Strickers.* Ed. Ute Schwab. Göttingen: Vandenhoeck & Ruprecht, 1959.

----------. *Karl der Grosse.* Ed. Karl Bartsch. Quedlinburg and Leipzig: Gottfried Basse, 1857.

----------. *Die Kleindichtung des Strickers, 5 Bände.* Ed. Wolfgang Wilfred Moelleken [*et al.*]. Göppinger Arbeiten zur Germanistik 107 I-V. Göppingen: Kümmerle, 1973-1978.

----------. *Kleinere Gedichte von dem Stricker.* Ed. Karl August Hahn. Bibliothek der gesammten deutschen National-Literatur von der ältesten Zeit bis auf die neuere Zeit 18. Quedlinburg and Leipzig: Gottfried Basse, 1839.

----------. *Liebe und Ehe: Lehrgedichte von dem Stricker. Mit Wort- und Sacherklärungen.* Ed. Wolfgang Wilfried Moelleken. Chapel Hill: U of North Carolina P, 1970.

----------. "Der Pfaffe Amîs." *Erzählungen und Schwänke.* Ed. Hans Lambel. Deutsche Classiker des Mittelalters mit Sach- und Worterklärungen 12. Leipzig: Brockhaus, 1872.

----------. *Tierbîspel.* Ed. Ute Schwab. Altdeutsche Textbibliothek 54. Tübingen: Niemeyer, 1960.

----------. *Verserzählungen I.* Ed. Hanns Fischer. Altdeutsche Textbibliothek 53. Tubingen: Niemeyer, 1967.

----------. *Verserzählungen II. Mit einem Anhang: Der Weinschwelg.* Ed. Hanns Fischer. Altdeutsche Textbibliothek 68. Tübingen: Niemeyer, 1967.

----------. *Von übelen wîben.* Ed. Wolfgang W. Moelleken. Europäische Hochschulschriften. Reihe I: Deutsche Literatur und Germanistik 25. Bern: Lang, 1970.

II. Critical Writings and Related Works

Adelung, Johann Christoph. "Chronologisches Verzeichniss der Dichter und Gedichte aus dem Schwäbischen Zeitpuncte." *Magazin für die Deutsche Sprache.* Ed. J. C. Adelung. Leipzig: Johann Gottlob Immanuel Breitkopf, 1784. 2.3 (1784): 58.

Agricola, Erhard. "Die Prudentia als Anliegen der Stricker'schen Schwänke." *Beiträge zur Geschichte der deutschen Sprache und Literatur* 77 (1955): 197-220.

Ahrendt, Ernst Herwig. *Der Riese in der mittelhochdeutschen Epik.* Diss. Rostock, 1923. Güstrow: Michaal'sche Hof- und Ratsbuchdruckerei, 1923.

Baker, Imogene. *The King's Household in the Arthurian Court from Geoffrey of Monmouth to Malory.* Diss. Catholic U of America, 1937. Washington, D. C.: Murray & Heister, 1937.

Bartsch, Karl. "Alberich von Besanzon." *Germania. Vierteljahrsschrift für deutsche Alterthumskunde,* 2 (1857): 449-464.

----------. "Wetzels heilige Margarete." *Germanistische Studien. Supplement zur Germania.* Ed. Karl Bartsch. Vienna: C. Gerold's Sohn, 1872. I, 1-30.

Bernt, Alois. Rev. of *Verhältnis des Strickers zu Hartmann von Aue, untersucht am Gebrauche des Epithetons* by Maximilian Mayer. *Zeitschrift für die österreichischen Gymnasien,* 60 (1909): 188-190.

Blosen, Hans. Review of Resler, *Daniel. Germanistik,* 27 (1986): 855.

Blumenfeldt, Albert. *Die echten Tier- und Pflanzenfabeln des Strickers.* Diss. Berlin, 1916.

Bode, Friedrich. *Die Kampfesschilderungen in den mittelhochdeutschen Epen.* Diss. Greifswald, 1909. Greifswald: Hans Adler, 1909.

de Boor, Helmut. "Der Daniel des Stricker und der Garel des Pleier." *Beiträge zur Geschichte der deutschen Sprache und Literatur,* 79 (1957): 67-84.

Brall, Helmut. "Strickers *Daniel von dem Blühenden Tal.* Zur politischen Funktion späthöfischer Artusepik im Territorialisierungsprozeß." *Euphorion,* 70 (1976): 222-57.

Brinkmann, Hennig. "Der Prolog im Mittelalter als literarische Erscheinung." *Wirkendes Wort*, 14 (1964): 1-21.

----------. *Zu Wesen und Form mittelalterlicher Dichtung.* Halle: Niemeyer, 1928.

von der Burg, Udo. *Strickers Karl der Grosse als Bearbeitung des Rolandsliedes. Studien zu Form und Inhalt.* Göppinger Arbeiten zur Germanistik 131. Göppingen: Kümmerle, 1974.

Caflisch-Einicher, Emma. *Die lateinischen Elemente in der mittelhochdeutschen Epik des 13. Jahrhunderts.* Prager Deutsche Studien 47. Reichenberg: F. Kraus, 1936.

Cram, Kurt-Georg. *Iudicium Belli. Zum Rechtscharakter des Krieges im deutschen Mittelalter.* Beihefte zum Archiv für Kulturgeschichte 5. Münster and Cologne: Böhlau, 1955.

Cramer, Thomas. "Normenkonflikte im 'Pfaffen Amîs' und im 'Willehalm von Wenden.' Überlegungen zur Entwicklung des Bürgertums im Spätmittelalter." Spec. issue of *Zeitschrift für deutsche Philologie*, 93 (1974): 124-40.

Curtius, Ernst Robert. *Europäische Literatur und lateinisches Mittelalter.* 5th printing. Bern and Munich: Francke, 1965.

Dreyer, Max. *Der Teufel in der deutschen Dichtung des Mittelalters, Erster Teil: von den Anfängen bis in das XIV. Jahrhundert.* Diss. Rostock, 1884.

Egelkraut, Paul. *Der Einfluß des Daniel vom Blühenden Tal vom Stricker auf die Dichtungen des Pleiers.* Diss. Erlangen, 1896.

Ehrismann, Gustav. Rev. of Rosenhagen, *Daniel. Literaturblatt für Germanische und romanische Philologie*, 16 (1895): 76-78.

----------. Rev. of *Geschichte der handschriftlichen Überlieferung von Strickers Karl dem Grossen* by Friedrich Wilhelm. *Anzeiger für deutsches Altertum und deutsche Literatur*, 30 (1906): 194-201.

----------. "Untersuchungen über das mittelhochdeutsche Gedicht von der Minneburg." *Beiträge zur Geschichte der deutschen Sprache und Literatur*, 22 (1897): 257-341.

Erben, Wilhelm. *Kriegsgeschichte des Mittelalters.* Beihefte der Historischen Zeitschrift 16. Munich and Berlin: R. Oldenbourg, 1929.

Fechter, Werner. "Absalom als Vergleichs- und Beispielfigur im mittelhochdeutschen Schrifttum." *Beiträge zur Geschichte der deutschen Sprache und Literatur*, 83 (1961/62): 302-16.

Fränkel, Ludwig. Rev. of Rosenhagen, *Daniel*. *Literarisches Centralblatt für Deutschland*, 30 (1894): 1068f.

----------. "Der Stricker." *Allgemeine deutsche Biographie*. 1st ed. Leipzig: Duncker & Humblot, 1875-1912. Berlin: Duncker & Humblot, 1967-1971. 36, 580-87.

Frenzen, Wilhelm. *Klagebilder und Klagegebärden in der deutschen Dichtung des höfischen Mittelalters*. Diss. Bonn, 1936.

Gerhards, Gisela. *Das Bild der Witwe in der deutschen Literatur des Mittelalters*. Diss. Bonn, 1962.

Grimm, Wilhelm. *Kleinere Schriften*. Ed. Gustav Hinrichs. Berlin: F. Dümmler, 1883.

----------. *Zur Geschichte des Reims. Gelesen in der Königlichen Akademie der Wissenschaften am 7. März, 1850*. Berlin: Druckerei der königlichen Akademie der Wissenschaften, 1852.

Gürttler, Karin R. *'Künec Artûs der guote.' Das Artusbild der höfischen Epik des 12. und 13. Jahrhunderts*. Studien zur Germanistik, Anglistik und Komparatistik 52. Ed. A. Arnold and A. M. Haas. Bonn: Bouvier, 1976.

von der Hagen, Friedrich Heinrich, and Johann Gustav Büsching. *Literarischer Grundriss zur Geschichte der deutschen Poesie von der ältesten Zeit bis in das sechzehnte Jahrhundert*. Berlin: Duncker & Humblot, 1812.

Hahn, Ingrid. "Das Ethos der *kraft*. Zur Bedeutung der Massenschlachten in Strickers *Daniel von dem Blühenden Tal*." *Deutsche Vierteljahrsschrift*, 59 (1985): 173-94.

Hardt, J. "Nachricht von den altteutschen Handschriften auf der Churfürstlichen Jesuiter-Bibliothek zu München." *Braga und Hermode oder Neues Magazin für die Vaterländischen Alterthümer der Sprache, Kunst und Sitten*. Leipzig: Carl Friedrich Barth, 1796. 1.2 (1796): 188-97.

Hart, Thomas Elwood. "An Afterword in Response." *Colloquia Germanica. Internationale Zeitschrift für germanische Sprach- und Literaturwissenschaft*, 13 (1980): 156-59.

----------. Review of Resler, *Daniel. Colloquia Germanica. Internationale Zeitschrift für germanische Sprach- und Literaturwissenschaft*, 17 (1984): 124-28.

----------. "'Werkstruktur' in Stricker's *Daniel*? A Critique by Counterexample." *Colloquia Germanica. Internationale Zeitschrift für germanische Sprach- und Literaturwissenschaft*, 13 (1980): 106-41.

Harward, Vernon J. *The Dwarfs of Arthurian Romance and Celtic Tradition*. Leiden: E. J. Brill, 1958.

Haug, Walter. "Paradigmatische Poesie. Der spätere deutsche Artusroman auf dem Weg zu einer 'nachklassischen' Ästhetik." *Deutsche Vierteljahrsschrift*, 54 (1980): 204-31 (esp. 216-22).

Haupt, Jürgen. *Der Truchsess Keie im Artusroman*. Philologische Studien und Quellen 57. Ed. Wolfgang Binder, Hugo Moser, and Karl Stackmann. Berlin: Erich Schmidt, 1971.

Heinzle, Joachim. *Stellenkommentar zu Wolframs Titurel. Beiträge zum Verständnis des überlieferten Textes*. Hermaea. Germanistische Forschungen ns 30. Ed. Helmut de Boor and Hermann Kunisch. Tübingen: Niemeyer, 1972.

Henderson, Ingeborg. "Arthurian Iconography in 15th-Century German Manuscripts." [Forthcoming.]

----------. "Die Frauendarstellung im nachklassischen Roman des Mittelalters." *Amsterdamer Beiträge zur älteren Germanistik*, 14 (1979): 137-48.

----------. "Stricker-Handschrift Dresd. M. 56: Zur Rezeption des Artusstoffes im Bürgertum des 15. Jahrhunderts." *Res Publica Litterarum*, 2 (1979): 109-21.

----------. "Stricker's *Daniel* in the Recently Found *Ms. Germ. 1340*." *Journal of English and Germanic Philology*, 86 (1987): 348-57.

----------. *Strickers Daniel von dem Blühenden Tal: Werkstruktur und Interpretation unter Berücksichtigung der handschriftlichen Überlieferung*. German Language and Literature Monographs 1. Amsterdam: John Benjamins, 1976.

----------. "Zur Zahlenkomposition in Strickers *Daniel*. Eine Erwiderung." *Colloquia Germanica. Internationale Zeitschrift für germanische Sprach- und Literaturwissenschaft*, 13 (1980): 142-55.

Holtzman, Adolf. "Der Dichter des Annoliedes." *Germania. Vierteljahrsschrift für deutsche Alterthumskunde*, 2 (1857): 1-48.

Jensen, Ludwig. *Über den Stricker als Bîspel-Dichter, seine Sprache und seine Technik unter Berücksichtigung des "Karl" und "Amîs."* Inaugural-Diss. Marburg, 1885. Marburg: Universitäts-Buchdruckerei, 1885.

Kern, Peter. "Rezeption und Genese des Artusromans. Überlegungen zu Strickers 'Daniel vom blühenden Tal.'" Spec. issue of *Zeitschrift für deutsche Philologie*, 93 (1974): 18-42.

Köhler, Erich. *Ideal und Wirlichkeit in der höfischen Epik. Studien zur Form der frühen Artus- und Graldichtung.* 2nd rev. ed. Beihefte zu Zeitschrift für romanische Philologie 97. Tübingen: Niemeyer, 1956.

Könneker, Barbara. "Strickers *Pfaffe Amîs* und das Volksbuch von *Ulenspiegel*." *Euphorion*, 64 (1970): 242-80.

Köppe, Walter. "Ideologiekritische Aspekte im Werk des Stricker." *Acta Germanica*, 10 (1977): 139-211 (esp. 143-51).

Krappe, Alexander Haggerty. "Le cri meurtrier." *Studi Medievali* ns 11 (1938): 173-79.

von Kraus, Karl. "Der rührende Reim im Mittelhochdeutschen." *Zeitschrift für deutsches Altertum und deutsche Literatur*, 56 (1918): 35f.

Krohn, R[üdiger]. Rev. of Resler, *Daniel*. *Wissenschaftlicher Literaturanzeiger*, 22/23xx (Dec. 13, 1984): xx.

Lambel, H[ans]. Rev. of Rosenhagen, *Daniel*. *Zeitschrift für die österreichischen Gymnasien*, 48.3 (1897): 231-247; and 48.4 (1897): 316-334.

Lecouteux, Claude. "Das bauchlose Ungeheuer. Des Strickers Daniel vom blühenden Tal, 1879ff." *Euphorion*, 71 (1977): 272-76.

----------. *Les monstres dans la littérature allemande du moyen âge. Contribution à l'étude du merveilleux médiéval.* Göppinger Arbeiten zur Germanistik 330. Göppingen: Kümmerle, 1982.

----------. Rev. of Resler, *Daniel*. *Etudes germaniques*, 39 (1984): 67.

Leitzmann, Albert. "Das chronologische Verhältnis von Strickers Daniel und Karl." *Zeitschrift für deutsche Philologie*, 28 (1896): 43-47.

----------. Rev. of Rosenhagen, *Daniel* and *Untersuchungen. Zeitschrift für deutsche Philologie,* 27 (1895): 543-547.

----------. "Strickerstudien." *Zeitschrift für deutsches Altertum und deutsche Literatur,* 81 (1944): 69-84.

Lütjens, August. *Der Zwerg in der deutschen Heldendichtung des Mittelalters.* Germanistische Abhandlungen 38. Breslau: M. & H. Marcus, 1911.

Mast, Hans. *Stilistische Untersuchungen an den Kleinen Gedichten des Strickers mit besonderer Berücksichtigung des volkstümlichen und des formelhaften Elementes.* Diss. Basel, 1929. Basel: n.p., 1929.

Meier, John. Rev. of Rosenhagen, *Untersuchungen. Literaturblatt für germanische und romanische Philologie,* 12 (1892): 217-220.

Menhardt, Hermann. "Der Stricker und der Teichner." *Beiträge zur Geschichte der deutschen Sprache und Literatur,* 84 (1962): 266-295.

Meyer, Elard Hugo. "Über Tandarois und Flordibel, ein Artusgedicht des Pleiers." *Zeitschrift für deutsches Altertum und deutsche Literatur,* 12 (1865): 478-82.

Moelleken, Wolfgang. W. "Die Bedeutung der Riesenvaterepisode in Strickers *Daniel von dem Blühenden Tal.*" *Spectrum medii ævi. Essays in Early German Literature, in Honor of George Fenwick Jones.* Ed. William C. McDonald. Göppinger Arbeiten zur Germanistik 362. Göppingen: Kümmerle, 1983. 347-59.

----------. "Minne und Ehe in Strickers 'Daniel von dem blühenden Tal.' Strukturanalytische Ergebnisse." Spec. issue of *Zeitschrift für deutsche Philologie,* 93 (1974): 42-50.

Moelleken, Wolfgang W., and Ingeborg Henderson. "Die Bedeutung der *liste* im 'Daniel' des Strickers." *Amsterdamer Beiträge zur älteren Germanistik,* 4 (1973): 187-201.

Müller, Dorothea. *'Daniel vom Blühenden Tal' und 'Garel vom Blühenden Tal.' Die Artusromane des Stricker und des Pleier unter gattungsgeschichtlichen Aspekten.* Göppinger Arbeiten zur Germanistik 334. Göppingen: Kümmerle, 1981.

Müller, Otto. *Die täglichen Lebensgewohnheiten in den altfranzösischen Artusromanen.* Diss. Marburg, 1889. Marburg: Joh. Hamel, 1889.

Müller-Ukena, Elke. "Rex humilis — rex superbus. Zum Herrschertum der Könige Artus von Britanje und Matur von Cluse in Strickers 'Daniel von dem blühenden Tal.'" *Zeitschrift für deutsche Philologie*, 103 (1984): 27-51.

Niewöhner, H. "Strickerhandschriften." *Beiträge zur Geschichte der deutschen Sprache und Literatur*, 77 (1955): 495f.

Pfeiffer, Franz. Rev. of *Grundriss zur Geschichte der deutschen Dichtung* by Karl Goedeke. *Germania. Vierteljahrsschrift für deutsche Altertumskunde*, 2 (1857): 498f.

Piquet, F. Rev. of *Reimwörterbuch* by Waelzel. *Revue germanique*, 19 (1928): 291.

Połczyńska, Edyta. *Studien zum "Salman und Morolf."* Prace Wydziału Filologicznego. Seria Filologia Germańska 4. Poznań: Uniwersytet im. Adama Mickiewicza, 1968.

Pörksen, Uwe. *Der Erzähler im mittelhochdeutschen Epos. Formen seines Hervortretens bei Lamprecht, Konrad, Hartmann, in Wolframs Willehalm und in den Spielmannsepen.* Philologische Studien und Quellen 58. Ed. Wolfgang Binder, Hugo Moser, and Karl Stackmann. Berlin: Erich Schmidt, 1971.

Quak, Arend. Rev. of Resler, *Daniel*. *Amsterdamer Beiträge zur älteren Germanistik*, 21 (1984): 197f.

Ragotzky, Hedda. "Das Handlungsmodell der list und die Thematisierung von guot. Zum Problem einer sozialgeschichtlich orientierten Interpretation von Strickers '*Daniel vom blühenden Tal*' und dem '*Pfaffen Amîs*.'" *Literatur—Publikum—historischer Kontext*. Ed. Gert Kaiser. Bern, Frankfurt and Las Vegas: Lang, 1977. 183-203.

----------. *Gattungserneuerung und Laienunterweisung in Texten des Strickers*. Studien und Texte zur Sozialgeschichte der Literatur 1. Tübingen: Niemeyer, 1981.

Reisel, Johanna. *Zeitgeschichtliche und theologisch-scholastische Aspekte im "Daniel von dem blühenden Tal" des Stricker.* Göppinger Arbeiten zur Germanistik 464. Göppingen: Kümmerle, 1986.

Resler, Michael. "Zur Datierung von Strickers *Daniel von dem Blühenden Tal*." *Euphorion*, 78 (1984): 17-30.

Rocher, Daniel. Review of Resler, *Daniel*. *Cahiers de civilisation médiévale*, 30 (1987): 87-89.

Rosenhagen, Gustav. "Der Stricker." *Die deutsche Literatur des Mittelalters. Verfasserlexikon.* Vol. 4. Ed. Karl Langosch. Berlin: de Gruyter, 1953. 292-99.

Rosenhagen, *Untersuchungen*: ----------. *Untersuchungen über Daniel vom Blühenden Tal vom Stricker.* Diss. Kiel, 1890. Kiel: C. Schaidt, 1890.

Schirokauer, Arnold. "Studien zur mittelhochdeutschen Reimgrammatik." *Beiträge zur Geschichte der deutschen Sprache und Literatur*, 47 (1923): 1-126.

Schlosser, Horst D. Rev. of Resler, *Daniel. Arbitrium: Zeitschrift für Rezensionen zur germanistischen Literaturwissenschaft*, 4 (1986): 33-36.

Schmidt, Wolfgang. *Untersuchungen zu Aufbauformen und Erzählstil im 'Daniel von dem blühenden Tal' des Stricker.* Göppinger Arbeiten zur Germanistik 266. Göppingen: Kümmerle, 1979.

Schnell, Rüdiger. "Strickers 'Karl der Grosse.' Literarische Tradition und politische Wirklichkeit." Spec. issue of *Zeitschrift für deutsche Philologie*, 93 (1974): 50-80.

Schönbach, Anton E. Rev. of Rosenhagen, *Daniel. Österreichisches Litteraturblatt*, 4 (1895): 13-15.

Schröder, Werner. "Der Text von Strickers 'Daniel' und seine Überlieferung." *Zeitschrift für deutsches Altertum und deutsche Literatur*, 114 (1985): 46-70.

Schultz, Alwin. *Das höfische Leben zur Zeit der Minnesinger.* 2 vols. Leipzig: S. Hirzel, 1879. Osnabrück: Otto Zeller, 1965.

Schultz, James A. *The Shape of the Round Table. Structures of Middle High German Arthurian Romance.* Toronto: U of Toronto P, 1983.

Schwab, Ute. "Beobachtungen bei der Ausgabe der bisher unveröffentlichten Gedichte des Strickers." *Beiträge zur Geschichte der deutschen Sprache und Literatur*, 81 (1959): 61-98.

Schwartzkopff, Werner. *Rede und Redeszene in der deutschen Erzählung bis Wolfram von Eschenbach.* Palaestra. Untersuchungen und Texte aus der deutschen und englischen Philologie 74. Ed. Alois Brandl, Gustav Roethe, and Erich Schmidt. Berlin: Mayer & Müller, 1909.

Seemüller, Joseph. Rev. of Rosenhagen, *Daniel*. *Zeitschrift für deutsches Altertum und deutsche Literatur*, 41 (1897) [= *Anzeiger für deutsches Altertum*, 23 (1897)]: 56-66.

----------. Rev. of *Über den Stricker als Bîspel-Dichter* by Ludwig Jensen. *Deutsche Litteraturzeitung*, 7 (Oct. 23, 1886): 1526-28.

----------. Rev. of Rosenhagen, *Untersuchungen*. *Zeitschrift für deutsches Altertum und deutsche Literatur*, 37 (1893) [= *Anzeiger für deutsches Altertum*, 19 (1893)]: 247-253.

Singer, Johannes. "Der Eingang von Strickers 'Karl dem Grossen.' Text und Anmerkungen." Spec. issue of *Zeitschrift für deutsche Philologie*, 93 (1974): 80-107.

Singer, S. Rev. of Rosenhagen, *Untersuchungen*. *Deutsche Litteraturzeitung*, 12 (May 9, 1891): 703f.

----------. "Salomosagen in Deutschland." *Zeitschrift für deutsches Altertum und deutsche Literatur*, 35 (1891): 177-87.

Sparnaay, Hendrik. "Hartmann von Aue and his Successors." *Arthurian Literature in the Middle Ages. A Collaborative History*. Ed. Roger Sherman Loomis. Oxford: Clarendon, 1959. 430-42.

Spiewok, Wolfgang. Rev. of Resler, *Daniel*. *Deutsche Literaturzeitung für Kritik der internationalen Wissenschaften*, 105 (November 1984): 863-65.

----------. "Der Stricker und die Prudentia." *Wissenschaftliche Zeitschrift der Ernst-Moritz-Arndt Universität Greifswald, Gesellschafts- und sprachwissenschaftliche Reihe*, 13 (1964): 119-26.

Suolahti, Hugo. "Der französische Einfluss auf die deutsche Sprache im dreizehnten Jahrhundert." *Mémoires de la société néophilologique de Helsingfors*, 8 (1929): 1-310; and 10 (1933): 360f.

Ukena-Best, Elke. Rev. of Resler, *Daniel*. *Beiträge zur Geschichte der deutschen Sprache und Literatur*, 110 (1988): 132-37.

Vietor, Karl. "Die Kunstanschauung der höfischen Epigonen." *Beiträge zur Geschichte der deutschen Sprache und Literatur*, 46 (1922): 85-124 (esp. 105f.).

Wailes, Stephen L. Rev. of Resler, *Daniel*. *Journal of English and Germanic Philology*, 83 (1984): 406f.

----------. "Der Stricker." *Dictionary of the Middle Ages.* Ed. Joseph R. Strayer. Vol. 11. New York: Charles Scribner's Sons, 1988. 492-94.

----------. "Stricker and the Virtue *Prudentia.* A Critical Review." *Seminar,* 13 (1977): 136-53.

Wechssler, Eduard. "Wechselbeziehungen zwischen den romanischen Litteraturen unter sich und romanischer und germanischer Litteratur. Einflüsse der altfranzösischen Litteratur auf die altdeutsche." *Kritischer Jahresbericht über die Fortschritte der romanischen Philologie,* 4 (1895-96): 382-472.

Wegener, Hans. "Der Stricker: Daniel vom Blumental. Ms. germ. quart. 1340." *Beschreibendes Verzeichnis der Miniaturen-Handschriften der Preußischen Staatsbibliothek zu Berlin.* Vol. 5. Leipzig: J. J. Weber, 1928. 27-30.

Werlin, Josef. Rev. of Resler, *Daniel. Leuvense Bijdragen,* 73 (1984): 379f.

Wilhelm, Friedrich. *Die Geschichte der handschriftlichen Überlieferung von Strickers Karl dem Grossen.* Inaugural-Diss. Munich, 1903. Amberg: Hans Böes, 1904.

----------. Über fabulistische Quellenangaben." *Beiträge zur Geschichte der deutschen Sprache und Literatur,* 33 (1908): 286-339.

Zieren, Helene. *Studien zum Teufelsbild in der deutschen Dichtung von 1050-1250.* Diss. Bonn, 1937.

Zwierzina, Konrad. "Mittelhochdeutsche Studien." *Zeitschrift für deutsches Altertum und deutsche Literatur,* 44 (1900): 1-116, 249-316, 345-406; and 45 (1901): 19-99, 253-313, 317-419.

----------. "Zur Textkritik von Strickers Daniel." *Zeitschrift für deutsches Altertum und deutsche Literatur,* 42 (1898): 83-93.

III. Reference Works

Arbusow, Leonid. *Colores rhetorici. Eine Auswahl rhetorischer Figuren und Gemeinplätze als Hilfsmittel für akademische Übungen an mittelalterlichen Texten.* Göttingen: Vandenhoeck & Ruprecht, 1948.

Bartsch, Karl. *Grundriss der Geschichte der provenzalischen Literatur.* Elberfeld: R. L. Friedrichs, 1872.

Select Bibliography

BMZ: Benecke, G. F., W. Müller, and F. Zarncke. *Mittelhochdeutsches Wörterbuch, I-III.* Leipzig: S. Hirzel, 1854-66.

de Boor, Helmut, [and Richard Newald]. *Geschichte der deutschen Literatur von den Anfängen bis zur Gegenwart.* 7th ed. Munich: Beck, 1966.

Brogsitter, Karl Otto. *Artusepik.* Sammlung Metzler M38. Stuttgart: Metzler, 1965.

Ehrismann, Gustav. *Geschichte der deutschen Literatur bis zum Ausgang des Mittelalters.* Handbuch des deutschen Unterrichts an höheren Schulen 6/2/2/1. Munich: Beck, 1927. II/2/1, 13-15.

Grimm, Jacob. *Deutsche Grammatik, I-IV.* Göttingen: Dieterichische Buchhandlung, 1822-37.

Grimm, Jacob, and Wilhelm Grimm. *Deutsches Wörterbuch.* Leipzig: S. Hirzel, 1854-1960.

Khull, Ferdinand. *Geschichte der altdeutschen Dichtung.* Graz: Leuschner & Lubensky, 1886.

Koberstein, August. *Grundriss der Geschichte der deutschen Nationalliteratur bis zum Ende des sechzehnten Jahrhunderts.* 6th rev. ed. by Karl Bartsch. Leipzig: Vogel, 1884. I, 173f.

Lexer, Matthias. *Mittelhochdeutsches Wörterbuch, I-III.* Leipzig: S. Hirzel, 1872-78.

Merker, Paul, and Wolfgang Stammler. *Reallexikon der deutschen Literaturgeschichte.* Berlin: de Gruyter, 1925-39.

Paris, Gaston. *Histoire littéraire de la France.* Paris: Académie des inscriptions et belles-lettres, 1888. XXX, 136-141.

PMS: Paul, Hermann. *Mittelhochdeutsche Grammatik.* 20th printing by Hugo Moser and Ingeborg Schröbler. Sammlung kurzer Grammatiken germanischer Dialekte. Tübingen: Niemeyer, 1969.

Piper, Paul. *Höfische Epik, Dritter Teil: Nachahmer Wolframs und Gottfrieds. Kleinere Epen und Chroniken.* Deutsche National-Litteratur 4.1. Stuttgart: Union deutsche Verlagsgesellschaft, 1894.

Schmitt, Anselm. *Stoff- und Motivgeschichte der deutschen Literatur. Eine Bibliographie.* 2nd rev. and expanded ed. Berlin: de Gruyter, 1965.

Schneider Karin. *Die deutschen Handschriften der Bayerischen Staatsbibliothek München*. Vol. 5, pt. III, Cgm. 351-500. Wiesbaden: Harrassowitz, 1973.

Schwietering, Julius. *Deutsche Dichtung des Mittelalters*. Handbuch der Literaturwissenschaften. Potsdam: Akademische Verlagsgesellschaft Athenaion, 1932.

Seiffert, Friedrich August. *Ein Namenbuch zu den altfranzösischen Artusepen*. Diss. Greifswald, 1882.

Waelzel, K. *Reimwörterbuch und Verzeichnis der Reimwörter aus 'Daniel von dem blühenden Tal' und dem 'Pfaffen Amîs' von dem Stricker*. Münchener Texte, Ergänzungsreihe Reimwörterbuch 8. Munich: Georg D. W. Callwey, 1926.

Weinhold, Karl. *Mittelhochdeutsche Grammatik*. 2nd ed. Paderborn: Ferdinand Schöningh, 1883.

West, G. D. *An Index of Proper Names in French Arthurian Verse Romances, 1150-1300*. Toronto: U of Toronto P, 1969.

DANIEL
of the
BLOSSOMING
VALLEY

by

DER STRICKER

Das er wol syns speres lang
Von dem roß nyder viel

Do wolt im her Daniel
Nit me tun do das ergieng
Wen das er das rosse gefieng
Und rette im offenlichen mitte
Ritter ist dz uwer sitte
Den ir do gelernet hat
So möhtent ir licht haben rat
Ob ir des sitten vergessent
Und uff uwerm roß gesessent
Bereitent ir sie alle
Mit eym solichen falle
Der sitte ist gar ane ere
Des gerumet ich nyemer mere

Plate 2. Daniel of the Blossoming Valley unhorses Sir Keii.
Ms. germ. 1340, leaf 54v.

I

KING ARTHUR

(1-6) He who gladly hears those things which are proper for men of virtue shall be always mindful of such tales[1] when he himself performs deeds of virtue. He, however, who is averse to literature is often slow to carry out noble deeds.

(7-22) Master Alberich of Besançon has brought to me a story from the French which I have translated[2] that it might be heard in German whenever entertainment suits the occasion.[3] Let no one criticize me: for only if Alberich has lied to me, do I pass falsehood on to you.[4] Thus begins this tale in which der Stricker[5] wishes to demonstrate his art with words, and bids you listen decorously and not interrupt with talking. Good breeding is so noble a virtue, for it does honor to both young and old.[6]

(23-33) "Any man who wishes to pursue praise and worldly acclaim ought not to despair should he perchance be wanting in material goods. For if others sense in him a certain zeal and also see evidence of that zeal, then they will speak of him just as they would of a man who possesses this same zeal and who also performs virtuous deeds. Yet he who lacks such zeal will seldom if ever find praise from others, no matter how much material good he boastingly lavishes upon them." These are the words of King Arthur.[7]

(34-46) Never has there lived a lord comparable to him. For he loved in great measure both generosity and acclaim as well as virtuous teachings, and he was never guilty of dishonor or disgrace. Hence his praise and his name live on and remain untarnished. Any man who desires to live the true courtly life should cherish King Arthur's good breeding in its every guise, for this is a bountiful fruit and a praiseworthy possession. From such virtue one can indeed become a worthy man.

(47-58) King Arthur was the paragon of all men. Whatever knowledge we have of kings throughout the ages was as naught compared to him. Save that I greatly wish to avoid conflict with others, I could very well tell of all which he did in his youth. I am altogether aware, however, that, were I to conjure up his excellence in words, people would say that I am a madman or a liar. Therefore I shall speak but little of this topic—and yet I shall not keep it wholly a secret either.[8]

(59-74) Hear now of the greatness of King Arthur's excellence: so fully truthful was he that he never once spoke a word less steadfast than a jewel which endures for all eternity. Hear now likewise of what other customs King Arthur observed. He considered all of his vassals—though they were subject to him—as comrades.[9] For this reason the finest knights from all lands came to be at his side. At his court they were made comrades of his and were, once back in their own lands afterwards, held in yet higher renown for having been in King Arthur's presence. Indeed, this is why they came to his court, for he who keeps company with a brave man can often thereby enhance his own esteem.

(75-88) King Arthur was greatly pleased to see that all the world bestowed praise upon him. And he vowed, for the sake of his comrades' good name, that he would each and every day refrain from food until such time as he should hear of—or else witness himself—a new tale of some deed worth recounting.[10] This he did only in order that his men should more actively pursue knightly deeds and not fall prey to indolence at his court. Thus, King Arthur brought to pass that they were in every way esteemed, which in turn led to his reaping the highest praise.

(89-108) All that he possessed was held in common, and his court was never so devoid of courtiers that a festival could not be celebrated. King Arthur's praise was rightfully heard both far and wide, and his retinue was countless. In his throneroom there stood a table which had the exquisite quality of refusing a seat to any man unworthy of becoming a comrade to the king. For whoever had at any time been guilty of villainy thereby lost the table's favor, and it scorned him forthwith, such that he never dared come near it. In such a way were those men chosen who were worthy of being King Arthur's comrades and who properly deserved to be called the men of the Round Table.[11] Moreover, they pursued at that court—and in more than abundant measure—all forms of entertainment and games in which men engaged.

(109-124) There at King Arthur's court they observed a custom which was seldom if ever disregarded: whomever ignominy had befallen was required to tell of it openly, and whomever fame had blessed was to hold it secret forever. Thus, each had to report his disgrace and conceal his gallantry. Any man among them who was desirous of esteem had to guard himself against and ever shun all infamy, such that he might be the more highly cherished. Hence it was commonly held as blameworthy to tell of another's disgrace or to boast of one's own valor.

(125-142) For each man who rode out in pursuit of adventure, there was a new shield held in readiness. As soon as he had accepted it, he dared not return until it was totally hewn to pieces, as proof of what he had been engaged in during his absence. No cause was ever so insignificant that those knights left it unaccomplished, and for this reason King Arthur was extolled in all lands. Because his men were ever accustomed to ride forth from his court, King Arthur's renown was magnified with each passing day. And because of this reputation, all of the most valiant knights from all lands journeyed there to King Arthur's court.

II

DANIEL'S ARRIVAL AT THE COURT

(143-159) Amazingly enough, King Arthur also had in his household the most deceitful man ever to gain the title of knight. This man was a calumniator who would hear nothing base said about himself. Had he slain one man, he would have claimed there had been three. Keii was his name, and he was at the same time the very boldest man who had ever joined the court.[12] One day he had ridden out arrogantly onto the field in search of adventure and to see what else he might find.[13]

(160-171) Now Sir Keii espied a knight riding toward him, and he headed in his direction. Daniel was this knight's name,[14] and the Blossoming Valley was his land. Daniel had heard tell that any knight—regardless how brave he might be—would, if once he sought out King Arthur's court, find an even more worthy knight in residence there.[15] Most intrepidly he rode off in haste toward Sir Keii in order to test the truthfulness of that amazing tale.

(172-187) As they approached one another, Daniel inquired whether he would have joust with him.[16] Sir Keii replied forthwith: "Indeed, but you could acquire greater fame elsewhere. For I have turned into cowards all who have ever done battle with me. No man has ever attacked me whom I have failed to unhorse. For this same reason all who have ever known me avoid me. Those who have nonetheless mustered the courage to oppose me have suffered the same fate as must now befall you. I shall show you at once a certain custom which I have learned!"

(188-212) They then lunged full tilt toward one another, their spears each lowered at the other's chest, each man[17] fervently desiring to unseat the other. With what fury did they slam together! Sir Keii was dispossessed of his knightly demeanor there and was, quite against his will, struck with great might, such that he fell a good spear's length from his horse. Sir Daniel was of a mind to do nothing further to him after this, save to retrieve his horse and to address him courteously: "Sir knight, if this be the custom which you have learned, then accept my advice and renounce this custom and remain seated on your horse the next time. Is this the sort of unhorsing you have imposed upon all of your opponents? Such a custom is indeed unlikely to bring you fame, and you would do well to boast no more of it."[18]

(213-232) Keii made no reply, but remained lying there on the ground, for he had by no means taken a gentle fall. Then spoke Sir Daniel: "Take your horse if you desire it, on the condition that you forsake this custom and not fall again unless truly you must." Sir Keii did what he commanded and took possession of his horse once more. Yet in the future he was often to fall in a like manner, which was again to be a source of much distress to him.[19] Keii then mounted his steed and rode to the court at Karidol,[20] where King Arthur asked him what had transpired. Keii would reveal nothing, save to exclaim angrily: "What happened to me happened to me!"[21] But since they knew of his ways, they inquired no further of him.

(233-253) Thereupon they cried out, one and then the other: "Bring forth the armor and the horses!" For all of them wished to ascertain what had happened to Keii. No man could begin to enumerate those knights who wasted no time in riding out onto the field in search of fame. On that field they spied Daniel of the Blossoming Valley and began trotting in his direction. The first to do battle with him was Troiman du Gereit, whom Daniel unseated with dispatch. Then came Sir Gressamant, whom he dashed down onto the very same spot. Gengemor and Linval, Alom and Schaitis, Pribandron and Belamis[22] (what good would it do for me to name them all?) fell at Daniel's hand, a fate which they were helpless to forefend.

(254-293) Finally, Sir Gawein and Iwein came riding up to the assembled knights, and I fancy the sun never shone on two finer knights than these. Sir Gawein then spoke up: "What is afoot here?" His comrades all replied: "Many a man has been mightily unhorsed here. We, too, have fared in a like manner." Then spoke Sir Gawein: "Sir knight, will you do joust with the two of us, so as to prove your courtliness?" Daniel was indeed eager to do so, and once they had agreed upon this, Daniel and Sir Gawein rode out straightway, the two of them alone. Their horses wheeled about, were given rein and made to charge one another fiercely. With a fury this game was pursued! Each knight thrust his lance through the other's shield with such intrepid fervor that it broke and flew apart. Yet neither man's esteem suffered on that battlefield; both remained seated, just as they wished and as excellent knights should. Thereupon Sir Iwein challenged him, and these two displayed such valiant riding and jousting that they both were able only with great difficulty to avoid falling from their steeds. And yet Daniel remained seated before them all, without a taint of disgrace. At the very last Sir Parzival came up, likewise anxious for the joust. Once again, this meant the end for their two lances, which at once flew asunder in splinters. But nonetheless each man remained firmly seated upon his horse.[23]

(294-304) The acclaim which fell to the stranger from these three knights (inasmuch as none had been able to unhorse him) gave the other knights cause to rejoice most heartily: they fancied their own excellence so much enhanced, since Daniel had remained amount even in combat with these three. Why is it that men are so? He who has himself experienced adversity gladly sees and hears of others with a similar lot, for thereby does his own ill fate appear to him diminished.[24]

(305-324) Those altogether impeccable knights Sir Gawein, Sir Iwein, and the noble knight Parzival desired to have Daniel as a guest at court. For Daniel had demonstrated his excellence to all by the fact that he had ridden in joust and had in so doing avoided the disgrace of being thrown from his steed. This wish of theirs they made most evident, for all three of them rode forward to him and spoke: "We bid you welcome! That you are an excellent knight, we must readily concede, for this much we have seen and heard. Now you shall no longer keep from us your business and your name, for we would all gladly hear of this. There is no need for you to feel reticent towards us, for we all stand most eager to serve you, as you have shown yourself worthy of such."

(325-344) Daniel replied: "It is not necessary that you stand in my service. Indeed, I should never shrink from performing such service as would be fitting for you, were I so excellent and esteemed that I were able to do so. *I*, then, shall all be the one to serve *you*, and I shall tell you whatever you wish to know. For I have indeed found here what it is that I was seeking. Many are the times I have heard tell of the excellence and great power of King Arthur's fellowship. And this is what I wished to witness. I shall speak the truth: I have come for no other purpose than to gain your favor. Daniel is my name, and the Blossoming Valley is my land, which my father, King Mandogran, bequeathed to me."

(345-357) The lords were all gladdened by this, and in all good faith they accepted Daniel into their fellowship, which was knit together so tightly that no peril, save death itself, could disjoin them. Merrily they rode off, for they had found a man who did honor to the court and who enhanced the number of their company. In great joy they returned to the court, where King Arthur inquired as to what had occurred.

(358-380) His nephew Sir Gawein related to him the news: "Here is one of the most excellent knights of whom we have ever heard tell. A fortunate hunt it was which we pursued this day, for God has provided us with a splendid catch! With this man we tested our knightly games, yet little benefit did we gain, for despite our bold determination, he thrust us all onto yonder grass. Indeed, I too am one of those whom he has unseated.[25] And not a one of us—lest he were to resort to falsehood—can rebuke his comrades for having fared any worse than he himself." This is why Sir Gawein spoke these words: he would have gladly done all he could to enhance Daniel's reputation even further. And Gawein, noble knight that he was, wished no greater praise for himself than for his comrades, for he had no desire to portray himself as more worthy than any of the others.

(381-394) Once this same tale had been related, King Arthur received Daniel with all the kindness befitting the reception of a good friend who is to be accorded warm hospitality. King Arthur rejoiced greatly that Daniel wished to remain at the court, and he ordered that hero enrolled forthwith in his fellowship. Great was the measure of King Arthur's excellence; he was praiseworthy and versed in all good qualities. His hospitality was endless, which in turn reinforced his own esteem.

III

KING MATUR'S CHALLENGE

(395-407) One day not long afterwards, as the men of the Round Table were pursuing the amusements which were seldom if ever lacking there (for merriment was a constant guest at the court), it occurred that they wished to partake of food. As you have already been told, the king had to hear of some new and unknown story before he would eat.[26] However, no such adventure had yet reached Arthur's ears, and so he bode his time in patient expectation of such tidings.

(408-435) After all had waited till nearly mid-afternoon,[27] there came riding into the courtyard a giant, powerful and great in size, who was bare of weapons and who wore neither helmet nor armor. The cloak of this giant was the most wondrous object ever sewn of silk and gold. In his hand he bore a club more massive than a roof-beam.[28] Whoever were to see this creature in a dream would be gripped indeed by fear, and as they saw him coming, many a brave hero shuddered in terror. So dreadfully enormous was the giant that they became vexed at the very sight of him. He did not even carry with him a shield, but rode barehanded atop a large camel,[29] which scarcely was able to carry him. As he rode on through the courtiers, he cleared a broad swath indeed. The skin of this giant was far from soft, but rather was harder than horn.[30] Had he truly become angry, he would have easily slain all of those present.

(436-461) The giant dismounted and had such things to tell the king that all were given over to despair. Thus did he address King Arthur: "King Matur[31] of Cluse has sent me here to investigate certain of your affairs. Many a noble story has he heard of your excellence. So perfect are you in all things which the world deems desirable that he considers you most worthy of ceding to him your land. Without resistance you must surrender yourself as a vassal to him and from that time forth hold your land as a fief granted by him. Such an honor he has seldom—if indeed *ever* before—offered to another king as now he does to you. This you can well believe: my lord is so powerful that any man can count himself forever fortunate whom he seeks out and deigns to choose as a vassal, as he has with you.

(462-476) "This would not have come about, save that he has often heard tell of your excellence. Many powerful kings there are whom he does not deign to count among his men, though they themselves have wished it. Not a one of them does my lord deem worthy of even being allowed into his land. Now, however, he has dispatched me here to you, with permission for you to visit his land—provided you are willing to accept him as your lord and to acknowledge that your esteem comes from him alone. Do not keep me waiting any longer now. Tell me forthwith what you think of this."

(477-493) Then spoke King Arthur: "Never before has a stranger tale been told at my court. If King Matur knows that I am as valiant as you have said, then he could well have anticipated that I would not agree to this. It would do me greater honor, I fancy, to be a free man (as now I am), the owner of my own land, than to hold it as a fief from another man. As long as God—it is from *Him* that I hold it as a fief!—grants me this, I shall beg no man for it. Should I have need of any defense, a powerful army shall carry out my request and my command.

(494-503) "Now tell me, in God's name, my friend, about your lord, as well as about his land and his people. You must relate to me everything, regardless whether or not it might please me.[32] If everyone in your land is as enormous as you, then I shall—Christ be my witness!—speak differently than I have thus far."

(504-526) Then spoke the giant knave in reply: "No king who ever wore a crown has lived as splendidly as does my lord. His land is well protected, such that your military campaign shall bring him no harm. This much is ensured by a mountain range which surrounds his land. Nothing living has ever been known to cross it, save for a bird which might fly over it. There is a road which leads through the mountain at the point whence I exited. Whenever it is desired to close off the road, a huge boulder is lowered in front of it. This entrance is such that I alone can lift it, while you with all your men would utterly fail to budge it. Ever since I rode out through it, the road has stood open and will continue to, until such time as I enter again.[33]

(527-549) "The land is large and broad and is verdant in all seasons. Of the women I shall tell you nothing,[34] for you shall see them there for yourself. So very winsome are they that neither I nor any other man could ever fully describe their beauty. One thing can be perceived there: even the least beautiful woman in that land is as lovely as a rose.[35] So delightful and so very fair are the women there that any man who dares observe them, be he young or old, is indeed crowned by the power of Lady Bliss. For these women are lacking in nothing at all: they are the very embodiment of both inward and outward perfection. Women have never before reached such a pinnacle; they are far beyond mere beauty!

(550-574) "There lives in this land a bird called the Babian.[36] The women—as well as anyone else who might wish one—have in their possession a great many of these birds, for the people prize them in no small measure.[37] Such a wondrous plumage has the Babian that I hear the women speak of seeing their own reflection in it—as clearly as in a mirror, perhaps even more so! What is more, they also utilize those same birds in this fashion: whenever the women go out into the sunshine—regardless of the time of day—the birds hover above them, for they are are trained (and indeed are naturally adroit at this) to provide them with cooling shade from the sun. At night when all are abed, wherever in the chamber the Babian may be, the people are provided with light emanating from that bird, such that they are able to see in the room, as though from a burning candle. And both night and day the Babian sings exquisitely, with so sweet a voice that people long to hear it.

(575-604) "For manifold reasons my lord is acclaimed by others. Wherever he journeys, regardless how far he may ride in a day's time, his entire palace accompanies him. No other king enjoys this reputation, that his dwelling follows him about. You may perchance find this inconceivable, for such a thing as this you have never witnessed. Yet it is accomplished without any great artifice, and I shall tell you precisely how: there is an animal (probably unknown to you)[38] called the elephant, whose strength is so enduring that it would not be harmed, nor even become fatigued, if one were able, by means of some device,[39] to place even a mountain upon its back. However much were to be loaded onto it, it would not so much as bend its legs.[40] It is one of the most massive creatures which the earth has ever borne. From its hoof to its shoulder joint it measures twelve double arms' lengths and more, and regardless of its burden it never senses any pain. Both day and night it remains standing, and it can be driven wherever one desires. So mighty is its strength that it survives any manner of adversity, even if one purposely attempts to slay it.[41]

(605-634) "Now there are artisans in this land who have these elephants brought together two at a time, but in a manner such that they do not come into contact with one another.[42] Thereupon they order a forest of trees to be felled, from which they fashion a great many sturdy beams, which in turn are lashed onto the elephants between the torso and the haunches. Regardless how many beams may come to rest atop this contrivance, it all holds together permanently, for they secure the beams so tightly that they could never give way under any burden (this custom is unparalleled and is the most extraordinary in that land). Onto these beams they then affix fortresses hewn both of marble and of ivory, which are marvelously embellished, in part with a great many precious ornaments wrought of gold. Never before was there such wondrous work crafted so as to depict birds and animals, battles and tournaments, dancing and flirting and courting of the ladies—all of which is engraved on the surfaces and spelled out with captions. My lord possesses a host of such palaces, any one of which follows him around as he pleases.[43]

(635-647) "Never was there so powerful a king who exercised his might so joyously as King Matur. Manifold pastimes does he enjoy, for there is a continuous festival in progress there. The land itself is broad and large, and he was so bold as to clear the empire of all those who had previously held this land, unless they were willing to serve him in fear and fall down at his feet.[44] Fiefs he then granted them, such that they might serve him well.

(648-673) "King Matur has divided his entire kingdom up into seven armies, one of which is required each day to journey to the

Wer gewesen in im zorn
Er hett sie alle wol erslagen
Er erbeiszet und begund sagen
Dem künige ein solich mere
Das sie alle duhte swere
Er sprach zu dem künige artuse
Der künig mattur von kluse
Hat mich her zu dir gesant
Und hette gern erkant
Wie getan din leben were
Er hat manige edel mere
Von dinen tugenden vernomen
Du bist so gar vollekomen
Alles des des die welt gert

Plate 3. The giant arrives at King Arthur's court.
Ms. germ. 1340, leaf 52v.

court and take part in tournament. Many a gleaming knight one can see galloping there, whose bearing and riding skills are marked by great artfulness, and who, with a knightly mien, fights for the sake of praise as though obsessed. The din of clanking swords[45] and the sight of the heroes pressing for worldly acclaim are to be found there. (Those knights possess no outward splendor unaccompanied by a corresponding measure of inner merit.)[46] There is for these knights no surfeit of such games. Furthermore, all of this is witnessed there by five hundred maidens, who must sit nearby on a green meadow and whose presence emboldens the knights. Above each of the ladies, sitting or standing, there hovers a Babian, which provides her with shade in ample measure. Well suited to joy is this place, with an abundance of bliss for all in attendance.

(674-690) "After such knightly game has carried on for a time, there follow various amusements without lance or sword. With dispatch the knights dismount and doff their weapons, whence a great many make haste to don their courtly attire and then go off joyfully to court the ladies. The sight of joy is manifest, for there commence dancing and singing and a festival blissful in so many ways. Joy alone is the object of all the competition, and each man finds there whatever pastime he can.

(691-715) "A short time afterward, the riding, the jousting, and the tilting commence once more. Shafts are seen broken for the ladies' acclaim, and fighting is performed with great ardor for the sake of their favors. When the riding is again ended, the knights take up whatever pastime they may choose. Thrice in the course of the day do they ride and make merry with courtly games. Glory is the reward for success, for their hearts are bent upon such joy. With the advent of evening, the knightly company takes its leave, but on the following day an army no less splendid arrives in great force and once more passes the day with the very same fanfare. Thus they all journey to the court each week, every day a different troop. The first assembly then returns anew, bringing with it many a handsome helmet-plume and both birds and animals crafted of gold and of precious stones.

(716-730) "Throughout all the land there is a commandment in effect that, at the risk of life and property, no maiden may be seen in the protection of her father, who is obligated to send her to the court once she turns eight years old, such that she may help[47] enhance this elegant way of life. For in such matters as these my lord takes the utmost interest. He desires to give to each of these maidens in marriage that man to whom she is drawn and who, of all the men, is most pleasing to her.

(731-737) "My lord is possessed of great majesty; his excellence and his physical strength are rare among all kings. Every man who has ever ridden into that land in search of adventure and who has lain in wait for my lord, has had death bestowed upon him.

(738-760) "Located there in Cluse is a finger of land, on which grows a magnificent limetree. Beneath this tree stands an object wrought of gold,[48] in the image of a fierce beast, which has, strangely enough, a banner in its mouth. Through this animal there flows water, which is brought there through an artful device by the force of the wind. Great skill and mastery are evident in this, for the beast is so devised that it possesses the power to imperil the life of any man who is so foolhardy as to remove the banner. For in that very instant the animal would raise such a din and would roar fiercely and with so thundering a voice that any man would fall down from his horse, so overwhelming is the blast.[49] Thereupon my lord rides up, in so fierce a rage that the intruder—even if he were greater in size than a mountain—would be beyond all hope.

(761-787) "The same artisan who wrought this beast likewise created me—as well as a brother of mine—and endowed us both with such enormity, for we are both his offspring.[50] Because of the close bond which ties him to us, he employed his craft to invest us both with an impenetrable skin, such that neither of us has ever suffered a wound. I have heard from his own lips that he is a good one hundred years in age, yet he is nonetheless still so agile that no creature has ever lived in flesh or fur upon this earth which could outrun or escape him. Indeed, I have come to see that he is far stronger than I (though he is much older and far smaller in size), and that he is versed in many an extraordinary art. And indeed his offspring bear full testimony to his artful skills, for neither I nor my brother—though we have been engaged full many a time in combat—has ever been cut by thrust of spear or by dint of sword.

(788-810) "You claim that you can dispatch a great throng of knights across the sea.[51] My own bare hands, however, are the only defense which I require. Even were your army so immense as to stretch beyond the reach of your eye, they should still have to suffer death at my hand. Therefore make an end to your threats. Before long you shall have cause to rejoice, for you must soon behold my lord face to face. However, if you fail to do so most willingly, your good name shall be entirely forfeited. For then I shall capture you and take you to Cluse, and I shall execute you straightway[52] and deliver your land to some other man, to whomever my lord grants it. Now, I have withheld nothing and have told you all, both the good and the bad. Now apprise me forthwith of your resolve. I shall not take leave of you until such time as you accompany me to that land."[53]

(811-823) Thereupon King Arthur summoned his wisest knights to court and entered into council with them.[54] Before they had even been asked for advice, the inexperienced youths among them spoke up: "However we may bring it to pass, this churlish devil shall never return to his land to recount how he has stood before you today and has cajoled and spoken with such insolence. This must be avenged here and now! His tale shall not follow him home!"[55]

(824-842) Then spoke Sir Gawein:[56] "Such talk and such advice as you have proffered can in no wise enhance our high repute. For you have all heard full well that no man can conquer this giant, whether by sword or by spear, whether by shots or by missiles. In truth, we have need here of sound advice. I counsel, therefore, that my lord act as though pleased by this affair, yet at the same time weigh the means whereby we might avenge this injury. My lord should declare his willingness to journey to that land, but should request that the giant first tarry here, for no more than a week and until such time as my lord has stated that he is prepared to depart.[57]

(843-855) "Then let us all bid him to grant us this entreaty, since my lord has a most faithful company of followers whom he must summon to undertake this bold venture together with him. All of these followers, we shall tell the giant,[58] have sworn an oath to confront any danger, whatever the circumstances may be—whether our king has been provoked to anger or wishes to defend his good name. These men, we shall say,[59] King Arthur must take along on the journey, for the renown which falls to him in Cluse shall likewise provide *them* occasion to acquire fame.

(856-884) "Were we to slay a messenger, we should have no less than disgrace itself to live with.[60] And even if we could contrive to take his life, I would nonetheless argue against such a course of action. In truth, if he were to be slain just now, I should forever lament this to God, for then there would be no one to show us the way into his land. My advice to all of you is that, once we are in this realm, we take aim at the giant's eyes, even if we cannot dispatch him with the sharp edge of our weapons.[61] Thus we shall shroud his knowledge both of light and of day, whether it be a sword or a spear that hits the target. If we cannot fully put an end to this giant, then we shall take flight from him. Bereft of his eyesight, he can inflict no great harm upon us. Then let us not fail to betake ourselves to the limetree and cause the beast to roar and the water to flow through it in full measure. And if the giant's brother[62] should then appear, we shall aim our bolts in search of *his* eyes as well. With both giants deprived of their eyesight, the king shall be quite fully stripped of his right hand."

(885-905) Gawein's counsel struck the king and the people as both chivalrous and sound.[63] All were of a resolve to win glory there in Cluse, or else to die a praiseworthy death. King Arthur, seated upon his throne, then spoke in reply to the messenger: "Your words please me more than all others which ever I have heard. Now bide time with us here for but a week. My comrades and I are united by staunch bonds of loyalty towards one another. In order to demonstrate my loyalty in this matter, I must assemble them here, so that whatever glory is allotted me in your land[64] might likewise fall to them. They ought all to witness the moment when[65] I surrender my land into your lord's hand, such that they—as well as I—may become his vassals.

(906-926) "I now bid you, good knight, tarry here for seven nights' time. For you can well grasp that I would be quite crazed if I were to break the oath, the loyalty, and the truthfulness which I have sworn to my comrades. What good would I then be as a vassal to any lord if I were to repudiate my loyalty and forsake my comrades? If King Matur were to see me arrive in such debasement, I should then have to live with eternal shame—since he knows of my name and has heard so much of me. Insofar as he holds me in such high esteem, I would like to arrive in a manner such that he might concede the truth of my reputation. And since I myself am to be so highly honored there, I wish to ride into his land in a way that will likewise confer honor upon him.

(927-935) "It has ever been my custom to celebrate at Whitsuntide,[66] and it is ill-fitting that I should pass this holiday in the absence of a festival. However, your lord, with his great glory, shall replace this festival, which I shall forgo on his account. Gladly will I journey to his land, for I am greatly pleased by this affair."[67]

(936-956) Therefore the knights all bade the giant delay there for seven nights, whereupon they would set out together with him. So resolute were they in their request that in the end the giant acceded to their will and spoke just as I shall tell you: "Seven days I shall remain here, inasmuch as you attach such great importance to this. However many knights you are able to convene within that same period you may take with you when you depart. Yet this shall be an easy game for my lord, and regardless how great a host of knights you may assemble, they cannot elude either sure defeat or else death itself. This is a fact which they cannot alter. Hence you ought not to fancy that any defenses will ever deliver you from my lord. Should he become at all ill-tempered, then you are lost, each and every one!"

(957-973) Once the giant had spoken these words and had pledged to them all to delay for a week's time, the king commanded missives to be written, which were then dispatched at once. Both petitions and decrees were sent forth throughout his entire land, saying that King Arthur was in quest of his friends and was in need of assistance and of a mighty combat force. Whoever had pledged friendship to King Arthur was to renew that pledge by now upholding his fidelity to it. Their loyalty he wished to examine and to test, for a circumstance had befallen him in which he had need of a stout defensive force.[68]

(974-986) Thus did King Arthur[69] amass his army, such that no king before him had ever procured so many an excellent man. He deemed it a misfortune, however, that certain of his comrades had already set out elsewhere in pursuit of adventure. Gladly would he have awaited their return or have sent after them, but they had ridden forth on too many diverse and unknown paths: Lanzelet and Erec, as well as an ample host of others who were bent upon winning acclaim.

IV

THE ADVENTURE OF THE DARK MOUNTAIN

(987-1017) King Arthur was now to host this enormous giant at his court for a week's time before commencing the journey. One of Arthur's comrades, who was spurred on by his own bold valor, felt so urgently pressed to launch the campaign that the week's delay seemed to him too long and the respite was unwelcome. This was the knight Daniel of the Blossoming Valley.[70] Out he slipped from the court and onward to the fortress gate, where he espied the trail visible from the hoofprints of the giant's camel. In his heart Daniel thought: "Once at the limetree, I shall not fail to remove the banner and loose the wailing of the beast. Should King Matur then appear, he shall have to deal with me, regardless whether this brings success or failure upon me. I shall suffer at his hand either injury or good fortune, for I wish to ascertain once and for all whether he is worthy to rule over his land. With that I shall seek to determine for my lord whether he ought to tolerate such haughty behavior."

(1018-1027) In the evening, as night approached and Daniel no longer could see the tracks, it became necessary for him to seek out a resting place. He endured such rest most unwillingly, and no other night ever seemed to him so long. Quite early in the morning he rode back toward the trail and followed the hoofprints. He made haste in his journey until night fell once more.

(1028-1046) Thus Daniel again had to delay his journey, until the third morning. A great trial was about to befall him! He rode in the direction of a mountain both craggy and high. Save for the fact that the tunnel passed through it, no one would ever have known what manner of land was inside. Now Daniel glanced here and there and quickly discerned that he should have to travel through the mountain if he wished to enter the land in which the beast was said to be. It pleased him greatly that the land was so close at hand. Eagerly he hastened onward toward the opening in the mountain, fearing no manner of affliction.

(1047-1072) Daniel spotted a creature seated there of whom he could well stand in awe:[71] a monstrous giant! His thoughts turned then to the other giant, whose trail he had followed to this place, and who had, in King Arthur's presence, claimed to have a brother invulnerable to all manner of weapons. "If I postpone the completion of my journey and do battle here with this giant," he thought, "I shall forfeit nothing more than my fame and the effort which I have thus far expended. — On the other hand, if I must some day confess that I shrank back in fear and did not dare[72] to determine whether this giant can be vanquished—if I am unable to report on this, then I shall be held a coward. — However, should I ride up to him now in order to put myself to the test, and should my sword fail to pierce him, then I must suffer both disgrace and death at his hand. I have need of sound counsel!"

(1073-1114) Thus Daniel weighed the dilemma in his mind, as the unfortunate circumstances compelled him to do. Then, however, he seized the courage of a lion.[73] "No good can come of my cowering in fear like a woman! I prefer[74] to lose my life valiantly than to live on in endless shame. Never could I risk my life for greater stakes than these, for I find twofold comfort in the teachings of my heart: if I am victorious, the victory shall ever bring me acclaim; yet I shall incur little if any disgrace if the giant defeats me. However great my injury may be, I shall willingly take on the risk! For I should gladly be seen[75] wounded in body, but with my reputation unblemished before I would ever shrink from battle or injury—and, what is worse, be laden with shame. Either I shall fall, or else I shall fell this giant! Even if my comrades had already arrived in full force, I should still yearn to be the first to take up the battle if I could arrange it so. If I should prove my mettle in this encounter, then I shall still have the same measure of determination and strength left in me. On the other hand, if I fail to gain the victory here and if the giant departs from me unscathed, then indeed all of King Arthur's army could not inflict upon him any harm. I am anxious to see how he defends himself!" Daniel dismounted, tightened the saddle girth of his steed, and, once again seated, assumed the air of a man about to take on all the world.

(1115-1138) All of this was being observed by a lady who was standing nearby and who took good note of Daniel's actions. Standing by a tree, she tied her horse's reins to a branch. Quickly she hastened toward Daniel and offered him her greeting; once having spoken these words, she then fell down at his feet. "What is the meaning of such a salutation as this?" spoke the splendid knight, for it was grievous for him that she had cast herself at his feet. Daniel dismounted onto the turf and was about to help her up, when he perceived that she was in grief. Her every feature had a hue of death, so that she could neither see nor speak. And she lay there in such a state that Daniel fancied she could not live much longer, but had already given up her life for lost. It rent his heart that she was unable even to speak.

(1139-1174) Daniel had been on the verge of riding off eagerly into battle against the giant, whom he so keenly wished to tame. His thoughts were filled with anger towards this giant, and he pondered to himself: "I shall depart here with great shame if I cannot determine whether this lady wishes to relate to me the cause of her lamentation—or whatever it is that troubles her, since she has humbled herself so astonishingly before me.[76] I can readily discern from her appearance that she has in her possession both great power and manifold suffering. This much she has demonstrated here. I do not know, however, what it is that she wishes. And even if I knew full well, I would be unable to come to her aid if I lose my life to the giant, with whom I am now to engage in battle. First of all, I shall determine my fate with him. If he then lies dead before me and I remain alive, I shall ride back to this place and hear what it is that she desires. For if I were to ride off from her forever, without even hearing of her distress, I should be the lowliest man ever to bear the title of knight, since a lady has demonstrated in so wretched a fashion her need of my help. If I am incapable of granting her what she desires, however, my reputation shall still be but meager."[77]

(1175-1200) Thus Daniel bent down to the ground with the intention of finding out what was afflicting the lady. He had abandoned his timid demeanor and, taking the lady's head, he laid it onto his lap. Her anguish was abundant, but after Daniel had sat there with her for a time, she felt in some measure better. She then sat up and spoke: "May God preserve your reputation and your life, my lord, in exchange for this comfort. Never before has a poor woman been so wholly divested of favor, and yet now I have been granted your kind help. There is no way in which you could better increase your esteem and your hope for good fortune than by aiding me, for I am utterly bereft of all favor." Daniel spoke: "This grieves me, my lady, and I tell you in all truth that I too have endured much hardship. If I can comfort you, however, I shall not fail to do so, as long as I am able to move a muscle in my body."

(1201-1220) The lady thanked him profusely and spoke: "My care and my affliction are so great as to be incalculable. Yet just now I took note of your intention to embark upon a journey[78] from which no one could have rescued you. For death would of necessity have fallen to your lot. If you now lose your life on account of me, then I shall not be so sinful a woman for having caused this, inasmuch as you would already have forfeited up your life. You could not have escaped alive, for so hard is the giant's skin that it has never been pierced at all, regardless what weapons were ever shot, struck, or thrust against it. No matter how ferociously one goes at this giant, no man who attacks him is so skillful as to come away alive.

(1221-1250) "Hear now, in God's name, good sir, what it is that afflicts me and how great my misfortune is. I am the daughter of the Duke of the Dark Mountain,[79] and I have incurred such travail from a certain dwarf that death would be a thousand times dearer to me than life. God would do well to grant me death, good sir, inasmuch as I am doomed to suffer such adversity. This dwarf wished to possess me as his own.[80] My father refused him this[81] and offered angry resistance, for he had no other offspring and desired to give me to someone my equal. (I could rightfully have acquired high esteem, but this is now no longer possible for me!) After the dwarf had made a great many entreaties (all of them in vain!), his threats then turned violent and became burdensome to my father, who aired his vexation to his men and proved himself not to be a coward. He did battle on the green with this dwarf, who then—my lament to God shall be unending!—slew my father!

(1251-1271) "All who have endeavored to avenge him there, as they rightly should, have likewise met with death. When my mother witnessed this dire event from atop the battlements,[82] her heart broke open with misery and she died a death of grief. Thus have I lost them both. Because the dwarf has inflicted this great distress upon me and has still continued to woo me, my heart shall never again know gladness, since I did not likewise die of grief. In anger I sent word throughout these lands: whoever should be so fortunate as to slay the dwarf and were to bring his head before me, that man would be chosen as lord over me and over my land, regardless how low he may be in birth.

(1272-1290) "After word of this had spread, there came many a valiant man, for all who yearned for glory and had heard of my proclamation undertook the journey. There came a procession of such proportions that I cannot describe it to you! All, however, were slain, without exception, so that not a one came away with his life—not a one of those knights who had been bold enough in strength and in skill to do battle with the dwarf. Death has been the fate of all of them! For the dwarf possesses a sword whose blows no man can survive:[83] even if a man were protected by twelve suits of armor, he could not withstand so much as a single blow from the dwarf, whose name is Juran.[84]

(1291-1309) "Now I am come here for this reason: I have often heard tell that no man has ever come to this place without meeting death, and I seek such a man as might deem it slightly preferable to die in my own land than here. God has always come to the aid of a just man, and since I am quite wholly without blame in this matter, such a man may perhaps profit from this endeavor. For whomever God grants the victory in my land shall acquire a sword with which to slay these monstrous giants who shun all weapons, but who have never been wounded themselves. Never was there a rock so hard that, once struck by this sword, it could resist being shattered into pieces like mere wood.[85]

(1310-1342) "For this reason the dwarf is so haughty as to maintain that, his will prevailing, I must become his wife. Since I am unwilling, he will force me, so that eventually I must fall at his feet. If he drives me to that, he claims, then he shall keep me as his wife for but two or three nights. My fortress and all that is in it I shall forfeit and must then depart from it naked. What is more, the dwarf has sworn a public oath that, if I leave under such circumstances as these, I can be certain that he will set upon me with birch twigs until I begin to bleed. Wherever there be skin on my body, he will flog it all off. Oh, wretched woman that I am, how shall I endure this? He also plans to cut off my nose and my lips and disfigure me to the point where no man will wish to rest his glance on me. Unless he can be dealt with in quick measure such that I might find some comfort, I shall sooner take my own life than endure such misery!"

(1343-1384) When Sir Daniel had heard this wretched tale—that the giant's skin was so hard as to render him invincible, and that the dwarf bore a sword with which he slaughtered all who parried with him, and when Daniel had heard from the lady's lament that she was so burdened with grief and with injury—he then thought to himself: "What a blessing it would be to me if I knew now of a prudent course of action! I fancy I have encountered a full measure of all that I ever set out for. I have clearly heard both choices, yet I can neither do battle here, nor ride off with the lady. It shall be a great salvation indeed if I can come away alive from these monsters, who commit such carnage that no man has engaged in battle with them without suffering death as a result. I have set out too early! Oh woe, would that I were still at home! Never have I become entangled in a more wretched strait—of that God the Allpowerful is well aware! — But no, my mind is filled with misguided thoughts. For no matter how much time I might spend lying peacefully at home enjoying my comfort, I could never accomplish anything for which people could ascribe to me any manner of valor. What matter that I am now enduring such hardship as this? It may be of value to me later! Yet if that cannot be, then it is better (as now seems my fate!) that I soon give up my life valiantly than that I live forever in disgrace."

(1385-1394) All concern for his own life Daniel dismissed from his mind and spoke: "My lady, your misery and your distress trouble me. In all certainty I shall either lie dead for the sake of your innocence, or I shall vanquish the dwarf. Ride forth and show me the way! He is not so fearsome that I dare not challenge him, since he has caused you such distress."

(1395-1402) The lady again offered Daniel her thanks and was most joyful for this consolation. Yet she wept out of anguish and for fear that she should see happen to him that which had befallen all whom the dwarf had ever slain. Thus she had ample sorrow to endure!

(1403-1423) They tarried there no longer, but mounted their horses and rode off. The lady was oppressed by grief, so that she rode along in great sorrow. This distressed Daniel, who wished to console her and spoke: "Trust in God, my lady, that I, with His command, shall overcome the dwarf. For God so loves righteous deeds that you can be assured that we shall survive unscathed any ordeal with this dwarf." The lady found comfort in this and comported herself with somewhat more cheer than was in fact present in her spirit. Yet heavy was her heart, so greatly did the thought of Daniel's death grieve her. He too felt pity for her in her distress. Thus, neither was disposed towards joy of any sort, though both made every effort to be happy.

(1424-1451) All day long they rode, until nightfall, when they arrived at their proper destination, the lady's homeland. Here they both were received most graciously, for well nigh sixty maidens came forth to meet them. Marvelous things can[86] be seen there: a host of knights and squires[87] received both the lady and her guest in a manner befitting their rank. Save for the fact that joy was lacking, all manner of glory ever witnessed elsewhere was to be found at this court. Now, however, the sorrow of all the courtiers grew deeper than before, and their hearts began to ache as they saw this knight whose death—should he fall in battle—they all said they should never cease to lament. Their anguish over this was so profound that no man equal to Daniel had ever before been more deeply lamented while still alive! Greatly did they fear for his life.

(1452-1474) The lady's dearest handmaidens, who were free to offer her advice, fervently entreated her to absolve Daniel (since he was so splendid a knight!) of losing his life to the dwarf. They advised her furthermore to take him as her lord[88] (since he would easily be worthy of her) and not to let him leave the lodgings. For they were confident that the fortress itself could always be defended against the dwarf, and they would concede whatever damage he might wreak outside the fortress walls. The lady then ceased to bewail her sorrow, since she had Daniel safely in the fortress with her. With a glad heart she spoke: "I would gladly accept this counsel, and I should be ever pleased with the outcome if only we could persuade this knight. However, the duel now so occupies his mind that he will refuse to withdraw, as ill fate would have it."

(1475-1490) When it came time for dining, they performed an act of courteous service which was most pleasing to Daniel: all manner of repast was brought forth in lavish quantity. I can well assure you that they were lacking in nothing there, and that they held their guest so dear that he luxuriated in their ministrations that evening. They showed him both zeal and such good works that he resolved forthwith—should he live to see the next day—to prove himself worthy of this hospitality, or else to die at the hand of the dwarf.

(1491-1506) During the night Daniel slept in comfortable lodgings until wakened by the glow of dawn. He heard an early mass[89] and readied himself for the duel with the dwarf and for the chance to perform knightly deeds that day.[90] To the Lady of the Dark Mountain he then spoke: "Send word to the dwarf and tell him to come, that you wish to see him. Whatever you then hear me say to him, you must be prepared to do. A man can often accomplish with wisdom full many a thing which he could not achieve by relying upon strength alone."[91]

(1507-1528) The dwarf was summoned, and Daniel proceeded with the lady out to the battlements. He wished to determine whether he could save his life through some act of cunning. Daniel then watched as the dwarf (whose name was Juran) approached and walked up to the fortress gate. Once there, the dwarf inquired as to what his lady desired, and whether he should ever win her favor. "Yes," spoke Sir Daniel forthwith from atop the battlements, "my lady and her land are yours if you are prepared to display whatever valor you possess. She is ready to offer you her love. If you demonstrate your bravery to her, she is willing to accept you as her lord."

(1529-1557) The dwarf answered him thus: "I should be most pleased indeed if I could deservedly earn her favor. Whatever task she can set for me whereby a man might prove his prowess, that I shall perform both willingly and well!" Daniel replied: "My lady has pledged to put an end to her anger so that you might demonstrate whether or not you are worthy of such an honor. Lay down your own sword and take up the finest sword which you can find here, and then do battle with the very weakest man whom my lady has to offer. Should you succeed in defeating him, my lady will drop the quarrel and do all that you desire. It is your sword alone which is credited with all the slaughter which you have wrought, for no man has been able to withstand that weapon. Now show my lady and her retinue whether or not you are capable of inflicting death on any man without the aid of that sword. Whatever you then desire shall be fulfilled."

(1558-1580) Then the dwarf Juran spoke: "Will I then possess her favor if I attain victory over that man?" Cheerfully the lady spoke up forthwith: "Indeed! If you win your life from him, then you may take dominion over all that I possess." Then spoke the dwarf Juran: "If this is so, I shall gladly do combat with your most excellent hero! Death must befall whomever you have chosen for this battle. I shall demonstrate to you that my prowess is in no way dependent upon the sword, but rather that it emanates from my body. Even if you call upon me to put down the sword and take up a club, I should not flinch with fear. On the contrary, I would rely upon my strength and would indeed be the victor. Even if my opponent were stronger than Samson,[92] I should challenge him for such a reward as this!"

(1581-1597) Lady Love proved here that any man whom she fails to entice into servitude for the sake of her reward must indeed possess a strong will in his steadfast mind. This lesson she can demonstrate quite fully with Solomon, who was the wisest man of whom I have ever heard tell, until she, Lady Love, destroyed both his wisdom and his senses. Lady Love has done the same to full many a good man. Hence you ought not to be amazed that she was victorious here too, for every man on whom she exerts her power has no choice but to subjugate himself to her.[93]

(1598-1620) Sir Juran did likewise: he surrendered himself to Lady Love's command. It seemed to him that our Lord God Himself could have no angel as replete with beauty as the lady whom he saw there before him. Laughingly he spoke: "I shall gladly perform all that you wish!" He removed his sword and carried it off a good distance to one side so that they all saw it, and then placed it on the ground. "Now I wish to see," spoke the dwarf Juran, "who it is who dares to engage in battle with me." The killing of his opponent as the price for the lady's promise of favor he fancied an easy task indeed.[94] He walked up to the fortress gate and in front of it drew a circle wherein they should fight if in fact it should come to that.

(1621-1653) The gates were seen opening and Juran watched as Daniel of the Blossoming Valley approached him. Daniel offered Juran the choice of two swords. The dwarf took the one which he preferred, and Sir Daniel took the other. Both men stepped into the ring. The courtiers gave their pledge that the fortress gate was to be closed and no one allowed outside save for Daniel and the dwarf. The two of them together commenced to perform manly deeds. With their shields they attempted to ward off the blows to their armor, which came apart at the seams. So fierce were their thrusts that they were in little time stripped of those shields. They fought such a bout that all who heard and saw it swore that neither opponent could come away alive, that both would have to die. They struggled in that ring with ferocity! Each strove fiercely for the other's death. Flashing red fire could be seen sparking from their helmets[95] as the swords which they held in their hands resounded and struck against their helmets and armor.

(1654-1681) The onlookers were unanimous in their hope that the dwarf would be defeated. Most courteously they beseeched God, for the sake of the Holy Trinity, to stand by the righteous man and to bring about a just outcome to the duel. The dwarf Juran then spoke: "May this blow be dealt, my lady, in your honor!" With that he battered

Daniel on his helmet so mightily that his own sword burst in two. At that moment the stranger Daniel dealt him so fearsome a blow that the dwarf slumped to the ground, yet Daniel's sword failed to penetrate his skin, a fact which vexed Daniel greatly. The dwarf was fierce and clever and immensely powerful. Just as Juran had recovered from that blow and was about to draw himself up, Daniel struck him again so that he fell back to his knees. In quick succession Daniel then dealt him four mighty blows, and yet—amazing to recount!—no matter how stoutly he battered away at the dwarf, he was able to pierce neither his helmet nor his armor.

(1682-1690) Once more the dwarf jumped to his feet and, forgetting his good breeding, took flight in the direction of his sword, for his life was most dear to him. Daniel, seeing his intentions, quickly betook himself in the same direction. Both combatants were in full sprint. Ah, what a race was on for that sword!

(1691-1705) Never was there any firm resolve which could be brought to fruition without the aid of favorable circumstances, which are always far more crucial (provided resolve itself does not lag too far behind!). Both men raced against each other. Their resolve was identical, but favorable circumstances smiled on the one, whereas the other, who fought without this advantage, was but the shadow of a man. No matter how he strained, Juran was unable to thwart the advantage which fell to Daniel. For Daniel's legs were so long that he outstripped the dwarf and took possession of that sword.

(1706-1733) Having gained this advantage, he wasted no time, but drew the sword and spoke: "If you desire to live another moment, then you must surrender as a captive to my lady's rule." Now the dwarf was so bold as to have no fear of death; in his vexation he quite fully lost his senses out of desire for the sword. He fancied himself so valiant that, relying solely upon his strength, he intended to seize the sword from his opponent. But Daniel kept him at a distance and drew back from him thrice, informing him repeatedly that he would kill the dwarf should he refuse to surrender. The dwarf paid heed to none of this and, offering Daniel no reply, persisted in charging at him. Once Daniel had sufficient proof that the dwarf no longer desired to live, he held back no more, but dealt him a blow with the sword, so that his head flew off and he never again uttered another word.

(1734-1745) As soon as the lady had beheld this, she bowed down deeply to God and offered thanks to Him for His ordinance, both with her heart and with her words. The gates were then opened and the lady assembled her court—a glorious multitude it was!—and walked up to Daniel, whom she graciously welcomed. Her heart was set free, for she had overcome her worry and her distress.

(1746-1764) Great and ample was the praise which they now heaped upon Daniel. And clearly evident was the proof of the lady's and the court's indebtedness to him as he carried forth Juran's head. All those present placed themselves at his command and rendered thanks to Daniel and to God for the victory that had befallen them there. Had Daniel set his mind upon any manner of reward, had he desired their service or their gifts,[96] you could have readily heard and seen that all of this would have been a joy for them to fulfill. They showed themselves eager to carry out his every request.[97] If the lady had possessed all the world, she would have deemed Daniel worthy of receiving it.[98] And had he desired her hand, as the story relates it, those courtiers would not have refused him.[99]

(1765-1781) Now, however, Daniel wished only to take his leave. They attempted to dissuade him from this and said that they should always regret it if he were to ride off unrewarded for his troubles. The lady besought him to linger at least until he had rested from the battle. But every request and every command which she made of him went unfulfilled. That he had acquired the sword from the dwarf pleased Daniel greatly, and he intended to determine conclusively whether it was capable of penetrating the giant's skin. Unwilling to be dissuaded from that, Daniel mounted his steed and rode off,[100] which brought great sorrow to the lady and all her retinue.

V

THE ADVENTURE OF THE BRIGHT FOUNTAIN

(1782-1800) After Daniel of the Blossoming Valley had delivered the Lady of the Dark Mountain from the dwarf and had taken his leave,[101] he made haste to depart. But just as his horse was trotting away from the fortress, he spotted before him perhaps forty maidens, who, once having descried him, dismounted onto the turf. Hastening toward Daniel, they all followed their mistress, all the while lamenting and weeping. Daniel saw that they intended to approach him, and so he dismounted onto the sand and led his steed by hand until he came close enough to hear their greetings.

(1801-1842) At that they fell at his feet one and all.[102] Immediately Daniel showed his friendly intentions and quickly bade them rise, inquiring as to what was troubling them. Their mistress spoke: "My lord, it is a heartache and an ordeal for me which I am forced to endure and which is in excess of all suffering. Once upon a time I was a powerful countess and held full dominion in the land of the Bright Fountain. Now this and all my good name have been taken from me, and I would never again find joy or comfort unless you can deliver me from my affliction. I had been filled with despair as to whether any man could ever help me. However, since you have just relieved this lady of the great anguish which she suffered, now I know in all truth that, if I am to encounter any manner of salvation, it will have to come from God through you. For God has taken from this world so many hundreds of men whom you have vanquished that my consolation depends upon you. Through your help—should I be so blessed!—I wish to replace with joy the sorrow which has fallen to my lot and which is soon to overwhelm me. If only I might find this from you! I swear upon my oath the full truthfulness of this: that if you do not save me, I shall never receive consolation!"

(1843-1851) Daniel spoke: "This is cause for much grief to me, my lady. For I have gone to great trouble and have expended much courage in a certain matter which I have still not yet completed and with which I must now occupy myself. If I fail to carry out that which I have undertaken, then I shall forfeit and lose all my reputation."[103]

(1852-1870) The lady wrung her hands and spoke: "Never mind this! I take it upon my soul that you could never augment your reputation and your good fortune more than by coming to my aid. Never have you been in a situation—nor will you *ever* be!—where your favor is more needed than here. And in so doing, you can acquire God's grace as well as worldly acclaim. Your good name shall multiply ever more and in all respects. For God and for the sake of your own courtliness, have mercy upon me, my lord, and harm shall never inflict itself upon you or your reputation. Help me to overcome my heartache, poor woman that I am! God will always help you in return."

(1871-1910) "Tell me, my lady," spoke Daniel, "what it is that you lament, and I shall right whatever wrong you have incurred if I am at all able." She fell at his feet and thanked him, compelled as she was by great distress. She wept profusely and spoke: "May God repay you for this, my lord. I am suffering shame and scorn from a devilish creature on whom no bodily harm can be inflicted. Truly he is the devil's[104] comrade! So immense is his head alone that two men could barely lift it. He wears no clothing and is covered from head to toe with hair.[105] Furthermore, he is wholly without a belly or a lap, so that his legs and arms grow directly onto his head. Believe me, my lord, his chin in all truth reaches down to his knees. Two larger eyes were never seen than those which grow on his head, and his mouth is more than a yard in width. One could search forever and not find a creature so monstrous! I doubt not a whit but that the loathsome devil himself has dispatched him here straight from hell. Whenever this creature wishes to commit murder, he picks up in his hand a head, and no matter how many men look this head in the eye, not one of them ever comes away alive. All of them fall dead in an instant. And this is the very direst torment of all: as soon as he kills off the men, he will turn to the women and children.

(1911-1927) "This demon leads a hideous army, all of whose members are in his image and who have come from the sea. They do battle wholly without the aid of weapons, of which they have no need, since immediate death comes to anyone who beholds that head. These creatures suck blood from the bodies of their victims. After retaining it in their mouths for but a short time, they spit it back out again. This is how they all live; there is no other nourishment which they take. In this same fashion the creature has laid waste to my land without once resorting to pillaging or burning, to sword or spear.

(1928-1961) "And yet the injury which I incurred from this was as naught compared to the loss of my six fine children who perished at his hand. But even this distress I have overcome. Until yesterday morning I still possessed my castle and a large retinue, along with a knightly spouse by whom I had born my children. Then yesterday at dinner as we sat in sorrow over the losses which we had suffered, that devil walked in upon us and slaughtered all who were present! I myself was scarcely able to survive by stealing off like a mouse through the rear of the palace—only I and my remaining ladies are still alive here. My lord was overcome by rage and took flight into a lofty tower in which he has barricaded himself. I am at a loss as to how I shall retrieve him. If he should lose his life, then I shall return there in order to behold the head—so that I too may find death and follow after my lord. But if you can carry out to completion all that I request, I shall surmount all sense of loss and shall consider myself most exalted. If my lord is dead, however, then I shall be freed from all affliction and shall surrender myself most willingly unto death."

(1962-1976) "Now ride forth along the road,"[106] spoke Daniel to the lady, "until we catch sight of the palace. Let me then ride up to it, and you shall see straightway whether I am able to assist you. I shall win back your husband or else lose my own life in the attempt." The lady and her women offered Daniel profuse thanks. They tarried no longer, but rode off quickly for a distance of four long miles, until they drew close enough to see the palace.

(1977-1999) Daniel then addressed her: "Await me here, my lady, until I determine whether God is willing to bestow His grace upon you. It is now altogether in God's hands as to whether or not I shall ever see you again. However wretched the nightmare that I may witness, I would gladly endure it, being spurred on by the commandment of your fear. How I shall accomplish this without the aid of my eyes (since they would bring down harm upon me), I do not, in God's name, know. Have you any sort of mirror[107] here?" The lady spoke forthwith: "Indeed, there are many; which do you wish?" "Bring me any one of them!" he replied. As soon as Daniel had spoken, she said to her women: "Bring all of the mirrors, and let him choose for himself which one he wishes!"

(2000-2016) This was accomplished in quick measure. Mirrors were shown to Daniel one after the other until he spoke: "This one will suffice!" Then Daniel grasped the one which suited him best of all and stuffed it into his tunic. He pledged to the lady to bring back good tidings unless prevented from doing so by such dire adversity that he himself should have to suffer hardship. Daniel made great haste to set out, and the ladies—to the extent they were able—wished him well as he departed. Many a tear streamed down from the eyes of the lady and all her followers.

(2017-2040) Daniel hastened on toward the fortress, where he saw that the loathsome intruders had barricaded themselves inside. Unflaggingly he rode on and dismounted at the fortress gate. There he rapped with the knocker and demanded in a loud voice that he be let in. With wrathful words the bellyless devil answered him forthwith: "Who is out there before the gate?" Daniel spoke: "It is I." The monster thought it curious that Daniel had avoided giving his name, so as not to be recognized. Flushed with rage he spoke: "Precipitate ruin shall be your fate if you persist in seeking it in this manner! I shall slay you on the spot if you fail to tell me at once your business—as well as your name and, if your life is dear to you, your lineage!"

(2041-2064) Such talk as this was a mockery to Daniel, who said in reply: "I much prefer to follow your bidding in these matters than to lose my life. Listen and I shall tell you my name, for I shall never be ashamed of it: I am called by the name which the priest gave me[108] when he baptized me. My family I can certainly reveal to you as well: my father was my mother's husband, and I am their son. This is how you shall know me!" Then spoke the bellyless demon: "Never before have I heard such reckless talk as what I hear you saying. I shall avenge this myself! You cannot fancy yourself so valiant that you will still be standing there when I come out. Even if you possessed all the valor in the world, I would not allow you to come away with your life. Of this you can be assured: you now face certain and unavoidable death!"

(2065-2081) In his irritation the demon jumped up angrily and, taking the head in his hand, made his way threateningly toward the gate. Standing before that gate, Daniel heard these ominous words and reacted as would any man of wisdom. First, he tied his steed to a limetree standing in a meadow a short distance from the fortress. He then undertook an act of cunning: he took out the mirror and, following the precepts of his wisdom, he turned his back to the fortress gate, which shortly afterward was opened.

(2082-2109) Carrying the deadly head in his hand, the creature, who was able to kill without the aid of weapons, then emerged. Daniel saw him in the mirror as he came out and made his way toward him, with the head held out in front. The creature would himself have perished had he beheld it face to face! Now he carried it before him with the intention of inflicting death upon the courageous hero. Daniel watched all of this in the mirror. Yet his heart was filled with joy at what he saw, for he deemed his chances most auspicious. Daniel took several quick steps backwards until he drew close enough that he thought he could reach the monster, to whom death was soon to be dealt. For Daniel unsheathed the sword which he had so bravely seized from the bold dwarf in the land of the Dark Mountain. He brandished it about behind his back and served the creature a gift which he would not soon forget: a blow beneath the chin that cleaved his legs in two!

(2110-2134) At this, the creature sank to the ground, his hideous voice shrieking in great wrath. He cried out to his men that he had been dealt a lethal blow, so that they might hasten over and take possession of the head. As soon as he had uttered these words, Daniel saw in the mirror precisely where he lay on the ground in his agony. Daniel now proceeded to sever the hand in which the creature held that head, which he then quickly snatched up. Though it faced him as he removed it, Daniel was mindful to look at it only from behind. A happy man was he that he had acquired this head! Addressing the creature lying there, he then spoke: "For full many a day now you have beheld this head only from behind. Now you shall find out how it is when one looks straight into its eyes. This much you shall not be permitted to forgo!" Daniel then held forth that head until the creature caught sight of it, whereupon he at once fell dead to the ground.

(2135-2164) Meanwhile, all the bellyless intruders held their eyes shut as they pressed hurriedly out from the fortress, for they were well aware that one frontal glance at the head meant certain death. It was a stroke of good fortune for Daniel that he, on the other hand, dared to keep his eyes open, for those others ran about blindly in search of the head. As soon as the first one of them found his master's body, he felt for that head in the dead man's hand. But his hand had been cut off, which the intruder reported to all of his comrades. Afterwards they explored the entire expanse of grass around them, as fast as they possibly could, but they were able to discover nothing. Then they all agreed to open their eyes. This was to be their downfall! For Daniel was standing there before them and thrust forth the head until they had all beheld it. At that, each and every one of them fell into the grass dead,[109] never to rise again.

(2165-2206) When Daniel had witnessed this, he said to himself: "What man could ever offer me any resistance, now that I am in possession of this head? Those giants, whom no man can slay, shall have to behold this thing—which will assuredly bring about their death, and with which I can be the victor in the land of Cluse and can assist King Arthur in his contest with King Matur. I shall show this head to all who wish to clash with us, and it shall be for them a bitter poison! — On the other hand, if I were to bring about mass death in Cluse, I would fall into disgrace and would acquire a notorious reputation.[110] Everyone would know that even a poor woman could easily massacre all the world by carrying about this lethal head and killing people with it. I would be branded a devil and a coward, and people would claim that I carried it out of fear, because I dared not take on any man in battle. I would be vilified and shunned by all. Indeed, it seems unavoidable that I should eventually incur misfortune from this head—misfortune which could even come in the form of my own death from having beheld it face to face. You have meant death for so many a man. The devil has sent you, now let him have dominion over you: I have no wish to keep you!" Whereupon Daniel cast it into the water[111] and spoke: "Never again shall any upright man have knowledge of you," and he let it sink down all the way to the bottom.

(2207-2220) Having cast away the head, Daniel then made haste toward the fortress. At the tower Daniel—well-born knight that he was!—shouted up to the lord of the castle in order to determine whether or not he were still alive. Daniel told him to be of good cheer, for his suffering was now at an end. The lord heard this and spoke: "Would that God had been willing to bring to pass such an outcome as that!" "Come, I shall show you that this has indeed transpired," spoke Daniel of the Blossoming Valley. "The intruders have changed their tune! The devilish head which they carried about for many a day has been the cause of their own deaths."

(2221-2237) The count then unbolted the door and came forth with great trepidation. Since he had still not heard tell how all of this had come about, he welcomed Daniel and besought him in the name of our Lord to relate how he had survived the creature and why he had ventured into this place. Daniel told him that his wife and her ladies were all still alive, and that he had come there at her request, which she had made as if from the very depths of misery. Daniel related to him furthermore how he had slain the creature which had stalked that land with the head, as well as how he had killed all of his comrades.

(2238-2260) Both men hastened out through the fortress gate,[112] where the count beheld all of their bodies lying there as proof of Daniel's story. "Oh woe, where is that lethal head?" spoke the lord of the house. "Never before have I suffered deeper agony than has befallen me from it. I should be forever content if the devil had taken it away." Daniel then replied: "Be not concerned about this, for I have hidden it in such a way that it can harm neither you nor any other man." The count then spoke: "May God grant you just recompense for this!" He placed at Daniel's disposal both himself and all that was his, and spoke: "You can help me greatly by now showing me to where my wife is. Never before has any other man accorded me such fine treatment as have you. If I am to live, I shall serve you for this, as well I should!"

(2261-2284) Both men mounted their steeds and rode out across the field, coming in quick measure to where they found the ladies. The countess, having spotted them, spoke happily: "God welcome you both!" Quickly she forsook her sorrow and her tribulation, and was overcome with joy. Her lord was likewise gladdened that his lady was still alive, and he hastened to tell her that their enemies all lay dead at the hand of the lord riding with him, who had freed them from all distress. Moreover, he informed her that the head would no longer cause her any harm, since it had been cast into the water. The lady then told him forthwith of how Daniel had rescued both the Lady of the Dark Mountain and her land from the dwarf, and how Daniel, with his valor and wisdom, had thereby acquired great renown.[113]

(2285-2315) Though their losses had been vast, they deemed themselves fortunate to have survived at all. Most earnestly the count said to Daniel: "Onward, noble knight! You shall come with us to our court and decide upon whatever reward you may desire, and it shall be fulfilled. For I proclaim to God on this day that I have received from you the greatest succor which has ever fallen to my lot." Daniel, however, countered by saying: "In God's name, my lord, it is my wish and my command that you not pursue such talk. What reward could I merit simply because your enemies lie slain? For they were every bit as much a threat to me as to you and your people. Had the monster killed you today, he would have killed me tomorrow.[114] Now we are, in all our sorrow, mercifully comforted, and it is God who has saved us all. Thus you should offer your thanks to Him. Now I must take up a trail which I already have followed far; it is a source of vexation to me that I have been off it for so very long."

(2316-2330) The Count of the Bright Fountain, however, said in reply: "Both my castle and my life you have redeemed for me, as well as my good name and my wife. Now it is fitting that I, in exchange, should evermore be your knight and your vassal. Whoever it be that you have been hunting, whether far or near, I shall help you undauntedly. If you wish to remain here no longer, then I shall set out together with you. Ride off to wherever you intend to journey, and I shall aid you gladly, for you have rendered me such great assistance."

(2331-2336) The countess then hastened to add: "This knight should be assured that if I could come to his aid, I would relieve his distress, of whatever sort, in the same manner in which he has allayed my own heartache."

(2337-2360) Both men then took their leave. With joy and yet with sorrow the lady and her lord parted company. Two thoughts occupied her mind. She pondered to herself: "This knight, I fear, is so courageous and so driven by his boldness that he may become entangled in a situation from which great sorrow might befall me, through the death of my lord. Ah! how could I ever live on without him?" At once, however, her thoughts turned in another direction: "Since the knight has overcome this devilish creature, he can easily vanquish whatever he desires. His guile ought not to be underestimated!" The lady rode back to court and resolved, along with those others who were still alive, that they ought all to be of good cheer since they still possessed what God wanted them to have. They were of one accord that they should be content with whatever God should ordain for them. For they could have nothing other than God's destiny for themselves.

VI

DANIEL SLAYS THE GIANT'S BROTHER

(2361-2383) Daniel and his companion, whom he had rescued from the tower, rode onward and came, a bit after noontime, upon a forest. There they followed hoofprints until the daylight ended and so dark a night fell that neither of them could see the other. Each of them now rode that much faster in anticipation of repose. A heavy weariness beset them, and the count was well aware that they probably ought to have arrived already at their resting-place. Now it came to pass (this was caused by their haste and by the fact that they were unable to see in the darkness) that they had lost the road to the castle and had taken up another path, which they pursued—as valiantly as their strength permitted—all through the night.

(2384-2395) Since they encountered nothing but forest and more forest, the brave heroes rode on until the first rays of dawn struck them. Then Daniel spotted the mountain at the foot of which he had previously seen the giant. He exclaimed at once to the count: "Our undertaking is faring well! Here is the mountain which I am seeking." Yet even after catching first sight of that mountain, they still had two long miles to ride before reaching it.

(2396-2415) In a short time, however, they came upon a field in which there was a tent pitched on the grass at the foot of the mountain. This was the most exquisite glade to be found anywhere. From atop a green limetree wafted the melodies of birds warbling sweetly, and beneath the tree a lovely spring issued forth, clear and pure. A trough, crafted of marble and most splendidly embellished, stood beneath the spring, brimming with water.[115] As they drew close enough to see all of this, Daniel said to the count: "This is a suitable place and an opportune time for the horses to rest. I wish also to ascertain what is in the tent."

(2416-2427) He dismounted forthwith and tethered his horse to the limetree. Walking straightway into the tent, he found neither man nor woman there, but a lone table heaped with all manner of food and drink. Sir Daniel looked about: the tent was so marvelously embellished with pictures and with inscriptions that he would gladly have remained there for as long as it would take to eat.

(2428-2443) Yet he felt a twinge of fear that something further might transpire to divert him from his journey, as had happened before. Furthermore, he feared that if King Arthur had arrived in the land of Cluse before him and should enter into battle against the giants without Daniel's aid, the king might well lose his life. For with his sword Daniel intended to bestow death upon the giants, as well as on whatever others might engage in battle with him. Thus Daniel felt a twofold distress: he would gladly have dined on the food there, if only he could have known whether he dared to linger any further.[116]

(2444-2460) At this moment the count spied a knight riding across the field. Immediately he cried out into the tent, saying to Daniel: "I discern a knight galloping fiercely in this direction. He is beginning to draw quite near, and I do not know what his intentions are!" Just as his comrade Daniel emerged from the tent, the knight galloped up before them. He had with him a prisoner who must have been most uncomfortable indeed, for he lay thrown across the horse in front of the knight, quite like a sack! Sir Daniel offered him a word of greeting, but the stranger merely looked ahead and rode on.

(2461-2476) Both men were vexed that the knight remained mute and neither spoke nor nodded. The Count of the Bright Fountain cried out angrily: "In truth, I shall find out what causes this knight to refuse us his greeting!" He put the spurs to his horse and wrathfully gave chase. A road, not even quite as wide as two men, led on into the mountain, and the knight bore down upon it. The count chased after him with drawn sword, but the stranger fled from him like a coward.

(2477-2495) Daniel, having mounted his steed, rode after the count as fast as he could, for he had no intention of remaining behind! But the knight was still ahead of them both and rode on to the gate, which consisted of a massive boulder, forbidding entrance to the mountain. At this point, the stranger spun around, but failed to lower that boulder. Yet as soon as the count had ridden on through, the strange knight let the rock (which was immense and bulky!) drop down into place. Thus the knight Sir Daniel was left there alone, cut off outside the mountain in front of the boulder. He was pained and vexed at this, and was unable to prevent his comrade from coming to harm.

(2496-2516) Now you shall hear an amazing tale of how Daniel barely escaped with his life intact, so close a brush did he have with death: as the rock shot downward into place, one could see a burst of water gushing forth from the rock—a cascade so powerful that wherever the surrounding terrain was lower in elevation, it became flooded with water. For a lakebed had been dug into that mountain, and whenever the boulder was raised, the water rushed in to fill the lake. Never before had Daniel heard tell of a more wondrous thing than this! The boulder was thus placed there for two purposes: whenever it was lifted, the water was cut off; and as soon as it was lowered, it blocked the road and the water poured forth. In this manner the passageway could be closed off.

(2517-2532) Now we can well believe, in all justice to Daniel of the Blossoming Valley, that his heart was torn with wrath, furthermore that such an ordeal as this had never before beset him, and that he had never been seen fleeing in the face of peril, however ominous. Had he been able to die an honorable death there, he would have sooner suffered such a fate than take to flight. Yet if, because of excessive stubbornness, Daniel had failed to retreat and had waited for death to

Plate 4. Daniel rides in pursuit of the unknown knight.
Ms. germ. 1340, leaf 91v.

overwhelm him, then such behavior would be reckoned more as foolhardiness than as valor.

(2533-2551) The flood waters rushing over him alarmed Daniel in no small measure, and he very much feared for his life. Despite his great distress, however, Daniel turned his steed around, but was unable, no matter how he tried, to traverse the raging water. Nevertheless he did not fall from the saddle and was able to remain mounted, while his horse stayed afloat and finally swam over to the safety of the meadow. From here he had only to ride back to the lime-tree. Tying his horse to it, Daniel thus managed to rest from his trial. He doffed his clothing and spread it out in the sun, and, having drunk of the water from the fountain, he entered the tent in order to partake of the food there.

(2552-2564) No man could reproach him for this, for Daniel had journeyed quite without food since doing battle with the dwarf (whom he had slain with the dwarf's own sword). Now Daniel found an abundance of food on the table inside that tent, yet he was unable to savor it fully because of the count, whom he had lost there. Daniel was wholly bereft of joy on account of the loss of his comrade. Had he only been able to reach the count, he would have rescued him, or else he would have given his own life in the attempt.

(2565-2595) After eating and drinking, as he sat there disheartened at his misfortune, Daniel said to himself: "I would have fared much better had I never set eyes on this knight. Even when he was locked away high in his tower, his lady's face betrayed deep lines of despair. And at that time he was still clearly alive! Now, however, if she should have to hear word of his death, I know in all truth that her anguish and her grief would be far more excruciating than before. Oh woe! she has been robbed of her joy on my account. I have compensated her with sorrow for the good which I had accorded her before. This shall be for me an everlasting heartache. "I have caused you such misery here that I shall not yet depart, but rather shall remain for a while longer. If any of these people should perchance reappear, then they shall be forced to let me see what is inside this mountain! And they shall hand over my comrade, if God is gracious enough to allow me to find any of them in there. However, if they have already taken his life, I shall never rest until I avenge him in such a way that men will tell of it for evermore!"

(2596-2630) Thus Daniel kept watch all day long, up until night began to fall, when he spotted four young men approaching the tent. They carried with them meat, bread, and wine, and every imaginable delicacy which a king might ever desire should he happen to dine here. All of this they brought in great profusion. Daniel did not know whether good or ill was drawing near as he watched them approach. He walked over to his horse, and—taking the harness and quickly slipping it on—he rode off to a safer position.[117] As soon as they came within earshot, he offered all four of them his greeting, which they quickly returned in a decorous manner, proceeding then on foot into the tent. Once inside, they removed all of the food from the table and replaced it with what they had brought with them. They carried away the original food which they had just taken, and were about to set out in the same direction from which they had come, when Daniel bade them stop.

(2631-2648) "What is your business here?" he asked. "To bring food to this place." "But who will eat it here?" "Whoever seeks the food," they answered. "Who has sent it here?" "He who is lord over this land." "Does he by chance come here himself?" "Perhaps he does, perhaps not. We shall tell you nothing more for certain than this. Tomorrow morning we shall return with different food." "Then God be with you," answered Daniel, "but first tell me more, and ensure your lasting good fortune by directing me to where I might find your lord. I should like to meet him in good time, since he is clearly a most courtly man."[118]

(2649-2670) "Do not ask too many questions of us, good sir," they said. "We know not the least about this matter. It has been a year now since our lord last spoke to us. He would have murdered any one of us whom he so much as spotted, had he been able to capture us. We do not know what it is that troubles him. So disturbed is he that every man whom he sees must die, provided my lord is at all able to bestow such a fate upon him. He was ever a courtly man, but this past year he has been of such a mind that he suffers no one to live. If you wish to see him despite all of this, then such a meeting can transpire only on this very spot." Daniel asked God's blessing on them for having apprised him of these things, which, however, were a source of vexation to him.

(2671-2701) They then departed forthwith. By now it had become so dark that Daniel could scarcely see. He felt gravely distressed, for four different reasons: that he was so utterly cut off from his comrade; secondly, that he had no way of knowing whether the count had suffered bodily harm; furthermore, it grieved him that he could do nothing at all to investigate this matter; and finally, he was at a loss as to how to prevent King Arthur's death in the land of Cluse at the hand of the giant. Thus Daniel pondered all of his alternatives. For a time he was about to leave, but then he decided to remain. Daniel would have preferred to be elsewhere; nonetheless he lingered there for nearly a week's time in hopes of rescuing or avenging the Count of the Bright Fountain. However, by the time King Arthur was to come on horseback into the land of Cluse together with a powerful army, no one had yet emerged from the mountain.

(2702-2735) Daniel thought to himself: "I have waited here as long as I can. Today is the day on which my lord enters the land where death awaits him. Though he will endeavor to defend himself, the giants possess skin so hard that he cannot slay them, and they shall inflict upon him that which ought rightly to befall them. I can remain no longer! I must set out for Cluse now if I am to come to his aid. I shall place full trust in this sword which fell to my lot at the Dark Mountain. Surely the giants are not so invincible that I cannot deal them an ample measure of harm with it. Then they shall never again compel any king to surrender his land and to subjugate himself to them. — Yet though I must now set out, how shall I ever rescue the count, whom I have lost here? If I depart here without him, I shall be in constant anguish. — On the other hand, this also worries me greatly: if my lord King Arthur is slain in Cluse, I can never cease to lament his loss. It is better that I leave, and that, once the battle is over in Cluse, I then return to this place. There is no use in my delaying any further. If I remain here even a bit longer, in truth I am certain to let slip the opportunity, both here as well as in Cluse."[119]

(2736-2746) Daniel then took his horse and embarked boldly on his journey. Great was his chagrin (and it was still to become greater yet!),[120] for his heart was heavy at having to depart without the count. Turning around full many a time to look back, Daniel said to himself: "God protect you now, my comrade! May His grace and His command soon bring us together again in good health!"

(2747-2775) Off he then gal ped in haste, coming in quick measure to the mountain, since it was but two short miles distant.[121] Once again the giant was seated there. As he saw Daniel drawing near, he asked at once where he was going in such haste. Daniel replied forthwith: "I am headed for the land at the other end of the passage-way!" "You are a fool!" replied the giant; "be silent and forsake your childish thoughts. If you ride ahead so much as one single foot, in all truth I say to you, I shall break you into pieces like a twig!"[122] "Show me then," spoke Daniel, "what you are capable of doing, for there is no question of my turning back." The giant leaped to his feet. His body was far from that of a dwarf! Daniel of the Blossoming Valley stood scarcely as high as his knees.[123] Inasmuch as the giant had never before been wounded by any weapon, he did not know that he should defend himself now. Unmindful of his coming fall, he raged with anger.

(2776-2804) As Daniel of the Blossoming Valley came riding toward him, the giant strode in the direction of his opponent. His fists were clenched tightly in rage, and he swung at Daniel, who, taking good note of this, angered him by holding forth his sword. Irately the giant thrust at Daniel's sword, so that it resounded loudly, and his hand—as well as a good third of his arm—were lopped off. This was the very first misfortune ever to befall him from a sword! Daniel cried out mockingly: "Tell me now, is this by chance the way in which you have killed so many men with your hand? Never before have I visited a land in which the fighting is done in so strange a fashion. Indeed, how would it be if I myself were the twelfth in line to do battle with you? You would need a great many fists before you could dispatch us all! And you would also have need, it seems to me, of many skilled physicians! Yet unless they are here in but an instant, you shall never again go into battle with *that* hand—on this I shall stake my word!"

(2805-2821) Now the giant was infuriated. He stalked over to a massive rock with the intention of hurling it at Daniel, who let him get as far as the rock before lopping off his leg. Nonetheless the giant seized that boulder and heaved it at Daniel's shield with such force that his horse fell to the ground with him, very nearly causing him great distress. The giant, thirsting for fuller revenge, reached for yet another rock, but was unable to remain standing any longer on his one leg. Down to the ground he slumped—though still prepared to defend himself from a sitting position! But to his great distress, God deigned not to save him.

(2822-2844) At that moment Daniel's horse recovered, and Daniel vaulted up closer to the giant and cut off his other arm. With that, the monstrous fellow toppled helplessly onto his back, with but one leg remaining of his four limbs. He flew into a rage over this and kicked Daniel's horse in its side so ferociously that it rolled over a good three times in quick succession. Daniel was well nigh injured by this, for he was unaccustomed to falling. Red with anger, he strode up to the giant and cleaved off his head, speaking these words: "I have now, I fancy, offered you just recompense for that blow! Now you are no longer so huge nor so invincible as before. Any man who does battle with you now shall defeat you easily—unless you have a very fine physician indeed!"

VII

KING ARTHUR SLAYS KING MATUR

(2845-2860) Following Daniel's duel with the giant, King Arthur arrived with a large assemblage of high-spirited knights well prepared for battle. Now three of his comrades had ridden on ahead and had come close enough to witness Daniel's final blow to the giant, as he lay there still alive. These knights were Sir Gawein, Parzival, and Sir Iwein. They recognized Daniel and rejoiced at the giant's death and at Daniel's survival. They were certain that, if Daniel were to be anywhere else but there on the battlefield with them, they would surely fare ill.

(2861-2890) Daniel bade them all three dismount and put their swords to the test, that they might ascertain whether or not they could fell the giant's comrade with their blades. They alighted forthwith, being curious about the truth or untruth of what they had heard tell of the hardness of that giant's skin. These knights unsheathed their swords and hacked away at the corpse, but failed to pierce its skin in the least. All three of them exclaimed: "His brother's words are true indeed. Let us now try your sword, for ours are worthless here." Daniel held forth his sword and spoke: "Here it is. I would just as gladly give it to whichever of you wishes it, as to keep it myself." "In truth," they answered, "you yourself must bear this sword. For you are far more worthy of it than is any one of us." Then spoke Sir Gawein: "We can linger here no longer, we must be off on our way!"

(2891-2912) They all four mounted their steeds and galloped off through the mountain at a fast pace. They wasted no time, but rode even faster once they had spotted the limetree and the golden beast, from whose mouth they then withdrew the banner. At once it raised such a cry, began to wail so deafeningly, and created such a din that not one of them could hear his neighbor. This roar was still thundering through the air when King Arthur entered the land through the mountain. Once hearing the voice of this beast, he made haste toward the limetree, accompanied by his many bold knights, all of whom were bent upon winning victory there, or else dying in the effort.

(2913-2919) The giant, who had conducted them to Cluse, waited at the foot of the mountain until they had all entered in. He did so in order to close the passage behind them, until such time as they had fulfilled all that King Matur desired of them.

(2920-2938) Only as he was about to follow them in at the end of the throng did he discover his brother lying there dead. He made the sign of the cross and raised a loud lament for his brother, saying: "Oh woe, how is it that I have lost you to so strange a death? Your skin was more impenetrable than horn itself! This could never have come about unless the devil himself had a hand in it! Now King Arthur and his men shall all have to sacrifice their lives to me for this. Each one of them shall make recompense for your death. Not a one shall ever return alive!" He then lowered the rock behind him and galloped after King Arthur's army, for he was flushed with anger and in great haste.

(2939-2958) As King Arthur and his men quickly assembled around the wailing beast, all that they had heard tell of this beast was verified by what then befell them: for the din buffeted those knights from their horses as though they had been slain. Each and every one of them lay on the ground before there was even a chance to muster any resistance. Never has a clap of thunder ever been heard that was as dreadful as this din! That noble knight Daniel of the Blossoming Valley, however, regained his senses and hurriedly stilled the awful roar by replacing the banner in the beast's mouth. Save for this, no man would have come away alive, for none of those present could have prevented his head from bursting at that deafening din.

(2959-2991) Now King Arthur's army made preparations for battle, for they had heard that King Matur would ride up in quick measure. Many a fearless knight began to request the first joust, anxious to perform marvelous deeds with his sword. Since so many of them were desirous of the first joust, King Arthur spoke: "All who were present at my court and heard the words of the giant know full well of his statement that no other king is so excellent as ever to be allowed to enter this land: I alone enjoy the good fortune to be admitted. Now I wish to determine whether I am so fully blessed that King Matur also deems me worthy of fighting a duel against him with sword in hand. My lords, you must willingly allow me this. Insofar as he desires me as his vassal and bestows upon me a great honor refused to many kings, I shall consider it my good fortune if he deigns to joust with me." All present deemed it chivalrous of King Arthur that he had taken this upon himself.[124]

(2992-3006) At that very moment they spotted King Matur approaching on a horse obedient to his every command. Ornately embellished was Matur's attire, as was fitting for a king who claimed to have no peer. He held before him his highly ornamented shield,[125] on which was perched a Babian (I have already reported to you of these birds). Thrusting his lance under his arm,[126] he spurred on his horse until it assumed the proper speed.

(3007-3040) King Arthur then vaulted forth with the rush of a storm. He bore a crowned eagle upon his shield, and his heart pounded with joy that he was about to do battle with this man who desired to subjugate him and seize his land. King Arthur wished to find out then and there whether or not he was worthy of this honor, for both men knew full well that the blows of their weapons would reveal the ultimate truth. They came flying at one another with such ferocity that both their saddles snapped as they collided.[127] Losing their grip on their horses, both of them fell off backwards and found themselves standing on the ground![128] They then demonstrated what it was they wished to accomplish: they embarked upon the fiercest swordplay which had ever been witnessed in their day between any two men. How they avenged blow with blow! Each man was valiant and showed skill and strength, both with body and with sword. For as long as their shields held out, they were well able to defend themselves, yet it was unavoidable that those shields should fast disintegrate, so that in short measure they were reduced to nothing.

(3041-3071) Once their shields were demolished, they no longer spared either helmet or armor. They set about hacking away at the choice steel of the armor, and they assailed one another for a long while indeed,[129] so that no man could discern which of them held the advantage. Then King Arthur had the good fortune to force such a blow through King Matur's helmet that it penetrated all the way to his very scalp. But Matur parried this straightway with a fearsome blow—a blow which came down with such might that King Arthur staggered to his knees. Never before had this happened to him! Thinking himself forever disgraced by this, King Arthur leaped back to his feet at once. He then brought to pass his opponent's downfall: for he dealt King Matur a blow which sealed his doom, since it was sent by Misfortune, from whom no man can defend himself. King Arthur battered him on the same spot as the earlier blow and sliced into him so mightily that his head was ripped off and fell lifeless onto the grass. King Arthur had survived, and King Matur lay slain.[130]

VIII

THE FIRST BATTLE

(3072-3087) At this moment they spied a royal company galloping up. These were a good two thousand knights—men who were to engage in tournament on this day, both at their own yearning and at King Matur's command. The sight of Matur lying there dead fanned their ire, and, spotting King Arthur there, they dashed forward in full force. With that, the good knights of the Round Table vaulted forth to meet them. Well over a thousand lances were broken to splinters in but a brief lapse of time. Each man who fell—be it this one or that one—was doomed!

(3088-3105) The fiercest fury of which you have ever heard tell was in evidence on the battlefield that day. With ferocity they hacked away at shield and armor, so that it all went up in a cloud of dust. Many a sturdy helmet was ripped apart by their swords. No man could relate to you how the fire flashed forth as one piece of steel penetrated the other! Even a man well protected so as to withstand the mightiest of sword-blows was on that day naked and bare.[131] Any man able to defend himself was blessed with good fortune. Yet there were a great many of them who were compelled to abandon their courage.

(3106-3121) All that we have ever been told of battle was a mere puff of wind in comparison to this encounter! As you have heard before, young knights well versed in the art of battle charged together from both sides. Not for the briefest of moments did they cease from the feverish tumult. Thus they strove to squeeze every ounce of strength from their bodies. Many a man met with his death as a consequence. Whatever those knights struck was slashed to pieces, and the weapons they bore were sharp beyond all belief, so that the steel burned just as though it were wood.

(3122-3145) So grave was their game and so miraculous the feats they performed, that all those present feared that the Day of Judgment was nigh upon them, and that the heavenly conflagration had come down over all the earth. Only when they saw that the fire burned upwards—towards the heavens—was this fear allayed, though the heat of the battle compelled many a brave man to waver in uncertainty. The combatants on both sides had the stamina to persist forever and to prevent their opponents from seizing the victory on that battlefield—save for the fact that Daniel of the Blossoming Valley brought to the ground many a splendid knight, with the sword which had once belonged to the dwarf. A full three times and more did he ride through the midst of that company! Many a man was wounded that day who could otherwise have boasted of his invincibility in swordplay. At Daniel's hand, however, even such a man as this was dealt the blow of death.

(3146-3176) Once the battle and all the anguish had begun in full earnest, they spied trotting in their direction the giant who had sealed off the mountain behind them. Great beyond all measure were both his body and the anger which he felt towards them. Once having heard the thunder of the battle and eager to be present there himself, the giant gave spur to his steed. But the horse[132] proved itself so sluggish that he thought it better to proceed on foot—and that giant was indeed possessed of immeasurably long legs! Thus he dismounted and took a number of long strides in the direction of King Arthur's army. At that, a host of young heroes ran toward him armed with bows and arrows. They had stored these up in preparation, and they used

Plate 5. King Arthur's knights assail the giant.
Ms. germ. 1340, leaf 106[r]*.*

them to take aim at his eyes.[133] Shooting off an unceasing barrage of more than a hundred arrows and other missiles, they robbed the giant in quick measure of his eyesight—this is no untruth![134] A frightful wrath overcame him, and whomever he struck, that man was doomed. Angrily he drew his club and wielded it with such force that every man whom he could reach lost his life.

(3177-3203) Those intrepid[135] and high-born knights, King Arthur's comrades, breathed revenge at this and were spurred on by their bold valor to seek the victory. With their trusty swords they applied brute force against the giant, yet however ardently they yearned to deal him his death, they remained unable to do so. They paid dearly for this, for once his club was so utterly hacked to pieces that nothing of it was left in his hand, he picked up all whom he found before him and snapped them in two like a twig. And any man whom he spared *this* treatment, he picked up by the leg—whatever his size!—and used him as a club to bludgeon the others. Though they strove to penetrate his skin, they were altogether without success. A great array of swords were tried out on this creature, but he was left unscathed. And regardless how many lances were thrust at him, how many arrows were shot at him, they were unable to harm him a whit.

(3204-3223) Once those knights saw that it was futile, they all took to flight from the giant.[136] This angered him and caused him to chase hurriedly after the throng wherever he could hear them. Any man whom he could lay his hands on was doomed to die, for he dealt with his victims in such a way that they could only be picked up in pieces afterwards. How could anyone have escaped with his life? And what havoc do you expect that this blinded devil would have wreaked were he still possessed of his eyes? (For even *without* them he slew so many men who were fully able to see!) It would have meant death for them all! That giant inflicted such woe upon them that no man dared approach him. In the face of their failure, they began to beat a retreat.

(3224-3238) After the others had been forced to flee, Sir Keii, who spotted the giant, but had not witnessed the fate of his comrades, came riding up. Keii confirmed once more his old reputation, for he relished nothing more than belittling an upright man. So rash was he with words that, even if he knew that his evil tongue should cost him his life, he could not silence it. Even when he himself was unable to win the victory, he never failed to deride those who likewise missed the mark.

(3239-3264) "What is this, King Arthur?" he exclaimed. "If you were sitting safely at home in your court, you would be surrounded by brave comrades thoroughly capable of bringing other knights to their knees. They would be given hearty brew to quaff, and all would drink to their health. As long as they were at your court, they would fight with lance and sword until they had avenged any ill that had ever befallen your family, even back in the days when your father was alive. — But how is it now that these men here are so feeble? I clearly see that their opponent is blinded. A small child could gain no esteem from doing battle with him. Your men ought to feel forever shamed for letting themselves be chased about like this. If your Round Table ever suffers these cowards—whom a blind man, without a sword, drives from their wits in this manner!—to be seated at it, then it is not worth a pittance. It is a good thing that I am alive, for I am a man who strives after fame! How can these weaklings deny me their esteem? I myself shall prove to you now that I am bold enough to oppose this man alone—this man whom none of the others can so much as touch!"

(3265-3288) With these very words Keii vaulted forth and broke his lance quite in two against the chest of the giant, who paid it no heed whatever. Hearing the jangle of the riding equipment on Keii's horse, the giant stepped forward angrily and grasped Sir Keii by the leg. This put an end once and for all to his fighting! He carried Keii quite like a stick, and his armor and tunic fell up over his head. So stupefied was Sir Keii that he very nearly had his fill of battle for the rest of his life. The giant's eye sockets were aching with pain, and he thrashed about furiously, wishing to club to death with Sir Keii yet more of those knights. No one can begin to tell you how dreadfully he swung! All of them beat a swift retreat, so that the giant's lunges missed them altogether. And the force of the swing enabled Sir Keii to slip out of the giant's hand.

(3289-3302) I shall tell you how it came to pass that Keii avoided death from his fall: it was near a limetree that Sir Keii escaped from the blind man's hand, and his good fortune stepped in to prevent him from plunging to his ruin. This is what helped to preserve his life: he dropped right onto a branch at the top of the limetree and tumbled rapidly from branch to branch till finally he lay on the ground quite like a sack![137]

(3303-3322) Listen now with pleasure as I tell of how the knights of the Round Table lamented Keii. With one voice they exclaimed: "The devil take this limetree and this blind man for letting Keii slip away! We have always heard tell that men who have lost their sight are powerful fellows indeed. This one, however, shall have to forfeit his esteem altogether! Why has he permitted Keii to escape? Had the devil himself not been protecting Keii, surely he would have fallen elsewhere than onto this tree!" Yet however great their chagrin, the fact remained that Sir Keii had come away alive. But he too was every bit as vexed, for he lay on his back in bed for twelve weeks and more before recovering from that tumble of his!

(3323-3344) Thrashing and hacking, the giant then avenged the loss of his eyes on King Arthur's men, who would gladly have been elsewhere, but were hemmed in and unable to flee. For so great was the pressing throng that no man could find room for escape. The giant let them charge at him and was delighted that no one could flee. They had not a horse among them so tall that the giant could not raise his foot above it. Thus he trampled and crushed the horses and all who sat mounted upon them. Moreover, the giant's foot was so massive that death unfailingly came to all who had to bear its weight for any measure of time. Listen and I shall tell you just how very heavy it was: if it lay upon a man—be he strong or weak—for even as long as it took to shut one's eye, that was enough to snap his back in two!

(3345-3359) Thus did that giant scatter all of King Arthur's army from its battle position—save for Daniel of the Blossoming Valley, who was on the other side of the battlefield,[138] amongst King Matur's men. Daniel could find no escape from them. For—however grave the harm which he inflicted upon them—Daniel had no choice but to do their will and remain there in their midst, as they would not permit him to slip away. Though they lunged with their pikes and let fly their javelins, it availed them but little, for Daniel buffeted them all to the ground with the very force of a hailstorm.

(3360-3381) Many a man lost the nails[139] on which he carried his shield, and once Daniel assailed him, his death was assured. The sword which Daniel bore in his hands rescued him from this dire strait, for he was under fierce attack by all of King Matur's army and he had need of a sturdy weapon. He comported himself with a ferocity, and he hacked to shreds like a mere sponge both his opponents and whatever armor protected them. Fortunate indeed was any man who recovered from the wounds inflicted by Daniel, who himself, to be sure, likewise endured great distress. It was a bold venture on Daniel's part that he summoned the courage to blaze a trail through two thousand men—a trail which carried Daniel so deep into their midst that not one of his own comrades could even see him to come to his aid.

(3382-3405) The enemy well nigh took Daniel's life, so fiercely did they defend themselves. But King Arthur's army began to retreat from the giant once they saw that he would crush to death as many of them as he could reach. Thus they fled from his clutches in the direction of the enemy, with whom they intermingled so as to escape the giant. When the creature stalked over to them, as soon as he picked one of them up and was about to maul him, each such victim would cry out in despair: "Hold off! I am here with *your* army!" The giant would then believe that man and would permit him to live. This same story they all then told him, from one captive to the next, so that he was deterred from crushing any of them. For the giant failed to see the truth of the matter and refrained from harming them at all.

(3406-3437) King Arthur's forces then launched into the enemy and were met with a counter-attack. Both sides summoned up immense fierceness, and only now did the battle really begin in earnest. Men shouted out from all directions, so that the giant knew not on whom to avenge his eyes. He heard all of them say: "Hold off! Why are you rebuking me? I am on your side!" whereupon he released them at once. Inasmuch as he was blinded, he could not know which of these men were speaking falsely. The first battle had been but a trifle, and the swordplay was only now beginning. It was true combat which was in evidence there as they brandished their swords with enough might to cleave through helmets and armor. These were lads unafraid to risk their lives and utterly in command of their stamina, which each one of them displayed to all of the others in full and unrestrained measure. There was no man among them who deemed his strength adequate to the task. And many an otherwise prudent man was seen caught up in the uncontrolled rage of battle. Anyone desiring to come away alive had to perform deeds of wonder!

(3438-3457) King Arthur's comrades executed marvelous feats with their swords. They had renounced their lives, and they wished to see the enemy put their own lives up for sale.[140] Onward they pressed with thrashing swords. A great number of their victims they felled without inflicting any wounds at all: for they bashed at these mens' heads through their helmets with such a ferocity that they were stunned and fell lifeless to the ground. Even those who were fully armed thought themselves utterly unclothed! The tribulation on both sides was horrendous. There was no postponing of retribution for the suffering incurred by King Arthur's men on that battlefield: their opponents paid for it most dearly!

(3458-3484) No man dared glance about in the firestorm of blows being exchanged, and none could claim that he had kept his head—or indeed that his head would survive much longer in that torrent of swords! All would have sworn that their heads had, in fact, already been cleaved in two. Many a man cried out in wrath when he failed to penetrate the steel armor with his blade. All of them were enduring great tribulation: even a man who at home was well-bred forgot his good breeding here in the face of dire distress. What one man spared another, he made three others pay for. Seldom if ever does one win games which have already been lost. On the line that day were both life and reputation—no more and no less! Anyone who gambled away both of those paid a very dear price indeed. Yet because they were loath to forfeit life and fame, they resolved to stand firm.

(3485-3513) Those knights—some of them over here, others over there—comported themselves with the bold and chivalrous air which they all shared in common. Regardless how harsh the punishment each side dealt out to the other, neither army could dislodge its opponent. Even a knight who had suffered a hundred wounds refused to renounce his fierce demeanor—provided those wounds were trifling enough that his bones were still whole! No man was asked to cease fighting unless he had first been accorded such painful injury by the sword that he was no longer able to retaliate. Even if he fell from his steed, he still continued to defend himself on foot. The sword was the sole form of greeting and reply—a fact which cost great numbers of men their lives. That battle endured for so long a time that many a man felt smothered by the heat of combat and by the pressing throng—to the extent that he truly feared a journey with death! He became as weak as a lamb, yet he fought on with the ferocity of a wild boar.

(3514-3528) King Arthur and his knights began to press forward and wrathfully avenge the harm that had befallen them there. Much bravado and much reprisal could be seen and heard on that battlefield, yet there were no insults exchanged among the men. Though they brooked nothing without paying it back in full measure, no one, strangely enough, requited his opponent with abusive words, regardless what suffering he had sustained at his opponent's hands: the *sword* was the means by which each man affronted his opponent, until such time as he had imparted to him a goodly measure of what he had in mind. Such taunts as these no man was able to silence!

(3529-3552) King Arthur pushed onward with his three finest knights: his nephew Sir Gawein, the noble knight Iwein, and the heroic Parzival. Each of these was an artist skilled in a wondrous sort of drawing,[141] and whatever man received one of his works had but three choices: to lose his life, to meet with death, or not to survive! Each victim was allotted in good measure whichever choice was best for him! King Arthur and his three companions were excellent scribes whose quills were weighty indeed, for they fashioned such letters as could never be erased or washed off by any man. However, they washed away many a man in such a way that he turned pale with death. Whomever the king wounded, that man had no need of a physician, for no sooner did he fall than he lay dead.

(3553-3570) King Arthur now spied Daniel of the Blossoming Valley far across the battlefield—Daniel, who had ranged about in a wide circle and had slain every man within a broad radius, performing with his sword such deeds as no man (no matter how sturdy a blade he might possess!) shall ever match for as long as the world exists. All about him Daniel had brought down with his sword a heap of dead men as high as a moat is deep, and he stood there upon it defending himself like an intrepid hero. All of the enemy focused their efforts on the battle with Daniel (as was indeed fitting for good knights), until such time as death overcame them.

(3571-3608) Upon seeing Sir Daniel's distress, King Arthur was gripped with rage. With swinging sword, he gave spur to his steed and galloped off toward Daniel. All who witnessed King Arthur's exploits proclaimed that never had there been a man born into this world whose might and whose wrath could so fully discharge his will. We are told that he fought in such a way as to instill terror in the hearts of his opponents. King Arthur crafted and performed such feats with the blows of his sword that they all cried out—independent of one another: "There is no doubt—this is the very devil himself! We are all doomed to die!" Before this, they would all have sworn that no man could defeat them,[142] but now he changed their minds and planted awe in their hearts. They would sooner have dared to come up against a thousand other men than against him alone. The noble King Arthur wielded his sword with both hands, and from that sword issued forth a din that penetrated their helmets, so that blood gushed out and his victims lay dead. With a deluge of mighty blows he was able to cut a path through a good thousand defenders. He could be seen blazing that trail through the very midst of the enemy—a trail which was bitter medicine for a great host of them!

(3609-3650) As soon as Sir Daniel had sensed (and later confirmed this with his own eyes) that King Arthur was so fiercely breaking through the throng in his direction, it pleased him greatly and infused him with an added measure of vigor. Making his way toward King Arthur, Daniel demonstrated beyond all doubt that he was glad to hear and see his dear liege lord. Death awaited all who were so foolish as to challenge him. Daniel was a great hero, and his sword was unique among all swords. He brandished it such that it raged onward, and neither armor nor helmet could offer protection to any man. Daniel became the most awesome forger of metal,[143] for his forging consisted of the following: out of every helmet which he struck he forged, without the aid of a blacksmith's fire, two separate helmets—though neither was as useful as the one had once been! What I mean to say is that he cleaved it in two, right down the middle. No man whom Daniel hit ever again cried out for help, for Daniel carved him up so thoroughly that he at once gave up all hope of ever being saved. Grave indeed was the alarm which swept through the enemy ranks! The knight Daniel buffeted them about so that all hope of survival escaped them, and their souls abandoned them. As he battered away at the enemy, such that their souls scarcely had time to make off, Daniel was not unlike the hunter who rustles the bushes above a rabbit's lair and causes the rabbit to scamper off.

(3651-3674) Oh! how his sword resounded as Sir Daniel forced his way through the knights toward King Arthur on that battlefield in Cluse! Lustily he swung his blade through their helmets! What Daniel had to dole out was a certain sort of sleep-inducing potion; whoever drank of this potion could do nothing to fend off the shades of slumber. The potion was Daniel's sword and the sleep was death itself. Such sleep was the dreadful affliction which compelled them to lie down against their will and await the Day of Judgment. Daniel hewed a path so wide that he confounded them all and burst right through their ranks. All who witnessed his feats stood back and made way for him. To anyone who hesitated, however, Daniel dispensed a precious tidbit as a gift, so that that man fell in great agony and expired before even striking the ground.

(3675-3693) Daniel thrashed and hacked his way through men and armor as though they were but water. And his sword raged no less turbulently, breaking through the steel of those knights' armor as though through a mere rivulet. He pelted wave after wave of the enemy, and the fire burned in the wake of his sword not unlike a white-hot flash from the heavens. All were terrified and made the sign of the cross whenever he brandished his sword. So powerful was its glow that hard steel broke open and split in two on contact. Daniel sawed and crafted his work without the aid of a gauge: there was no more delicate a craftsman than Daniel.[144] Whatever he hit shook with the anger of his hatchet.

(3694-3707) Daniel now rode on at will through the ranks of his opponents, suffering no harm himself, but dealing out injury to a great host of them. Finally he reached King Arthur, who joined his comrades in showing Daniel their good will and bidding him welcome. Though Daniel scarcely heard their greetings above the deafening roar of that frenzied fighting, nonetheless they let him know through words how happy they were to see him unharmed, for they were deeply glad to have him there.

(3708-3733) The king then lamented to Daniel the great tribulation inflicted upon them by the giant. "Many of our men lie dead upon the battlefield. Beyond putting out his eyes, we cannot harm the giant. Since losing his eyesight, he has retaliated against us with such wrath that we have scarcely escaped him." At this point the king did not yet know who it was who had slain the other giant, whom he had found dead at the foot of the mountain. But King Arthur was soon to find out, in consequence of the words which he then spoke: "We are all too weak for this giant. No one can kill him—save for the man who slew his comrade at the base of the mountain. For in all truth that man bore a sword well capable of dispatching this second giant. I would take home with me to my court and would bestow gifts and fiefs upon any one of you who is so deft as to find that man for us, so that he might help us escape this ordeal. For otherwise we shall all lose our lives."

(3734-3752) Sir Gawein then spoke up: "It was Sir Daniel who slew the giant! And indeed he would have accorded this one the very same fate had he been in our company. The hardness of his skin would avail the giant naught, and he would have no hope against Daniel." The king then replied: "If this is so, then I am free of all care!" All three knights spoke in reply: "Believe us when we say that it was indeed Daniel who accomplished this! We witnessed it as he sliced off the creature's head neatly with a single swing. The giant was still wrestling with death as we dismounted nearby. It shall be the second giant's downfall that Daniel still lives. For after setting out on his own, Daniel acquired through his valor a sword with which he was able to cut through the giant just as readily as through a stream of water."[145]

(3753-3780) The king was overjoyed and exclaimed in his delight: "Hail, Daniel, glorious hero! Now help us to bring about a just end to this creature who this day has wrought death upon so many of my excellent men." They then joined ranks with one another and, leaving behind all frivolity, returned once more to the raging throng. No man who wished to challenge them on that battlefield was so fine a warrior that he came away alive. Dead men could be seen falling, and helmets and armor being frightfully cut to bits, as well as feats of valor which opened up many a deep gash. King Arthur and his comrades proved that they could comport themselves as knights and deal out powerful and deep blows with their swords. Many a weeping man cried out: "Oh woe! that I was ever born!" The battle grew so grim that no one expected to survive. They were certain that these were devils on horseback fighting so viciously!

IX

DANIEL'S SEARCH FOR THE COUNT

(3781-3813) Daniel spied the giant and proclaimed straightway to his riding-companions: "I shall waste not a moment's time, by God, for I see standing yonder the creature who has inflicted upon us this harm!" He put the spurs to his steed and made his sword clank through many a suit of steel armor. All whom he encountered were swiftly cast down from their horses. So enraged was Daniel at the sight of that giant that no helmet could offer protection to any man's head, for Daniel ran his sword through it with such fury that not a single victim survived. However well protected a man was, it availed him no more than would a layer of morning dew. Oh woe! how wretched was the man who awaited the blows of Daniel's sword! For Daniel imparted to each such man a lesson which would ever ring true. So remarkable was Sir Daniel's sword that a delicate shirt of flax was just as good a shield against it as were helmet and armor. Neither iron nor leather could fend it off any differently than would a blanket of shrubbery. Whatever Daniel struck went up in a cloud of dust.

(3814-3824) Thus rode the illustrious hero until he made his way up to the giant. Clenching his trusty sword in both hands, he then lopped off both of the giant's legs with a single blow. At this, the creature dropped like a rock. He groaned and roared in a manner so painful to Daniel's ears that he could bear it no longer and severed the giant's head.

(3825-3833) The king and his three knights had now drawn close enough to witness the giant's fall and to hear the din which he raised, and then to see how Sir Daniel so fiercely silenced him. The king bowed and offered Daniel his gratitude and his thanks.

(3834-3858) In quick measure King Arthur's comrades returned to the battlefield together, where many a man fell dead that day. The giant's death emboldened them such that they put out of their misery all who attacked them. They helped their opponents down to the ground and shrouded them most decorously! No longer did they fear the enemy; rather, in their exuberance they now had them encircled on all sides. The king commanded them to keep a sharp eye upon the foe, that none of them might escape. The enemy ranks became so thinned that they realized they could neither escape nor fight on. It was a host of splendid warriors against whom they had defended themselves so grimly that day! And now that they had been so utterly overwhelmed that the specter of death stared them straight in the eye, they all surrendered into the king's dominion. Only by this act did they come away alive.

(3859-3892) It was at about the time of vespers that the horrid battle at long last drew to an end. The king then entered into council to determine whether it was advisable for them to wait there or to journey onward into the land of Cluse. As all of the knights were pondering this, Daniel of the Blossoming Valley spoke up: "It is better that we remain at this spot. For if we can hold our ground here, then we shall have conquered the entire land. Grant our men a respite for the remainder of the day. You have heard the giant speak of the seven regiments in this land, one of which journeys to this place each day, having been granted fiefs for that purpose. Because of this I am convinced that an army every bit as vast as the one with which we have contended today shall come riding up on horseback at dawn tomorrow. By summoning them with the beast, we shall bring them here with great dispatch. In the meantime, however, we ought to rest. From my own experience I know full well that all of the men have need of respite. It would surely be our death if we were to ride on into the land, for we would be discovered and observed at once. The six remaining armies would join forces and attack us in concert. Inasmuch as this single army today held its ground against us for so very long, we ourselves should not have long to live."

(3893-3905) Daniel's advice was lauded by all. Each and every one of them was glad to have occasion to rest, and set about making himself comfortable for the night. Many a splendid tent did they then pitch upon the field. And they had brought with them marvelous stores of food; indeed, they had provided for everything of which they might possibly have need: they had wine and bread, meat and fish (both dried and fresh) as well as mulberry wine and clear spice-wine.

(3906-3921) All of them showed their gratitude to Daniel, who had slain both the giants and had shielded them from the suffering which those creatures would have inflicted upon them. Had Daniel not killed them, King Arthur's men would themselves have lain dead upon the battlefield. For all of this they thanked Daniel and praised their good fortune. Daniel's own joy, however, was constrained, and he was not unlike a man who stifles his vexation and laughs even while his heart is bleeding with sorrow. For never again would Daniel be happy except it should come to pass that he could locate the count, whom he had lost outside the mountain when the torrent of water had driven him back.

(3922-3936) Daniel remained there with King Arthur's army until around midnight. He began then to reflect upon how he yearned to set forth (this was a part of his very temperament!) and to ride off to the mountain, so as to determine whether or not the boulder was in a raised position. If so, he would search for his comrade who, in his bold valor, had become separated from him there. Should the tunnel still be closed off, however, Daniel would return to King Arthur's camp and would, during the battle on the following morning, remain vigilant and continue to return to that boulder until such time as he found the mountain open and passable.

(3937-3947) Daniel now mounted his steed and set out. It was most fitting indeed that he concealed himself and stole off from King Arthur's company, so that no one was aware of his secret journey. Daniel now gave spur to his horse with all the more vigor, with one thought foremost in his mind: he desired to return to the encampment without anyone's knowledge of his trip—provided he were not to lose his life while underway.

(3948-3976) Daniel soon came to a spot where the trail was blocked and rendered impassable. This the giant had done by rolling an immense rock into the pathway. None of them had knowledge of this until Daniel now saw it. Angrily he cried out: "Good Fortune has denied me her company on this journey! King Arthur and his men have benefitted little indeed from the fact that the count became my comrade. So many of these accursed rocks—may the devil take them!—stand in my way that I cannot be certain whether I or any man shall be able to come to the aid of the count! How I long to find him if at all possible! Alas, my good friend! I shall vow to God this very day to renounce all other earthly joy if only I might ever set eyes on you again! My life is worthless and despicable to me unless I wreak vengeance for this ordeal upon the knight who has separated us. Little does that knight divine what is in store for him!"

(3977-3994) Spurred on by his valor, Daniel dismounted and strained to lift the rock, that he might continue his journey. Yet even a hundred men of Daniel's strength would have failed in that venture, and so he was compelled to leave it unmoved. Daniel was angry and troubled at this and drew his sword in a rage, slashing away at the rock with it; for he had heard the Maiden of the Dark Mountain proclaim that that sword would not fail to penetrate any substance which it struck. Wishing to verify this, Daniel brandished it with fearsome might. Luck was on his side in every regard, for he hacked the rock into splinters as though it were made of ice.

(3995-4000) When Daniel saw that this caused no harm to his sword, he quickened the pace. And in but a short time he had hewn an opening so high and so wide that he could lead his horse on through it.

(4001-4014) This Daniel deemed a sure sign of good fortune. He mounted his steed and set out in haste to resume his journey. He had but a short distance to traverse, and just before daybreak he arrived at the field near the magnificent tent—the one in which he had dined after escaping the flood. Even before arriving there, Daniel discerned that the torrent was obstructed—that torrent with which the mountain pass could be blocked off.

(4015-4048) As he drew closer and closer, Daniel spotted the same man approaching who previously had isolated him from his comrade. Daniel's valor spurred him on to the attack, and the stranger followed suit. Both lowered their lances, Daniel over here and the stranger over there. They took aim at one another's chests and crashed together with such might that their lances no longer remained whole. Thus they clutched their swords and in quick time hacked apart the shields and then each other's armor, so that their very lives were hanging in the balance! Each of them dealt the other many and fearsome blows—until the duel reached such a pitch that never before had either of them incurred such dire punishment from another man. Daniel's opponent was possessed of overwhelming strength, which he displayed with his skillful swordwork. Beneath his armor he was wearing a durable skin, one which was precious and dear to him and which had been flayed from the body of a water sprite. This skin helped him to stay alive, for it was steeped in the blood of a dragon, so that he could freely do battle with whomever he wished without ever sustaining injury.[146]

(4049-4078) Once Daniel perceived that—even with that fine sword of his—he could still not defeat this knight, he began to fear that this very hour might witness his own death. Thus he began to mete out fearsome blows with his sword—blows such as might rightly have been messengers of death, save that he still failed to pierce his opponent's skin. The stranger likewise requited Daniel for this punishment, extracting such a heavy toll that he, for one, could hardly be thanked for their both being still alive! Even if they had sworn an oath and pledged one another equal doses of anguish, they could not have raged any more furiously than they did. Both men strained at the stirrups as they stormed against one another, each breathing the fire of revenge.[147] High into the air did they hoist their swords, and deeply did they arch their backs with the strength of their hearts, in order to execute those blows! Both men were intrepid fighters. Sir Daniel battered his opponent so savagely that the knight's armor and helmet flew off and fell to the dust in shreds. Yet he still wore on his body the skin from the water sprite, which afforded him sure protection.

(4079-4095) Now they were compelled to fight on foot, for both their horses lay dead. With firm resolve each man served out whatever injury he could to the other, until such time as their blows no longer availed them and Daniel began to fear death. Spurred on by the will to live, he sharpened his defense all the more. He then dealt a sword-blow to the stranger's head—a blow that caused his opponent to shrink back in fear and fall at Daniel's feet. With that, Daniel captured the man and enjoined him to tell at once whether or not he had murdered the count—and if not, what had otherwise been his fate.

(4096-4108) Though he had not been wounded, the man had not a word to say. His silence and his refusal to speak at this point ruffled Daniel, since there was no cause for it. Daniel stood over his prisoner and said: "I shall permit you to live, but I shall determine straightway what it is that you have done to my comrade, and that very same fate shall be yours as well. This I pledge to you in all truth: only by escaping from me can you avoid this!"

(4109-4123) Daniel then followed the path on to the mountain, toward the spot where that remarkably contrived boulder had cut him off from his comrade. As he came nearer, Daniel perceived from the appearance of the rock that he could very likely move it alone. He then lowered it, causing the torrent of water to rush forth. This he did for no other reason than that the stranger not be able to follow him once he had regained his senses. Daniel was still burning with wrath about the count, whom he had lost at that same spot. Now he had returned there, determined not to leave again without him.

X

THE ADVENTURE OF THE GREEN MEADOW

(4124-4144) Daniel proceeded on his way until he reached the end of that mountain tunnel,[148] where the path was blocked by a most wondrous sort of portal. Before the opening there hung a finely woven net,[149] which was artfully devised so as to be invisible both day and night. Whoever was so foolish as to attempt to pass through this gate—whether entering or exiting—without permission, would fall to the ground and would become so inextricably ensnared in the net that, even if placed over a hot fire, he could have stirred neither his hands nor his feet. Such a straight-jacket was this net that its victims could not so much as move forward or backward! Except that someone versed in the operation of the net should free them, they would have lain there trapped forever.

(4145-4160) Daniel approached this spot and alas! how stricken with horror he was as he stepped straight into the net! He dropped to the ground, and in quick measure he lay there so entangled that he lost all hope of coming away alive. He was certain that it was the devil himself who had captured him. He tried to move his hand so as to cross himself, but was forced to give up, unable to budge even so much as a finger. So fully constrained was Daniel that he could stir his eyes and his tongue, but nothing more.

(4161-4188) A maiden, who had erected that net following the unknown knight's departure, spotted Daniel in his distress. Daniel had become entrapped just as she was withdrawing from the net. Glancing over her shoulder and seeing him enmeshed, she ran back and exclaimed: "Sir knight, your days are numbered. You could not have chosen to undertake a more unfortunate journey than this! You have done a wretched job of defending yourself. Alas! what is it that you seek here?" "Noble lady," he replied, "tell me first what has befallen me, such that I lie here like a piece of lead! What is it that has sapped me of my strength?" "You are trapped in a net," said the maiden, to which Daniel replied: "How is this net so contrived (or else what is it that has happened to me?), such that I am unable to see it?" "That is indeed impossible for you!" she answered. "Had you been able to see the net, you would not have fallen into it. No one can see it. For this very reason it has been the undoing of so many a man!"

(4189-4206) The knight of the Blossoming Valley then responded: "Help me out of this net in return for a pledge which I make to you with all knightly fidelity: that I shall be your prisoner willingly and without rancor. I shall shun no suffering, great or small, which you command me to endure. You must grant me but one request, which I ask of your mercy and am willing to beg for at your feet: if I must suffer death, then first grant me occasion to avenge any harm done to you by any man still alive on this earth, so that I may sacrifice my life valiantly and not die here like a helpless woman!"

(4207-4238) The maiden agreed to grant Daniel this wish. She accepted his pledge that he would refuse nothing which she enjoined him to do. Then she extracted him from the net and, taking him by the hand, led him into a nearby cave. It was a most comfortable refuge, yet Daniel saw no one else there save for himself and the maiden. This seemed most strange to him until he later heard tell of what had transpired. The lady then bade him to be seated at a table which stood ready in that cave. Had Daniel refused to comply, he would have breached his word and his fidelity, for he had sworn an oath to her to perform all that she ordered until such time as she might set him free. There was food in ample supply on the table, but Daniel was not of a mind to partake of it until he first knew what was to become of him, and until he heard word of his comrade whom he was seeking. For he wished to discover whether or not the count was still alive and if so, how he was faring.

(4239-4276) His great concern for the count drained Daniel of all appetite. Once the maiden discerned, however, that he drew no pleasure from all the food, she resolved to delay her story no longer, and said: "I wish to lament to you,[150] my lord, the state of affairs in this land: how our heartache has multiplied and deepened, and how our joy has been replaced by sorrow in the past year. In truth, never before have you heard tell of greater sorrow than this. My father was lord over this land. So courtly a man was he that at a moment's notice he would have given away to any man desiring it all that was his, no matter how precious—save for his own life and that of my mother, his wife. It is he who had that tent erected on the field at the foot of the mountain. And it is he who granted fiefs to those knights who excellently tend the table inside (once early in the day, and then again later),[151] which is piled high with foodstuffs suitable for each day. All of this my father enacted in order that travelers journeying that way and desirous of food should find in readiness whatever they were seeking. Things are arranged such that all of the food which stands there during the day is removed from the tent at nightfall and other dishes are then carried in. These then remain there until daybreak, when once again different food is delivered.

(4277-4328) "Because my father enjoyed the reputation of a man courtly in so many different ways, one day a mermaid, whose entire body was as exquisite as a rose, journeyed to this land. In her company we beheld a most wondrous army arriving both on horseback and on foot, for she was queen in the ocean over all the sea-creatures, who stood at her service, each and every one. She remained here for four days exactly, until such time as she could put to the test my father's courtly renown, both by what she saw and by what she heard here. She swore on her life to the truthfulness of all that she had been told for so many years concerning him, and she affirmed the report that no more perfect man could be found, save for King Arthur himself. For, as she said, no man can compare with King Arthur and his court; all must defer to him. She then departed, bestowing upon my father, as a sign of her esteem, a skin so excellent that, whenever he wears it, he is well protected against wounds from all manner of weapons. Moreover, she gave him this net which I have erected before the portal here. Never has there been a beast—whether wild or tame—so fierce that it could extricate itself once it had become ensnared in this net.[152] And never was there a sword, moreover, so finely crafted or so excellent that it could cut through the net. Along with this the mermaid also presented him a salve so exquisite that any man who applies but a small portion of it to his eyes is no longer prevented from seeing just as clearly at night as during the day. Even this net itself is then rendered visible. What is more, that salve would make any man's eyesight so very sharp that he could easily split a small hair lengthwise into nine strands. This same salve I have here in my possession.

(4329-4347) "Hear now, for the sake of God, how it is that the devil himself has mocked this land. (Our day has turned into a never-ending night!) In all truth it was but a year ago this very day, alas! that the devil dispatched his messenger here to us. He has banished joy from our land and has invested us with this great sorrow in which we shall have to live for evermore. No foe who ever assaulted us with sword or with regiment could have imposed any manner of harm upon us, for our land borders on the sea in one direction,[153] and is so safe on that side that we are impregnable to all onslaught. On the other side, this mountain stands along the border; whenever we close off the passageway, we are likewise secure.

(4348-4375) "This land was named the Green Meadow, and it is two miles in breadth. Many a noble lady has lost her husband here in the course of this past year. We could readily have survived any ordeal—even if all the world had conspired against us. Now, however, we shall no longer retain our joy or our good name, for the devil has exerted the full measure of his power and has won the victory here. During this past year all men whom you ought to see in this land have, in all truth, lost their lives—the warriors as well as the young infants.[154] Each and every one of the male children born to us has at once met with death. All the men, both young and old, have been murdered by the power of the devil. Only the women are now left alive. The men have so utterly vanished that, were you to search throughout the land, you would find not even thirty men. No mortal has ever witnessed such wretchedness! Yet even these thirty shall themselves lie dead before the passing of this very day.

(4376-4409) "As I have related to you already, it has been exactly a year this day. Yet we were to blame for none of this: it was the malice of the devil! At that time my father was hosting a festival—the most splendid which he had ever held—when a man came up, bald-headed and ruddy. The guests were then compelled to do whatever this man commanded them: however unjust it may have been, they dared not refuse! Just as they were seated at the tables caught up in the merriment, this creature appeared and ordered them to waste no time, but to proceed on foot and on horseback to their homes, and to bring back with them all of the inhabitants of the land, both lords and peasants. All were quick to arise from the tables (many of them leaping up!) and to hasten back to their homes, just as he had decreed. They brought back to him the entire population, both rich and poor alike. Even the sick were placed on horseback in stretchers, and all returned to the court—in such numbers that not a man could be found throughout this land who had failed to journey to the court as ordered.

(4410-4444) "Once the intruder saw them all assembled there, he told them in truth that he intended to remain here for a year's time. For he was afflicted with an illness that required his bathing once a week for an entire year; after that his affliction would then fully subside. All of the men of this land were to come before him each and every day without fail. Right there on the spot he slew—whether this pleased them or not!—a hundred men and as many more as he needed to fill a vat with blood. In this vat he was then to bathe himself. No man could impart to him any harm, and so he carried out this massacre. For all who heard his voice were rendered as feeble-minded as geese and were unable to think or act so as to impair this ogre. Each and every man whom he ordered to step forward straight into the fire would have no choice but to comply. Moreover, whomever he commands to stand still is incapable of budging an inch from that very spot. If he wishes to carve them up, they are forced to endure such treatment. As soon as a week had elapsed, he desired yet another bath. And since that time he has persisted in this, until now there are none left alive save those whom he intends to slaughter today. And there are painfully few of them!

(4445-4464) "When he came here the very first time and delivered his dismal message, I happened to be in bed deathly ill, although I was, as he had commanded, brought before him sick. My own affliction had so deadened my hearing that I never heard him as he spoke. When I was later recovered from my sickness and discerned that all who had heard his words had so utterly lost their senses, I stole off alone to this cave, where I have remained ever since. I never have heard this creature's voice while possessed of my senses.[155] But all others in this land have indeed heard it and have become more mindless than newborn infants.

(4465-4472) "What is more, this ogre enjoined my father to don his armor and to roam about morning, noon and night on horseback, bringing back for the intruder's bath the blood of all whom he defeats in battle. It is for this selfsame reason that the net stands erected on this spot: whomever my father traps in it suffers the same fate.

(4473-4497) "A week ago this very day my father set out in the morning in pursuit of such booty as this and attacked a knight, whom he defeated. Just as he was about to return here following his splendid success, he spotted two men on horseback. They had found the tent and were of a mind to strip my father of his prisoner and to kill him as well. Yet he barely escaped from them by riding into the mountain near the boulder. Then he waited until such time as one of them had already passed by that boulder and had entered into the tunnel; at that point he lowered the boulder and blocked the second knight's path. Had they both found their way in, my father would have been unable to defend himself against them. One of them had already proven this by attacking my father near the boulder and inflicting great distress on him—such that never before had he experienced so close a brush with death!

(4498-4518) "Whatever combat my father had ever known before was but a pittance in comparison with this battle, and all his previous opponents were mere children. Throughout that long day and right up to the evening I watched them struggle so very fiercely that I could never begin to relate it. Both their steeds were killed, and my father was pelted so many a time that he was to lie in bed for four full days—and indeed would have lost his life had he fought on any longer. But they were close by the entrance to the mountain, and my father then took flight into the tunnel. Onwards he galloped, heading straight past the net. The one knight fell into it and was entrapped. Thus my father defeated him and brought him before the diseased ogre, whose voice then rendered him senseless and tame."

(4519-4545) "Tell me in God's name, my lady," Daniel interrupted her, "is this knight still alive?" "This I say to you in all sincerity," she replied, "his life is worthless, and I shall tell you why: his blood would have been added to the ogre's bath on the same day as their duel had my father managed to overcome him before the bath had already been accomplished. But they fought on until nightfall, and the knight was captured only after the ogre had already bathed. It is for this reason alone that he still lives. But on this very day his blood must be mixed in with the bath. I too shall on this day suffer a sorrow which I shall never be able to forget. God help me that I may never see this day to the end! May God in His mercy grant me this much! Four of my brothers are still living. My father has ridden out in search of them and shall soon be returning. Then the ogre will delay no longer, but will butcher them all! How shall I ever overcome this grief?

(4546-4562) "You have been too rash in your actions, and now, just as you have sworn before God, you must carry out my command—if that is not too much for you. I shall now offer you a choice: either slay the diseased ogre, or endure the same fate that so many before you have suffered here—or else cut off my head, that I might sacrifice my life along with my family and not live to experience such heartache as this. The choices are three, my lord, now make your decision from among them. Whichever one of them you may choose, if you are an upright and excellent knight and set out to accomplish this, I shall then set you free."

(4563-4583) Daniel then answered her in the manner of a true hero: "The choice is easily made: I shall avenge you on the diseased creature! However, if I fail to do so, then my blood shall have to be added to his bath before I would ever consent to do you any bodily harm. Never shall I consent to kill you. Now tell me, my lady, is there any way for me to draw near to the diseased ogre? For I have concocted a plan whereby he shall fail to render me senseless no matter how he may chatter on: I shall obstruct my ears with a well-molded plug of wax. I have in my possession an excellent cutlass, and if I can draw close to the creature, he shall fare the worse for it. Both my sword and my zeal are so sharp as to enable me without fail to hack him to bits!"

(4584-4609) "It is impossible to come close to the ogre," the maiden replied. "As soon as he catches sight of you, you shall be compelled to halt on the spot—unless he bids you to draw nearer, or else walks up to you himself." "Advise me as to what I ought to do," Daniel then said. "For I shall never slay him if I cannot approach him." "I tell you in all truth," the lady then answered, "if you approach him with your hearing obstructed, he will pose a great many questions to you, of whatever sort he pleases. If you stuff your ears with any substance, you shall be unable to hear what manner of answer you must give him. Then he will permit you to live no longer. So foul a creature is he that he will turn you into a stone on that very spot—or an animal, or whatever else he pleases. So great is the power which he has from devils that he is sure to invoke such a curse upon you!

(4610-4636) "I shall tell you how it is that I verified all of this: a good twelve weeks ago I captured another man who was willing to avenge me by likewise stopping up his ears. To his great misfortune this made him so deaf that he heard nothing of what the diseased one was saying. Once the creature perceived that this knight was deaf to his words, he became so enraged that he cast a spell upon him. The creature stopped him dead in his tracks with the power of the devil. A more horribly martyred man than this could never be found, no matter how long one were to search. For then he commanded that knight to fall to the ground, and made him both deaf and dumb, as well as blind and disfigured. All of this befell that wretched man! I had stolen up close by, so that I could easily make out his gestures. Yet I heard nothing of what was being said, for I had blocked my ears so as not to be rendered senseless."

(4637-4662) "So it appears to me from what you have said," replied Daniel, "that in order to stay alive, one must hold back a good distance, and that no one can survive in close proximity to this ogre. — But pray tell me where I might now find the diseased one." She replied: "He is not far from here." To which Daniel answered: "Now tell me, where are the brave men whom he intends to butcher today? How has he guarded them? And when are they to die?" "They are, just as he ordered, by the house located in the orchard," the beautiful maiden replied. "Save for the fact that he desired to delay the bath and determine whether my father might acquire a victim to perish along with the others (and is therefore awaiting his return), the bath would already stand prepared, and they would all be dead by now—if indeed they are not already! Since my father shows no sign of returning, it may be that he has lost his life elsewhere. Nor would I object to that, inasmuch as he still faces death today from the creature."

(4663-4677) Daniel was greatly alarmed that he might lose not only the count, but also his own life and reputation. He could think of no means of averting this, nor did he know of anyone who could grant him protection from the creature's curses. No less than Daniel's very life now stood in the balance. "I shall go, my lady," he then said, "and permit myself to be slain along with the others and let him bathe in my blood. For I have no hope of inflicting injury upon this man. Since he is able to do battle by means of spells, there is no way for me to capture him. It is in this manner that I shall carry out your commandment."

(4678-4699) "No, my lord," said the lady in reply, "for the sake of God not this! You are a most knightly gentleman, and I am but a wretched woman who has lost all of my family, my only source of comfort. I shall gladly permit you to live for the purpose of killing me, so that I might not experience this grim ordeal. Why would you sacrifice your own life, which is—and ever shall be, for as long as you are alive—of far greater worth than mine? You must never permit your life to be taken without good cause. I would think no more highly of you for suffering death merely on my account. When I see that I must live without my brothers and my father, then I wish only to strike myself dead!"

(4700-4730) She urgently besought Daniel to put an end to her life, yet he refused. "In truth, I shall shear off my hair and at once don men's clothing," said the lady. "The ogre will then mistake me for a man. I shall accompany you there, so that death may befall me along with my father and brothers." With all his charm Daniel entreated the maiden to abstain from this, but she refused to grant him as much. "Your tresses are radiant and blond,"[156] said Daniel of the Blossoming

Valley, "you must not cut them off. If you will for my sake but renounce your intention, then I shall solemnly pledge to do all that I can today, even unto death. I would not gladly quit this world; I prefer to live if at all possible. Do this for my sake: remain hidden near to where this ordeal is to take place today, until such time as you see how we shall fare. What need is there now of more words? I shall gladly do all that is in my power, so that we might remain alive!"

(4731-4769) The lady was pleased at such comforting words as these and promised to do what he bade her and to stand concealed at a certain spot until she saw his fate. She then showed Daniel the way to the orchard, which he adroitly entered, quickly finding the good knights who were to suffer great torment that day. Wishing at all costs to locate his comrade, he contemplated the splendid knights one and all until he descried the count, whom he quickly recognized. Daniel was offered no form of welcome whatever as he approached; for they neither spoke nor bowed. Since the others were so very mute, he too fell silent and said nothing. This he did out of fear that, should he utter even the first word, the diseased creature might perchance be close enough to hear it and would foil Daniel's mission. Seeing that no one addressed him there, Daniel perceived that they were utterly robbed of their senses, and he began to imitate them in their gestures. He glanced all about and carefully observed all that they did, then assumed the same mannerisms himself.

(4770-4800) The diseased ogre wished to delay no longer, but rather to make preparations for his bath. He now came up and ordered all of them over to a vat at which he was standing. They all hastened to do his bidding. Daniel of the Blossoming Valley was cunningly hidden in their midst, fearful of being discovered. Underneath his cloak he carried his bare sword thus hidden from view. In quick measure they were standing at the vat, where the diseased creature—in all truth!—grabbed the nearest man by his hair and tore off his garment, till he was as naked as the back of his hand: this was to be

Plate 6. Daniel prepares to slay the diseased creature.
Ms. germ. 1340, leaf 135[r]*.*

the first victim! The ogre stabbed at him as at a swine and raised him over the vat, hideously digging with his knife at the man's heart. While the creature was still occupied with this, Daniel slipped up behind him in the very nick of time and lopped off his head. Never again was that creature to butcher men or to utter words harmful to their ears! Thus was an end put to his bathing once and for all![157]

(4801-4824) All of those who were standing around him then regained their senses and exclaimed: "What has happened to us?" Though they had witnessed everything occurring before their very eyes for that entire year, nonetheless they in fact had no inkling of any of it—up until such time as Daniel had slain the diseased ogre and come away with the victory. Daniel now began to relate to them how this creature had dulled their senses from the very moment of his arrival there. He also told of the harm he had inflicted upon them, and how he had bathed in their blood during the past year. "All of this is so," they replied in unison. "We watched it happen day in and day out, but never did we once think of escaping from him or mustering our courage in common defense. Death was inevitable for us here. No man could have averted it had you yourself not done so!"

(4825-4850) The Count of the Bright Fountain, meanwhile, had also come to his senses[158] and proclaimed: "Welcome in God's name! In truth, you are His messenger, and He has dispatched you here. Likewise, your hand rescued me from the tower in my own land. Both times I would have been lost. Never before have I received such great succor from any one man. Now I desire nothing more than to be granted the occasion to serve you in return. For this indeed would please me." Daniel then replied: "I shall soon show you a venture in which you can easily requite me three times over for the favor I have accorded you." "Onward then!" replied the count. "I have you to thank for the soundness both of my body and of my mind—this I shall proclaim for evermore. Show me now, for the sake of God, where it is that I might prove myself deserving of all of this. See for yourself whether I am worthy of being called a knight!"

(4851-4879) "This man has given us back our joy," cried out all the knights with one voice. "We shall all set out together with him and shall most gladly test our fate alongside him, for it is because of him that we are now alive." The fair maiden who had captured Daniel there now walked up to him and offered him a gracious welcome unsurpassed by any of which I have ever heard tell. Her eyes became wet with joy. She then went to her mother, to whom she related all that had transpired. The mother returned straightway and received Daniel, bidding him to tell her whether her lord was slain, and if not, then what had befallen him. Daniel told her in truth: "I saw him this very morning as I came here on horseback. When I offered him my salutation, he thrust me to the ground and well nigh killed me. But my good fortune plucked me from his grasp, so that I barely broke away and escaped through the passageway into this mountain. I then blocked the entrance before such time as he was able to follow me in. Otherwise he would have slain me."

(4880-4886) Daniel chose not to tell them what had in fact transpired. His heart was seized with joy in great abundance that he had not slain that knight, and that he knew him to be still alive, for thus was it best.

(4887-4892) A blessed man indeed is he who can keep his wits about him and not lose his self-restraint when overcome by anger. For had Daniel slain the knight in their clash, he would now have felt deep heartache at having done so.

(4893-4908) Both knights and ladies proceeded to the field at the foot of the mountain to see what was happening there. The lord of the land then entered the tent healthy in both body and in mind,[159] and they at once presented to him[160] Sir Daniel, their source of comfort. "This is the man who has redeemed us," spoke the lady. "Give thanks to him that I am still possessed of my senses. We have all been mindless for this long year now past. Not a man has survived save for you and your children and the knights present on this meadow. You owe this knight thanks for the fact that you are still alive."

(4909-4928) The lord of the land bowed deeply to Daniel and spoke: "Show me, my lord, how or where I can repay you for my life, which you have restored to me. It was my derangement which beguiled me into trying to kill you. Yet even then, sir knight, you defeated me in a most praiseworthy manner, such that I was compelled to surrender my life into your hands. May God reward you for permitting me to live and for helping me to survive this creature, who was bent on murdering me! I was utterly doomed, and you have saved me. You must therefore allow me the chance to make recompense for this. I have every kind intention to repay you, as well I ought. You will do well to grant me this much."

(4929-4944) "Excellent!" Daniel replied. "You speak with the tongue of a courageous man. Order the horses to be fetched! For I shall take you at once, if you are willing to go with me, to a place where I too must undergo a bath—one which, if I cannot fend it off, is the most deadly that any man has ever endured. This bath is none other than death itself, and I have great need of your aid." "Onward then!" the lord said. "Bring up the horses! Coming to the aid of this man is something for which I profoundly thirst, for he has rescued me from certain death this very day. If I am at all able, I shall indeed help him in return!"

(4945-4958) There commenced a great flurry of activity then as the men went for the horses, once having heard their lord's desire to set out with Daniel. In very quick measure the horses were ready, and all began to take their leave. The Lady of the Green Meadow took Daniel by the hand and spoke: "If my land had in it as many knights as a year ago, in truth, they would be accompanying you now, each and every one. May God Himself now be the one to protect you!"

(4959-4968) Daniel now rode off with twenty-six men who were every bit as valuable to him in their prowess as born kinsmen would have been. They placed in the balance both their lives and all that was theirs. He who gladly does his utmost for others is well deserving of all manner of gratitude, for gratitude sweetens his sense of fulfillment.

(4969-4990) As they rode up to the mountain, the giant, whom Sir Daniel had slain, still lay there hacked to pieces. Daniel's companions marvelled greatly at this and exclaimed: "Whoever was able to fell this creature was indeed a stout-hearted hero against whom there could be no defense!" Daniel, however, did not betray the fact that he was this selfsame hero. Then they rode on into the mountain and came to the rock, where they all cried out: "Alas! the man who carved this opening through such a rock must bear a marvelous sword indeed!" Sir Daniel comforted them, saying: "He who hewed[161] this cavity does whatever I command him. He shall aid us valiantly in our very midst even today." At this, his comrades declared: "Then no man can oppose us and come away alive!"

XI

THE REMAINING BATTLES

(4991-5013) It was an act of great valor on Daniel's part that he had left King Arthur's camp around midnight to fight for his comrade, the Count of the Bright Fountain, whom he had now rescued. Daniel also displayed an intrepid spirit by returning to King Arthur's encampment before the resumption of the fighting. For it was soon time for the next army to arrive and engage in tournament.[162] As the men of this army were approaching through the mountain, they listened and heard the beast wailing with the roar of an abyss opening up over all the land and with a din so deafening that it seemed as though the heavens were about to come crashing down to earth on that very spot. Those who were near the beast soon reached the limit of their endurance and hastily placed the banner back in its mouth.

(5014-5026) Daniel now came riding up robustly with his followers; he would have been eager to let them show[163] their good will towards him in whatever ways they could. When King Arthur saw them approaching, he was amazed and exclaimed: "When did Daniel ride out?" But there was no one in King Arthur's retinue who could offer an explanation, for Daniel had set forth in secret. The king, however, showed Daniel his good intentions and bade him welcome.

(5027-5051) After the greeting there was precious little time for King Arthur to hear of all that had transpired, for at that very moment they spotted a good two thousand knights galloping toward them on horseback. Once they caught sight of these men, they wasted not a moment's time. Many a bold hero vaulted into the saddle without the aid of his stirrup[164] and scarcely waited long enough to grab his lance and shield. They held back no more, but took off like a rush of wind. From the other direction came a great host of men, fearlessly hurtling toward King Arthur's company. They yearned to be at the very front ranks of the army, and in their zeal to push ahead of their comrades, many a man fancied his steed far too sluggish. There commenced a cracking of lances as though an entire forest were thundering to the ground. And there followed the clanking of swords banging away against the tops of the helmets, just as though they were all blacksmiths pounding upon their anvils.[165]

(5052-5070) Oh! what powerful blows King Arthur dealt out by the dozens! He acted as a plow for the others,[166] for he burst through in front and opened up a furrow wide enough for all his men to follow him on their steeds. Both horses and their riders did King Arthur mow down! He was not unlike a farmer making a clearing in the forest: for such a man focuses his every energy upon that task, chopping down whatever is harmful, until such time as the field is of value. In the same way did King Arthur slash down everything—be it horse or man!—that was in his path and that offered him injury, until he had carved out a wide and excellent field all around him. Proudly and defiantly did he fight!

(5071-5088) Sir Gawein, his sister's son, was among the most splendid of all knights. He proved—both that same day and at other times and places—that he was indeed a valuable warrior. For Gawein had it in his power to cast such a spell that all who were mesmerized by it fell to the ground and perished: this spell was the mighty sword-blow which cut through bones and bone-marrow with the force of a windstorm. Many youths did he silence on that battlefield, so that they never again uttered a sound. He slashed away at their skin so fiercely that they had no need of weeping. All throughout that day Gawein showed his mettle at jousting[167] and proved that he was indeed no mere beginner!

(5089-5100) As his comrade Sir Iwein broke through the enemy ranks, he cut down so many of his opponents that each one of them felt himself much too close to Iwein—regardless how far off he really was! All would have preferred to take on three other men together than Iwein alone! All whom he fell upon, from the front or from behind, were doomed as soon as they came within range of Iwein's sword.

(5101-5116) The bold hero Parzival bashed away at the finely wrought gold fittings on his opponents' helmets, so that the skulls beneath were split and broke open. Every man whom he struck, were he ever so ardent in battle before, soon took on the coldness of death. For Parzival's victims were reduced to such utter poverty that they forfeited all they owned, not only life and possessions, but even their very blood as well—in short, all that God had ever entrusted to them.

In the end, it was just as though they had never existed at all! Many a man's back sagged under the weight of the heavy burden which that fine warrior Parzival had imposed upon him.

(5117-5144) Daniel of the Blossoming Valley could likewise be seen riding through the battlefield, which was the very most glorious path[168] ever trod upon by any man. At his side rode the Lord of the Green Meadow, whose every taunt was followed up by a death-blow. How very joyful he was to repay Daniel for all the travail Daniel had undergone on his account while delivering him from the ogre's bath! In consequence, many a man came to harm that day, for the count battled with the fierceness of a lion. All four of his sons, moreover, were distinguished heroes and fought with such a fury that Daniel remarked: "How fortunate for me that I ever set eyes upon you!" And the rest of his companions, how bravely they too defended themselves! The Count of the Bright Fountain had also won the chance to prove whether or not he could bring death to other men that day, and to show whether he himself was worthy of being called a man.

(5145-5160) An upright man will eagerly return in double measure whatever good or evil is imparted to him. Thus the count made such restitution time and again and accomplished all that he had ever boasted of. For he had pledged to serve Daniel with a willing heart if his help should be needed, and he was fervently glad that it had come to this. He extracted the breath of life from all whom his sword carved up. So mightily did he slash away at his opponents that the red juice[169] spurted forth from their steel helmets. They were utterly incapable of defending themselves, and all who came to him hale and hearty were fast dispatched weak and sickly.

(5161-5174) Hear now of a wondrous thing: though there were many men present there on that battlefield, there was but one referee who watched over them all. Whenever one man vanquished another, this referee separated the two, as is the custom with such judges. This referee could take on ten men at a time, yet those opponents were all just as fully disengaged from one another. For that judge was called death. Thus were the combatants forced by dire necessity to be disjoined. Yet if they entertained thoughts of slipping away, death stepped in and reunited them.[170]

(5175-5199) Oh! how they raged on that battlefield! How each man strove after fame! Many a man died, I fancy, who had little expected death. What tales were born there of feats which had never before been told! Many a man was crippled there, many a man was slain; many a man turned coward, many became as fearless as a boar; and many a man displayed his wrath.[171] King Arthur's knights all demonstrated their courage,[172] which furthered their cause in battle. Because they were all of one mind, their venture met with success. This was all the more proof that, to a man, they loathed their opponents and would gladly have used their own hands to bring them all to the ground at once. And those others, who had ridden up haughtily on horseback, would have willingly accepted the lowly fate of coming away alive on foot, yet even this was denied them.

(5200-5212) The harsh were pitted against the harsh in this battle, the strong against the strong, and the sly against the sly.[173] Whatever blows each man dealt out were met with firm resistance, for as long as his opponent was able. All of them received their fill of this fare, and vast strength was expended in the killing and the frenzied tempest. Anyone who had assumed a gentle air on that battlefield would have been scorned outright—and indeed it may even have brought him some measure of harm as well!

(5213-5232) As these excellent knights set upon one another in desperate self-defense, they pressed together until both sides were fully intermingled. Many then brandished their swords as if desiring nothing less than to kill off all the enemy single-handedly and to bear alone the strength of twelve men or more. No man emerged victorious who could not rise to the occasion and fight better and better, and with a might surpassing that of all the others. Those men of the

Round Table—King Arthur's companions, who had the greater endurance—could be seen pressing onward, spreading death on all sides. All of this was a battle to exceed all battles!

(5233-5272) After the combat had raged on for a long time indeed, all of them—Daniel of the Blossoming Valley, King Arthur, and the knights from his court—converged on horseback in the midst of that battlefield. Fearless lads were these! They all came together and rode in formation through the opposing army with a great clamor, freeing many a man from his suffering. The medicine which they dealt out was death itself,[174] with which they knew how to cure all opponents. No man who was numbered among the dead that day was treated any more mercifully than the rest—be he young or old, weak or strong, generous or miserly, be he armed or weaponless, great or small, short or tall, be he dark or light, inexperienced or wise, scorned or acclaimed, be he a liar or a man of truth, bold or timid, agile or sluggish, or be he lord or servant.[175] Each of them was accorded the selfsame judgment and was forced to come face to face with death. After a time, however, as their ranks began to thin, such that they feared death, they were compelled to give up the battle and all thoughts of victory. Thus they surrendered themselves, as was high time, into King Arthur's hands, whereupon the battle came to a close.

(5273-5284) King Arthur's men then made preparations to rest for the night. For as you have already heard tell, it was their plan to remain there for seven nights' time, since King Matur had assembled seven armies in his land, each of which journeyed to the tent on separate days. Had all seven armies marched upon them at once, King Arthur's men would have had but scant hope of holding up in battle. Thus they camouflaged their encampment, as they planned to join issue five more times with the enemy. Only then would they march on into the land of Cluse.

(5285-5303) After they had doffed their armor, they were in high spirits at their success. They laughed and sang and were cheerful and merry. After resting a bit until they had overcome their fatigue, they gathered about King Arthur, some sitting and others standing. They all spoke of how Sir Daniel had performed most admirably on the battlefield of Cluse. Daniel, they said, was courageous and wise and was alone responsible for their victory; they would all have fallen in battle had he not slain the giants. It was because of his valor, others claimed, that such renown had fallen to their lot in Cluse. All present declared that Daniel had been indispensable to their triumph.

(5304-5329) The king then bade Daniel to divulge whither he had ridden off alone during the night. He likewise enjoined Daniel's companions not to keep silent, but to tell him where they had made Daniel's acquaintance. The Count of the Bright Fountain then related the story of the dwarf's demise at Sir Daniel's hand in the land of the Dark Mountain; he told of how Daniel had acquired the sword from him, and how Daniel had come to his—the count's—aid by rescuing him out of the tower from the creature bearing the lethal head. He related how Daniel had slain the ogre who was to bathe in their blood; and he finally told the king of all the losses that the Lord and the Lady of the Green Meadow had suffered from that ogre's bathing[176] and how desolate their land was, since the only men who had survived were those who had come along on this journey.[177]

(5330-5353) When the king had heard this report, he deemed it all most amazing and yet very fortunate, and indeed a great act of cunning that Daniel had slain opponents whom no other man could withstand. "Of all that I have ever heard tell of brave feats," said the king, "no tale has ever come to me of so monumental a deed so easily performed as that which Sir Daniel has accomplished!" All of the valiant heroes then exclaimed merrily: "May Christ in all His power protect you, Daniel! Everything about him is upright and courageous, and it is just that he should be acclaimed. For he is able to come to grips with all manner of hardship, as a brave and good knight should. It is meet and just that he should never endure failure. Never has there been, and never will there be, a knight with such good cause for joy!"

(5354-5376) It was the custom at King Arthur's court that no man should tell of his own honorable deeds. Yet such feats were not left untold, for as soon as another man heard of them, *he* was the one to relate them, to the glory of the knight who had performed them. All of them strove therefore, in whatever ways possible, to augment the next man's fame and praise. Sir Daniel's companions, whom he had brought there with him, all then asked what man it was who bore the sword which had cut down the giants and had hewn the great opening through the rock. "All wondrous things that have been performed here," said Sir Gawein in reply, "were done by Sir Daniel,[178] who has rescued you from adversity in your own land. Surely we would all have suffered death had he not slaughtered the giants. It is he too who cut through the rock. Let no one tell you otherwise!"

(5377-5404) The rest of the day they passed in this same manner, and they remained merry all through the night, until daybreak. As the hour drew near when their opponents were to arrive for the tournament, King Arthur's men lured them to the battlefield by once more causing the beast to emit its wail. In a short time they spotted the army galloping up in great haste toward them, and they rushed out to welcome them with such a greeting and such a throng and such jousting that many a man longed to save his life! Each of them set about giving sharp rejoinder to the blows of his opponent. They strewed the field from one end to the other with corpses, for many a man dropped to the ground, never to rise again. They fought in the manner of men giving full vent to their anger. Some of them won and some of them lost, but none lost as much as those who tasted death. These were the ones who truly lost everything: all else was a mere child's game.

(5405-5423) Seen following Daniel of the Blossoming Valley through the midst of that battlefield were both the Count of the Bright Fountain and that other band of men—the ones whom Daniel had assembled in the land of the Green Meadow, where the maiden had captured him in her net. These men, whom Daniel had once accompanied to the bloodbath, now rode here for the sake of Daniel's fame. They were fighting so fiercely that it was a most honorable thing to see, and that the enemy, unable to outrival them, was forced to concede the victory to King Arthur. Those who wished to remain alive had no choice but to give themselves over into his power as captives. Thus the battle ended, and King Arthur's men rested once more.

(5424-5443) As this great ordeal was besetting the knights of the land of Cluse (that in the three battles waged thus far, they had suffered injury both to body and to honor at the hands of their opponents), word of this began to spread. Soon it had been heard throughout all the land. Every man able to ride a horse and skilled in the use of the sword made himself ready at short notice. As soon as they heard tell that, in all truth, their king had been slain, they deeply feared that they should have to forfeit both their land and their reputation and face inescapable death as well. Thus they made great haste toward the court, where they heard their queen's deep lament.

(5444-5467) This came to pass on the same day on which the third battle was concluded. It was with great impatience that the enemy awaited the dawn of the fourth day. When that time came, all who meant to defend the land rode forth to meet King Arthur, swearing fervently either to avenge their king or else to abandon the land after that for evermore. They rejoiced greatly that King Arthur, who had wreaked such havoc on their court, was still present in the land, for they knew full well where they could avenge their suffering. Out of their hatred of King Arthur was hatched a savage plot for the assault on him: their numbers as they rode off together into battle were four times as great as those with whom Arthur's men had previously fought. Yet they too were now faced with the boldest warriors ever to sit astride their steeds!

(5468-5482) King Arthur, intrepidly leading a veritable forest of lances and swords, now came riding up against the fourth army. Had any man been present who was desirous of death, he would have been granted his wish in quick measure. Many a man who desired to live, on the other hand, lost his life as well. Spurs dug into the horses on both sides, and they could be seen vaulting toward one another, the lances splintering as they crashed together. Swords were then unsheathed and came cracking down on their opponents' shields.

(5483-5501) King Arthur's men undauntedly took up the fight, pummeling the enemy with such mighty blows that their shields flew to bits in their very hands. They slashed and struggled and they battered and fought[179]—until many a man reached the point where he would have much preferred to be elsewhere that day! They forsook all raillery and demonstrated their resolve with grimness of purpose; they proved that they would willingly tolerate neither subjugation nor disgrace. The enemy, however, possessed the same firm resolve and performed in a like manner.

(5502-5532) A battle of immeasurable scope was playing itself out![180] The path through that battlefield was strewn with the dead, yet there was no rest there for the living either, who exchanged blow after blow. Little did they tolerate anything that could be avenged! Each and every one of them brought woe to his opponent, arching frightfully with each sword-blow and forcing his sword down through steel and iron. Both horses and men could be seen hurtling to the ground. The blood ran everywhere. The heat of the battle was cause alone for agony. Many a man made the leap from life into death, and every youth, however green in years, turned quickly and inexorably old once he had tasted, even briefly, the sort of pleasure enjoyed upon that battlefield. A grim day it was indeed! They renounced all idle chatter and spoke only in terse words, but chiefly with the sword alone. So many suits of armor were hacked open by the onslaught of their blades that even the experienced men amongst them stood aghast.

(5533-5552) All who could see this were quick to arm themselves with swords which were sturdy and sharp and capable of killing a man regardless what manner of armor he wore. Hence there arose on both sides an epidemic parting of body and spirit. Many a man was compelled to do his enemy's bidding and to choose death, which was a most formidable command indeed. Renouncing all scorn and all contempt, yet equally devoid of all joy and all laughter,[181] they pursued this pastime of theirs, which was utterly without gentility. Any man who was not hale and hearty would have been a fool to partake of such a battle as this!

(5553-5576) Daniel of the Blossoming Valley made no effort to conceal his own valor, for he felled the enemy right and left as he rode onward through their midst. Unless he were in the very pits of hell, no man could endure such agony as Daniel meted out with his sword. Daniel did this with such mighty blows that each victim lost all memory then and there of all that had ever happened to him, be it sweet or be it bitter. For Daniel knocked them senseless and taught them what it was that he bore in his hand! Whatever he struck with that sword was pierced as if by a bolt of lightning. I shall tell you why it was that his sword penetrated so deep into the enemy ranks: it was amazingly sharp, and Daniel himself was possessed of such great strength and such craftiness, and he wielded that sword so zealously that it began to cut ahead—all on its own!—so that nothing was able to withstand it!

(5577-5582) It was a grim toll indeed which Daniel paid out. Even helmets hard as flint offered no protection in the face of that warrior! Any man who desired to live had to keep his distance, else Daniel would have slain him in quick measure.

(5583-5609) The Count of the Bright Fountain wielded a sword covered to the hilt with blood. All whom he encountered were compelled to hand over their bodies and their lives in exchange for death. A ruinous purchase was this indeed! He mowed down both the horses and their riders, and he sliced open the skin of all who rode at him. Thus they not only had to forgo their revenge, but they were utterly silenced for evermore. King Arthur's comrades were goaded by their bold courage to surge onward toward their lord, cutting down a whole host of men along the way and leaving them altogether unaware of the battle that raged on. Present on the battlefield that day were both fierceness and hatred, suffering and distress, displeasure and sorrow; there were animosity and immoderation, unrest and great violence, discomfort, ire, and wrath.[182] So much was lost that was never again regained!

(5610-5627) Those who were able and who knew how to fight fared well. Thus King Arthur could be seen performing marvelous feats. Thus, in turn, did the men of Cluse, many of whose saddles were empty, pay dearly. King Arthur's brave helpers gave full proof of their valor and followed him wherever he rode. Many a man's helmet was notched and dented there. This was no undertaking for a coward, for any man who feared his enemy would have done better elsewhere! King Arthur's companions displayed such knightliness and such fortitude that any man who wished to confront them was compelled to back up his challenge with firm resolve and with daring feats.

(5628-5637) They rode through blood up to the horses' knees, and all who were unhorsed drowned in it.[183] Yet not a one of them displayed cowardice: so great was their collective burden that even those who were mortally wounded dwelt not on their pain, for on both sides they yearned so fervently for the victory!

(5638-5656) In both his hands King Arthur carried into battle against that enemy a certain salve. Once applied to a man, it penetrated throughout his body, driving out his soul such that it remained within him no longer. This salve was the sword which King Arthur bore, and which he brandished so mightily that many a hero lay dead. Never had any living man endured greater tribulation than this. Those warriors battered away with their swords, so that everything which was on or around them glowed red-hot, and whatever their swords touched went up in flames like straw. In the end, there were many amongst them who would have been happy to escape, whether dead or alive, from this holocaust.

(5657-5681) Yet there was proof enough of unbending, manly courage: though a great host of them went sprawling into the blood, not a one of those remaining flinched in fear. No one was called upon to give chase to his opponent, for neither of them shrank back an inch from the fight. The very grimmest of all greetings ever offered by any man was meted out that day: this greeting was death, which was imparted nearly free of charge. Whoever eluded death's call had surely to credit that to his good fortune! Helmets clear as glass became covered with the red of blood. Those whom King Arthur had brought there in his company were intrepid heroes who fought with one accord. They extracted from their opponents such liens as cost them their lives. (A most formidable collateral was this indeed!) Many a man was brought to shame when struck down from his horse, yet he was never heard to lament his disgrace, for—even while bathing in the pool of blood!—he bewailed his injury to no one, up until the final moment in which he drowned.

(5682-5692) All throughout the long, hot day they battled. Finally night fell and fatigue sapped their strength so utterly that neither side was able to carry out the full vengeance which they were bent on wreaking. A truce was then arranged until the following day. The countless and mighty blows which each side had delivered made them glad to lay down their weapons and rest for the night.

(5693-5714) Though both sides had agreed upon the truce for that night, King Matur's men nonetheless decided not to quit the battlefield. Instead, they dismounted on the meadow not far from their enemy, from which spot they could see King Arthur's tents already pitched. For they were so bold as to assert[184] that, once they had regained their strength, they would easily be the victors. Thus the men of Cluse camped near King Arthur. They posted sentinels who kept careful watch throughout the night, so that he might not flee before they could defeat him. In fact, there was no need for them to guard against King Arthur's escape, for even if they had tried to drive him away, he was bent upon remaining there until such time as he should either perish or else win the victory.

(5715-5753) Late in the night King Arthur entered into council with his men to determine the best course of action. The illustrious hero Daniel of the Blossoming Valley spoke up and said: "If you are willing to follow me in every detail, I have devised a clever scheme which, if we can carry it out, shall reap for us the victory and shall cast the enemy at our feet in submission. Indeed, I fancy that they shall be forced to concede the victory without even once putting up a fight. In this fashion we shall both fare well: they for not losing any further lives, and we for no longer having to endure the agony of battle. We are killing far too many fine men who, in my view, ought not to die. My plan, however, shall preserve their lives, yet force them to surrender unto you both themselves and all that is theirs. Listen now to my scheme and see whether or not it is pleasing to you. Before daybreak tomorrow we must all obstruct our ears.[185] Then, when the truce comes to an end, we shall merely remain where we are and allow the enemy to advance. As soon as they commence the assault, we shall then cause the beast to cry out. We ourselves shall not be harmed in the least by this din, but it will roar so thunderously through their heads as to deaden both their senses and their bodies. This shall be to our advantage, for they shall be thrown to the ground and be compelled to surrender. Thus both the land and its inhabitants shall be ours."

(5754-5778) The lords all proclaimed the wisdom of Daniel's advice, and they made haste to carry out what he had proposed. By daybreak they were all in readiness, and the truce was withdrawn. King Matur's troops mounted the attack against King Arthur, whose

Plate 7. Daniel removes the banner from the wailing beast's mouth.
Ms. germ. 1340, leaf 154^r.

men then pulled the banner from out of the beast's mouth, causing it to emit its wail. It raised so ear-splitting a din (as well it was able!) that it shot through the heads of all who heard it, and jolted them from their horses down onto the ground. This same agony befell all of King Matur's men: not a one could escape, nor defend himself any longer. All who wished to save themselves were forced to surrender their swords and beg for their lives.

XII

DANIEL'S CORONATION

(5779-5797) The battle ended in such a way that King Matur's men surrendered both their swords and their oaths of allegiance, whether it pleased them or not. They had tasted defeat, but avoided death in battle. King Arthur's companions then replaced the banner and thereby silenced the beast. The men of Cluse approached King Arthur and yielded to him both themselves and their land, as well as their children and their wives. All of this he then turned back over to them as fiefs. They knelt at King Arthur's feet and, hoping for his mercy, they swore an oath that they would never knowingly commit any act which could bring either harm or disgrace upon him.

(5798-5812) Thus did those enemies become good friends. They saw to it before nightfall that the slain King Matur was borne from the battlefield and inhumed in a manner befitting his position, along with all the other dead. A great many pious priests were quickly summoned to help lend the burial propriety in the eyes of God. The king then turned all his thoughts towards a timely end to the animosity between himself and the Queen of Cluse.

(5813-5848) After the dead had been buried, they called at once for excellent physicians to minister carefully to the wounded, who had been carried off the battlefield. (Those who lay there dead had suffered the ultimate harm!) The king now summoned before him the knights of that land, who earlier had been his foes. Their conduct towards King Arthur was most conciliatory, for they possessed sufficient excellence and wisdom, once they had in fact witnessed first-hand his valor, to proclaim with one voice: "This king is indeed a good and upright man!" With these men before him, King Arthur spoke: "Why did I first depart from my palace in order to journey here? This I shall relate to you with great lamentation, lest you fancy that I did so out of haughtiness. I had never once heard of this land until that giant was dispatched to me—the one who lies slain here. The giant relayed to me a message from your lord, who likewise lies here dead: that I was to set out forthwith on a journey to this land and surrender myself and my territory to King Matur and live under his command.

(5849-5878) "My recalcitrance so irritated the giant that he led me here as his captive. Now matters have unfolded as you have all seen. I speak truthfully when I say that I would have gladly remained at my court, and that I was driven here contrary to my will. Now your queen bears hatred towards me. To be sure, I have not served her well, and cannot therefore reproach her for this. However, you must now set about winning me her favor. Tell her of my innocence, and that I came here a prisoner. If she sets aside her animosity, I shall treat as my very own sons all who aid me in this endeavor—and I shall do so for however long I am as well in body and in mind as I am now. I shall compensate you for whatever harm I have caused, and I shall make each of you so happy that you shall have to agree that I have treated you well." They were most pleased at King Arthur's words and replied: "In truth, this shall be accomplished in quick measure. The queen shall have to put an end to her anger."

(5879-5896) Those lords then rode off. King Arthur, however, remained there, in accordance with a certain custom: if a man were engaged in battle and it came to pass that he was victorious, then he was required to stay close by to the battlefield for three days and three nights if he wished to win an honorable victory. Whoever failed to do this, and deserted the battlefield prematurely thus gave rise to talk that he had run away.[186] Hence the king bode his time there. The assembled knights of Cluse, however, he enjoined to show their good faith by speaking well of him before the queen and by commending him to her favor.

(5897-5920) The men of Cluse now rode off to call upon the queen. They found the noble lady (this was unavoidable!) overcome by deep heartache, for she was enduring misery and woe at her dear lord's death. Her lament and her distress and her dire grief had very nearly robbed her of life. Ever since the tidings had come that her lord was slain, she had lain in woe both day and night, doing nothing but weeping and lamenting, and proving in many ways that no woman had ever undergone greater sorrow. All who heard her words and saw her gestures were certain that such wretchedness as this had never before befallen a woman. No one fancied that she would ever recover from her distress, but rather that she should have to die of grief.[187]

(5921-5950) Her closest counselors, who had advised her all her life as to the proper course of action, were at great pains to comfort their lady and to free her from her suffering.[188] In numerous ways and with great zeal they directed all their efforts towards this end. Her very dearest vassals, who well dared to offer their counsel, besought her for the sake of God to be of good cheer; they vowed that, for as long as she lived, they would serve her willingly and would never abandon her or withdraw their material support. With one voice they proclaimed: "It is our common will, my lady, that you now fall silent.

Plate 8. The Queen of Cluse receives her vassals.
Ms. germ. 1340, leaf 157r.

Your lament has been long and excessive, and we beseech you to suppress it. If you grant us this and forsake your weeping, we shall evermore undertake to augment your fame and to execute your will. Moreover, we wish also to inform you that, if you fail to follow our advice, you shall incur our displeasure."

(5951-5986) Tearfully the lady replied: "Do I not even dare to lament my distress in your presence, my lords, without thereby forfeiting your service and your favor? If so, then I shall lose both undeservedly. I can readily see and hear that a twofold misfortune has beset me: that I must be deprived of my lord and that, in addition, you are to deny me your favor at such quick notice. This I shall ever lament to God! I would have none of this to wrest with if I still had my lord! Am I supposed to be glad to hear so foolish a threat from all of you, that if I do not at once assume an air of bliss, I shall forfeit your favor? Any woman beset by a lesser burden than this is surely permitted to weep and lament. Yet I have lost the most precious lord the earth has ever seen. Never has a woman acquired so good a name by her husband as did I. For this reason I shall never again be happy! If you were possessed of any understanding at all, you would not reproach me for my weeping. I shall prove to my lord that I cannot forget him, and I shall weep until the very day I die! Never again shall I think well of you, for my grief does not affect you in the least, and you are so quick to oppose me."

(5987-6005) One of her ministerials,[189] who fully grasped the predicament, then spoke up: "This you must believe in all truth: that we too have never suffered (and never *shall* suffer!) so great a loss as this. Yet what would it avail us to die of grief, since we should gain nothing thereby? Listen carefully therefore to what we have to say, or else you shall utterly forfeit your people and your land and be left quite empty-handed, bereft of your last ounce of esteem. For this very reason you ought not to permit yourself to scorn our advice so rashly.

You are acting in too great haste and may miscalculate and have to abandon your land and your court.

(6006-6039) "What right did our lord have to demand that King Arthur become his vassal? All kings living on this earth are but a puff of wind in comparison to King Arthur. We had eight thousand knights in our army, yet we still were forced to concede the victory: how do you now hope to defeat King Arthur? If you wish to be responsible for two more such blights in addition to this one,[190] you shall rue it, but only after it is already too late. You ought not to disregard our advice so contemptuously, for you have long heard the saying that a person who scorns the advice of others can be helped by no one. Indeed, many a man has had to forfeit all his happiness because of a grudge. Weigh this in your mind, my lady! Your esteem will not be thereby diminished; rather, if you follow our counsel, you stand only to gain in benefit and fame.[191] Your anger towards us is without foundation. For we shall now zealously act so as to augment and expand your good name—no less so than we once did in enacting my lord's commandments. Consider now this advice, which each of us deems wise. Thus it shall ever be our resolve, both publicly and in private, to perform all that you command."

(6040-6052) "Even if your advice may be ill-weighed," spoke the queen, "I shall now follow it and do as you counsel me—but only because you have in the past always shown nothing save good intentions towards me. May God dispose all of you to maintain your allegiance to me and never to swerve from standing by me with full loyalty. Speak now your wish, and I shall have to grant it, for I cannot dispense with your favor."

(6053-6099) All of her ministerials[192] then spoke up: "You have only to gain from this, my lady. If our lord had acted in a like manner, he would still be alive today. But he would not act according to reason, and now he lies dead in consequence. What possible need could he have had to enjoin King Arthur to journey here at once with the giant and to surrender on the spot both himself and his land? When King Arthur refused, the giant took him captive—in his own court and in the midst of all his men!—and led him off as his prisoner. Now, however, King Arthur has demonstrated here the greatness of his valor, of which we have always heard tell. He has slain our lord, along with many a fine knight. But he has acted justly in doing so, and it is for this reason that success has smiled upon him. Now he has compelled us—those of us who had any remaining will to live—to surrender both ourselves and our possessions into his power; he has permitted us to retain our lives, which we have received from him. That which we have done, you too must now do. Since we were overcome in battle, we can be glad that he even suffers us to live and to keep what we possess. You are well protected with King Arthur, for he is fully blessed with all good qualities. We have heard from his own lips that he wishes, in truth, to compensate you for your sorrow,[193] provided you are willing to dismiss from your thoughts all that has happened. It is for this reason that we have been so bold as to endeavor to win for him your favor. For our sake you ought now to abandon all blame and do as we counsel you, if we are at all dear to you."

(6100-6128) The queen then replied: "I shall follow you, just as I ought, in your advice and in your actions, and in whatever appears best to you. I have full trust in you that you will not betray me in the end. King Arthur has inflicted great suffering upon me. Since I have served all of you well in lamenting my lord, I am now willing to assume a new bearing and for your sake to make the best of things—in order that I might not lose[194] my land or your favor. It is an act of incalculable loyalty that you do not abandon me or forsake me now that I have suffered such misfortune. If indeed this advice of yours—that I drop all my animosity—is given in good faith, then you must all pledge to me here and now to remain ever at my command in word and in deed, and never again to do anything which might be so displeasing to me."

All of them swore to this, and the queen said: "I shall now permit you to do whatever you wish."

(6129-6144) The men of Cluse then rode back to King Arthur and brought him the good tidings, that their lady had undergone a change of heart. Hearing this, he and his men welcomed them graciously. Then the noble King Arthur set out with them in great joy toward the court. When the lady saw him approaching, she arose and greeted him. Her grief still so oppressed her, however, that she was unable to forget all that had transpired, and she burst into tears.

(6145-6161) King Arthur, whose eyes, unbeknownst to the others, welled over with tears of sorrow, then spoke: "Try to be of good cheer. For in truth, if I live to see it, I shall demonstrate to you that all of your suffering indeed touches me to the quick. Never would I have inflicted any harm upon your lord here in his own land, save that he left me no choice but to slay him. For in my eyes it would have been a disgrace to surrender to him as a vassal—as long as I could live as a free man. Your grief moves me to great pity. Now, however, you must forgo any further sorrow for the sake of my loyalty, and you must forgive me my transgressions.

(6162-6191) "I wish to win your favor in a fashion that shall augment your good name. I shall spare no pains to atone for your damages and for the death of your husband, so that you will once more become happy. My own heart shall have to dwell in the shadow of sorrow until such time as I have devised a means of bringing gladness into your heart. I am afflicted and pained by all that I have done to harm you, for never before have I inflicted injury or distress upon a lady! God is my witness that what has transpired could not have been avoided with my good name intact. It had to happen and it did happen! In all truthfulness, if you are willing to overlook all that I have done to trouble you, then I shall not fail to make amends for your unhappiness. Either I shall rise so high in your favor that you will justly pray that God might reward me for it, or else I shall never again wear my crown! Now have no fear of me, for, in truth, all shall turn out well for you."

(6192-6199) "This I shall entrust to your grace," spoke the queen. So consoled was she to hear that it was self-defense which had compelled King Arthur to slay her lord, and so gladdened was she to hear the promises which he now made to her, that she forgot all her anger and kissed him on his lips.

(6200-6219) Listen now and I shall tell you of what bliss held sway, once this sorrow had come to an end. King Arthur entered into council with all of those whom he had brought there from Britain, and spoke: "I shall inform all of you of my plan. Assist me now in carrying it out with the teachings of your loyal hearts, and advise me as to how to deal with this lady in a manner commensurate with my good name. Give thought, all of you, and tell me which man it is who can free her of her woes. See to it that your advice is not unwise; for whomever you choose by common consent, to him I intend to confer both the lady and the land. Such a man may indeed call himself happy!"

(6220-6243) "I myself wish to offer counsel on this matter," spoke King Arthur's nephew Sir Gawein; "there is not a man alive today who is right for this land and whom I would advise her to accept, save for Daniel of the Blossoming Valley. Indeed, there is no other plan of action which will more favorably transform the queen's circumstances, if you all agree to follow my counsel. For had Daniel not slain both giants with his own hand, we would never have lived to tell at home the tale of what has transpired here. Now we should requite him for saving our lives. Do my bidding therefore, and agree that he is well deserving of such reward! None of us could have won the sword from the dwarf as did he, nor saved the Count of the Bright Fountain, nor the Maiden of the Green Meadow. This land and this lady are well provided for with Daniel!"[195]

(6244-6261) All of them concurred and bade King Arthur with one accord to grant Daniel of the Blossoming Valley both the land and the lady. They were glad to see Daniel rewarded for all that he had done while fighting alongside them. The king praised Sir Gawein's advice, saying: "I myself was disposed towards precisely what you have counselled me. Since I have now heard that this is your common will, you shall be granted it, for you have advised me well in this matter. My life and all that I possess shall evermore be shared with you and ventured for the fame of each and every one of you."

(6262-6273) King Arthur then inquired of Daniel as to whether he desired the land, saying that Daniel had won acclaim in battle with his sword, that he was well deserving of this reward, and that he was Arthur's very own choice for such an honor. Daniel replied merrily: "Indeed I do! May God Himself reward all of you for according to me alone that which we have together won in battle. This is indeed a sign of your vast loyalty. I shall prove myself ever worthy of this if I am granted long enough to live!"

(6274-6297) No other man had ever received a greater benefaction, and this gladdened all their hearts. With a jubilant fanfare the king and his retinue returned to the queen, where King Arthur proclaimed: "My lady, the very finest men from all lands seek out my court. And the most noble of them ever to come to me or my court—or of whose manly deeds I have ever heard tell—is Daniel, who stands here now, and whom I wish to bestow upon you in atonement. Aside from our heavenly reward itself, no better lot could befall you—and you yourself will yet agree that this is so! Never would we have survived the battle had Daniel not defeated your two towering giants, whose skin was hard as stone. Daniel could easily have vanquished and slain your entire army single-handedly!"

(6298-6310) King Arthur then began to recount how Daniel had rescued the Lady of the Dark Mountain from the dwarf, how he had consoled the Lady of the Bright Fountain, and how he had saved the Maiden of the Green Meadow. "Tell me now," interrupted the lady, "am I at all to be tainted with disgrace for calling so quick an end to the mourning of my husband? This you must tell me before all else."[196]

(6311-6327) King Arthur then replied: "How could it come about that you should incur shame from this? Inasmuch as this counsel is urged upon you by all who are intent upon your welfare—both by your kinsmen and by your followers, free men and vassals alike—what dishonor would there be in so doing? What is more, I and my men offer you quite the same advice. Be certain of this: I know of many a brave and upright man, but I have heard tell of no knight as excellent as Daniel. Be therefore of good cheer! You can truly speak of good fortune, for you are receiving here the very finest knight now living!"

(6328-6338) "Then let there be no further resistance," spoke the queen. "May God will that he should desire me, since you hold him in such high esteem! I shall gladly be wedded to him if he wishes me." Present amongst them were a great many priests, who then gave the queen to Daniel in marriage. Yet by that act they granted him even more than a wife: they bestowed upon Daniel the kingdom and the crown as well.[197] All of this was Daniel's reward!

XIII

THE FESTIVAL BEGINS

(6339-6370) All these precious words of praise earned Daniel of the Blossoming Valley such acclaim that the people received him as lord over the land of Cluse. Thereupon he went aside with King Arthur and sent for all his other comrades, who came up in quick measure. Daniel then spoke in good faith: "I shall no longer conceal my wish to hold a festival here, since joy has crossed my path and I have become lord over this land. I now desire to gladden the hearts of all whom I can assemble here, both men and women. In keeping with your position of renown, you must now, God willing, help me to consummate my festival. All that you have done on my behalf in choosing me as lord over this land will be for naught if you fail to assist me further, so that I might bring to fulfillment all that has been embarked upon. Because of the tales which my lord King Arthur has told of me, my lady has forgone her grief. Prove now that what one hears is true, namely that King Arthur is always in pursuit of acclaim.

(6371-6389) "For while King Matur ruled over this land, he held each and every day a festival. Hence the people are well accustomed to having festivals. Should we neglect, while all of you are still present here, to make our own festival as praiseworthy as those the populace is wont to see, then we shall be forever disgraced; nor will I ever be acclaimed or praised throughout this land. Though we have thus far striven with great zeal to achieve worldly reward, all of this can quite readily be lost. Instead of thanking us, the people of Cluse would forever lament King Matur's death all the more. Thus I have need of your aid in winning the esteem of my people.

(6390-6420) "You have always been courageous and wise, and you are widely renowned for this. Show now the truthfulness of your reputation. You have all fought to conquer this land, and you suffered great adversity before taking it by the sword. I now have among my subjects five hundred maidens, who, by all accounts, are perfect in every sense of the word beauty, both inward and outward. For they are both pure in character and comely in appearance. Never have I heard tell of women so splendid. All of you who desire to remain in this land I shall permit to choose from among these women. No one could begin to count up for you the number of them who were widowed here, but who still retain their maidenly beauty. Each of you who desires one of them may, in addition, take sufficient land to sweeten the prospect of settling here. Thus this festival is yours as well as mine. Let me charge you to act in a manner ever favorable to our common esteem. You have been chosen as members of a circle of the most excellent men ever born, and you are famed for that excellence. See to it now that you prove the truthfulness of your reputation!"

(6421-6447) They all laughed and spoke: "We shall gladly work to augment your fame, just as you wish and in whatever ways we are able." Daniel then made a request of the Count of the Bright Fountain, the Count of the Green Meadow, and the others who had come there with him, leaving their ladies at home. He asked that they hasten to journey homeward and bring back their wives, so as to prove their friendship and service; and he also asked that they be mindful of the loyalty which Daniel had already shown and still intended to show to them. Daniel cherished the hope that those men's wives would delight in his joy and in his festival and not begrudge him what he had acquired there. He charged the Count of the Bright Fountain, upon his loyalty, with fetching the Duchess of the Dark Mountain, whom he had rescued from the dwarf. This the count solemnly promised to Daniel.

(6448-6458) They tarried there no longer, but took their leave and journeyed almost until noontime of the second day. No man can know, I fancy, how they were then received! All things flourished for Daniel of the Blossoming Valley, who in the meantime had dispatched messengers in all directions to summon his own fellow countrymen. The festival soon began.

(6459-6475) All three of the ladies whom Daniel had rescued were seated alongside the queen. The Maiden of the Dark Mountain recounted to her the story of the dwarf[198] and lamented her great distress and told her of how many men the dwarf had slain, until Daniel avenged her. The Lady of the Bright Fountain in turn told the queen of all the harm which she had suffered at the hands of the creature who carried about the lethal head, until Daniel slew it. And the Lady of the Green Meadow related to her all of the misery caused by the ogre who bathed in blood, until Daniel overcame him.

(6476-6492) Upon hearing this, the queen's eyes at once became tearful with sorrow, so great was the pity that she felt for them at having endured this tribulation. Her heart, however, was most joyous that the same man who had slain both of those tough-skinned giants had fallen to her lot, for she rejoiced to hear that others had survived great adversity because of Daniel's efforts. Thus her joy became so great that she was able to banish her dead husband from her thoughts. As she heard Daniel's praise ever more enhanced, she would have been mad not to hold him in high regard! That Daniel was worthy of her was evident from what all of them had to say of him.

(6493-6534) As soon as Daniel had heard that all the people from his own land had arrived there, a great array of splendid tents was pitched with much dispatch on a lovely field nearby. Elephants then trudged up carrying on their backs a good twenty-four palaces. Neither King Arthur nor any other man had ever before witnessed such lavish elegance as that![199] All of this took place out on a green meadow, which was broad and long[200] (easily a mile or more!), and which was covered year-round with nothing but flowers and clover and with the most exquisite grass the earth has ever borne. The season was likewise most splendid, for this festival of which I tell commenced on Whitsunday.[201] The men of the Round Table were clothed from head to toe in the garb of their own lands; they had brought with them the very finest raiments to be found anywhere in all the world. Early on Whitsunday the principle liegemen arrived, and unbounded joy held sway. Daniel of the Blossoming Valley was crowned that day. His subjects were anything but scorned for having as their ruler a lord so excellent! Five hundred maidens were seen standing round about the queen; even the least comely among them was laden with such beauty that Venus, standing next to her, would have been put to shame and would have had to acknowledge the other's radiance as superior.

(6535-6544) After a mass had been sung, they prepared the food: there was meat from beasts both wild and tame, cooked in all the different styles ever heard of. Mountains of food were served up—and in such abundance that all of the guests were well provided for and no one was left wanting for more.

(6545-6568) After they had dined on that Pentecost day, the equipment with which they were to ride for the joust was seen glittering with silk and gold and with precious stones. They were all engaged in many forms of entertainment, and every game ever devised was played there. The men of the Round Table strove to win praise and entertained the spectators, just as courtly knights should do. In whatever activity they pursued, their skills seemed flawless on every count. The noble maidens observed all of this eagerly. Any man who beheld these maidens can forever speak of joy! Though one might ponder for years on end, one could never picture all of the splendid and wondrous raiments which they wore. They were every bit as radiant at night as during the daytime!

(6569-6595) Wool of scarlet and dark brown hues would have been among the basest of their garments. What is more, dyed silk and silk interwoven with gold, fine white linen and yet more dyed, interwoven silk were the very thinnest of their fabrics. Even ermine, brightly colored or gray, was as naught to these ladies.[202] They all wore robes (which are foreign to *our* taste!), and each of them had on a tunic of white silk. Not a single woman could be seen who failed to wear costly silk, for they would have been forever shamed were they not each to have two stockings sewn of that fabric. Their cloaks and frocks, in which emeralds and chrysoliths were skillfully inlaid, were likewise stiff with gold. Hyacinths, amethysts, and pearls were similarly in abundance, as well as jasper and topaz, carbuncle and sapphire, agate and onyx, a great many rubies and almadine.[203] Their downy furs were fashioned of sable and the edges were of beaver skin.

(6596-6604) All of the ladies stood pointing their fingers at this or that knight, each indicating which one she would like to have, if it should come to that. Above each of the maidens, shielding them from the sun, hovered a Babian whose entire plumage was more lustrous than a mirror.

(6605-6630) Once Daniel was mounted on his steed, he proved to his lady and to all others present there that he was well able to comport himself as a fine king should. All were of one mind, that no man present was Daniel's peer. For he went on to display his skill in so many different pursuits that the queen could not but praise him, saying that God had in every respect granted her compensation for her slain husband. Never again, I fancy, will there be a king so engaging as Daniel! The assembled multitude, men and women alike, all exclaimed to one another: "God has bestowed upon Daniel all that a knight should have. Never has a woman encountered such good fortune as has our lady!" All of them agreed that she could indeed count herself blest, since she had been made so happy and compensated so readily for her suffering.

(6631-6671) When it came time to rest, King Arthur's men dismounted and merrily walked off the grassy field together—off to where they were graciously welcomed by the maidens. Sweet laughter could be heard, and many wistful glances of love were to be seen. They observed one another's conduct and demeanor, yet they were also careful to take note of their words and their dispositions, until they all were able to find a lady willing to praise them. No man who desired one of them, whether she was a widow or still a maiden, was spurned. Finally, four hundred of the women were chosen to take in marriage the knights who had journeyed with King Arthur from the land of Britain. These were the men who were to remain there with Sir Daniel in Cluse. In addition, the Duchess of the Dark Mountain selected for herself a duke, one who was good and faithful to her. Belamis[204] was his name, and he possessed as much fame as a knight

Plate 9. The knights of the Round Table engage in jousting.
Ms. germ. 1340, leaf 170[r]*.*

could possibly have. He became her very dear husband, was never inconstant towards her, and reaped great reward in return. Moreover, the Lord and the Lady of the Green Meadow had four sons, each of whom soon chose for himself a wife well able to gladden him in every way.

(6672-6686) This festival was celebrated on so regal a scale that joy unblemished by any hatred poured forth from the very bottom of all their hearts. Daniel of the Blossoming Valley performed in the manner of men who, in their quest for the highest acclaim, strive to invest their undertakings with perfection. To such men as these Good Fortune, along with all her retinue, spontaneously pledges a clear measure of her good favor. Thus their endeavors are praised by all. Daniel hastened unflaggingly to pursue this selfsame esteem.

(6687-6726) Hear now of a most wondrous matter. Daniel of the Blossoming Valley took all of the women aside from the other guests. Once he had assembled them all there, he spoke in a most courtly fashion: "I shall refuse my favor and my salutation to all of those in your midst who have lost their husbands and who refuse to choose another here. Any such ladies shall incur my lasting disesteem![205] There are a great many brave heroes present here who are my very dearest friends. I shall treat as my very own offspring as many of you as may now accept one of them.[206] Dwell not on the fact that your lords have been laid to rest during the past seven days' time. Rather, let whatever disgrace there is be mine alone. You need look no further than at the queen, who did not disdain to accept this same advice when it was offered her. You have before you the opportunity for happiness. Let these men, who took your husbands from you, now make amends, so that they in return might be yours in body and in soul. Be free of the fear—whichever ones of you choose a husband—that this will ever bring down harm upon you. For even the very least among those whom we have brought here is a finer man than whoever was previously deemed the very most excellent in this land. I wish now to make recompense for the loss of your husbands. Do not fail to make the most of this, and do not rebuff any man here who is without a wife. For in these men you shall find everything for which a woman could possibly wish in this world.

(6727-6744) "If you should bring shame upon yourselves by refusing, and if they should be compelled to ride off alone to their own lands, you would never again have the chance for such great fame as can now be yours. Therefore, choose a husband, each and every one of you, so that a great host of them will remain here in Cluse. I shall reward you with gifts and with favors. Whoever rejects this and disobeys my instructions, however, shall stand in disfavor with me. Accordingly, it is my decree that none of you should hang her head in shame, that there be no disgrace at all attendant to what transpires here today. For my full favor is granted to all who now carry out my wish."

(6745-6766) Whatever joy was at first held back was now unleashed in full measure. To be sure, the women would have raged angrily in protest, save that Daniel had pledged that there was no dishonor in what they were to do that day. Hence, a ceremony was held there which seldom if ever took place anywhere before or since: each lady asked a knight whether or not he had already trothed himself to any woman. If he replied no, then the lady asked straightway: "Then do you wish me, my lord?"[207] Thus did each such knight forfeit both his heart and his mind at a lady's willing offer of love. Not deeming himself worthy of that love, he otherwise would never have dared wish for it for as long as he should live.

(6767-6789) By the time the decree had circulated throughout the court that each knight should take whichever lady he wished, those courtiers experienced for the first time a deep joy which brought tranquility to lodge within their hearts. Their discourse and their entreaty on that happy day were conducted in this fashion: the knight approached the lady and, embracing her, spoke: "Do you wish to have me, my lady, as your husband?" "Indeed, my lord, and I shall give praise to God if you have set your heart upon me." "Yes, my lady, you may be certain that my love for you is yet stronger than yours for me." Thereupon they kissed one another in a manner utterly devoid of disrepute. When was there ever another day so resplendent with joy! Such a day as this, I fancy, shall never again be seen![208]

(6790-6812) He who was to be lord in that land was both courtly and brave. This he demonstrated in manifold ways. For Daniel now found his knights insufficient in number to make recompense to all of the ladies for their lost husbands. Yet he quickly devised a remedy for making amends to those ladies: six hundred of his squires he took aside, wishing to grant them their will and thereby win their good favor. All of them were nephews of King Arthur's comrades. Striving to enhance the security of his land, Daniel dubbed them knights on the spot. He also bestowed upon them, once having found the proper moment, garments so splendidly radiant that all who beheld them thought and said aloud that the angels in heaven could be forever joyous if God were to clothe them in such gowns as these!

(6813-6832) Moreover, Daniel ordered them to be given such fine horses that no one claiming to be at all generous of heart, whether man or woman, can deny Daniel his praise. Wherever one might expect to find wood or iron on the riding equipment, there stood pure silver, on which were embellished with the most exquisite skill all such decorations as the mind could ever imagine. The men of the Round Table thought this all to be most marvelous indeed! And they agreed amongst themselves that though they had in many lands seen splendid riding accoutrements and lavish clothing in which the highest mastery was evident, nonetheless all of that had been but a trifle in comparison.

(6833-6846) As the young knights rode off together to court, many a tongue spoke of how no man had ever beheld clothes as rich and elegant as those which they wore. The horses, whenever spurred into motion, glistened brightly with the reflection of the sun. Indeed, so blindingly did they sparkle and burn that those charged with tending the horses were scarcely able to endure the brilliant shimmer!

(6847-6862) These lads, invested in their newly acquired order of knighthood, deported themselves so skillfully and so decorously that no one who beheld them could deny that they fulfilled every demand of perfection. For this reason the ladies of Cluse held their new husbands dear. And once those ladies saw that their spouses were possessed of all good qualities, many a courtly stranger in that land was accorded the sort of welcome reserved for the head of a household. It had turned out well for both the men and the women alike that they were to remain there together.

(6863-6884) Once the widows had been provided for, and once their every lamentation had been duly banished, all the sights and sounds of entertainment and games expected at a festival were now evident in great abundance there. Lady Bliss was granted her will in so many ways, for it was she who was praised and esteemed and who wore the crown upon her head that day. It was Bliss who had so splendidly extracted obedience from all of those courtiers, and her virtuous name was most worthily honored. All of the assembled guests fixed their hearts upon her alone. So mightily did Bliss hold sway that she could not possibly have hoped to fare any better, and she sat there enthroned in her lofty dignity.

XIV

KING ARTHUR IS ABDUCTED

(6885-6899) Then suddenly Bliss was rudely struck, so that the crown dropped from her head and she herself, quite against her will, fell sprawling before the throne, landing in a puddle of water. In her place, though uninvited, sat Care, who trampled Bliss beneath her feet. This was most unjust, and Bliss was at once so disdained that no one missed her or even bothered to see where she lay. This was a frightful blow, which robbed her of all her sublimity.[209]

(6900-6932) Listen now and I shall tell you how it came about that this misfortune befell Lady Bliss. Just as all the guests were caught up with joy, there came walking up a most peculiar man who wore but a silken tunic and silken breeches, being bare of all else that men are wont to wear.[210] He was neither unduly large nor unduly small, his complexion was most radiant, and his hair was well-kempt, gray and white, and with curls. As he strode into the court, he bore a club in his hand and knocked the people back away from him, commanding them to clear a path. All—both the poor and the rich alike—who saw him pushing forward in this manner, swinging his club about with mighty blows, were quick to make way for him. Finally he came before the throne. He cried out so that he was heard by all, and he commanded them to fall silent. Then he asked to be shown to the loftiest man in their midst. Sir Gawein was the first to speak up; he pointed out King Arthur and gestured the stranger to where Arthur was seated, for he was undisputedly the most exalted of them all.

(6933-6947) The wondrous man then spoke: "Make room for me, all of you! I wish to show you a game which you shall all have to agree is most exceptional. For I am well convinced that no man has ever observed a game so extraordinary as this." They fancied this would be an amusing sport, and so they quickly stepped back to make room. The man then said: "I must be able to see the field, or else this game cannot be undertaken." They now cleared a path for him in the proportions which he himself prescribed.

(6948-6973) Hear now of what then happened to them: the man walked up to King Arthur and, placing his arm around him, snatched him up like a wisp of straw (a most amazing theft was this!) and carried him off right under their noses! So swiftly did he run off that there was no one in their midst able to catch up with him on horseback, though many made the attempt. King Arthur's men found this game not only disagreeable, but quite loathsome as well! Daniel and Gawein, Parzival and Iwein, all greatly dismayed, were soon off in hot pursuit. With lowered lances, they were most eager to requite this man for his actions by taking his life. And they swore in their hearts to accomplish as much! Even the horses were compelled to shed some blood,[211] for many fine heroes set out in angry pursuit.

(6974-6982) It was in this manner that Bliss was dislodged, such that no one searched for her, nor even cared what had become of her! For they had lost the one man whom they had chosen to be a crown of joy and the mirror of all valor. "Oh woe!" they all cried out, "we shall never again set eyes upon the king!"

(6983-6996) That man who bore the king off ran with immense speed: with Arthur in his clutches, he darted like the very wind itself! Those two giants who had been slain there were his sons. (King Arthur's men had heard one of them speak of his father's speed and cunning, which were unsurpassed in all the world!) No creature was ever endowed with such properties of body and mind that it could have outstripped that man. Not even a bird could have outflown him as he ran!

(6997-7006) Nonetheless King Arthur's men continued their pursuit, hoping to prevent him from proceeding any farther once they came to the mountain. But they quickly discerned that the man was carrying King Arthur up onto the mountainside. Seeing this, they were filled with desolation in no small measure, for they were unable to pursue him onto such terrain.

(7007-7026) They dismounted from their steeds in an instant and were about to climb up after him, for no one could prevent them from doing so! Those who wished to live, however, were forced to give up the idea, since no man could do so without falling to his death. They were all left standing there gaping in dismay! The ascent up to the place where he had carried the king would have been dizzying enough even for an ape. Had it been of any avail, there was a great host of archers who would have readily shot the man. But no good would have come of that either, as King Arthur and his abductor would both have plunged to their deaths. Thus they all chose to allow him to abduct the king rather than to kill them both.

(7027-7036) Once the intruder had scurried up the mountainside nearly out of the range of their bows, he set King Arthur down onto a terrifying ledge from which he could move neither up nor down, nor to one side or the other. Had Arthur budged but an inch from that ledge, he would have taken a plunge which he could not have survived even if made of steel.

(7037-7050) The sight of this was enough to make all of the courtiers—men and women alike—sink into immeasurable gloom. The old man then climbed back down the same dizzying path until he was well within earshot. Hear now his words: he commanded them all to fall silent and to forgo all talking.[212] Not a one of them made a sound, for great was their distress as to why the king had been abducted and how he should ever escape from that ledge.

(7051-7067) The old man then spoke: "For as long as I still have the use of my God-given senses, you shall all pay with your lives—you who are to blame for my dear sons' having been so horribly hacked to pieces! I shall not rest until such time as I avenge this on you and shatter your joy, just as you have done to me. You shall not escape punishment for the demise of my sons!" They were about to shoot the old man, but Daniel admonished those foolish people against taking his life.

(7068-7078) "The king has been placed out onto a ledge," he said to them all, "from which he will of necessity plunge to his death if we cannot peacefully convince this man to bring him back down to us. If you possess any good sense at all, you will desist from shooting him. As long as he holds the king captive, I advise you to let this man live, regardless of what may happen to us in consequence."

(7079-7094) Daniel then turned to the old man and spoke: "It appears you can use any means you wish against us (nor do you appear averse to doing so!) without our being able to harm you in the least. Your armor is so sturdy[213] that you will easily hold your own against us—no matter how long the king may sit up there on the ledge. However, if we should manage to win him back, then you would most certainly have to give us a full accounting of your behavior:[214] of why your courtesy prompts you to appear before us unarmed (we had not even seen you coming!) and to threaten an entire army single-handedly. Why do you wish to harm the king, and how is it that you intend to kill us all?"

(7095-7122) The old man then replied: "I shall apprise you of this:[215] each one of you I shall drag up onto this mountain and set down on a spot where you would grow old and gray before any man devised a scheme to bring you back down again.[216] You shall all die of starvation first![217] This is how you shall have to perish—as many of you as I can capture—and believe me, I shall gladly endeavor to catch a great many of you! In truth, as a result of your designs the ground is well washed with the blood of my sons, whom you have slain. Hence the wind will parch and emaciate on this mountain as many of you as fall to my lot. I shall cut my prey off from all that they ever possessed, such that they shall enjoy not the least bit of pleasure from any of it—

until finally they are ravaged by the sword of hunger and lie dead. This is an even more wretched torture than if I were to requite them with lance or sword!

(7123-7134) "Is there is any man amongst you who is of such a mind that, alone and unarmed, he dares to draw close to the rock, so that I can grab him by the hand? If so, then let him determine thereby whether he is able to wrench me down—or whether I possess the strength to haul him up to a spot where he shall be bereft of all help. Is any one of you so brave as to approach me and put this to the test?"

(7135-7149) Many a volunteer did the old man find amongst them, for over a thousand cried out: "Yes, I shall go, I shall go!" Thus did they all clamor, yet nothing came of it, and this is why: none was willing to see the next man go, and as a consequence they all were forced to forgo the challenge. Seeing this, the old man demanded their silence and spoke: "You are *all* free of fear! Now tell me in truth, however: who is the very finest man amongst you? Such a man ought surely to thirst for the fame which is to be won here."

(7150-7165) There was not a man among them who would presume to speak up, for it would have been unseemly to say: "I am the finest!"[218] Likewise, they were aware that it would be misbecoming to name any other man as capable of taking on such a challenge. For if that man were to die in pursuit of fame, or even if he encountered great tribulation, others might distort things and perchance assert that he who named him had done so out of animosity or out of desire to see him lose his life—even though he may simply have meant to do him honor.

(7166-7186) Thus for a good while many a man's lips remained sealed—out of the courtly misconception that anyone would fall into disrepute who said openly: "I am the finest of all who have journeyed here." On the other hand, if one said: "This or that man is the finest," then he would be blamed if that man were slain as a result. Hence, no one was willing to speak up. At long last Parzival, that excellent hero, broke the ice of their good breeding. He was too courageous a knight to leave the king trapped up on the mountainside, and he spoke: "If I am to tell the truth, I myself am the most praiseworthy man present here. I have no witness to this, but I wish instead to praise myself. If this is considered madness on my part, then I am willing to endure such a charge, as long as I may do battle with you."

(7187-7215) Leaving his sword behind and showing no trace of arrogance, Parzival walked toward the old man in his armor. Seeing this, the intruder scrambled down from the mountainside. A battle then took place that was free of swords, but short of duration. For the old man leaped down from the rock and, grabbing Parzival with one arm, climbed back up to where he had previously stood. Never have you heard tell of such fierce gestures as those Parzival then made, for he was most outraged at being forced to follow that man! Most furiously did he defend himself! So frenzied was Parzival's struggle that no devil ever existed who could have restrained him gently. Yet this was to be the cause of great distress for Parzival, for so vehemently did he resist that the old man, angered by this, hurled Parzival down onto a rock—a blow which left Parzival pallid as though with death. So mighty was the impact that his heart very nearly burst in two!

(7216-7242) With that, a loud clamor arose down below. All of them, save for Daniel alone, cried out that this man should be killed. Why, then, did they permit him to live? Daniel entreated them to forgo this and to await his return there, for he would bring back help which would be their salvation. He then set out in haste, for it was his plan to win a truce from the old man, once he had acquired that same net in which the Maiden of the Green Meadow had once found him entrapped. To this end Daniel departed at once, concerned about the outcome and in haste to secure the net. He was most vexed that the king was a prisoner under such wretched circumstances, and that

Parzival himself was little better off. It was a journey of but two miles, and Daniel's steed raced along paying full heed to his spurs.

(7243-7256) When in a crisis, a courageous man spares neither his own safety nor his possessions. He, however, who shamefully refuses to risk what he owns has acquitted himself in such a way that, if it were up to me, I should never let him call himself a man. For I would checkmate[219] any esteem which he might have enjoyed and I would refuse him all claim to integrity. It is a nefarious man indeed (whether anyone wishes to agree with me or not!) who possesses material goods, but lacks a sense of honor.

(7257-7266) Daniel's steed was obedient, and in a short time he arrived at the Green Meadow, where the maiden spotted him as he was riding up to the court. There he received, in truth, a most worthy reception: the maiden recognized Daniel straightway and came running (not walking!) out to meet him.

(7267-7284) Before he had even fully dismounted, she embraced him most nobly and exclaimed: "Welcome, in God's name!" She kissed him sweetly and pressed him to her bosom, with the words: "I wish to lament to God the fact that neither I nor anyone else can fully value the service which you have accorded me. And I further lament my ignorance as to how to requite you for this service, so that I might gain your favor and thereby become as precious to you as you are to me. Nothing more grievous has ever beset me than that I might fall the least bit short of achieving this. For I would willingly serve you if only I knew how!"

(7285-7301) The knight Daniel then said in reply: "If you are pleased by what I have done for you, then by all means show me so! For you now have occasion to gain my full favor. Indeed, the service which you can render me in a very short time, if you are willing, far outweighs any service which I could ever expect of you. Unless you help me to elude the distress which has beset me, my joy will have been relinquished for all eternity in exchange for everlasting death."

Von der grünen owe
Also gebunden ynne fant
Des endes kerte er zu hant
Im was ernst und gach
Der von und dar nach
In begunde sere belangen
Das der kunig gefangen
Also gar jemerlichen saß

Und her parcifal lutzel baß
Do waren zwo mylen dar
Die lieff das rosse gar
Das es nye anders getratt
Den als er es mit den sporen batt

Plate 10. Daniel seeks aid in the Land of the Green Meadow.
Ms. germ. 1340, leaf 182ʳ.

"How has this come about?" she asked. "Is my father still well?" "I left him this very hour," Daniel replied, "free of all care."

(7302-7330) Daniel then told her the tale of how the outlandish man had captured first King Arthur and afterwards Parzival. "Hasten now and journey there together with me," he then said. "There is so much at stake here for me that—for as long as I shall live—I can never hope to requite you for your good will. Never did you need me as urgently as I now need you! I am quite convinced that if you bring your net to that spot and place it in the path which he takes as he descends, then you shall put a stop once and for all to his climbing about! Then God would force him to spare our lives and to surrender to us his two prisoners. It is for this reason that I have come here. Do not tarry now any longer, for I am most eager to be off! I shall requite you for your aid, in whatever way you wish." "Fear not," she answered, "and be of good cheer. For I shall capture this man for you in but an instant!"

(7331-7346) Not a single man was present there save Daniel. Thus it was her damsels whom she addressed, ordering them to make great haste and to bring her a horse. As they were trying to ready the steed as rapidly as possible, not a one of those damsels was able to apply the saddle or the bit, try as they may. Daniel himself then quickly stepped in and busied himself with these tasks. He thought it none too soon, for he could scarcely wait until it was all accomplished. When the lady saw this, she hastened all the more in her own preparations, as Daniel was glad to see.

(7347-7362) It was meet and proper that a powerful king should so willingly prepare the lady's horse and lead it up to her like an eager squire; for it was critical to Daniel that they waste not a moment's time. And there was no cause for Daniel to blush with shame on account of the lowly tasks which he had performed there. God Himself is of such a mind that He finds fault with nothing which a man does when compelled by proper circumstances. Whoever finds disgrace in such actions is wanting in good sense!

(7363-7382) Once helped into the saddle, the maiden set out at a fast amble—one that was in fact well nigh a trot! For she was well aware from what Daniel had said that, no matter how quickly they might arrive there, it would not be soon enough for him. Daniel continued to whip his horse on harder and harder. The lady was greatly troubled by the anguish which he voiced and by the deep concern which he displayed for King Arthur's safety. Thus they arrived at Cluse in a very short time. Assembled at the foot of the mountain they found both the men of the Round Table and all the inhabitants of that land who could rightly distinguish between honor and shame.

(7383-7394) All of them were lamenting the harm that had so cruelly fallen upon the noble King Arthur. They feared that Arthur might have to send home to Britain a most dismal tale, for the distress which he was suffering dashed all hope that he might come away unharmed in body. They were grieved not only by this harsh stroke of ill fortune, but also by the fact that no one knew how to fetch him down from the ledge safe and sound.

(7395-7416) In the midst of their woe Daniel, and with him the Maiden of the Green Meadow, both came up on horseback. Her father spotted them and cried out with unbounded joy: "Welcome, both of you!"[220] The assembled knights and ladies followed suit. Wasting no time, they set about the preparations: as soon as the maiden had dismounted onto the turf, she made ready her net. Daniel led her to the spot where she was to set it up. Gladly did she go about doing this, spurred on by her sense of duty and by Daniel's bidding! Yet no one could see what she was doing, save her mother and her father. And both of them Daniel enjoined to say nothing until such time as they should behold the old man entangled in that net.

(7417-7434) All of those present had shuddered at the sight (this I have already related to you!) of Parzival's being dragged so roughly up the mountainside. Since then the old man had been standing there fiercely taunting them with questions as to whether any one else among them wished to try his luck. No one dared to go near the old man since they had all just witnessed the apparent death-blow to Parzival. This was the excuse which they all proffered: "There is not a man among us who is brave enough. Wait, however, until King Daniel returns. He shall spar with you forthwith!" The old man then sat down on the face of the cliff, awaiting Daniel's arrival, so that he might slay him.

(7435-7453) Daniel was apprised of this, and he remained silent for safety's sake. Nor did he reveal himself until he had heard the maiden say: "The net is now in place. Go and stand at that spot, and bid him descend. He shall be unable to lay a hand on you!" At this, Daniel of the Blossoming Valley cried out at the old man: "They all say that you wish to engage in a tug-of-war with me. Can you assure me that this is so? I am also told that you intend to inflict misfortune upon me. Are you still of such a mind?" "Indeed I am," he replied. "Then on with it!" said Daniel, who then ordered that his sword be carried off.

(7454-7486) This was to the old man's utter satisfaction. He commanded the people to stand back, whereupon he flew at Daniel at an immense speed, rushing like a blind man straight into the middle of the net. He would gladly have taken Daniel as his third captive, but a different outcome was awaiting him: he became so utterly enmeshed in that net that he lost all hope of survival; he was in such agony that he cried out for help and thrashed about in an attempt to rip the net apart. But try as he would, he was compelled to abandon all hope of that. He would not, however, refrain from his fierce outburst until he had rendered himself incapable of moving even his hands or his feet in this straitjacket hold. He was completely held in fetters. Once more, however, his heart, which was robust and wrathful, smoldered with anger at being so crippled, and he squirmed about like a netted fish. Finally he was reduced, despite all his strength, to such timidity that he lay there as if dead, so overwhelming a nightmare was this for him!

(7487-7503) Whatever man has exquisite cunning at his command is deserving of all the more praise from everyone, both men and women alike. For one man alone can accomplish with cunning that which a thousand men, however strong they might be, could never do together. You may see an example of this in the old man: for had he been able to gain the upper hand, he would have carried Daniel up the mountainside, where none of that knight's helpless lamentation would have been of any avail. Yet if the old man had proceeded using cunning, all their strength combined would have been utterly useless. Thus, by having the maiden so effortlessly capture the old man in this net, Daniel had made most excellent use of his cunning.

(7504-7522) Whoever takes issue with what I say ought to be considered a foolish man: for it should be viewed as good and honorable that one be possessed of cunning, provided it is applied justly and prudently. Many men are vehemently opposed to learning upright things, claiming in the manner of fools that one might come to know too much. Such men are not wise enough to marshal their own good sense! If a man learned all of the skills which God has ever conceived and created on this earth, what harm could come of that? He who is laden with the burden of wisdom bears an easy load indeed. Never has there been, I fancy, a burden so easily borne, for the burden of wisdom is heavy, yet also supple.

(7523-7548) Whoever places both skill and wisdom into his coffer can expect an ample supply to keep for himself and to share with others. Even if he should live to be a thousand years of age, he can learn as much as he wishes from such a coffer, yet it will never become empty. He can readily give of it to whomever he wishes and still have the same portion left in his coffer. If he is of upright character, his propriety will win him both fame and material goods, as well as friends in abundance.[221] If a man were ever so constituted that he could possess the beauty of Absalom and the strength of Samson,[222] and yet if he were at the same time a fool, then even three such men together could not compare with a man possessed of good breeding. What good is a man who cannot distinguish between good and evil? Far better is the character of an upright man who is able to discriminate between good and evil: for such temperament provides splendid teaching as to what one ought and ought not to do.[223]

(7549-7573) Hear now of what those courtiers did once they saw the old man enmeshed in the net (this was a great blessing for them!): they ran up to that spot amidst great clamor, and in unison they praised both God and the maiden that they should see the intruder entrapped before their very eyes. The maiden was then received a thousand times more warmly than before. Indeed, they would have gladly lifted her onto their shoulders with gratitude had they been asked to do so! They were all beside themselves with joy! All of those present offered their fealty to her, and she was acclaimed in a manner befitting a goddess. Queen Danise,[224] who wore the crown there in Cluse, offered the maiden most proper thanks for having arrived so gallantly and for having delivered them from their fear of the old man.

(7574-7584) "If I live to see it," said the queen, "this service which you have rendered us shall be for you a shield against all care. I shall not rest until such time as I have amply demonstrated my appreciation for this favor which you have shown me!" Thus the Maiden of the Green Meadow came to be so highly praised that it benefitted her for the rest of her life.

(7585-7605) Those fine knights, as they raced up to the net, caused such a clamor that it could be heard far and wide. Indeed, so deafening was their hue and cry that nothing else could even be distinctly heard. Finally, that din of theirs was silenced upon command. Thus a hush fell over the gathering, and Daniel addressed

Plate 11. Queen Danise thanks the Maiden of the Green Meadow.
Ms. germ. 1340, leaf 188v.

the old man: "You are responsible, both directly and indirectly, for great misery on our part. Why ought we even to spare your life, now that we hold you prisoner? Instead, we ought to insure once and for all that we will be safe from your wiles. You have so ruthlessly wrought death upon us[225] that you yourself shall without fail reap the selfsame reward! If you could hold us captive as we do you, then you would certainly deal us the final blow.

(7606-7616) "Therefore you must likewise suffer death straightway. If my sword will not penetrate your skin, then I shall turn it around and dash in your skull with the hilt, before I will ever allow you to live. You have practiced intemperance against us, and since we have captured you, you shall most surely die for having dealt in death yourself."

(7617-7642) The old man then replied: "You shall be forever laden with my ingratitude if I am to live as much as half a day. I prefer to die than to live on, and I ask nothing of you save death alone. I am so pained in body and in spirit that I no longer desire to live. My only wish is this: to test my luck against you with all my faculties and then (if I should come away from here alive) to realize my fate by bringing about your demise. For you have burdened my heart with everlasting sorrow, and life is worthless to me. Do not prolong my suffering, for you have turned my life into such deep anguish! I shall be glad the sooner you put an end to it. It is foolish of you to fail to do so, for if you do let me live, then your own death shall be inescapable!"

(7643-7661) Vexed by these words, Daniel then replied: "You are most certainly a man of good sense! How is it that you could ever be so bereft of reason? How do you dare *ask* to be killed on the spot? You yearn for a woe which no man should hasten to experience. It is fitting that a wise man know what it is he speaks. Even if for twenty-four days on end he spoke the wisest words of wisdom ever uttered, nonetheless, if but a single word of that were false, others would take note of the falsely-spoken utterance a thousand times more keenly than of all his wisdom. Thus he would incur the loss of his acclaim and of his good name.

(7662-7695) "I condemn you in no small measure for your lack of wisdom in the counsel which you offered your king. For whether out of sincere loyalty to him or out of desire for some reward, you advised King Matur to undertake this base scheme (which was to be his downfall!): you had him dispatch your son to King Arthur and order him seized in a most disgraceful fashion at his own court; and you furthermore counselled him to threaten King Arthur's life if he refused to surrender himself and all his possessions. In great arrogance did your son then set out toward King Arthur's court to fulfill the command of your lord. Neither God nor man could have prevented our returning with him to this land. As soon as we arrived here and confirmed that he intended to subject us to oppression unbecoming to us, we rejected this on the spot. In consequence he has taken nearly all our lives. However, we have rewarded him in turn with the selfsame ruin. Had we spared him despite his persecution of us, then whatever scheme might have entered his mind would have been the vehicle of our death.

(7696-7716) "A blow in self-defense was never forbidden an angry man, for if he cannot otherwise survive, he must defend himself. If he wishes to live, then he eagerly retaliates before he himself lies vanquished on the ground. This is all that we have done! We are not like you, who would willingly surrender your life. We endured great hardship in order to vanquish your sons after they had attacked us and had violently extracted a great toll of life from us. They offered us death, and we declined it. We wreaked no further revenge save to fight off an entire army—but only in self-defense and with but a narrow margin of victory!

(7717-7732) "I wish to say in all truth that none of this would have come to pass, were it not for this one fact: that it was their very iniquity which killed them and which forbade them—in all their haughtiness!—to wrest from us either our lives or our possessions. God has granted them just recompense for their actions. Any man who finds fault with us for this is a fool! Now tell me in truth, if God and your loved ones be at all dear to you: was it at *your* advice that King Matur committed this act of immoderation against us?"

(7733-7759) The old man then said in response: "If indeed they have suffered this misfortune at your hands as a consequence of their own acts of violence, then they rightly deserve all which they have endured. I myself had no part in their actions. If my lord had included me at all in his plans[226] (and he did not!), I would not have permitted this to transpire. Even if I had been unable to thwart their plan, I would have sooner delayed its inception than have aided in carrying it out. If what you claim is true—that they were in pursuit of you—and if they forced you to kill them, then indeed you had no choice but to retaliate just as you have done. There was no other way. Since this is so, I shall now gladly embrace my salvation from death. For if you desire a reconciliation, I shall not be the one to refuse it, inasmuch as it was King Matur who sent my sons (as well as himself and full many a bold hero!) off to their death.

(7760-7782) "I had fancied that it was your own arrogance which brought you here. Much to my misfortune, I was not apprised of their plan and knew not that it was being carried out, until such time as I beheld my children lying on the ground bereft of life. Since I have lost them on account of my lord, I shall now forgo my anger. Grant to me now your gracious favor as recompense for my great loss and as evidence of your goodness. For you have greatly impaired my joy, and you can reap lasting fame by now treating me with all the more favor, provided I forswear my wrath. I can prove myself well deserving of this in whatever way you wish. If you are now in need of counsel, I can offer you advice straightway which shall serve to augment your good name."

(7783-7808) Daniel rejoiced at this and bade the maiden make haste to release the man forthwith and to disentangle him from the net. His command was soon fulfilled, and the old man, once freed, then asked: "What manner of thing is this, oh noble lady? Do tell me more of it." "It is a net," she replied. "Any man for whom I set it, be he strong or weak, suffers the very same fate as you." "Are you able to see it?" he asked. "Indeed! How could I do anything with it if I could not see it?" "How is it then that I am so blind?" he inquired; "this I ask of you: can everyone present here view the net?" "There are but three persons present who are able to see it." "If it could ever come to pass," the old man responded, "that I were to be so blessed as to behold this net, then I would be happy beyond all measure!"

(7809-7820) "If it will be at all pleasing to you," she said, "I shall not refuse you this request. I have with me here an ointment more excellent than any other which you or I have ever seen. If I apply but a small portion of it to your eyes, your eyesight will become so sharp that even the blackest of nights will be to you as a summer day, and even the net will thereby be rendered clear and easily visible."

(7821-7830) The old man answered: "I would be willing to part with all which I have in my possession, a thousand marks in gold and more! All of that I would gladly relinquish in order that these two objects, the net and the ointment, might belong to me. Indeed, if they were for sale, I should give half the world, were it mine, in exchange for them!"

(7831-7842) The Maiden of the Green Meadow then said in reply: "Keep your possessions, but bring down for us your captives from atop that cliff! As soon as that has been accomplished, I shall give you both the net and the ointment, so that we may all live in friendship with you and in an everlasting bond of loyalty unmarred by animosity."

(7843-7859) Once the old man had heard that he was so close to possessing that which he prized so highly, he bowed down at her feet as a sign of his willingness to aid her, and he then vaulted off with the swiftness of a hart. He exerted all his energies to assist those to whom he had previously denied his favor and whom he had disgraced. Thus was his scorn transformed into loyal friendship, for he most willingly bore the king back down from atop the cliff. Then he scrambled back up and carried Parzival down as well.

(7860-7873) All were full of joy that they were now freed from their anguish, and King Arthur spoke: "All favors which I have ever incurred were as naught compared to this. Only now do I know what true bliss is! For so overjoyed am I now that I shall for evermore be happy! It is a godsend that I have been so graciously rescued from the mountain. Only scarcely did I come away unharmed in body and in mind."

(7874-7883) The king then turned to the old man and said: "I give thanks to God and shall gladly reward you for bringing me down from this ledge. Know likewise that you shall never leave here before I offer recompense, of whatever manner you please, for the grief to which you have been subjected." The maiden then presented to the old man both the net and the ointment.

(7884-7888) Sir Daniel then addressed him: "You have now brought things to a favorable state—so much so in fact that no act of service more pleasing than this has been performed at any time or in any place. If I am at all able, I shall prove to you the truth of this!"

(7889-7904) They delayed no longer, but returned on horseback to the king's throne. No man who ever read of joy, no man who ever witnessed joy, no man who ever heard tell[227] of perfect joy, has ever experienced such bliss as then awaited them there. They bestowed upon Bliss a yet more splendid welcome than before, and they seated her once more upon her lofty throne of grandeur. Her authority then took on so genial an air that all of the courtiers obeyed her command before it could even be issued![228]

XV

THE CONCLUSION OF THE FESTIVAL

(7905-7922) Daniel, who was host in that land, saw to it that they were well contented; he let no one amongst them cast away mirth, for he made certain that they were lacking in nothing. Daniel had many a dear guest at this festival, yet their joy still seemed to him less than whole. He therefore spoke most decorously to King Arthur: "You have accorded me great honor here in Cluse by making me lord over the land. Aid me now in banishing any remaining traces of shame, and I shall be justly grateful to you for evermore. Only then shall I have both material possessions and a good name as well."[229]

(7923-7934) "I should be most delighted," replied King Arthur, "and I would gladly help[230] you to confirm your reputation now, such that no man would take note of any imprudence which you might henceforth commit (something which—although distressing—any man can easily be guilty of).[231] Indeed, I would gladly see done whatever may be proper for you. Tell me now, what is it that you desire?"

(7935-7944) "That my comrades and I might ride to Britain to bring back Queen Guinevere, in order that she should witness the joy now reigning over my land. In so doing, she will in turn invest me with such good fortune that all of my countrymen whose esteem I seek shall forever impart to me even more of that esteem. Thus I shall fare well in all respects."

(7945-7955) "I am well disposed towards you," answered the king. "If you do not possess sufficient stores of gold and precious stones and silken clothing here in Cluse, then I shall give you this advice, which will work to your advantage and will bring no loss to me: when you arrive in Britain, order my courtiers to load for you twenty-four beasts of burden so that you need not impoverish your land of such goods."

(7956-7969) "Have my thanks for this," Daniel laughed, "but I need to import neither gold nor fine clothing. For so rich are my provisions that I am well furnished with everything that is sought after in all the world." Daniel then asked as many of his comrades as were present and still without wives that they willingly ride off with him to Britain. This was a request easily fulfilled, for they did whatever Daniel bade them.

(7970-7974) "I entrust it to you," spoke Daniel to the king, "to see to it that my guests be lacking in nothing that is needed for their enjoyment." To this King Arthur replied: "I shall certainly pledge my word to accomplish that!"

(7975-7987) Hear now the number of men whom Daniel selected to accompany him: there were six hundred of them who embarked upon the journey with him. He allowed to remain in Cluse all of those who had so recently chosen wives. This he did not out of any ill-feeling, but merely that the festival might proceed with undiminished joy in anticipation of his return. Daniel was a man well skilled in cultivating his own good name!

(7988-8007) While underway, Daniel bade his companions, as a favor to him, to permit their wives to accompany the queen back to Cluse. All of them pledged to do so without objection. Thus they rode with great fanfare into the land of Britain. Once there, they wasted little time before setting out upon the return journey. Lanzelet and Sir Erec were now at court, as well as the others whom King Arthur had had to leave behind because they were out on diverse paths in search of adventure. They now lamented the fact that fate had failed to bring word to them of King Arthur's campaign.

(8008-8026) Another brave hero, whose heart pumped solely with thirst for fame, had in the meantime arrived at King Arthur's court. This man was the Duke of Zone. He had travelled there because he had often heard tell that any man who had once been in Britain would become so excellent that the shadow of dishonor would never once darken his path, regardless where his adventures might lead him thereafter. He could not banish this thought from his mind, and he had often fancied at home in his own court that the mighty King Arthur might dub him a knight. It was to this end that he had journeyed to Britain. Beladigant was his name.[232]

(8027-8043) Upon seeing him, Daniel inquired as to his name and his business there. This he told Daniel forthwith, adding that he was a man who eagerly strove after knightly repute, and that he would gladly enhance his reputation at King Arthur's court. He was prepared, he said, to do whatever was necessary for this if the king would display such courtliness towards him as to receive him into his fellowship of knights. "I have heard tell," he said, "of the greatness of King Arthur's valor. This is why I am come here, in the hope of benefitting from his excellence."

(8044-8053) "You need have no misgivings," replied Daniel forthwith, "about having departed your land in search of this. You have not arrived too late, indeed you have come at an opportune moment! Inasmuch as you have set out in search of reward and fame, I shall take it upon myself that you might find all of this in ample measure."

(8054-8056) "You give me good cause for comfort, my lord," replied Beladigant. "May God reward you for that! I shall gladly and earnestly prove myself worthy of it."

(8057-8078) As soon as Daniel saw that all of his comrades had arrived with their ladies, they all embarked with him upon the journey. They were most eagerly intent upon this—and not merely because it was expected of them.[233] With much jubilation Queen Guinevere (a lady unparalleled in excellence!) was borne off along with eighty maidens. A splendid entourage they were, arriving joyously in Cluse without incident. Great acclaim fell to King Arthur's lot there. The guests all hastened and ran out to greet the ladies, as was wholly befitting their lofty name. For they were greatly pleased at Guinevere's arrival.

(8079-8102) The festival then resumed with yet louder jubilation than before Queen Guinevere's coming. Daniel's esteem was likewise greatly magnified because she had come there for his sake. Whatever man struggles undauntedly in the quest for fame will attain his goal. For this reason did they speak that day of Daniel's good fortune. Thus, thanks and appreciation are due both to God and to Daniel that King Arthur was able to celebrate there in Cluse that same sumptuous festival which he had in previous years always held in Britain. My advice is that all of you should see a just outcome in this. On the other hand, you might well be distressed if Daniel's acclaim had been but meager, for he had striven with unstinted mettle in quest of such acclaim.

(8103-8109) As soon as King Arthur had heard of Sir Beladigant's wish to be inaugurated into knighthood, he gladly granted him his request and dubbed him a knight on the spot. Sir Beladigant was thus made a comrade of King Arthur.

(8110-8121) The strains of music now swelled up—the fiddle and the flute, playing in all the chords ever devised so as to please the ear. Thus those courtiers could not have imagined[234] that anyone whose heart soared with joy could be as blissful as they were there in the land of Cluse. Wondrous things could be seen and heard there, things which would be long in relating. Be not loath, however, to hear some of what they enjoyed as entertainment.

(8122-8140) A man who can listen well to a story is truly a blessed man, and I shall tell you why: whatever time he spends in such pursuit (once his mind has already disposed of practical matters) is time which cannot be devoted to melancholy thoughts. Thus he is free of any such dismal preoccupation. For as long as he sits there and listens attentively, his time is not spent in vain. Even when he makes no great gains, as long as he also loses nothing, he keeps himself occupied. It is by no means a waste to pass one's time with entertainment if such brings joy to the listener.[235]

(8141-8151) Three hundred French fiddlers[236] were in attendance there, and they were both skilled and renowned. These I have selected, for they were true masters of their art. Indeed, I discern not a single one amongst them less than fully proficient. Yet I shall nonetheless speak no further of them, lest I should lose your good favor. Artistic dexterity has ever been a source of edification for man. Therefore it is good that one be able to call upon such talents.

(8152-8167) Sixty German minstrels, unequaled in their art, were heard there bowing their strings, and the jangle of tambourines with little bells filled the air. Flutes of diverse types[237] melted away all the cares of the guests, and a hundred harpists[238] fashioned a most exquisite melody, for which they were well rewarded. And twenty vocalists, who sang songs of love to banish all distress, and whose throats warbled sweetly, could likewise be heard at court.

(8168-8182) People were seen engaged in extraordinary dances,[239] and lances were being hurled. What man could fail to enjoy all of this? Pages scurried about to win prizes, no one amongst that gathering was in ill humor, and readings were held from various works in French.[240] Physical prowess is likewise a worthy pastime, and it was common to see a man capable of lifting with one arm a fortress of immeasurable girth. Whoever grew weary of watching this could observe men able to run with the speed of a bird.[241] The entertainment was augmented by bows and cross-bows which fired off arrows and bolts.[242]

(8183-8201) Not to be missed were the knightly jousts with the crack of splintering lances. The horses cantered about high-spiritedly, pages[243] cried out (of them there were a great many on hand!), and all manner of board games were also played. Falcons and sparrowhawks likewise flew about. Minstrels told lovely tales of knights in combat and of the flowers which adorned the ladies' many wreaths and garlands.[244] They held the widest round-dance of which I have ever heard tell in all my days: more than twenty hundred knights and ladies could be seen taking part! Lady Bliss was awakened and forbidden to fall back asleep!

(8202-8213) Many a wondrous document did they read out—documents which told of knowledge and of learning.[245] Any man who wished to cast off his cares surely found occasion to do so there. The ladies all had shade from the exquisitely plumaged Babians which constantly hovered over them. The elephants which in that land bore palaces on their backs were driven here and there.

(8214-8228) The blaring peal of ever so many trumpets[246] was to be heard far and wide, so that a man could whisper into his neighbor's ear and not even be overheard by others—as long as his neighbor were not deaf! If ever you have heard tell of anyone who has been present at knightly festivals and who claims to have witnessed one more splendid than this, surely he is lying to you—or else he has beheld the very realm of heaven itself! Such a festival as this could never, I fancy, find its equal. Joy of vast proportions was attendant upon them all![247]

(8229-8238) Sir Beladigant's knightliness was recognized here as exceptional. Thus did King Arthur (who, along with Sir Daniel, watched Beladigant riding his steed) exclaim that that knight was indeed possessed of all manly attributes. The whole multitude of them saw the truthfulness of this. Thus Beladigant acquired the reputation as one of the most excellent of knights—a renown which no man was able to wrest from him.

(8239-8257) The king then summoned him, and Sir Beladigant hastened to join the assembly of knights. Their words were warm with friendship from the outset, and Beladigant was seated between Daniel and King Arthur, who inquired of him: "Have you, at home in your own land, already taken a lady in marriage, sir knight?" "No," came the reply, whereupon King Arthur inquired further, saying: "Tell me this: if you are of such a mind that you wish it, then I shall grant you a wife, possessions, and joy in abundance. All of this I shall bestow upon you in such full measure that surely you shall have to consider yourself a powerful man indeed—unless there is nothing which could *ever* satisfy you!"

(8258-8271) "May my good fortune be put fully to the rout," Beladigant answered, "if I were so dull-witted as to refuse this kind an offer! I am most ready to accept with a willing heart all that you do in my behalf. Indeed, if you so desire, I shall swear an oath that this is all a source of gladness to me! The saying is true: that no man who comes to your court in search of resources shall go astray. For truly you are a noble lord. I have ever heard tell of that, and I am a fortunate man to have seen it confirmed and to have my own name so splendidly aggrandized in consequence."

(8272-8296) King Arthur then had the Maiden of the Green Meadow summoned. He wished to see her forthwith, so as to reward her for having purchased his life with her net and for having saved him. For she had rescued the king just as he had been so utterly engulfed in dire distress. The Maiden of the Green Meadow, who was called Sandinose by name,[248] appeared before King Arthur. She possessed the loveliness of a rose painstakingly fashioned in hues of red and white. No man wishing to possess a maiden embellished with perfection could ever in a thousand years have imagined a damsel crowned with more excellence or more exquisitely adorned with beauty than was she.

(8297-8309) When King Arthur had beheld her, he said to the knight Beladigant: "What do you think of this damsel?" "In truth," Beladigant replied, "I would be blind in all my senses were I to refuse her!" "And how does this knight please you, my lady?" "Very well, my lord," she spoke. This made King Arthur happy, and he bestowed them upon one another with his own hand, commanding that Beladigant be made duke over the land of Cluse.

(8310-8322) King Arthur thereby proved to that maiden his ability to confer a generous reward. He was said to have at his disposal the crowns to a thousand different kingdoms! So manifold was King Arthur's excellence that, even if he has ever suffered bodily death, his name has never perished, but instead shall live on in lofty acclaim for as long as a single upright man remains alive.[249] For King Arthur was always well disposed towards the valiant. He rewarded them for doing their best and for winning both happiness and fame.

(8323-8354) Once having requited the winsome lady so amply for her net and for her efforts, King Arthur inquired forthwith as to where the old man was, and ordered that he be summoned without fail. This was accomplished in quick measure, and the old man, upon hearing this, came at once before King Arthur with the words: "What do you desire of me?" The king had him seated right at his side and inquired astutely as to what he possessed of material goods. "Are you of such a mind," asked King Arthur, "as to return with me to my court in Britain? If so, you shall never leave my side. However, if that is not your will, then whatever I possess—whether far or near—is yours for the asking, regardless how dear to me it may be. I do not reward you for dragging me up the mountainside, for this seemed to me an act of immoderation and caused me great discomfort! I shall gladly requite you, however, for bringing me back down again. Tell me now what manner of recompense you desire from me."

(8355-8364) "I ask for nothing of what you possess," he answered, "save that you permit me to retain the fief which King Matur once granted me—King Matur who never denied me his friendship. Indeed, he was ever well disposed towards me and treated me well. Would that he had but refrained from leading my sons astray and seducing them from my teachings! Never did King Matur disregard my advice—save for this one single time, which was to be his downfall.

(8365-8384) "Beyond this mountain there lies a land which King Matur, by his own hand, once bestowed upon me as a fief. This land is a mile in breadth and is encircled by mountains so craggy and so towering that nothing—be it wild or tame—which I have ever brought there has escaped.[250] Nor can any man or beast enter into this land; I alone am agile enough to be able to come and go as I please. I have assembled there all manner of things which I enjoy as entertainment and as game. My lord enfeoffed me with this land. Now prove your goodness and grant it to me at this time as a fief, since it has now fallen into your possession. I shall gladly serve you in return, as has always been my wont."

(8385-8400) King Arthur then said in reply: "Since no one save you alone can enter or leave this land, I should be a most wretched man to deny this request. Hear now what it is that I mean to say: I should rather own the most frivolous trinket than two such inaccessible lands! Take my hand as a pledge that this land is your own for evermore, and that you are freed from the service which you have thus far performed in return for it. For you shall receive this land as a reward for having cast me into the straits of death and then having helped me out of my tribulation."

(8401-8411) The old man was joyful and bowed most decorously at King Arthur's feet, giving him heartfelt thanks and saying: "My cares are now at an end!" Arthur the mighty king was a just man indeed. How could his praise and his fame ever die out? Indeed, how could they fail to endure for evermore and to be deservedly proclaimed both far and wide?

(8412-8423) Thus the festival lasted for exactly four weeks' time. So rich was that land, however, that they would have been wanting for nothing which they needed even if the festival had continued on for a full year. The guests finally took their leave in a courtly fashion and rode off in high spirits. So richly rewarded were the minstrels that, had they lived for all eternity, they would have remained forever wealthy.

(8424-8443) Ah! how fully had King Arthur garnered the praise of all those present! The Queen of Cluse embraced him just as he was about to take leave of her, and said to him: "May God's blessing be with you! I could not have wished for a finer husband than Daniel even if all the kingdom of earth were mine and I were in my youth and were possessed of the beauty and excellence of all women! Never has a woman received a more splendid reward than that which you have accorded me. I, along with all whom you leave behind here, stand at your command." King Arthur now entrusted her to God's keeping and departed merrily. Twelve hundred of his most cherished men, who had journeyed there with him and had taken wives in the land of Cluse, remained behind.

(8444-8458) There is one thing which shall ever amaze me: that King Arthur was so generous a man and the lords nowadays are so miserly. King Arthur did well to relinquish so readily a land as wealthy as Cluse. For he granted it to a man who always performed King Arthur's will—to a man whom he never needed to petition, since they often rode their steeds together. Whenever the king had need of him, Sir Daniel was already at hand, before even being summoned. Thus King Arthur did not relinquish the land of Cluse, but instead retained both his vassal Daniel and the land as well.[251]

(8459-8469) Daniel dwelt in bliss ever after with a never-ending festival there in his land of Cluse. His life remained without blemish, and he invested his subjects with the very same fiefs which the slain King Matur had granted them, so that they might engage each day in tournament. Daniel bestowed upon them even more than that, so that they would strive yet more zealously than they had in the past. And indeed they fulfilled his will in this regard.

(8470-8478) Never has there lived a man to whom God has conferred a more excellent existence in this world than Daniel, whose life was passed amidst acclaim and without the slightest taint, up until the very day he died. Hence Daniel was—and is even now!—numbered among the very finest of knights. For this reason did his praise spread far and wide.

(8479-8483) Now must I make an end to my story. You have heard all that has reached my ears. May God vouchsafe that we should all enter into His kingdom! Amen.

NOTES

Abbreviations recurring frequently throughout the following notes are: BMZ = Benecke/Müller/Zarncke, *Mittelhochdeutsches Wörterbuch*; Lexer = Lexer, *Mittelhochdeutsches Wörterbuch*; MHG = Middle High German; NHG = New High German [modern German]; PMS = Paul/ Moser/Schröbler, *Mittelhochdeutsche Grammatik*.

CHAPTER I. KING ARTHUR

1. (Verse 3) *der wirt es selten âne muot.* This is an especially enigmatic verse which has been the source of some considerable confusion over the years, coming as it does at the very beginning of the work. Rosenhagen (*Daniel*, p. 175) was unable to explain it fully, and merely stated, somewhat casually, that its meaning is more or less clear from the context. The difficulty is caused by the unusual construction, which—as is obvious from the widely divergent manuscript variants—must likewise have been unfamiliar to the fifteenth-century *Daniel* scribes. Rosenhagen's proposed reading of *anemuot* as an adjective is clearly erroneous, as this would reverse the meaning. The construction can perhaps be adequately—albeit not with any final sense of definitiveness—interpreted as "to have in mind," "to be mindful of." See also Lambel (p. 328).

2. (10) The MHG text actually reads *betwungen* ("mastered," "tamed"), the notion being that the translator must first "overcome" the vagaries of the original language in order to be able to present the story in a second language.

3. (12) *swenne kurzwîle gezimet.* In response to Zwierzina ("Mhd. Studien," pp. 84f.) and Leitzmann ("Strickerstudien," p. 74), Schröder

(p. 65) proposes the emendation of this verse to: *swem kurzwîle gezimet*. In this case the final clauses of the sentence would have to be rendered somewhat differently: "that it might be heard in German by anyone for whom entertainment is proper."

4. (7-14) As Rosenhagen (*Daniel*, p. 175) first pointed out, der Stricker consciously attempted to model this part of the prologue on that of Pfaffe Lamprecht's *Alexander*. Even the notion (v. 14) that any falsehood in the present story would have its roots in the purported original by Alberich (der Stricker: *louc er* [Alberich] *mir, sô liuge ouch ich*) appears to stem nearly verbatim from the *Alexander* (v. 18): *louc er, sô leuge ich*; see Kern (p. 27).

5. (16) This is the only passage in *Daniel* in which the poet explicitly names himself. For a full discussion of the name der Stricker, see INTRODUCTION (p. xii).

6. (1-22) The first twenty-two verses constitute the prologue of *Daniel*. In the manner of his predecessors Gottfried von Strassburg and Wolfram von Eschenbach, der Stricker begins his work with a somewhat enigmatic, proverb-like statement, which is intended to limit his audience to those inclined towards the educative effect of literature. The relationship between *wort* (which I have translated here variously as "literature" and "words") and *werc* ("deeds") is of paramount importance, for the poet posits that whoever hears stories of great deeds will himself go forth and perform such noble feats. Brinkmann ("Prolog," p. 7) refers to this part of the introduction as the *prooemium*—or the "pre-prologue," in which the poet has not yet turned to the task of introducing his work *per se*, but rather, as Brinkmann ("Prolog," p. 10) says, "establishes the conversational situation, the connection between the author and his recipients" ("stellt die Gesprächssituation her, die Verbindung zwischen dem Autor und seinen Empfängern").

Then, with v. 7, der Stricker proffers his almost surely false source, Alberich of Besançon. For a full discussion of the question of the source, see INTRODUCTION (pp. xi, xxiif. and xxviiif.) and esp. Wilhelm ("Fabulistische Quellenangaben," pp. 335f.). Certain critics (in particular Wilhelm and Kern [p. 26]) are of the opinion that der Stricker, rather than merely attempting to establish the authority of his story (which is virtually canonical for works of this age), is in fact satirizing the common practice of claiming a French source. Since the opening lines of the *Alexander* were surely known to at least some of our poet's listeners, this theory appears by no means implausible. Ultimately, however, there are no final answers to the question: to what degree was der Stricker consciously aware of what he was doing in composing *Daniel*? (Is, for example, *Daniel* to be interpreted as the conscious, almost picaresque parody of an Arthurian romance, or was the poet merely unwilling—or unable—to adhere to the established conventions of the genre?)

With v. 12, der Stricker introduces the entertaining aspect of literature, but a scant six or seven lines later he reverts to his true purpose: to educate. For in his admonition to the audience to refrain from colloquy during the performance, we perceive the same didactic poet heard in the *prooemium* as well as in all the many instructive passages which are to ensue during the course of the story itself. Both purposes—*prodesse* (instruction) and *delectatio* (entertainment)—are, as Kern (p. 20) points out, commonly invoked in the prologues of post-classical romances.

7. (23-33) Although der Stricker does not overtly state it, these verses represent a transition to the dilemma faced by our protagonist Daniel in the course of the work: a knight wholly without *guot* (material possessions) of his own possesses the necessary zeal to set out and acquire not only *guot*, but also *êre* (acclaim). On the other hand, the poet claims that any man who possesses wealth, but is lacking in the proper frame of mind, will fail to gain success. Der Stricker introduces in this passage one of the central themes of *Daniel*, one which has become the focus of numerous scholarly interpretations of

this romance. See for example Moelleken/Henderson (pp. 197-99) and Ragotzky ("Handlungsmodell," pp. 186, 189f., 194).

8. (50-58) The narrator engages here in the conventional topos of praise of character, in the process maneuvering through several curious twists and turns in his narrative. First of all, he claims knowledge concerning King Arthur's youth, yet he opts initially not to report on that topic, stating, in effect: "I could tell you more, but no one would believe me." The intended effect of such a statement is apparently to underscore the truthfulness of the original claim. (As Rosenhagen [*Daniel*, pp. 176f.] points out, however, der Stricker would in all likelihood have had to resort to poetic fabrication had he presumed to report on King Arthur's youth.) In the final sentence the narrator appears to transform the whole issue of reporting on this subject into a *præteritio*—which would ultimately require that at least *some* of the details of King Arthur's youth be divulged (cf. v. 58). In the ensuing passage, however, the narrator drops the subject altogether, for although he goes on to relate marvelous things about Arthur as a king, he tells nothing whatsoever of Arthur's youth. On the topos of praise of characters, see Curtius (p. 169); for literature on the *Wahrheitsbeteuerung* ("claim of truthfulness"), see Heinzle (p. 133, n. to 83,1).

9. (65f.) As Kern (p. 23) notes, the idea that King Arthur's men were his *gesellen* ("comrades") appears to stem from Hartmann von Aue's *Iwein* 887f.

10. (78-82) Although der Stricker was indebted to Hartmann von Aue for much of what he knew about Arthurian romance, it is clear from this passage—in which is described Arthur's custom of not eating until he has heard a new tale of adventure—that Hartmann was not our poet's sole source. For this connection between food and tales of knightly bravery does not occur in either of the Arthurian romances of Hartmann. As Kern (p. 24) points out, however, it is present in Chrétien's *Perceval*, Wolfram's *Parzival*, Ulrich's *Lanzelet* and Wirnt's *Wigalois*. See also Rosenhagen (*Daniel*, p. 178) and Baker (p. 69).

11. (94-105) This notion—that the Round Table itself possesses the property of refusing a seat to anyone unworthy of membership in the Arthurian fellowship—appears to be der Stricker's own invention, as I have been unable to uncover it elsewhere. Rosenhagen (*Daniel*, p. 178) offers several possible outside sources for this idea.

CHAPTER II. DANIEL'S ARRIVAL AT THE COURT

12. (143-62) Der Stricker's depiction of Keii in *Daniel* is not only quite consistent with the portrayal of this character in the classical Arthurian romances, but is also strongly reminiscent of corresponding passages in Hartmann (especially *Iwein* 2566-69), who adopted the Keu of Chrétien and depicted him in yet more negative terms. For further elaboration of der Stricker's Keii figure, see Haupt (pp. 108-11).

13. (143-59) For reasons of logic and clarity I have altered the sequence of verses in this passage. The lines are translated in the following order: 143-146, 155-159, 147-154.

14. (163) With this verse, the protagonist finally makes his appearance. Kern (pp. 22f.) sees in this delayed introduction of the hero a parallel to Hartmann's *Iwein*. For discussion of the name Daniel, see INTRODUCTION (p. xxvii).

15. (168) *ern fünde noch tiurren dâ ze hûs.* The exemptive suffix -*n* (in *ern*) of my critical edition must be emended to *er* in this verse. Otherwise the passage would yield quite the opposite reading: "[he] would [...] *not* find a more worthy knight in residence there."

16. (170ff.) It is characteristic of Arthurian romance that even the title hero is seldom described either in terms of concrete physical features or in the more abstract sense of "personality." Indeed, the characters populating medieval literature tend to distinguish themselves not through their appearance (though the women must typically

be beautiful, at least in a very general sense) or their psychological constitution, but rather through their external deeds. Hence, in the present passage Daniel is introduced to the listener/reader solely within the framework of his encounter with Keii.

17. (190) *daz was ietweders gelust.* Schröder (p. 65) would insert the genitive third person plural pronoun *ir* between *was* and *ietweders*. If adopted, this would require the reading "each of them" in place of "each man."

18. (204-12) Daniel's sarcastic scorn of the defeated Keii appears to have been modelled on a similar scene from Hartmann's *Iwein* 2591-2600.

19. (222f.) Foreshadowing is a technique far more characteristic of the heroic epics, which are frequently marked by an historical or at least pseudohistorical time frame. Only seldom does this device occur in the largely ahistorical Arthurian romance; see Pörksen (p. 208). This present instance of foreshadowing—virtually the only such in *Daniel*—is, of course, by no means even crucial to the unfolding of the story.

20. (225) Karidol is in all likelihood the German form of Carduel, which in turn is the Welsh equivalent of Carlisle, the present-day capital of Cumberland in northern England.

21. (230) Keii's evasive reply here is strikingly similar to Daniel's later response (vv. 2045-52) to the questions posed by the bellyless demon.

22. (244-50) For a detailed treatment of the proper names, see Rosenhagen (*Daniel*, p. 181). The less than favorable manuscript tradition of *Daniel*, of course, raises questions as to the reliability of the spelling of certain of these names. On the question of origin of proper names in the French romances (from which many of der Stricker's names derive), see Baker (p. 61 and n. 56). Baker's suggestion that Chrétien himself may have simply invented the names of certain of his characters might well apply in some instances to der

Stricker's handling of proper names in *Daniel*. For despite der Stricker's broad eclecticism, which is evident throughout this romance, it may in certain cases be more efficacious to acknowledge the possibility of free invention, rather than expecting to uncover an exact prototype for each of the names occurring in *Daniel*.

23. (254-93) The encounter with Gawein, Iwein and Parzival is apparently an episode devised independently by der Stricker. Although all three jousts end in a draw, the mere fact that Daniel is able to avert an unhorsing by these three most famed of the Arthurian knights is sufficient to gain him acceptance into the fellowship of the Round Table. As Henderson ("Ms. germ. 1340," pp. 354f.) points out, the scribe of MS. b, in what appears to be a conscious attempt to further glorify knights and knighthood, deletes the entire passage (vv. 257-394) in which Daniel manages to hold his ground against these three ultimate representatives of Arthurian knighthood.

24. (300-04) In this, his first real excursus in *Daniel*, the narrator characteristically attempts to explain a common human foible—one which might, in the modern idiom, be summed up with the phrase "misery loves company."

25. (368f.) As der Stricker goes on to explain in the following verses, Gawein is exaggerating the details of his report at this point. For it is explicitly stated (vv. 278-280) that Daniel, while he is able to remain on his own horse, does *not* manage to unseat Gawein (nor, for that matter, Iwein or Parzival).

CHAPTER III. KING MATUR'S CHALLENGE

26. (402-06) On this custom, see note to vv. 78-82; see also Baker (pp. 56, 69, 86 and 90) and Müller (*Lebensgewohnheiten*, p. 14).

27. (408) The MHG text (*vil nâch unz ze nône*) actually reads: "almost until nones." Since in medieval times the hours of the new

day were reckoned beginning at six in the morning, nones (or the ninth hour) signified three o'clock in the afternoon.

28. (412-19) As Ahrendt (pp. 108-12) points out, it is not uncommon for giants in medieval literature to be armed only with a club. In fact, the brother of this giant so fully trusts his own invulnerability that he carries no weapon whatsoever, striking at his opponents with his fist alone (vv. 2779-804).

29. (428) As Ahrendt (p. 112, par. 141 and nn. 2 and 3) notes, giants are most frequently depicted in MHG literature as fighting on foot. However, when they do ride a beast, it is more commonly an elephant than a horse or, as here, a camel. (Presumably the elephant would be more readily capable of bearing the extra weight of a giant!) Albeit by no means a common animal in Europe during the high Middle Ages, camels are nonetheless recorded as having been brought back to Germany from the Crusades: in March of 1235 Emperor Friedrich II conveyed a number of these beasts to Colmar; moreover, in the year 1289 Rudolf von Habsburg is said to have had in his possession a rather large camel; see A. Schultz (I, 348f.).

30. (432f.) Ahrendt (p. 100, par. 122) points out that in MHG literature giants—while they often possess certain qualities which *appear* to endow them with absolute invulnerability—are ultimately almost always conquered.

31. (440) Rosenhagen (*Daniel*, p. 182) sees in the name Matur a conscious parallel to MHG *Artûs* ("Arthur") and rejects the derivation from the Latin *maturus*, which Singer (Rev., p. 704) favors. It appears not at all implausible that der Stricker may perhaps have had both of these connections in mind. Also, Rosenhagen (*Daniel*, p. 182) notes a parallel between this scene, in which the giant's challenge is delivered, and the corresponding passage in the prose romance of *Lancelot* 485-90.

32. (499) *swie mir der site gevalle.* This line might also be read: "however things may turn out for me." The ambiguity arises from the

fact that the verb *gevallen* can, in this context, mean (see Lexer [I, 955]) either "to turn out, happen," or "to please."

33. (508-26) Rosenhagen (*Daniel*, pp. 182f.) discusses the land of Cluse and its similarity to other "adventure lands" in the works of this age. Although the Latin *clausus* ("closed") quite accurately describes the chief geographical feature of Cluse, der Stricker did not need to have a knowledge of either Latin or Old French in order to encounter this name, since there are several locales in the German Alps bearing the name Kluse. Even these, however, need not necessarily have been der Stricker's source, for the very same name also occurs in *Parzival* 382,24. — In MHG literature there is a strong preference for mountain ranges and oceans as the surrounding geographical characteristics of giants' habitats, rather than for the forests which are otherwise the typical setting in such works; see Ahrendt (p. 93).

34. (529) The giant employs *præteritio* here, for despite his claim to say nothing concerning the women in the land of Cluse, they are in fact the sole subject of his discourse in vv. 530-49.

35. (537) For literature on the very common comparison of beautiful women in courtly literature to roses, see K. F. Kummer, ed., *Die poetischen Erzählungen des Herrand von Wildonie und die kleinen innerösterreichischen Minnesinger*, Vienna: Hölder, 1880, pp. 213f.

36. (550) On the possible origins of the bird described in the following passage, see S. Singer ("Salomosagen," pp. 185f.; and Rev., pp. 703f.), Meier (p. 219) and Rosenhagen (*Untersuchungen*, pp. 66f.; and *Daniel*, pp. 183f.). Of these, Rosenhagen's explanation of der Stricker's *babiân* as deriving from MHG *papegân* ("parrot") is probably the most convincing; see also Suolahti (p. 174) for explanation of the final *-n*. Rosenhagen (*Daniel*, p. 184) claims that tales of wonder were probably told in the Middle Ages concerning the parrot, but that few people living in Germany during the early thirteenth century had ever actually seen such a bird. However, A. Schultz (I, 348) uncovers several literary references to parrots, some of which are even trained

to speak; of course, their occurrence in the literature may or may not mean that such birds really existed in Germany during the high Middle Ages.

37. (553) *dâ enist niht widere.* This verse (which reads somewhat more literally: "they are not repugnant there") might also be rendered: "for there is no reason for them not to have these birds."

38. (586) During the Middle Ages the elephant was not entirely unknown in Europe. In the year 802, for instance, Charlemagne brought to Aachen an elephant which he had received from the king of Persia. And in 1237, within just twenty or so years after the composition of *Daniel*, Emperor Friedrich II exhibited in Parma an elephant presented to him in the year 1228 by the Sultan; see A. Schultz (I, 348). Nonetheless, for the average person living in Europe during the Middle Ages—and apparently for der Stricker as well—such a creature must have seemed quite alien and exotic.

39. (588) The prepositional phrase *mit geræte* is of uncertain meaning in this verse. I have chosen to translate it "by means of some device," but it might also mean (see Lexer [I, 871]) "by some scheme," or it could even be linked to "mountain" to signify "a mountain of [household] furnishings."

40. (592f.) *swie vil man darûf lüede, / ez gebüeget niemer sîniu bein.* Schröder (p. 65) proposes changing the subjunctive *gebüeget* to indicative *gebiuget*. In this instance the English text would read: "it *does* not so much as bend its legs."

41. (604) *man enwelle im gerne tuon den tôt.* Alternatively, this verse might also be translated: "unless one wishes to kill it intentionally."

42. (608) This final clause (*daz sie sich niht mugen berüeren*) might also be rendered: "that they are unable to move." However, since the giant is reporting the means by which King Matur's palace can be moved about, such a reading, though syntactically possible, appears inappropriate to the context. Schröder (p. 65) suggests

gerüeren in place of *berüeren* of my critical text, but inasmuch as neither Lexer (I, 198 and 889) nor BMZ (II/1, 814f.) lists any significant semantic differences between these two verbs, Schröder's proposed emendation—whether or not it is adopted in the MHG text—would have no effect upon the English translation.

43. (585-634) Concerning the giant's tale of the elephants which bear entire houses upon their backs, see Rosenhagen (*Untersuchungen*, p. 67), who uncovers a clear influence from *Wigalois* 10,345ff. and 10,497ff.; see also S. Singer (Rev., p. 704).

44. (643-45) *die rûmen im daz rîche / ob sie im vil vorhtlîche / niht welnt dienen unde flêhen.* Schröder proposes (p. 63) to emend these verses to read as follows: *die rûment im daz rîche, / ob sie im niht vorhteclîche / mit willen dienen und vlêhen.* Schröder is able to cite important manuscript evidence from the recently rediscovered MS. b—evidence which, if considered with a blind eye towards the surrounding context (particularly the immediately ensuing lines), would speak convincingly in favor of just such an emendation in the critical text. However, in the process vv. 646f. would be rendered meaningless. More specifically, Schröder's changes in vv. 643-45 would require the following translation for vv. 641-45: "he [King Matur] has acquitted himself so boldly that those who previously held the land—if they are not willing to serve him in fear and fall down at his feet—abandon his empire altogether." The problem with this is, quite simply, that Schröder's indicative *rûment* (v. 643) would seem to imply that no one still remained in the land as potential recipients of the fiefs which, as der Stricker explicitly states in vv. 646f., King Matur grants to those willing to submit to his hegemony. Finally, in this particular context the genitive *des* of v. 642 seems to anticipate more properly the subjunctive *rûmen* than the indicative *rûment* (which might have necessitated in v. 642, in place of *des*, an adverb such as *sô*).

45. (659) Schröder (p. 65) proposes—*inter alia* in this verse—the placement of the definite article before *swert*, such that one would then have to read: "*the* clanking swords." Such a change would bring *swert* more closely into a parallelism with the noun *helde* ("heroes") of the following line, which in the MHG text is also preceded by the definite article.

46. (662f.) *sien hânt deheine schône, / sie erfollent den muot nâch ir staten.* Here, Schröder (p. 63) correctly points out that the indicative *erfollent* must be altered to subjunctive *erfollen*. This allows for the exemptive nature of the second clause; see PMS (§ 340, pp. 417f.). — On a different point, the noun *schône* is a Middle German form of *schœne* ("beauty," "splendor"), and not *schône* (= "forbearance," "indulgence"); see Lexer (II, 768). Such Middle German forms as this are by no means uncommon in der Stricker's language.

47. (724f.) *daz si diz minneclîche leben / helfe volbringen.* Schröder (p. 65) would emend *helfe* to plural *helfen*, which would then change the meaning of these lines to: "such that *they* may help enhance this elegant way of life." While Schröder presents a certain measure of manuscript evidence to support such a change, the entire surrounding context speaks in favor of the singular *helfe*. For one thing, in the brief passage dealing with these maidens (vv. 716-730), no single reference is made to them which is unambiguously in the plural. Perhaps most importantly, in v. 722 (*sô si wirt aht jâr alt*) the verb *wirt* is unmistakably singular. Furthermore, the same clearly singular usage is evident in vv. 728, 729 and 730. The emendation to plural *helfen* would therefore impute to der Stricker an unlikely measure of stylistic inconsistency.

48. (741) The MHG text actually reads here *ein golt* (literally "a gold"), but as Rosenhagen (*Daniel*, p. 186) points out, this noun can be used to signify "an art object crafted of gold"; see also Lexer (I, 1047).

49. (740-56) For discussion of der Stricker's possible models for this beast, see Rosenhagen (*Daniel*, pp. 185f.), who points out two

particularly likely sources: *Iwein* 565 and *Lanzelet* 3888f. Furthermore, the effects of the creature's deafening roar (as depicted in the present passage as well as in vv. 2900, 2942, 5746 and 5766) may have been borrowed from *Karl* 772-81 and 7096-8000 and/or from the *Rolandslied* 10,4-10; 18; and 214, 30-32. Cf. also Kern (pp. 30f.) and Leitzmann ("Chronologisches Verhältnis," p. 45).

50. (765) In MHG literature giants most commonly appear in groups of two (as here) and twelve; see Ahrendt (p. 93 and n. 2).

51. (789) The prepositional phrase in the critical text reads *umbez mer* (literally "around the sea"). Although neither Lexer (II, 1721f.) nor BMZ (III, 178-181) lists the meaning "across" for the preposition *umbe*, I have nonetheless translated *umbez mer* by "across the sea"—as though the MHG text contained *über mer* or *überz mer*. Since there is no subsequent mention of a journey undertaken by King Arthur on the open sea, it may be that *umbez mer* is intended to describe quite literally a trip *around* the sea—that is, an expedition along the coastline of some body of water. Curiously, however, the poet never again mentions any large open body of water along the direct route to King Matur's land.

52. (801) The clause *[ich] rihte über dich zehant* might also be mean (see Lexer [II, 435]): "I shall pass judgment on you straightway."

53. (810) The protracted report by the giant finally comes to a conclusion with this verse. Direct speech of such exaggerated length as the giant's story—here amounting to just over 300 lines—is, as Mast (p. 12) points out, quite atypical of the works of der Stricker, perhaps an indication of the relatively early date of *Daniel*.

54. (811-13) As Baker (p. 90) indicates, the council of Arthur and his knights is a relatively uncommon topos in the works of Chrétien, but becomes more and more frequent in the later romances.

55. (823) *ez envolget im niht dar hein.* Lambel (p. 329) interprets this verse as: "he [the giant] shall not bring home any success" ("er bringt keinen Erfolg nach Hause"). However, the paramount concern

of the assembled knights at this juncture is that King Arthur's reputation not suffer in the land of Cluse—an idea which is specifically expressed in v. 817-21 and is reintroduced here. Hence, the line can be better translated: "His tale shall not follow him home," i.e. the "inexperienced youths" among the members of the Round Table are advising that the giant be slain on the spot. Gawein, in fact, expressly derogates this very plan in vv. 856-63.

56. (824) As the foremost knight among King Arthur's comrades, Gawein quite naturally assumes the role of advising the others here. Daniel is at this point in the story but a recent initiate into the fellowship and as such takes no part in the deliberations. At later councils (vv. 3867, 5720, 7068), however, Daniel—who has in the meantime further distinguished himself—is the one who speaks up to offer counsel.

57. (842) The final clauses in this paragraph ("until such time as my lord has stated that he is ready to depart," or in the MHG text: *unz er daz habe gesprochen*) might also be linked to the subsequent verses, as in the Rosenhagen edition. In such a case, this clause would, in the translation, have to be read together with the following paragraph: "Once my lord has stated this, then let us all bid him..."

58. (849-52) The clause "we shall tell the giant" is not present in the MHG original, in which the ongoing indirect discourse by Gawein is clearly marked by means of subjunctive verb forms—a function which the English subjunctive does not allow.

59. (853) As in vv. 849-52, I have interposed the clause "we shall say" in order to compensate for the lack of an English subjunctive to indicate indirect speech.

60. (856f.) Messengers were customarily accorded special hospitality in medieval times. Before presenting their message, for instance, they were often permitted to be seated and to drink a cup of wine. Because they were merely acting as agents for a third party, they were protected against any sort of retribution, even if the tidings

they bore were less than providential. In the literature of the high Middle Ages, only barbarians are commonly portrayed as infringing upon such privileges; see A. Schultz (I, 135-138). Hence, it would be, as Gawein correctly points out, a source of shame and dishonor if the men of the Arthurian court were to act contrary to this established code of behavior and to inflict harm upon the giant.

61. (866f.) As Rosenhagen (*Untersuchungen*, pp. 72f.) first pointed out, the plan being hatched here is quite clearly reminiscent of the Polyphemus story.

62. (881) The MHG text actually contains the noun *geselle* ("comrade"), which I have translated as "brother" so as to preclude any confusion with King Matur, who is clearly not intended here.

63. (887) While Gawein's plan—given the apparently dire circumstances which face the Arthurian court at this juncture—may well be sound (or at least practical), it is difficult to imagine that such a scheme (most especially the notion of fleeing if need be!) would have been depicted as chivalrous in the older, classical Arthurian romances of Hartmann von Aue or Wolfram von Eschenbach. Central to the ethos of *Daniel*, however, is the concept of *list*, or cunning. Indeed, in the "post-classical" *Daniel*, such *list* is just as important a knightly virtue as are the more traditional qualities of prowess and strength in earlier Arthurian romances. For some time it has been fashionable among literary critics (cf. especially Agricola, Spiewok ["Stricker und Prudentia"], Könneker, and Moelleken/Henderson) to see in der Stricker's emphasis on such "new" virtues a direct response to the changing social realities of the thirteenth century, most specifically to the incipient rise of the middle class. In more recent research, however, this theory has been challenged by certain scholars (cf. Cramer, Ragotzky ["Handlungsmodell"] and, somewhat indirectly, Brall). Among these, Ragotzky convincingly demonstrates that *list* may indeed have nothing whatsoever to do with emerging middle class values, that in fact the enhanced significance of *list*—and the

concomitant problem of *guot*, or material possession—actually reflects a reaffirmation and modernization of traditional feudal/noble norms.

64. (900) *swaz êren mir dâwider var.* The adverb *dâ*, rendered in my translation by the prepositional phrase "in your land," is erroneously subsumed in the compound *dâwider* and can best be recovered by reverting to the spelling of Rosenhagen's edition. Thus, the critical text ought to be emended here to read: *swaz êren mir dâ widervar* (or even *dâ wider var*).

65. (902-04) *sie sullen ez alle ansehen / swenne ich lîp unde lant / gibe in dînes herren hant.* The conjunction *swenne* can also assume a conditional meaning (see PMS, §351:2, pp. 430f.). Hence these verses might also be translated: "They ought all to be on hand as witnesses *if* I surrender my land into your lord's hand."

66. (928) In the courtly literature, knightly festivals typically take place at Whitsuntide, or Pentecost. This holy day, which occurs in late May or June, coincides with the final blossoming of spring and is associated in the literature with the outdoor activities of jousting and feasting. See A. Schultz (I, 308f. and 489) for a full listing of such festivals.

67. (927-35) In the interest of enhanced clarity I have translated the lines in this passage in the following sequence: 932, 927-931, 933-935.

68. (960-76) The sort of mutual pledge of assistance described here parallels in many regards the feudal relationship between a lord, who provided his vassals with land, and the vassals, who in turn owed their lord a military obligation.

69. (974) *sus gewan der künic Artûs ein here.* With express reference to Leitzmann ("Strickerstudien," p. 75), Schröder (p. 66) inexplicably proposes deleting the proper name *Artûs* from this verse, although each of the manuscripts, including the most recently rediscovered MS. b, contains *Artûs*.

CHAPTER IV. THE ADVENTURE OF THE DARK MOUNTAIN

70. (996f.) Rosenhagen (*Daniel*, pp. 186f.) compares the setting out of the impatient hero—alone and in secret—to *Iwein* 945. See also Kern (p. 31), who notes that in both romances—*Daniel* and *Iwein*—a tale told by another character at the Arthurian court provides the initial impetus for the unfolding of the plot. Major differences in the middle sections of *Daniel* and *Iwein* notwithstanding, both works also show striking similarities in the final outcome: after an abbreviated period of mourning by the widows of their slain opponents, both heroes end up married to those widows; also, Daniel and Iwein are both made lord over the dead opponent's land.

71. (1047f.) *Dô sach er dâ sitzen / den er wol mohte entsitzen.* The poet uses identical rhyme to make a play on words here—one which is unfortunately lost in the process of translation.

72. (1062f.) The MHG text actually contains present tense "shrink back" (*verzage*) and "do not dare" (*tar*), both of which I have rendered here in the past tense.

73. (1075) Bode (pp. 274-76) notes that, in both the heroic and the courtly literature of the Middle Ages, the lion is a favorite symbol of personal valor and undaunted courage. Surprisingly, however, the three greatest romance poets of the age—Wolfram, Gottfried and Hartmann—employ this image only very rarely.

74. (1078) *ich wil gerner mînen lîp.* Schröder (p. 66) would emend the comparative adverb *gerner* to the positive *gerne.* In this case vv. 1078-80 then would read: "I am willing to lose my life valiantly, rather than to live on in endless shame."

75. (1092) *ich würde gerne gesehen.* Here, Schröder (p. 66) proposes changing the positive adverb *gerne* to the comparative *gerner.* If adopted, this emendation would require that the English text read: "For I should prefer to be seen."

76. (1148f.) Although the ideals of high *Minnesang* ("courtly love song") had already begun to fade somewhat by the time *Daniel* was being composed, the act of a noblewoman's casting herself at the feet of a stranger must still (as Daniel's reaction would tend to suggest) have appeared rather extraordinary to der Stricker's audience.

77. (1144-74) This is the first of several monologues in which Daniel considers the consequences of postponing his chief pursuit in order to undertake a secondary adventure which has been thrust upon him. Each time he is initially overcome by despair, but eventually resolves to assume the responsibility of assisting the petitioner. Cf. vv. 1354-84, 2167-2202, 2569-95, 2702-35. Rosenhagen (*Daniel*, p. 188) and Kern (pp. 32f.) see the model for each of these scenes in *Iwein* 4825-4914.

78. (1206) *daz ir woldet eine vart.* MSS. d and m read: *daz ir woldet han tan eine vart.* This verse offers supporting proof for Rosenhagen's contention that MS. d is a copy of MS. m, and not vice versa. For, as Rosenhagen notes in his critical apparatus, *han tan* is added to the margin of MS. m. In MS. d, however, the scribe, copying directly from m, incorporated *han tan* smoothly into the line itself.

79. (1224f.) *ich bin des herzogen kint / von dem Trüeben Berge.* On the proper name, see Rosenhagen (*Daniel*, p. 179), who notes that such appellative place names and character names as der Stricker likes to employ in *Daniel* (e.g. Daniel of the Blossoming Valley, the Maiden of the Dark Mountain, the Count of the Bright Fountain, etc.) are more characteristic of the French than of the German romances. — Also, Rosenhagen (*Untersuchungen*, p. 75; and *Daniel*, p. 188) sees the story told by the Maiden of the Dark Mountain as stemming from the episode of Gawein's relatives in *Iwein* 4455-4506.

80. (1226-33) Rosenhagen (*Untersuchungen*, pp. 75f.) argues that this dwarf, with his sword and his other peculiar powers, must have originated not in the French stories (which to such a striking degree informed German Arthurian romance), but rather in the indigenous

Germanic heroic epics. For unlike the dwarves of French romance (who, though every bit as malicious and insidious as in the German tales, are generally portrayed as inferior), Germanic saga tells of many dwarves who hold positions of responsibility, and who (like Juran in this episode of *Daniel*) are able to engage in combat with valiant heroes on a more or less equal footing. — Lütjens (p. 57) sees this dwarf as a variation of the giant Harpin in *Iwein* 4494f. Lütjens also points out (pp. 100f.) that the winning of a sword from a dwarf is a relatively common motif in the Germanic literature of the Middle Ages. Finally, as Lütjens (p. 108) notes, the mixing of widely divergent elements and characteristics under the general designation "dwarf"—as here—is common in numerous works of the MHG period. Ahrendt (p. 115, par. 144) provides further information on the confusion of giants with dwarves.

81. (1234) Cf. *Iwein* 4470-73, where a giant sues for a maiden and is likewise refused by her father.

82. (1255) This part of the medieval castle consisted of a smaller wall which was built atop the main castle wall and was provided with numerous openings. The battlement had a primarily military function, as the openings were used in times of war by the castle's defenders to shoot down at the attacking enemy. In tournaments or (as here) in cases of individual combat, the battlements were a convenient place for onlookers to congregate. See A. Schultz (I, 19 and 21f.).

83. (1284f.) Rosenhagen (*Daniel*, p. 188) elaborates upon the motif of the magic sword. Among other things, he makes particular reference to the deep Germanic roots of the common topos that a hero, in order to overcome some especially foreboding opponent, must first acquire a sword possessing marvelous properties.

84. (1290) Rosenhagen (*Daniel*, p. 188) examines the name Juran and concludes that, though the ultimate origins of this particular name are unclear, the final syllable *-an* appears in numerous literary proper names, most especially in the *Spielmannsepen* still popular during

this period. In addition to providing convenient rhyming possibilities, the suffix *-an* appears to have had—by virtue of its foreign sound—a somewhat fantastic ring to the German ear.

85. (1302-09) Harward (pp. 67f.) notes that the dwarves of Celtic tradition often possess such supernatural objects. — In v. 1309, Schröder (p. 66) proposes emending the verb *zersnite* to the simplex *snite*; if accepted, this change would require that the final clause in this paragraph read: "it could resist being cut like mere wood."

86. (1432) *ouch mac man dâ wunder schouwen.* Der Stricker's use of the present tense modal auxiliary *mac* ("can") in the midst of his overwhelmingly past-tense narration appears, at first reading, somewhat abrupt and out of place. The effect, however, is to create a sense of immediacy—an illusion that the story is only now, during the moment of narration, unfolding.

87. (1433) *vil ritter unde knehte.* Schröder (p. 66) inexplicably proposes deleting *vil* from this verse (the three words "a host of" would then drop out of the English text), despite the fact that this is not substantiated by any of the five manuscripts which he cites.

88. (1458) This is the first mention (albeit fleeting!) of marriage in relation to the protagonist. Characteristically, the topic is broached not by Daniel, whose mind is never occupied with such affairs, but by the maiden's court ladies. Although Daniel, in his subsequent adventure, unquestionably earns the right to her hand, the matter is never again pursued.

89. (1493) The hero's attendance at a mass prior to doing battle is a common topos and reflects the church's practice of allowing a Christian burial only when the slain man had gone to mass beforehand. See Bode (pp. 170 and 174) and Müller (*Lebensgewohnheiten*, pp. 7 and 11).

90. (1491-97) Cf. *Iwein* 4818-24, where the protagonist likewise spends the night in the fortress, hears a mass the next morning, and then prepares for battle; see Kern (p. 35).

91. (1504-06) On the often recurrent question of cunning versus strength, see above (INTRODUCTION, pp. xxxi, xxxvi-xli, xliiif. and lf.), Moelleken/Henderson, and Kern (pp. 35f.).

92. (1579) Cf. Hartmann's *Erec* 2817f., where Samson's strength—proverbial during the Middle Ages—is also alluded to; see Rosenhagen (*Daniel*, p. 189).

93. (1581-97) In this excursus on the destructive power of love, der Stricker personifies *frou Minne*, who, he says, was responsible for Solomon's downfall, and who will in like manner bring about Juran's destruction. In his depiction of *minne* as a destructive force, our poet follows the lead of Heinrich von Veldeke in the Dido scenes of his *Eneide*. For a fuller treatment of the question of love in *Daniel*, see above (INTRODUCTION, pp. xxxi and xlvi-li).

94. (1613) In the MHG text this verse is actually still part of the dwarf's direct speech. Because der Stricker employs a very peculiar and difficult transition (between vv. 1613 and 1614) from direct to indirect speech in this passage, I have incorporated the final verse (1613) of Juran's direct speech into the third-person narrative flow—i.e., I have translated v. 1613 as though it belonged to the following segment of (indirect) discourse.

95. (1648f.) The hyperbole of armor emitting sparks is a common one in the literature of this age; see Bode (pp. 197 and 211).

96. (1756) *wolde er lîp unde guot.* The MHG text actually reads: "had he desired body and material good." Since MHG *lîp* ("body," "self") has a very broad field of meaning (see Lexer [I, 1930f.]), I have translated it here as "service," i.e. that which they would perform physically.

97. (1758f.) *sie begunden im die gebære / zuo den werken zeigen.* Lambel's proposed change (pp. 318f.) in Rosenhagen's critical text of *die* to *diu* is unnecessary, as *gebære* can be either feminine or neuter; see Lexer (I, 747). More problematical, however, is Lambel's suggested alteration of *worten* for *werken*. Although *worten* better fits

the context, and although the corresponding idea is contained in analogous phrases in the very passages from Hartmann which Rosenhagen lists as der Stricker's probable sources (*Iwein* 3821, 4618, 3671), nonetheless none of our manuscripts contains *worten*. The most satisfying solution is simply to leave the critical text unaltered and to translate: "They showed themselves (*gebære*) eager to carry out (*werken*) his every request."

98. (1760f.) *wære diu werlt ir eigen, / der dûhte er sie wol wert.* The ambiguity of the possessive adjective *ir* and of the accusative pronoun *sie* means that these two verses might also be read: "If they had possessed all the world, they would have deemed Daniel worthy of receiving it."

99. (1755-64) Rosenhagen (*Daniel*, p. 190) points out the parallels between this passage and *Iwein* 3797-99, 3805-09 and 3819-24. Also, the question of matrimony is once again alluded to here. As before, the protagonist himself fails to come to terms with this issue. On the narrator's position at this point, see Moelleken ("Minne und Ehe," pp. 47f.).

100. (1774-79) Cf. *Iwein* 5086-92 and 5133-38, where the protagonist likewise refuses the offer of hospitality because he is obliged to take up another adventure; see Kern (p. 35).

CHAPTER V. THE ADVENTURE OF THE BRIGHT FOUNTAIN

101. (1782-85) Here der Stricker offers one of the many summarizing passages which not only help to guide the modern reader through the work, but which also must have been an important aid for the listener of medieval times. Such passages as this remind us that *Daniel* was most certainly too long a romance to have been performed in one single night, and that it must have been necessary at numerous points to recap the earlier events of the story.

102. (1801-03) This is the same gesture of entreaty as is accorded Daniel in v. 1127, when the Lady of the Dark Mountain first seeks Daniel's aid in her fight against the dwarf Juran.

103. (1848-51) Once again Daniel is about to be moved to action by the possible consequences to his reputation by lack of such action; cf. vv. 1171f.

104. (1881) Zieren (p. 42) sees the devil as the ultimate incarnation of all which threatened the courtly way of life. Such phrases as *tiuvels geverte* (*Iwein* 4675) or *tiuvels kneht* (*Iwein* 6337) are common to the courtly romance. For a listing of other occurrences of these phrases in the literature, see Dreyer (pp. 46f.). Der Stricker, in particular, is fond of the image of the devil as the embodiment of all evil. This is, of course, in keeping with the pronounced didacticism found in his works. See Mast (pp. 26-28) for a listing of the various phrases and expressions which der Stricker employs with regard to the devil. In *Daniel* alone, the word *tiuvel* occurs no fewer than 22 times.

105. (1885) As Ahrendt (p. 96) observes, extensive body hair is a trait common to the monsters of MHG literature. — Rosenhagen (*Daniel*, pp. 190f.) sees in this beast a variation on the Greek myth of Gorgon, a female whose face is so hideous as to turn to stone anyone who views it.

106. (1962) *nû rîtet für an den strâzen.* Here Schröder (p. 66) correctly suggests the emendation of the plural *an den strâzen* ("along the roads") of my critical text to the singular *an der strâzen* ("along the road").

107. (1991) Mirrors in the thirteenth century consisted of glass which was coated on one side with a sort of tin foil. See A. Schultz (I, 175f.) and cf. Wolfram von Eschenbach's *Parzival* 1,20. S. Singer (Rev., p. 704) points out that the motif of a mirror in place of a shield has its roots in the literature of the ancients; Athena, for example, presents Perseus with just such a mirror.

108. (2047) Cf. Keii's answer in v. 230 and also Wolfram's *Parzival* 406,14.

109. (2163) *tôt nider in daz gras.* Schröder (p. 66) advocates emending the prepositional phrase to *an daz gras* ("onto the grass").

110. (2182) *ich hæte dester bœser wort.* On der Stricker's usage of *wort* ("word") in the sense of "reputation," see Hahn (ed., *Kleinere Gedichte von dem Stricker*, p. 85) and Rosenhagen (*Daniel*, p. 192), who notes that *wort* can be used both positively and negatively in this sense.

111. (2203) Since, in terms of both meaning ("lake" vs. "ocean") and gender, MHG *sê* is not as fixed a noun as NHG *See* (see Lexer [II, 840f.]), and since the present context offers no clues as to its meaning here, the word is perhaps best translated as "water"—a rendition which is equally ambiguous to modern readers as *sê* must have been to der Stricker's audience. See also Rosenhagen (*Daniel*, p. 192), who conjectures that the poet himself may well have simply employed this noun in imitation of whatever source he was using for this episode—in other words, without any clear notion of what sort of body of water was intended.

112. (2239) *beidiu durch daz bürgetor.* Schröder (p. 66) favors the preposition *vür* in place of *durch*, which is attested in the lead manuscript. If this change were adopted in the critical text, the passage would then translate: "Both men hastened out before [in front of] the fortress gate."

113. (2273-84) Once again, der Stricker employs the indirect speech of one of his characters as a device to summarize and to remind his audience of all that has previously transpired. Such a passage as this might well have afforded the poet a convenient beginning for the next "installment" of his tale following an intermission during the performance or following the break from the previous night's recitation.

114. (2307) *sô tœte er mich morgen.* Relying solely upon MS. k, Schröder (p. 66) curiously advocates the replacement of the verb *tœte* by the verb *tæte.* This would alter the final clause of the sentence to: "he would have done the same to me tomorrow."

CHAPTER VI. DANIEL SLAYS THE GIANT'S BROTHER

115. (2398-408) This passage contains der Stricker's description of the *locus amœnus* (literally "pleasant place") so common to Arthurian romance, and to courtly literature in general.

116. (2443) *daz er iht lenger törste bîten.* Schröder (p. 67) would emend the verb *törste* to *dorfte,* which, if adopted, would change the final clause to: "whether he had reason to linger any further."

117. (2614) *und reit an sîne gewarheit.* This last verse might also be translated: "and [he] rode off to see what they wanted."

118. (2631-48) These lines constitute the only instance of stichomythia in *Daniel.* This device is an important stylistic feature of the French works of the period. The fact that such rapid-fire dialogue occurs so infrequently in *Daniel* lends further credence to the notion that der Stricker was not working from a direct French source while composing *Daniel.*

119. (2711-35) The time constraint, which centers on Arthur's arrival in Cluse seven days after the giant's delivery of the challenge, may well have derived, as Kern (p. 33) points out, from Hartmann's *Iwein.*

120. (2738) *vil zorn im was unde wart.* Schröder (p. 67) prefers the reading of MS. b: *wie zornig er wart.* There appears to be no compelling reason to undertake such a change in the critical text. However, if this suggestion were to be adopted, the verse would then read in English: "How great was his chagrin."

121. (2749) *kurzer mîle niht wan zwô.* As Blumenfeldt (p. 26) observes, this is the only occurrence of the form *zwô* (for "two") in the works of der Stricker. Since, like virtually all of the romances of the MHG age, *Daniel* is composed in rhymed couplets (a feature lost in the prose of the present translation), it is safe to assume that rhyming necessity must have moved the poet to employ such a (for him) relatively unusual variant.

122. (2761) *ich zerbriche dich als ein huon.* The MHG text actually reads: "like a *chicken.*" Der Stricker also employs this phrase in v. 3191; the *huon* is used in comparisons in vv. 3512 and 4429; cf. also der Stricker's *Karl* 4643.

123. (2769) Ahrendt (p. 94, par. 113 and n. 8) observes that the heroes of MHG literature, when engaged in battle with a giant, are quite frequently depicted as standing only as high as the knees of the taller opponent.

CHAPTER VII. KING ARTHUR SLAYS KING MATUR

124. (2990f.) On the unusual circumstance of King Arthur's personally taking part in battle, see above (INTRODUCTION, pp. xlii-xlvi).

125. (3000) Bode (pp. 17 and 19) reports that the knight's shield, which generally extended from the knees up to eye level, was held in the left hand and the weapon in the right.

126. (3004) Upon impact the lance was held in place under the right arm by a disk which was fastened to the lance and drawn up to the chest; see Bode (p. 15).

127. (3020ff.) Rosenhagen (*Daniel*, pp. 193f.) sees the ensuing battle as modelled on the duel between Charlemagne and Baligan (*Rolandslied* 88,19ff.).

128. (3024f.) *und [sie] fuoren beide hinden abe / und gestuonden ûf der erden.* The verb *gestuonden* ("stood," "came to stand") in v. 3025 is, as Bode (p. 101) notes, used here with sarcasm.

129. (3047) *ein vil lange stunde.* This line might also be translated: "for well over an hour."

130. (3017) As Müller-Ukena (p. 47) points out, King Matur, up to the very moment of his death, never speaks a single direct word in the story. In fact, the duel with King Arthur is the only scene in which he even appears in *Daniel.* All information about Matur is assembled indirectly—through various second-hand reports (by the messenger giant, his widow, his vassals and the giants' father).

CHAPTER VIII. THE FIRST BATTLE

131. (3099-101) Der Stricker employs a similar metaphor in vv. 3450f. On a synonymous doublet such as *nackent unde blôz* ("naked and bare"), see Arbusow (pp. 32f.) and cf. v. 6425.

132. (3155) An apparent narratorial discrepancy is evident in this verse, for whereas earlier (v. 428) the giant is reported to be riding a camel, here he is depicted mounted on a horse.

133. (3164ff.) Rosenhagen (*Daniel,* p. 194; and *Untersuchungen,* p. 73) traces the ensuing episode back to the Polyphemus myth, though he conjectures that der Stricker's knowledge of this legend was probably not based upon any direct, first-hand acquaintance with the literature of classical antiquity. See also S. Singer (Rev., p. 704).

134. (3170) For literature on the *Wahrheitsbeteuerung* (or "claim of truthfulness"), see Heinzle (p. 133). In this and other passages in our story, der Stricker appears to be very much intent upon convincing his listeners that he has not invented the story of Daniel—although in fact this is precisely what he has done! Such appeals to truthfulness are commonplace throughout the literature of the MHG period. In a

broader sense, these invocations of the authority of a clearly fictional story point to a much larger phenomenon: the characteristically medieval appeal—on the part of poets and other writers and thinkers of the Middle Ages—to the validity of established *auctoritas*, or authority.

135. (3178) *den ellenden rittern wolgeborn.* In place of the adjective *ellenden* ("intrepid"), Schröder (p. 67) would read *edelen* ("noble").

136. (3205f.) *dô fluhen sie balde / von dem risen alle.* These verses, which are transmitted only in MS. k, contain a consonantally impure rhyme and may or may not actually belong in the critical text. Rosenhagen (*Untersuchungen*, p. 23) outlines his reasons for including them. If these lines were to be deleted from the text, v. 3207 could be readily adapted to the new context by emending *im* to *in* (cf. vv. 1947f.); vv. 3204-09 (minus vv. 3205f.) would then read: "Once those knights saw that it was futile, they were both angered and hard pressed [to escape?]. Now the giant chased after the throng wherever he could hear them." See Zwierzina ("Textkritik," p. 90) for translation of v. 3207; see also Seemüller (Rev. of Rosenhagen, *Daniel*, p. 57).

137. (3271-302) This grotesquely comic scene underscores the post-classical tendencies of our work; for in the earlier, classical Arthurian romance, whose world is carefully held in check by *mâze* (or "moderation"), such slapstick humor is not as common. On the question of irony and humor, see Pörksen (p. 184). See also Haupt (pp. 110f. and 128) on this scene. Concerning the image of Keii's being dumped from his saddle like a sack (v. 3302), cf. *Erec* 4729 and *Iwein* 2584; see Rosenhagen (*Daniel*, p. 194).

138. (3348) Der Stricker employs here the somewhat archaic noun *wal* for "battlefield." As Heinzle (p. 160) points out, neither Hartmann nor Gottfried makes use (Wolfram does, albeit sparingly) of this particular substantive, which tends to occur more often in the older heroic poetry than in courtly literature.

139. (3360) *dô verlôs vil manger sîner nagel.* Schröder (p. 67) advocates the (accusative) singular *sînen nagel* in this verse. Though only the lead manuscript transmits the plural "nails," the adoption of Schröder's singular would yield a misreading of the verse. For since (as A. Schultz [II, 108f.] points out) the knight's shield normally contained *four* such nails, the partitive genitive plural is clearly called for here. There need be no accusative object in such a construction (see PMS, §218a, pp. 290f.), and *vil* modifies the subject *manger.* See Leitzmann (Rev., p. 545).

140. (3441) On this somewhat peculiar metaphor, see Bode (pp. 292 and 294).

141. (3534) *sie entwurfen seltsæniu mâl.* Lambel (p. 333) notes the affinity between this verse and *Parzival* 765,5—compelling evidence that, while Hartmann von Aue clearly exerted the most palpable influence on der Stricker, our poet was nonetheless in all probability also acquainted with the works of Wolfram von Eschenbach as well.

142. (3591) *daz in nieman möhte betouben.* Compelled by the surrounding context, I have translated this verse as though *betouben* (here "to defeat") were a dative verb—although there is no clear lexicographical evidence to support this assumption (see Lexer [I, 238] and BMZ [III, 61f.]). Thus I have treated the personal pronoun *in* as a dative plural ("[to] them") object of *betouben.* If, on the other hand, *betouben* were to be handled as an accusative verb, then its object *in* would have to mean "him"—i.e., "they would all have sworn that no man could defeat him [= Daniel]." Based upon all that follows, this would yield an unambiguous misprision of the verse.

143. (3626) On the image of the knight as blacksmith, cf. der Stricker's *Karl* 5124-26 and *Rolandslied* 145,18; see Rosenhagen (*Daniel*, p. 195). Cf. also *Daniel* v. 5050. For more on the comparison of the warrior with a blacksmith clanking at his anvil, see Bode (p. 182).

144. (3691) *ezn was niht wæher zimberman.* In accord with Schröder (p. 67)—and with MSS. h, b, and d—this verse might alternatively be read: *ern was niht wæher zimberman.* By this reading, *wæher* would be not a comparative, but rather a positive adjective with the strong nominative masculine singular ending. Thus, v. 3691 would state that Daniel was *not* an artful or delicate (*wæhe*) craftsman, but rather (cf. v. 3692) that he swung his hatchet wildly about, striking whatever he could. See Zwierzina ("Textkritik," p. 90) and cf. Wolfram's *Willehalm* 394,13. See also Rosenhagen (*Daniel*, p. 195) and Bode (pp. 291f.).

145. (3717-52) Following the example of Hartmann, der Stricker again employs the hero's aversion to self-praise as an opportunity for *recapitulatio* of Daniel's deeds by other characters. The Count of the Bright Fountain (vv. 5313-21) and Gawein (vv. 6220-43) likewise extol Daniel's acts of bravery in a way that summarizes all that has just transpired. See Kern (p. 38).

CHAPTER IX. DANIEL'S SEARCH FOR THE COUNT

146. (4038-48) As Rosenhagen (*Daniel*, p. 196) indicates, various older traditions seem to be fused together in the topos of the impenetrable mermaid skin. The notion that dragon's blood has the power to confer such impenetrability is a common topos, particularly in the heroic literature.

147. (4068) *die zwêne wunder zurnden!* I have translated this verse somewhat freely as: "each breathing the fire of revenge." It reads more literally: "the two [of them] became wondrously angry." On *wunder* used as an adverb, see the many compounds listed in Lexer (III, 988-94).

CHAPTER X. THE ADVENTURE OF THE GREEN MEADOW

148. (4124f.) *er begunde für sich gân / unz des berges ende wart.* These lines literally read: "He proceeded on his way until there was an end of the mountain." However, since Daniel must travel through a tunnel in order to reach the other side of the mountain (cf. vv. 4345-47, 4484-89 and 4511-13), I have altered "mountain" to "mountain tunnel."

149. (4128) *dâ stuont ein kleinez netze vor.* Uncertainty as to the exact nature of this net presents a translational problem which centers on (and is exacerbated by) the ambiguity of the MHG adjective *kleine*: in NHG *klein* means "small," but in MHG times *kleine* also bore (see Lexer [I, 1613-15]) a connotation of "thin" or "fine." Hence, since a "small" net would hardly be capable of ensnaring a knight and his horse, I have chosen to translate *kleine* as "finely woven." On a closely related issue, Rosenhagen (*Daniel*, pp. 196f.), in searching for der Stricker's possible literary model for this net, notes that the poet would likely have been acquainted with the net of Vulcan from Heinrich von Veldeke's *Eneide* (ca. 1170-90); in this early courtly adaptation of the *Aeneid*, Heinrich states that Vulcan's net is invisible not because of any magical powers, but because of the fact that the individual threads are so thinly woven. This lends further support to my own reading of *kleine*. However, Rosenhagen posits that the invisibility of the net in *Daniel* is due not to any such minute craftsmanship, but (in keeping with the net's ultimate origins in Germanic saga) to supernatural properties. (Certainly the supernatural is very much in evidence in the salve which accompanies this net in *Daniel*.) While der Stricker's exact wording in the present passage (containing, as it does, the ambiguous adjective *kleine*) fails to clarify the actual reason for the net's invisibility, my translation of *kleine* as "finely woven" at least does not exclude the supernatural properties which Rosenhagen claims for this net.

150. (4244) *si sprach: "herre, ich wil dir klagen."* As Rosenhagen (*Daniel*, p. 197) points out, the familiar pronoun *dir* in this verse, though it is attested in the lead manuscript and therefore belongs in the critical text, represents an apparent oversight by the poet himself. For normally only the giants, their father and the dwarf are addressed with the familiar second person pronoun *dû* in *Daniel*.

151. (4262) The MHG text actually reads: *beidiu spâte unde fruo*, literally "both late and early." Cf. v. 573.

152. (4311f.) *daz iemer dâ für gefüere, / swenne ez sich drin gewürre*. The rhyme here appears to be impure. None of Lambel's attempts (pp. 235f.) to purify it is convincing, nor does Rosenhagen's reference (*Daniel*, p. 197) to Weinhold (§ 73, p. 69) suffice to explain it as an Austrian rhyme. See also Leitzmann ("Strickerstudien," p. 73), Seemüller (Rev. of Rosenhagen, *Daniel*, p. 61) and Ehrismann (Rev. of Rosenhagen, *Daniel*, pp. 76f.).

153. (4342ff.) On the landscape described here, see note to v. 508-26.

154. (4362) *die knehte und die knebelîn*. This verse might also be translated: "the men and the young boys." See Lexer (I, 1644-46).

155. (4460) Instead of: *swenne* (or with Schröder [p. 67]: *wann*) *ich mich versinne*, this verse may also be read (with MSS. k and d): *daz ich mich kan versinnen*. In that case, this and the following line would mean: "The fact that I am still possessed of my senses is due to my never having heard his voice." — The *wand* of Rosenhagen's critical text is clearly wrong, since v. 4460 is not causal in nature, but rather temporal. Lambel (p. 322) engages in speculation which proves ultimately unacceptable because of its lack of adherence to the manuscripts, especially when *daz* of MSS. k and d would fully suffice as an alternate reading. See Leitzmann (Rev., p. 545) and Seemüller (Rev. of Rosenhagen, *Daniel*, p. 58).

156. (4715) Brown and (as here) blond are the chief hair colors associated with beautiful women in the works of the courtly period. See Heinzle (p. 62) for literature on this topos.

157. (4800) Just how Daniel is able to avoid the baleful effects of the creature's voice in this episode is unclear. Having already been warned (vv. 4594-631) of the dangers of stopping his ears, he does not, we must conclude, follow this particular course of action. Hence, v. 4774 (where the creature *hiez sie alle dar gân*, or "ordered all of them over to [the] vat") is problematical if we assume that this command is given orally and not, for example, through hand motions; for vv. 4776f. tell us that Daniel was already among the group of captives, from which position he should have been able to hear the creature's command. In the final analysis, it appears that der Stricker is simply guilty of an oversight in this passage.

158. (4825) *unz hâte er sich versunnen.* In a different passage, Rosenhagen (*Daniel*, p. 192, note to v. 2452) incorrectly translates *unz* ("meanwhile") with NHG *als* ("when"). In the present passage, however, as Lambel (pp. 240 and 245) points out, MS. h (which contains *unz* in v. 4825) yields a perfectly acceptable reading for this verse, since MHG *unz* is (see Lexer [II, 1992]) not only a conjunction (*als* or "when"), but also an adverb meaning "during this time," "meanwhile."

159. (4897) *beidiu sinnic und gesunt.* In accord with MSS. h and b, Schröder (p. 68) proposes inserting the adjective *siech* in the critical text in place of *sinnic*. This would introduce an oxymoron and would change to meaning of vv. 4896f. to: "The lord of the land then entered the tent both sick and healthy."

160. (4898) *dô zeigten sie im an der stunt.* Schröder (p. 68) would emend the verb from the plural *zeigten* of my critical text to the singular *zeigte*. Vv. 4898f. would then read: "and the maiden at once presented to him Sir Daniel, their source of comfort."

161. (4984) *der diz loch hie durch hie.* According to Blumenfeldt (p. 24), this is the only occurrence in all of der Stricker's works of *hie*

as the preterite of *houwen* ("to hew"). The necessity to rhyme this verse with the preceding line must have been the compelling factor in der Stricker's choice of this unusual form.

CHAPTER XI. THE REMAINING BATTLES

162. (5002) Although the two sides are about to embark not upon a sporting event, but upon serious warfare, der Stricker uses the verb *turnieren* ("to engage in tournament"), which would imply quite the opposite intent. Despite the fact that this verb appears somewhat out of place in this particular context, I have retained the original wording in my translation.

163. (5016) *die er gerne lieze schînen.* Schröder (p. 68) reads this verse along with MSS. b, k and d: *die gerne liezen schînen.* If this emendation were to be incorporated into the critical text, v. 5016 would then mean: "they were eager to show."

164. (5034f.) The ability to leap directly into the saddle, without using the stirrups, is a common motif in Germanic literature of the MHG age. It serves to epitomize the *hôher muot* (or "high-spiritedness") of the heroes who typically populate these stories.

165. (5050f.) The comparison of warriors to blacksmiths is also to be found in v. 3626, in the *Rolandslied* 145,18 and 174,8, and in der Stricker's *Karl* 5124. See also Bode (p. 182).

166. (5054) *er was der andern pfluoc.* As Leitzmann (Rev., p. 546) points out, this line need not necessarily—as Rosenhagen (*Daniel*, p. xi) insists—indicate a direct influence from Wolfram's *Parzival*, since both poets most likely derived this metaphor from earlier literature of the twelfth century. It is, however, highly likely that der Stricker knew *Parzival*, although Wolfram's stylistic influence on *Daniel* does not appear as strong as Leitzmann asserts.

167. (5087) Schröder (p. 68) prefers to read—in place of the verb *justen* ("jousting") of the lead manuscript (MS. h)—*strîten* ("fighting"), which is attested in the other manuscripts.

168. (5119) *daz aller hêrste phat.* In place of the superlative adjective *hêrste* ("most glorious") Schröder (p. 64) proposes *hertest* ("hardest," "most formidable"), which is attested in MSS. b and k, and which Rosenhagen incorporated into his critical edition.

169. (5156) Bode (pp. 249f.), who catalogues the various phrases employed by der Stricker to describe blood, speculates that the relative frequency of such "uncourtly" images in *Daniel* is attributable to the poet's close familiarity with the *Rolandslied*—the heroic epic which underwent a reworking at the hands of der Stricker in his *Karl.* The largely anonymous heroic poets generally showed a far greater affinity for sanguineous imagery than did the more refined poets of the courtly age.

170. (5161-74) The metaphor which der Stricker introduces in this passage is not entirely felicitous in its execution. Much hinges upon the translation of the MHG noun *griezwarte*, which signified the "judge" present at a judicial duel, and which I have also variously rendered into English as "referee" (in the sense of "umpire"). The idea here seems to be threefold: (1) that since death is the only force capable of separating two combatants (just as would the referee in a duel, though in a more definitive sense), this battle inevitably involves a fight to the death; (2) that this one single referee (death) has power over all of the many dueling warriors on this battlefield; and (3) that—in what is the least clearly developed part of the metaphor ("if they entertained thoughts of slipping away, death stepped in and reunited them")—either (a) anyone who tried to flee was killed, or (b) death, in its role as referee, prevented those knights from fleeing the battle. For further discussion of this passage, see I. Hahn (pp. 190f. and n. 55).

171. (5182-84) *dâ wart manger ungesunt, / dâ wart manger erslagen, / dâ wart manger zeinem zagen.* The poet employs lengthy anaphora in the triple repetition of *dâ wart manger.* Also, in v. 5186 he introduces the line with nearly the same phrase: *dâ tet manger.*

172. (5187) *sie zeigten ieclîches muot.* This verse reads literally: "They showed [the] courage of each." Because der Stricker, in the ensuing passage, employs no nouns (proper or otherwise), but rather only third person plural pronouns to refer to the combatants, it is not immediately clear whether he intends to praise the knights on both sides or only King Arthur's men. Indeed, the final outcome of the battle is not established until vv. 5268-71. However, in the present paragraph in the translation the eventual victory by the men of the Round Table is twice alluded to: first when the poet says that their valor "furthered their cause in battle" (v. 5188), then later when he states that "their venture met with success" (v. 5190). Hence I have translated v. 5187 somewhat freely so as to indicate that Arthur's men alone are intended: "*King Arthur's knights* demonstrated their courage." Furthermore, I have rendered v. 5196 (*der mit schalle dar reit*; literally: "he who rode thither with [loud] noise") in such a way as to make clear that it is the *opposing* army which is being described here: "And those others, who had ridden up haughtily on horseback."

173. (5200-02) *dâ was hart wider hart, / dâ was starc wider starc, / dâ was karc wider karc.* Der Stricker once again employs anaphora in these three verses, as well as a form of identical internal rhyme.

174. (5244) *ir arzât* [or: *ir arzenîe*] *was der tôt.* Here Schröder (p. 68) correctly points out that the substantive *arzât* ("physician") of my critical text ought to be replaced with *arzenîe* ("medicine"), which is attested in MSS. b and k. This emendation is reflected in the English translation.

175. (5248-61) Note the particularly extended anaphora in these verses. Only in vv. 5256 and 5260 is this interrupted. The antithetical adjective/noun pairs are reminiscent of vv. 5200-02.

176. (5325) *von sînem badene hâten.* In place of the gerund *badene* ("bathing"), Schröder (p. 68) suggests the pure substantive *bade* ("bath").

177. (5313-29) Once again, Daniel's previous deeds of bravery are presented in capsule form by one of the other characters. On the function of such recapitulative passages, see note to v. 3717-52.

178. (5370) Gawein finally informs the others here of the fact that it was Daniel who had hewn the hole through the boulder—a fact which Daniel had previously (vv. 4984-87) concealed out of modesty by answering them in a sort of riddle.

179. (5490f.) *sie hiuwen unde rungen, / sie sluogen unde vâhten.* Der Stricker employs in these lines not only anaphora, but also synathoismos in the four more or less synonymous verbs.

180. (5502f.) *dô wart ein strît volbrâht, / der gar was âne mâze.* Since *mâze* can mean either (1) "measure," "scope" or (2) "moderation" (see Lexer [I, 2064f.]), this passage might also be read: "They were fighting a battle of intemperate pitch."

181. (5546f.) *âne schimpf und âne spot, / âne fröude und âne lachen.* The poet employs here anaphora as well as synonymous noun pairs within each verse.

182. (5602-07) Once again der Stricker resorts to anaphora and to the amassing of more or less synonymous nouns in these verses.

183. (5628-30) The motif of knee-deep blood flooding the battle-field and of warriors drowning in that blood is common in the heroic epics of the day: it is present in the *Rolandslied* 146,17; 153,1; 28,25; 152,31, as well as in the *Nibelungenlied* 2114. Bode (pp. 219, 221, 226f., 231, 244 and 249) lists further detail concerning this image. See also Rosenhagen (*Daniel*, pp. 198f.).

184. (5700) *wande sie des alles jâhen.* This verse might also be read, with Schröder (p. 68): *wande sie des alle jâhen* ("For they all asserted").

185. (5739) The remedy for the unbearable din may, like the din itself, have derived from the *Rolandslied* 214,33; see Rosenhagen (*Daniel*, p. 199).

CHAPTER XII. DANIEL'S CORONATION

186. (5880-90) While this custom—that the victor remain on the battlefield for up to three days—was in reality often skirted, nonetheless it was, according to Erben (p. 101), a commonly cited ritual during the Middle Ages. Moreover, it provides evidence that medieval warfare was deeply rooted in the legal system of the day: for this notion of spending three days' time at the site of a battle derives from the concept of *sessio triduana* (literally "a three days' sitting"), a legal principle which held sway in juridical affairs involving the citizenry as well as in issues centering on the rightful possession of the throne. See also Cram (pp. 166f.). — As a poet perhaps travelling among various courts, der Stricker would have encountered this idea quite readily and quite naturally.

187. (5920) As Frenzen (p. 26) points out, only women die of grief in courtly literature. In fact, most scenes depicting lamentation and weeping are centered around women, whereas men are seldom cast in such a role.

188. (5952ff.) The ensuing debate as to whether or not the queen of Cluse should remarry must be viewed against the overall backdrop of the theme of the widow's remarriage in medieval literature. For although the reasons leading up to Daniel's subsequent marriage to Matur's widow are extraordinarily materialistic and lacking in emotional overtones (see vv. 6262-65), this is in fact the rule and not the exception in medieval literature. In *Daniel* the marriage of political convenience is, to be sure, presented with almost burlesque exaggeration, but, as Gerhards (pp. 216f.) points out, the emotional effect

of love is almost never depicted in connection with a widow's remarriage. See Gerhards (pp. 191, 196-202, 204f., and 216f.) for a full discussion of this question as it relates to the works of Chrétien, to Hartmann's *Iwein* and to *Daniel*.

189. (5987) During the course of the twelfth century, the ministerials (MHG *dienestman*) had developed into a distinct class of serving knights (though probably not all ministerials were actually members of the chivalric order) peculiar to Germany. Albeit originally in the service of the older nobility, the ministerials had by der Stricker's day amassed for themselves many of the privileges of their lords. Thus, while legally they remained serfs, for all practical purposes they had achieved the status of noblemen, constituting the lowest ranks of the German nobility.

190. (6015) The two other blights alluded to here by the queen's counselors are the loss (1) of her land and (2) of her people, each of which would be unavoidable if she were to refuse a reconciliation with King Arthur's forces. Both of these dangers are expressly specified in the preceding paragraph (vv. 5996f.).

191. (6027f.) *volget ir unser lêre, / ir hât es frome und êre.* Alternatively, the subject pronoun *ir* of the first verse might be deleted, with Schröder (p. 68) and in accord with MSS. h and b: *volget unser lêre, / ir hât es frome und êre.* This would transform v. 6027 from a condition to an imperative; the English would then read: "indeed, follow our counsel, and you shall gain in benefit and fame."

192. (6053) On the significance of the ministerials in medieval Germany, see note to v. 5987.

193. (6091f.) *er wil iuch mit triuwen / ergetzen iuwer riuwen.* The verses might also be translated: "that he wishes to replace your sorrow with [proof of his] fidelity."

194. (6112) *daz ich drumbe niht verliesen.* The first person singular inflectional ending *-en* (as here) is not unusual in der Stricker's Middle German dialect of MHG.

195. (6220-43) On the recapitulation of Daniel's deeds of bravery, see note to vv. 3717-52.

196. (6306-10) Cf. *Iwein* 2300-03, where the same concern is expressed by Laudine. Whereas in Hartmann's work, however, the queen speaks directly to Iwein, in *Daniel* the newly widowed queen addresses not the protagonist himself, but rather King Arthur. This accentuates the central position which King Arthur occupies in our story, a position which closely approaches that of co-protagonist. Müller-Ukena (p. 28), in fact, goes so far as to refer to the "two protagonists" in *Daniel*.

197. (6334-37) Cf. *Iwein* 2418-20, where Hartmann states: "There were many priests present, who at once joined them [Iwein and Laudine] in marriage and who bestowed upon him [Iwein] both the lady and the land"; see Rosenhagen (*Daniel*, p. 199). These lines underscore, through the contrast with *Daniel*, the striking absence of *minne* (or "courtly love") in *Daniel*. For further discussion of this question, see Moelleken ("Minne und Ehe," pp. 49f.).

Chapter XIII. The Festival Begins

198. (6461f.) *und ir von dem getwerge / diu von dem Trüeben Berge.* These two verses are in reverse order in all of the manuscripts. Following Rosenhagen's example (see *Daniel*, p. 199), I have rearranged them in my own critical edition as well as here in the translation.

199. (6504) *der gezierde gemach.* Rosenhagen's translation of this line (*Daniel*, p. 199) as *Gemächer von solcher Zier* ("rooms of such elegance") appears to miss the point. Lambel (pp. 329f.) and Leitzmann ("Strickerstudien," p. 76) are almost certainly closer to the intended meaning, which I have incorporated into my English translation.

200. (6505f.) *dâ was ein grüener anger, / breiter unde langer.* As Rosenhagen (*Daniel*, p. 199) correctly points out, *breiter* and *langer* of v. 6506 are not comparative adjectives, but rather strongly inflected predicate adjectives in the positive degree. Such adjectival inflection outside of the noun phrase, albeit somewhat unusual in MHG, is by no means unheard of (see PMS, §259-61, pp. 316f.).

201. (6514) Cf. v. 928, where King Arthur's custom of holding the festival on Whitsunday is initially reported.

202. (6569-75) Two different fabrics of wool are described here: First, *scharlachen*, produced in the Netherlands, may or may not have been—despite its name (see Suolahti, pp. 228f.)—of a scarlet color; see A. Schultz (I, 269f.). The second woolen fabric, *brûnât*, was indeed brown, as the name (see Suolahti, p. 71) suggests; see A. Schultz (I, 267). *Pfeller*, on the other hand, is a general designation for expensive silken fabric which originated in the Orient and which came in various colors and designs; see A. Schultz (I, 249-51). *Plîât* is also a type of silk, usually consisting of two different colors and interwoven with gold thread. It was imported from Greece or from the Orient; see A. Schultz (I, 261f.) and, for the etymology, Suolahti (p. 68). The next fabric listed by der Stricker, *saben*, is problematical chiefly because of the fact that it is not uniformly transmitted in the manuscripts; only MS. k comes close to giving the correct orthography. *Saben*, at any rate, is a fine white linen; see A. Schultz (I, 269). *Ciclât* appears to have been nearly identical to *plîât*; see A. Schultz (I, 249 and 263f.) and Suolahti (p. 237). On the use of ermine in medieval clothing, see A. Schultz (I, 272).

203. (6585-93) Several of the names of the precious stones mentioned in these verses are of Latin derivation. As Caflisch-Einicher (pp. 302f.) points out, the use of foreign designations for such costly objects was consciously intended in MHG literature to heighten the sense of marvelous and lavish exoticism. Rosenhagen (*Daniel*, pp. 199f.) lists other works of the period in which such catalogues of gems

occur. Rosenhagen (*Daniel*, p. 200) correctly identifies *berlen* as pearls and not beryls, which Bartsch (ed., *Karl*, p. xxvii) asserts. *Sarmihel* is most likely not, as S. Singer (Rev., p. 704) and Schönbach (p. 14) maintain, *sarmius*; nor is it, as Ehrismann (Rev. of Rosenhagen, *Daniel*, p. 77) claims, *carniol*, but rather carbuncle; see Suolahti (pp. 221 and 117f.). *Calcedonius* is clearly agate or *achates chalcedonius*; see Lexer (I, 1495) and Suolahti (pp. 115f.). Rosenhagen's *onihilus* (*onichilus* in my critical text) apparently does not occur with that orthography anywhere other than in Rosenhagen's edition; see Lexer (II, 156f.), BMZ (II/1, 437) and Suolahti (p. 169). Rosenhagen (*Daniel*, p. 200), Schönbach (p. 14), Caflisch-Einicher (p. 282) and Lambel (p. 330) all link this misspelling to *onichilus* / *onichinus* (= onyx). And finally, the *almedîn* must be almadine, a purplish-red garnet; cf. Rosenhagen (*Daniel*, p. 200), Lexer (I, 47), Suolahti (p. 48), and Schönbach (p. 14).

204. (6659) The name Belamis is first introduced in v. 250. Rosenhagen (*Daniel*, p. 181) notes the tendency of der Stricker to employ pairs of personal names which are phonetically similar: e.g., Belamîs and Beladigant (v. 8026), Daniel and Danîse, and Artûs and Matûr.

205. (6696) *daz si ir iemer darben muoz.* This verse might also be translated: "Any such ladies shall be reduced to starvation!"

206. (6701) *diu hie einen mac behaben.* Schröder (p. 69) correctly points out that the genitive plural personal pronoun *ir* (which is not present in my critical edition) must be inserted into the text between *hie* and *einen*.

207. (6751-58) Cf. *Iwein* 2328-33 and *Daniel* 6779f., where the marriage proposals are similarly worded; see Rosenhagen (*Daniel*, p. 200). Der Stricker concedes here that such mass marriages are unheard of. More importantly, the entire episode is, once again, wholly devoid of *minne* ("courtly love") and its inner workings upon

lovers (although the poet does finally employ the word *minne* in v. 6762).

208. (6789) *iemer sider ûfkome.* Schröder (p. 69) prefers the comparative adverb *ofter* (of MS. h) in place of *sider.* If adopted into the critical text, this would alter the meaning of the verse to: "shall not be seen very often."

CHAPTER XIV. KING ARTHUR IS ABDUCTED

209. (6872-99) As Rosenhagen (*Daniel*, p. 200) points out, the personification of Bliss in these lines is not only carefully developed here, but is quite skillfully reintroduced in vv. 7898-7904. These two passages thus serve as a sort of frame around the entire episode of the giants' father.

210. (6902ff.) Der Stricker seems to have obtained the episode beginning here from the Provençal Arthurian romance *Jauffré*, in which King Arthur is carried off by a strange creature who is swift of foot and who likewise drags the king up a steep and dangerous mountainside. As in *Daniel*, the other knights are forbidden to shoot. See Rosenhagen (*Daniel*, p. 200; and *Untersuchungen*, pp. 69-72). Insofar as I have been unable to find this specific episode in any contemporaneous MHG works, it appears likely that der Stricker must have known *Jauffré*, in one form or another. On other possible sources for the giants' father and on the curious mixture of dwarf and giant characteristics, see Ahrendt (pp. 84f.). For further interpretation of this episode, see Moelleken ("Riesenvaterepisode").

211. (6970f.) These two verses appear to suggest that Arthur's knights, in their haste to catch up with the intruder, must have dug the spurs into their horses with unaccustomed force.

212. (7045f.) *er hiez sie alle swîgen / und ir rede vermîden.* The impure rhyme of these verses might prompt us to read this couplet,

along with MS. k (and, in part, with MS. d): *er hiez im machen eine lust / des wart an niemanne brust.* In this case, the translation would have to be adjusted to: "he commanded them to heed his words, which no man failed to do." See Rosenhagen (*Daniel*, pp. 200f.), Ehrismann (Rev. of Rosenhagen, *Daniel*, p. 77) and Waelzel (p. 56, n. 4).

213. (7084) *dîn halsperc ist sô guot.* Daniel's reference here to the armor (*halsperc*) worn by the giants' father is curious in light of the earlier passage (vv. 6906-09) in which this man is described as wearing only a silken tunic and silken breeches. It appears that either der Stricker is guilty of an inconsistency here, or else that Daniel is alluding in a very general fashion to the overall defensive capabilities which derive from this intruder's physical superiority. However, since the word *halsperc* has a narrow (rather than broad) field of meaning (see Lexer [I, 1156] and BMZ [I, 159-61]), the former explanation is probably more likely: that der Stricker simply overlooked this minor discrepancy.

214. (7088) *dû müestest uns bringen innen.* Schröder (p. 69) advocates the reading attested in MSS. h and b: *dû muost uns bringen innen.* Such a change from subjunctive to indicative would alter the meaning of the verse: "then you shall most certainly have to give us a full accounting of your behavior."

215. (7095) *Er sprach: "daz wil ich dir sagen."* Rosenhagen, in his critical text, places the open quotation marks at the beginning of v. 7096 and emends the familiar second-person pronoun *dir* (present in all manuscripts) to the formal *iu*. In my own critical edition I have moved the quotation marks up to v. 7095 and have retained *dir*, despite the inappropriateness of such familiar address in this situation. Not only is fidelity to the manuscripts thereby better served, but prefatory introduction to direct speech in *Daniel* more often leads into that speech within the same line as the introduction itself (34.8%) than in the following line (26.2%); see Resler ("Datierung," pp. 19-21).

216. (7100) *wie man in dannen bræhte.* This verse might alternatively be translated: "...a scheme to bring him [King Arthur] back down again."

217. (7101) *dâ suln sie hungers sterben.* This line literally reads: "*They* shall all die of starvation [first]." Throughout this speech, the giants' father refers to King Arthur's men variously in the third person and in the second person.

218. (7150-53) Kern (pp. 38-40) treats at length the ossified code of honor which prevents the knights from taking action to rescue King Arthur. Der Stricker clearly presupposes that his audience is familiar with Wolfram's *Parzival*, for of all the knights present only Parzival—who in Wolfram's work had already learned the fallacy of overly strict adherence to the rules of knightly conduct—dares to speak up (vv. 7180-86) in defiance of the knightly code. We can detect in this circumstance further evidence that Daniel's role in this work is not that of the traditional Arthurian hero, for he, like the other knights, stands by helplessly, handcuffed by an exaggerated sense of *zuht*, or courtly good breeding. See also Ragotzky ("Handlungsmodell," pp. 191f.).

219. (7250) *ich seite im schâch unde mat.* Chess is an ancient game which came to Europe from the East. Once established on the European continent, it became very popular among members of the nobility. During peacetime chess provided the warrior with a battlefield on which to practice his martial strategies; indeed, chess sets—sometimes very costly ones—were frequently carried on campaigns by kings and barons. Hence the use of chess terms, as in this passage of *Daniel*, is not uncommon in German courtly literature. Suolahti (pp. 156f. and 222f.) reports that the terminology (Persian *šâh mât[a]* = "the king has died"; cf. MHG *schâch mat* and English "checkmate") came into Germany, along with the game itself, by way of the Romance languages.

220. (7401) *sît beidiu wol willekomen.* Alternatively, this verse might also be read, in accord with Schröder (p. 69): *sît beidiu gote willekomen.* In that case, the English would have to be rendered: "Welcome in God's name, both of you!"

221. (7531-34) With these lines we have a restatement of Daniel's own dilemma at the beginning of the work: in the prologue (vv. 23-25) the poet first introduces his theme that knightly fame can be acquired even by a man lacking in material wealth. And indeed it is precisely this which Daniel has accomplished, by means of both prowess and cunning, over the course of the work. See Moelleken/Henderson (pp. 198f.).

222. (7537f.) Hartmann's *Erec* 2816-18 seems once again to have been der Stricker's model here. Absalom's handsomeness and Samson's great strength were proverbial in the Middle Ages, so that our poet could certainly count on his audience to grasp a comparison such as this. See Rosenhagen (*Daniel*, p. 189) and note to v. 1579. On Absalom as a topos in MHG literature, see Fechter.

223. (7487-548) In this lengthy excursus on *list* (or "cunning"), the poet develops his ideas on this virtue, which is so very essential to all of Daniel's successes. It is of course not at all accidental that this didactic passage follows so closely on the heels of Daniel's final adventure, a fact which underscores the summarizing character of this excursus. For more on the question of *list*, see above (INTRODUCTION, pp. xxxi, xxxvi-xli, xliii f. and l f.) and Moelleken/Henderson.

224. (7569) Finally Daniel's queen is named. On the occurrence in *Daniel* of phonetically similar proper names, see note to v. 6659.

225. (7600f.) Daniel's characterization of the intruder's offence is, of course, somewhat exaggerated: neither King Arthur nor Parzival has been killed as a result of his abduction by the giants' father.

226. (7739) *hæte mirs mîn herre gedâht iht.* This verse might also be read, in agreement with Schröder (p. 69) and MS. b: *hæte mirs mîn herre gesagt iht.* In the case of such an emendation, vv.

7739f. would then read: "If my lord had told me anything of this (and he fully excluded me from his plans!)."

227. (7892-94) *swer von fröuden ie gelas, / swer fröude ie gesach, / swer ie gehôrte daz man sprach.* Der Stricker once again employs anaphora in these lines.

228. (7898-904) In this passage the topos of personified Bliss is once more taken up. See note to vv. 6872-99.

CHAPTER XV. THE CONCLUSION OF THE FESTIVAL

229. (7922) In this line Daniel states his present situation in terms of the predominant theme of the story: that a man possessed of the proper qualities of character can strive for and achieve both *guot* ("possessions," "wealth") and *êre* ("esteem"). See notes to vv. 23-33 and to vv. 7531-34.

230. (7925) *und hülfe es gerne sêre.* In concert with Schröder (p. 69) and MSS. h and b, the indicative *hilfe* might be read in place of the subjunctive *hülfe* of my critical edition. The line would then mean: "and I shall gladly help."

231. (7930) *daz lîhte ein man unsanfte tuot.* This verse might also be translated: "or which might perhaps be vexing to another man." However, two factors argue against this: (1) *ein man* is in the nominative singular, not (as such an alternative reading would demand) in the dative singular (see PMS § 151, p. 178, n. 2); and (2) *unsanfte* is an adverb (see Lexer [II, 1930 and 1935]) and not a noun (which would likewise be required for such a change in the English text).

232. (8008-26) The introduction of an entirely new character at this late point in the story may in some respects appear as an afterthought on the part of der Stricker. Particularly curious is the extravagant degree to which he is later rewarded by King Arthur (vv. 8305-09), when in fact he has played no part whatsoever in the conquering

of Cluse. In another sense, however, Beladigant is drawn to the Arthurian court for the same reasons (vv. 8014-18) as was Daniel (cf. vv. 334-37), and so serves as a sort of counterpart to Daniel. See Rosenhagen (*Daniel*, p. 201) and Kern (p. 25). On the name Beladigant, see notes to vv. 244-50 and 6659.

233. (8057-63) Seemüller (Rev. of Rosenhagen, *Daniel*, p. 65) would strike these seven verses as a later interpolation. He bases this proposed emendation upon what he believes to be an irreconcilable contradiction: in v. 7965 Daniel invites the six hundred men who had not taken wives to accompany him to Britain to fetch Queen Guinevere; this is reiterated in v. 7979. In vv. 8057-62, already in Britain, once Daniel saw that "his comrades had arrived with their ladies, they all embarked with him upon the journey [back to Cluse]." How, asks Seemüller, can these unmarried knights suddenly have wives in Britain? Zwierzina ("Textkritik," pp. 92f.) provides one plausible explanation by pointing out that these men did not marry in Cluse precisely because of the fact that they already had wives back in Britain; the substantive *gesellen* of v. 7964 does not necessarily mean "bachelor." Perhaps even more convincingly, the poet may, in v. 8058, be referring to those of Arthur's knights who had not initially made the journey to Cluse (cf. vv. 7998-8003). At any rate, there is certainly no justification whatsoever for striking vv. 8057-63 from the text, as Seemüller proposes.

234. (8114) *sô beliben sie ungeletzet.* This is a very enigmatic line. It reads literally: "Thus they remained unimpaired." My translation of it as: "Thus those courtiers could not have imagined" is as much respondent to the demands of the surrounding context as to the dictates of the MHG text itself.

235. (8122-40) Just as in *Iwein* 47-59, the description of the festival is interrupted by an excursus on the effect of literary entertainment. Bartsch (ed., *Karl*, p. xxxi) calls this passage "a reflection which alludes to the purpose of epic poetry" ("eine reflection [...], die

sich auf den zweck der epischen dichtung bezieht"). See also Rosenhagen (*Daniel*, p. 202) and Kern (p. 25).

236. (8141-43) As Suolahti (pp. 7f.) documents, several of the German poets of this age, der Stricker included, make a point of referring to French fiddlers and to the French way of playing this instrument. While we cannot say with any assurance just why the German courtiers so admired the French for their skill with the fiddle, such admiration is certainly in keeping with the broader German fascination with French culture and French taste of this age. See A. Schultz (I, 432f.) for descriptions and illustrations of the various sorts of fiddles in use during the high Middle Ages. Cf. *Erec* 2158-62, where Hartmann employs similar wording to describe the minstrels in attendance at Erec's wedding festival; see Rosenhagen (*Daniel*, p. 202).

237. (8156f.) A. Schultz (I, 433f. and 437f.) details the different types of flutes (MHG *pfîfen*) and tambourines (MHG *sumbere*) in use at the courts during the high Middle Ages. The various flutes differed from one another chiefly in the number of holes which each such instrument had. In the case of percussion instruments (such as the tambourines in the present passage), small bells were commonly attached along the sides.

238. (8160) The harp was one of the most popular musical instruments at such festivals as this. In one form or another, the European harp dates back at least as far as the ninth century. For illustrations and descriptions of the various types of harps, see A. Schultz (I, 429-32).

239. (8168) *man sach dâ verre springen.* The precise meaning of this line is unclear. The verb *springen* may possibly indicate less specifically directed activity than the dancing with which I have chosen to translate it. Rosenhagen (*Daniel*, p. 202) suggests that *knappen* ("squires," "pages") is the understood subject of *springen*; thus: "pages could be seen engaged in contests of leaping." It is also

possible that the poet is merely describing a more general sort of activity, and that the line might therefore be rendered: "People were seen bustling about."

240. (8173) The reading aloud of French stories was, as Suolahti (p. 7) documents, a common pastime at such festivals in Germany. — As regards the more private, individual sort of reading, it was still chiefly the women who were able to read during the thirteenth century. See Müller (*Lebensgewohnheiten*, pp. 25f.); also A. Schultz (I, 439f.).

241. (8179) *der sach dâ liute die flogen.* Rosenhagen (*Daniel*, p. 202) reads this line (the latter clause of which translates literally: "people who were flying") rather differently; he explains these courtiers as *Luftspringer* ("high jumpers"), although he wisely appends a question mark to his interpretation.

242. (8180-82) The knights are more likely merely practicing here than engaging in actual contests with bow and arrows; see Lambel (p. 330) and Rosenhagen (*Daniel*, p. 202).

243. (8186) As A. Schultz (I, 140, n. 1) points out, *garzûn* is another designation for "page." Given the pervasive influence of contemporary French literature on the German poets, it is not at all surprising (and certainly not unusual) to encounter such Romance words in the German tales. See Suolahti (p. 93) for etymology and usage of this particular word.

244. (8192f.) Although the MHG text states only that "they" wore wreaths and garlands, I have in the translation replaced the pronoun with the substantive "ladies," since, as A. Schultz (I, 181 and 232f.) indicates, it was primarily women (and young people) who wore such head covering in courtly circles. On the etymology and usage of *schapel* ("garland"), see Suolahti (p. 227).

245. (8202f.) *mangen seltsænen brief / lâsen sie von listen.* The exact meaning of these two verses is unclear. Rosenhagen (*Daniel*, p. 202) and Lambel (p. 330) attempt to affix very specific interpretations

to the phrase *brief von listen*. However, insofar as neither the poet nor the context yields a clue as to precisely what is meant here, it appears advisable to read these lines—as I have done, along with Ehrismann (Rev. of Rosenhagen, *Daniel*, p. 77)—in the broadest possible fashion: "documents which told of knowledge and of learning."

246. (8215) For a description of such trumpets (MHG *bûsûnen*) in the thirteenth century, see A. Schultz (I, 436f.). The instruments in question in this passage probably more closely resembled the modern trombone than the trumpet, since they were curved rather than straight in form. For orthographic variants, etymology and usage of *bûsûne*, see Suolahti (p. 74).

247. (8110-228) The description of the courtly festival appears to have been modelled on *Iwein* 31-95. Compared with Hartmann's romance, however, der Stricker's account is characterized by a much more confused listing of the various activities, and appears to depend to a great extent for its effect on the massing of large numbers of courtiers and entertainers; see Rosenhagen (*Daniel*, pp. 201f.).

248. (8285) Once again, the poet withholds a proper name until very near to the end of the story. On the use of this technique, see Arbusow (p. 121).

249. (8314-18) Der Stricker's use of the conjunction *ob* ("if") in this passage is vaguely reminiscent of a facet of the Arthurian legend which was present virtually from the start: that King Arthur was not dead, but would some day return from the island of Avalon to lead the British people to renewed glory.

250. (8365-72) On the landscape described in this passage, see note to vv. 508-26.

251. (8458) This, in a nutshell, is the central tenet of feudalism: that land was held by vassals in exchange for military and other assistance given to their overlords.

INDEX OF NAMES FROM *DANIEL*

Included in this INDEX are both place names and personal names from *Daniel*. In addition, the following are also indexed: personified abstract qualities (for example, Bliss or Lady Love); poets' names; and certain non-proper personal designations (such as the bellyless demon and the father of the giants). Of the personal names, generally only those designating actual characters in the story are listed; those invoked solely in expletives or in other formulaic expressions (such as God or the devil) are excluded. For all entries, page references are given only for their occurrence in the TRANSLATION, not in the INTRODUCTION or the NOTES.

Index of Names from Daniel

Index of Names from Daniel

The Garland Library of Medieval Literature

Series A (Texts and Translations); Series B (Translations Only)

1. Chrétien de Troyes: *Lancelot*, or *The Knight of the Cart.* Edited and translated by William W. Kibler. Series A.
2. Brunetto Latini: *Il Tesoretto (The Little Treasure).* Edited and translated by Julia Bolton Holloway. Series A.
3. *The Poetry of Arnaut Daniel.* Edited and translated by James J. Wilhelm. Series A.
4. *The Poetry of William VII, Count of Poitiers, IX Duke of Aquitaine.* Edited and translated by Gerald A. Bond; music edited by Hendrik van der Werf. Series A.
5. *The Poetry of Cercamon and Jaufre Rudel.* Edited and translated by George Wolf and Roy Rosenstein; music edited by Hendrik van der Werf. Series A.
6. *The Vidas of the Troubadours.* Translated by Margarita Egan. Series B.
7. *Medieval Latin Poems of Male Love and Friendship.* Translated by Thomas Stehling. Series A.
8. *Barthar Saga.* Edited and translated by Jon Skaptason and Phillip Pulsiano. Series A.
9. Guillaume de Machaut: *Judgment of the King of Bohemia (Le Jugement dou Roy de Behaingne).* Edited and translated by R. Barton Palmer. Series A.
10. *Three Lives of the Last Englishmen.* Translated by Michael Swanton. Series B.
11. Giovanni Boccaccio: *Eclogues.* Edited and translated by Janet Smarr. Series A.
12. Hartmann von Aue: *Erec.* Translated by Thomas L. Keller. Series B.
13. *Waltharius* and *Ruodlieb.* Edited and translated by Dennis M. Kratz. Series A.
14. *The Writings of Medieval Women.* Translated by Marcelle Thiébaux. Series B.
15. *The Rise of Gawain, Nephew of Arthur (De ortu Waluuanii Nepotis Arturi).* Edited and translated by Mildred Leake Day. Series A.

16, 17. *The French Fabliau:* B.N. 837. Edited and translated by Raymond Eichmann and John DuVal. Series A.

18. *The Poetry of Guido Cavalcanti.* Edited and translated by Lowry Nelson, Jr. Series A.
19. Hartmann von Aue: *Iwein.* Edited and translated by Patrick M. McConeghy. Series A.
20. *Seven Medieval Latin Comedies.* Translated by Alison Goddard Elliott. Series B.

21. Christine de Pizan: *The Epistle of the Prison of Human Life*. Edited and translated by Josette A. Wisman. Series A.

22. *The Poetry of the Sicilian School*. Edited and translated by Frede Jensen. Series A.

23. *The Poetry of Cino da Pistoia*. Edited and translated by Christopher Kleinhenz. Series A.

24. *The Lyrics and Melodies of Adam de la Halle*. Lyrics edited and translated by Deborah Hubbard Nelson; music edited by Hendrik van der Werf. Series A.

25. Chrétien de Troyes: *Erec and Enide*. Edited and translated by Carleton W. Carroll. Series A.

26. *Three Ovidian Tales of Love*. Edited and translated by Raymond J. Cormier. Series A.

27. *The Poetry of Guido Guinizelli*. Edited and translated by Robert Edwards. Series A.

28. Wernher der Gartenaere: *Helmbrecht*. Edited by Ulrich Seelbach; introduced and translated by Linda B. Parshall. Series A.

29. *Five Middle English Arthurian Romances*. Translated by Valerie Krishna. Series B.

30. *Les Cent nouvelles nouvelles*. Translated by Judith Bruskin Diner. Series B.

31. Gerald of Wales (Giraldus Cambrensis): *The Life of St. Hugh of Avalon*. Edited and translated by Richard M. Loomis. Series A.

32. *L'Art d'Amours (The Art of Love)*. Translated by Lawrence Blonquist. Series B.

33. Giovanni Boccaccio: *L'Ameto*. Translated by Judith Serafini-Sauli. Series B.

34, 35. *The Medieval Pastourelle*. Selected, translated, and edited in part by William D. Paden, Jr. Series A.

36. Béroul: *The Romance of Tristran*. Edited and translated by Norris J. Lacy. Series A.

37. *Graelent* and *Guingamor*: Two Breton Lays. Edited and translated by Russell Weingartner. Series A.

38. Heinrich von Veldeke: *Eneit*. Translated by J. Wesley Thomas. Series B.

39. *The Lyrics and Melodies of Gace Brulé*. Edited and translated by Samuel Rosenberg and Samuel Danon; music edited by Hendrik van der Werf. Series A.

40. Giovanni Boccaccio: *Life of Dante (Trattatello in Laude di Dante)*. Translated by Vincenzo Zin Bollettino. Series B.

41. *The Lyrics of Thibaut de Champagne*. Edited and translated by Kathleen J. Brahney. Series A.

42. *The Poetry of Sordello*. Edited and translated by James J. Wilhelm. Series A.

43. Giovanni Boccaccio: *Il Filocolo*. Translated by Donald S. Cheney with the collaboration of Thomas G. Bergin. Series B.

44. *Le Roman de Thèbes (The Story of Thebes)*. Translated by John Smartt Coley. Series B.

45. Guillaume de Machaut: *The Judgment of the King of Navarre (Le Jugement dou Roy de Navarre)*. Translated and edited by R. Barton Palmer. Series A.

46. *The French Chansons of Charles D'Orléans*. With the Corresponding Middle English Chansons. Edited and translated by Sarah Spence. Series A.

47. *The Pilgrimage of Charlemagne* and *Aucassin and Nicolette*. Edited and translated by Glyn S. Burgess and Anne Elizabeth Cobby. Series A.

48. Chrétien de Troyes: *The Knight with the Lion*, or *Yvain*. Edited and translated by William W. Kibler. Series A.

49. *Carmina Burana*. Translated by Edward Blodgett and Roy Arthur Swanson. Series B.

50. *The Story of Meriadoc, King of Cambria (Historia Meriadoci, Regis Cambriae)*. Edited and translated by Mildred Leake Day. Series A.

51. *The Plays of Hrotsvit of Gandersheim*. Translated by Katharina Wilson. Series B.

52. *Medieval Debate Poetry: Vernacular Works*. Edited and translated by Michel-André Bossy. Series A.

53. Giovanni Boccaccio: *Il Filostrato*. Translated by Robert P. apRoberts and Anna Bruni Seldis; Italian text by Vincenzo Pernicone. Series A.

54. Guillaume de Machaut: *La Fonteinne amoureuse*. Edited and translated by R. Barton Palmer. Series A.

55. *The Knight of the Parrot (Le Chevalier du Papegau)*. Translated by Thomas E. Vesce. Series B.

56. *The Saga of Thidrek of Bern (Thidrekssaga af Bern)*. Translated by Edward R. Haymes. Series. B.

57. Wolfram von Eschenbach: *Titurel* and the *Songs*. Edited and translated by Sidney M. Johnson and Marion Gibbs. Series A.

58. Der Stricker: *Daniel of the Blossoming Valley*. Translated by Michael Resler. Series B.

59. *The Byelorussian Tristan*. Translated by Zora Kipel. Series B.

60. *The Marvels of Rigomer*. Translated by Thomas E. Vesce. Series B.

61. *The Song of Aspremont (La Chanson d'Aspremont)*. Translated by Michael A. Newth. Series B.

62. Chrétien de Troyes: *The Story of the Grail*, or *Perceval (Li Contes del Graal)*. Edited by Rupert T. Pickens and translated by William W. Kibler. Series A.

63. Heldris of Cornwall: *The Story of Silence (Le Roman de Silence)*. Translated by Regina Psaki. Series B.

64. *Romances of Alexander*. Translated by Dennis M. Kratz. Series B.

65. Dante Alighieri: *Il Convivio (The Banquet)*. Translated by Richard H. Lansing. Series B.

66. *Jaufre*. Translated by Ross Arthur. Series B.

67. Lives of 13th-Century French Women Saints. Translated by Brigitte Cazelles. Series B.

Printed in the USA
CPSIA information can be obtained
at www.ICGtesting.com
LVHW041725311223
767818LV00002B/226

9 780976 087311